Praise for Julie E. Czerneda and *Search Image*:

"After some 15 years away, Czerneda returns to the Web Shifters series and the ever-entertaining shapeshifter Esen for this first volume in the Web Shifter's Library series. Esen and her human friend Paul Ragem have built a special library intended to help the various alien races understand each other, despite some major physiological and cultural differences. . . . As always, there are plenty of oddball alien hijinks, misunderstandings, and intrigues, all illustrating how badly the library is needed while providing excellent entertainment."   —*LOCUS*

"[*Search Image* is] a fun story with a lot of heart and a densely packed plot."   —SciFiMoviePage

"Czerneda has long been my favorite sci-fi author, and amazing, funny, awkward, compassionate characters like Esen are a big part of why I recommend her books so often. . . . I can't wait to see what fun she comes up with next!"   —The Obsessive Bookseller

"Julie Czerneda's novels ignite my sense of wonder, from the amazing worlds she creates to the fully realized aliens and likeable characters. I eagerly await her next."
   —Kristen Britain, *New York Times*-bestselling author of *Green Rider*

"*Search Image* is the guaranteed most delightful and fun SF read of the year."
   —Marie Bilodeau, author of the Aurora-nominated *Destiny* series

SEARCH IMAGE

Web Shifter's Library #1

Julie E. Czerneda

DAW BOOKS, INC.

DONALD A. WOLLHEIM, FOUNDER

1745 Broadway, New York, NY 10019

ELIZABETH R. WOLLHEIM

SHEILA E. GILBERT

PUBLISHERS

www.dawbooks.com

First Paperback Printing, October 2019
1 2 3 4 5 6 7 8 9

Dear reader and friend of the Little Blue Blob,
This one's for you.
(She's noticed.)

Acknowledgments

Esen's back.

It feels as if that's all I need to say, but you know I've more. To start with, in case you didn't know, I told just two "people in the biz" about Esen, the summer of 1998. The first told me to forget about an alien blob main character.

The second?

Was Sheila Gilbert, my Hugo-winning editor at DAW. Sheila loved Esen the way you do, bought her first book, and we've been happily blob-ing together ever since. We all thank you, Sheila.

There are not one but two new Esen covers by Matthew Stawicki. Both are brilliant, and both are Esen herself. Really. Take a look. Alien Blob of Blue! There's also a statue on our mantel, courtesy of Matt. Ersh, aka Phil, now stares at me. (I love my life.)

I've dedicated this book to you, dear readers, each and every one (Hi, Evan and Hal), because you've poured out your love of this particular, peculiar character of mine from the beginning. Janet Chase, the real and very nice one, even made me a line of Web toys. I've my own Blue Blobs! With Duras, of course. And more.

Suffice to say, I'm delighted you're pleased. Esen's special to me as well, being about messy biology.

And friendship.

So, to my dear Kiwis. Our friends from New Zealand

who've only grown closer with distance. It was my joy to populate this book and Esen's shiny new Library with you, as it's a place you'd appreciate. And, after dropping the future alien entry point for Earth on the South Island, it did seem the least I could do. (*Species Imperative*.)

The Roll Call: Barbara and Peter Clendon (Captain Petara Clendon); Helen Lowe (Continent of Lowesland); Jan Butterworth (Jan Terworth, cousin); Joffre Horlor (Joffre Sorbet); Kevin McLean (Senior Political Officer Aka M'Lean, because I added Haka to it); Lance Lones (Lance Largas); Lisa Marie Horner (Lisam Horner, security); Louise McCully (Cully Grass); Lyn McConchie (Red-tipped Conchie, a hedgerow); Lynelle Howell (Lynelle Owell, security); Malcolm Fletcher (Constable Malcolm Lefebvre); Maree Pavletich (the Mareepavlovax, because I remembered Pavlova, too); Mike Hansen (Ambassador Cichally Hansen); Nalini Singh (Alini Dove, who sings in the Garden); Peter Hamilton (Petham Erilton, embassy staff); Russell Kirkpatrick (Carwyn Sellkirk, transport wrangler); Sally McLennan and Norman Cates (Ally Orman, Response Room); Simon and Stephen Litten (Sammy Litten, xenopathologist); Taz/Harry/Syd (*THS Trailside Treasures and Oddities*); Henri and Steve Reed (Henri Steves, Assessment). Oh, the things I do to my friends. (Thankfully, they're understanding.) If I've missed anyone, let me know. There's more Esen coming, after all.

There is one official Tuckerization in this book: Celia Van Vliet donated generously to the FFANZ for the privilege of having me turn her into Celivliet Del, the Anata who causes Esen some very interesting moments. Thank you!

Here, 2017 was the year of unpacking, settling in (with renovations), visitors, and while Roger did most of that, I wrote more than I ever have before. Urban life has inspired! Or maybe it's just being happier than I've ever been. (And I'm a happy person, which says something.) Thank you for that, family-mine, always.

In between, I did get to some special events, and my thanks to their organizers and those who came out. Sandra Kasturi and Crew of ChiZine Colloquium in Toronto;

Andrea Dunn of the Toronto Library Association; and Matt Moore of the Ottawa Chiaroscuro Reading Series.

My heartfelt gratitude—on behalf of myself, and the family and friends of Ruth Stuart—goes to Ad Astra ConCom, starting with Mary-Ellen McAlonen and Amy DeRuyte, along with Taz and everyone involved in the wonderful celebration of Ruth's life you hosted. That so many of her dearest friends could gather, across oceans and continents, to share our stories and love of her on what would have been Ruth's birthday? A demonstration of the best of our community. Friendship *is* fandom. (And we wore "Ruth" smiley buttons. Thank you, Jana Paniccia, for those.)

Summer zoomed by and time to launch another book. I squeezed in a blog tour and major kudos to all involved, my hosts and especially publicists Alexis Nixon, Nick Seliwoniuk, and the amazing Mackenzie Filson. As always, Bakka-Phoenix Books (Toronto, ON) was flooded by Czernedas and friends. Thank you! We'd another excellent adventure at Flights of Fantasy (Albany NY), plus new stops at Librairie Clio (Pointe-Claire, QC), and Novel Idea Bookstore in Kingston.

Then came Can*Con 2017. Or as we DAW authors came to think of it, Sheila-Con, because our beloved editor, Sheila Gilbert, was a GoH! So we came. Yes, we did. Every one of Sheila's Canadian authors. Having taken the brunt of this outpouring of utter DAW-ness, I must—for myself, Sheila, and the gang—shout out all possible thank yous. In no order: Derek "Mr. Cool" Künsken, Brandon "Can't Catch Me" Crilly, Nicole "Ever Smiles" Lavigne, Marie "Glitterbombs" Bilodeau, Evan "You're Doing It Here?!" May, Jaggy "No Problem" Sue, Kate "Anything At All" Heartfield, Tim "Can I Help?" Sellmer, Farrell "Twinkle-Eyes" McGovern, Caycee "Saw That Coming" Price, Marie "Call The MP!" Pier Bouchard, Tyler "The Gazelle" Goodier, Gisele "The Gracious" Thomson; Dario "I Got This" Sciola, Lisa "Let Me Look That Up" Toohey, 'Nathan "Don't Miss This" Burgoine, Adam "Party Guy" Shaftoe, Etienne "Ever Ready" Price, and the student "Pick Me!" volunteers.

Dear Readers. Friends of Esen. I wrote these final paragraphs to *Beholder's Eye,* her first story, years before I wrote the rest.

I think it works here, at the start of her new adventures, and ours.

"... *I stepped out on my porch, seeing the future and completely content with what I saw. We would guard this gateway together. He would show me how to enjoy life as only an ephemeral could. In return, I would share with him whatever he wished to learn of other species, possibly even satisfying his inordinate curiosity—though I somehow doubted that.*

"*We would be together as long as he lived.*

"*And after that, I would remember Paul Ragem, my first friend, until the hearts of stars grew cold.*"

CONTENTS

Inception

BELIEF comes first.

This we are taught. Belief is the fuel, the lure, the guide. With it, each of us shall succeed in our quest to be made whole. To live in the Light. To Rise.

There are no promises when, you understand. Eventually is as good as we ever get, and the Ever Dark is rife with despair and rumor. We do not know if those who left before us succeed or Fall. Only that each of us must leave when it is our turn.

You can see why belief helps.

And why I keep my tooth sharp.

1: Garden Morning

WHEN my birth-mother Ansky answered the seductive howls of masculine desire as a Lanivarian, she didn't have far to go, being at a seaside resort for lonely singles.

Not, as Ersh expected, at a modern art fair gathering information on that species' trends in aesthetics and new materials for her Web.

Mind you, neither Ansky nor Ersh expected me to be the result, a genetic combination resulting in a Web-being not having occurred before. Proving you can plan ahead all you want, but biology? Will win.

I faced my version of the same quandary now.

Something had consumed every leaf, tendril, and bud from my jamble grape vine. The forthcoming lack of grapes, a favorite of my Lanivarian-self, wasn't the point. Well, it was in the long view, which I usually took, but the problem was more immediate. *What.*

As for who? My name is Esen-alit-Quar, Esen for short, Es between friends or in a hurry. It's my true name, as the canid Lanivarian is, thanks to Ansky, in a sense my true form—being the one I was born as and the one I resumed the way a Human might snuggle into a blanket.

Much to my web-kins' dismay. For I am that as well, a Web-being, able to manipulate my molecular structure at will. With practice. Occasionally I miscalculate, and all that stored energy is released in a contained but startling—

even to me—explosion. Not a Lanivarian problem; another reason I sought the form when upset.

As today. I poked at the nearest denuded vine. I should have played it safe with a small experimental arbor somewhere else, but no. Having recently been reminded of jamble grapes, I'd ordered a full overarching trellis with seats and a table, along with a patio tiled in a mosaic featuring, yes, grapes overflowing rustic baskets, and it was all now a thorough mess.

"I doubt staring at it will help, Es." My companion made an earnest attempt to be helpful. "Maybe a local bug took a liking?"

"Can't be that. The field's intact." He knew I'd mean the Kraal military bio-eliminator field I'd had Skalet install over, under, and around the Library Garden, much to my web-kin's paranoid satisfaction. "Nothing in, nothing out. That was the agreement."

One I'd signed with every level of government on our host planet who'd cared that I was importing alien-to-Botharis plant life, as well as a couple who hadn't but didn't want to be left out, given the tariff I was willing to pay for the privilege.

My companion and friend, Paul Antoni Ragem, was technically an import, born in space, but he'd been raised from infancy on this very spot, give or take a hill, by a large and close family. Botharans like the Ragems assuredly did not consider themselves imports. Being polite, I kept quiet on the topic, though Ersh, Oldest of us, had been a bemused spectator when Humans arrived in space, and Skalet, who'd conspired to be the Kraal version of Human for generations, remembered the conflict over which twig of humanity would first settle this world.

History notwithstanding, today Botharis was officially a Human planet, almost part of the Commonwealth, sometimes aligned with the Kraal, its people cheerfully imagining themselves independent and remote, until we'd invited the universe to visit on a daily basis.

Suffice to say most Botharans weren't entirely sure who'd let *us* in and maintained their distance. Until today.

The fine lines at the corners of Paul's gray eyes crinkled. "Then it's a puzzle that isn't going anywhere. Correct?"

Laughing at me, that was. *Might deserve it,* I admitted to myself, if not aloud, but I wasn't ready to stop glaring at the vine. "Today of all days. I want everything to look its best," I muttered. *Plants never cooperated—*"I can transplant a rose in time."

"Don't bother, Old Blob. They aren't coming."

My head whipped around so quickly my ears flapped. "What? But—" There were tables. I'd sacrificed flowers for each. There were—"Why?"

Paul gave a little shrug, nonchalant to someone who didn't know him. To me the movement was so full of hurt and disappointment I snarled in answer. Wanted to *bite*.

"It's not like that," he said, reading me with equal ease. "Just bad timing. Everyone's busy. My aunts have problems at the farm. My cousins—" Paul stopped and gave a more honest grimace. "It's my fault, Es. It was too soon to invite them here. They aren't ready."

Too soon? It had been over a year since we—I—bought this land from Paul's family, among others, bringing him back from "presumed dead" when I'd put his name on the deed with mine. I'd anticipated a blissful reconciliation. Paul's Human Web restored.

Ersh had warned me, *Look before you leap and drag everyone with you.*

Paul's first and, so far, only face-to-face meeting with his family had taken place the very next day, outside the Deed Registry Office of the Hamlet of Hillsview.

To my naïve amazement, the news had already spread throughout this rural community, and a small crowd was waiting. Outside, there being only room for two plus staff inside the office and that if you didn't want to sit. A crowd filled with a rich array of faces, forms, and voices, each with their tantalizing echo in Paul's own. Names he'd told me—or hadn't. Ragems and Lefebvres. Powells and Terworths. Camerons, too.

When they first saw Paul, faces had lit with wonder and deep-felt joy, as I'd fondly hoped, and Paul began to open his arms.

Then they saw me.

In hindsight, I grasped I might have been a shock; none

would have encountered a Lanivarian on their planet before.

At the time, all I could think was *I shouldn't be here*.

For each and every face had filled with anger. At Paul. They looked at my dear friend as though he'd recently eaten babies or committed some other heinous act—in Human terms—when he'd been returned to them and why weren't they still glad?

Then they'd turned to glare at me.

I didn't like remembering what happened next, how Paul had tucked me behind him, how he'd tried to speak, offered to explain—to these, his family, the people who'd raised him, people he'd lost and given up and who should have been glad—

A shouted "Monster-lover!" ended it. Despite the many who hushed the speaker, the hands held out in apology, Paul pushed through those gathered without another word, entering the deed office with me in tow. When we'd finished our business inside, his family was gone.

I didn't like remembering the look on his face then, or his silence the next day and the next. By the third, he appeared to put it all behind him. I'd doubts of that, but Paul hadn't needed to tell me to stay out of it. Even I understood there was nothing his "monster" could do that wouldn't make things worse. *Until they got to know me.*

Maybe his family had gathered to talk, and sensible heads prevailed. Or they'd felt a burden of guilt—as they should, in my admittedly biased opinion. Whatever the impetus, it wasn't long before a great-aunt called the Library and asked to speak to Paul. I didn't know what was said in that likely tense conversation, nor in any of those to follow, because "speak to Paul" soon became a distracting flood. Aunt after aunt taking their turn. Uncles. Cousins—Paul had so many cousins, he had trouble getting work done. Including, at last, his Uncle Sam.

My friend would recite their names to me, including new nephews and nieces, as if to prove his family—his life—was mended.

I knew better. It wasn't, not yet. Not when all they did was talk at a distance. I knew Humans better than that, especially this one, and I'd seen his hope for today's re-union.

"Not even your Uncle Sam?" Sam Ragem was Paul's mother's brother, and they'd been close, once. I loved Paul's stories about him. Especially the one where Sam had a sofa in his attic purportedly made from the remains of his mother, Paul's maternal grandmother, Delly Ragem having insisted she be recycled into something useful. Unfortunately, no one could bring themselves to sit on her. I planned a discreet nibble, to test the truth of this for myself.

"Sam has company staying over. I told him they'd be welcome, too, but it's a Ragem rule. You don't bring added guests," Paul said heavily.

We'd no guests at all now, and *bite* remained an option, an undertone affecting my voice. "While I've experience with the stubbornness of Ragems," I dared grumble, "you've been home a year. When will be long enough?"

"I let them believe I was dead for fifty, Old Blob." Flat and grim. Then he sighed. "It might take a while longer."

I whined at the grief in his tone. The guilt. Shared it. "You did it for me." To protect what I was from everyone else and I knew, deep down, that if nothing had changed in our lives—

Paul Ragem would have let himself remain "dead" to his family.

I feared they knew it. That be it Uncle Sam or cousin, they kept their distance because they knew Paul hadn't come back for them, however much he'd felt their loss. However much he now wanted to fix this. *Not something I'd say aloud.*

"What's done is done." His eyes flashed with something stern. "My family and friends will argue over who's to come first till they wear themselves out, then they'll all simply show up at the door one day."

"And we'll be ready," I said promptly. "I'll keep the tables out. Cut flowers daily. I can sleep by the door." I paused. "I'll need a comfy mat."

Paul laughed as I'd intended. "What would I do without you, my friend?"

"Not be ready," I replied smugly.

His mood had lightened, I could tell, if not how much was because of me, and how much he did for me. As far as I was concerned, this upsetting business of his reluctant family and so-called friends wasn't over.

Likely suspecting it, Paul changed the subject. "Speaking of ready—it's time to get to work."

"I'll meet you there."

"There" being inside the All Species' Library of Linguistics and Culture, ready for the first trainload of new clients already inbound from the landing field. In the early days, Paul would greet each arrival, relishing the chance to practice his language skills, after which I'd guide them to their respective habitat zone, relishing the chance to observe each species at close range. If the item of information the client brought was new to the Library's collection, it'd be accepted, and they'd be allowed to ask it a question. Answer received, they'd head back to their ships.

I missed those days. It had been so civil, before the word got out. Which might have had something to do with the pamphlets being given out at Hixtar Station—suffice to say, now hourly trains, usually full, disgorged a stampede of eager clients who raced to learn if they'd get their question, as if we ran a contest. If they "won," they waited impatiently for the answer. If not, they milled around in a disgruntled mass, waiting for the next train out.

Paul and I still interacted with clients and delegations, only now our time was reserved for those either experiencing problems our staff couldn't handle or being a problem our staff didn't deserve. *Senior academics were the worst.* Closely followed by industrial spies, but at least they were professional.

Many asked why we didn't make the collection available through the usual tech channels. There were times I could see the attraction, especially when I had to coax maintenance to clean up what non-Humans left behind to show they were disgruntled—or happy.

But no matter the challenges, Paul and I were in accord. Insisting clients travel this far off the lanes—and by Botharan insistence, they had to come through Hixtar Station first, making the trip even longer—to ask one question per visit about linguistics or culture winnowed the number to the serious—*mostly.*

To me, it also *felt* right, something my friend understood. In person was how my kind exchanged information, admittedly a more painful process. *Ersh would approve—*

Paul's finger scratched that soft spot behind my ear. I leaned into the caress. "So, Old Blob. What will you be today?"

It being a benefit of the Library's influx of clients from species far and wide that I could show up in any form without question. *Almost.* There'd be some issues giving orders to staff safely unfamiliar with my ability to be any form at all, and not every version of me was, to put it bluntly, old enough to be out alone, but as long as I could keep Skalet from installing bio scans and alarms?

I'd the freedom to be anything.

As did she, but Skalet only appeared as S'kal-ru the Kraal Courier, wasting a perfectly good opportunity to smile and shed pheromones for once.

"This me," I told Paul, leaving it at that. To staff and clients, my Lanivarian-self was his counterpart as the Library's curator, and the more visible me. "As soon as I'm done here."

His gaze fell on my poor plants, but he charitably refrained from declaring the situation hopeless. "See you there."

The thing about being a Lanivarian? I could follow Paul's progress along the winding path to the nearest Garden gate, my large, mobile ears turning slightly to hear the reassuring hum of the gate opening, then closing. Next, he'd pass through the field portal into the Library itself, but I slanted back my ears to stop listening.

Instead, I moistened my nostrils with my tongue and inhaled slowly, eyes half-closed in concentration. My surroundings became a painting composed of odors, both those being emitted, and, significantly for my purpose, those left behind.

Time travel by nose. The Panacians were best at this, collecting the merest trace from anywhere their kind had stepped, recording those in their shared history before tidying up. Given the cloying sweet of severed jamble grape, what I sought had been here shortly before my arrival.

There.

I bounded forward—bounding being another talent of this me—hard on the scent. I thrust my head inside a clump of fystia, lips curled back to show my fangs in a most unfriendly manner.

Doelike eyes blinked up at me from the hollow within the clump, completely unimpressed. "You didn't bring breakfast, Es. I got hungry."

"You're always hungry," I pointed out, knowing my Anatae. Lying down without breaking stems took some care and squirming. When done, I rested my chin on my paws to gaze at my guest. As Anatae went, Celivliet Del was a slender fellow, when his cavernous *revis* wasn't full of plant material being digested. *Thin, not slender,* I observed with a twinge. "You can't hide here forever, Celi. I've only so much garden." *And wasn't willing to part with much more of it.*

"I understand." Another blink, the lids crossing left to right. "Perhaps you could hide me in your house instead? Close to the kitchen?" This with an interested revis rumble.

Oh, and explain that to Paul? Who paid inconvenient attention to what my Lishcyn-self snuck from the cupboards as it was. "You need to go home."

"I can't." Wide supple nose flaps turned pink with misery. "I need the Library."

We'd hoped, Paul and I, that our clients would be satisfied with what they learned from us. Impressed by our professionalism. Perhaps share glowing reviews I could put in the next pamphlet. I hadn't thought our new minimum standard would be for them to leave, but here we were.

I'd found Celivliet Del when I'd first noticed missing plants and, to my regret, been too softhearted to grab him by the scruff at once and march him back to his ship.

A ship that had lifted without him. According to Celi, he wasn't popular with the others—

The pink faded. "You should get me lunch." A digging claw snapped open, the tip at the end of its strong curve tapping the nearest root suggestively. "Or let me nibble."

—*I couldn't imagine why.* I growled deep in my throat. "Don't you dare." It'd be another year and a half before the fystia could send up its first flamelike blossoms. "I'll bring you something," I promised.

I'd allowed a problem to take up residence—Celi had three dens, that I'd discovered, each a tidy hollow lined with whatever he'd thought I wouldn't miss—and knew it was my fault, not his. Something Paul and Skalet would confirm at tedious length.

If they found out.

How to make sure that didn't happen, while protecting the Garden, left me with one option. "Better still," I said cheerfully, "why don't you come inside with me?"

Paul awaited my help with the latest flood of clients.

What was one more?

Perception

HIXTAR VII was predominantly Human, one of the thousands of such worlds forming that species' Commonwealth. Some Humans viewed the Commonwealth as more than the sum of its parts, considering it the mighty collective arm of humanity reaching into space—but they tended to be those in need of strong-armed help with a local issue. Help they rarely received, because in truth the Commonwealth had little to do with planetary governance, being a relic of the time when Humans began their move across space and discovered they needed a common voice to get a word in edgewise among those already there.

Space, it turned out, was crowded.

The present-day Commonwealth, this leading edge of it at least, continued to represent the Human species in the great still-unknown, maintaining a fleet of Survey ships with their First Contact Teams. You never knew who'd you'd find out there, and Humans, it turned out, were unusually curious—or didn't know better, depending on who you asked. The Commonwealth continued to mediate disputes with their non-Human neighbors, plopping embassies on any world that would let them pay rent. Humans, it turned out, were rather good at diplomacy. And crime, necessitating a third arm, the Patrol. Who, to be fair, did pay attention to local issues, preferring those to interstellar squabbles; Humans felt better knowing they'd somewhere to leave an urgent message about their problems.

Though a world of little consequence in the greater scheme of things, around Hixtar VII orbited Hixtar Station. By happy circumstance, for those who'd invested in it, Hixtar Station proved a convenient stopover for miners working in nearby systems. Miners often flush with credits, leading those who ran the station to adopt a no-rule-but-safety policy and invite anyone with the finances to attach their useful bits to the station.

Leading to a bustling concoction of loading docks, repair shops, temp housing, entertainment facilities, and shopping. It wasn't a boast to say you could buy anything here. Finding it was the problem.

On Hixtar Station, the Commonwealth was represented by a handful of docked ships and a bored clerk behind a tiny info desk, who squinted up at Evan Gooseberry from his vidplayer as though wishing the tall young Human were a mirage. "I don't have that information. Next!"

There being no one behind him, Evan eased his carryall to the floor, rolling his shoulder. He'd carried the thing for what felt like hours, thoroughly lost after disembarking from the transport from Dokeci-Na. He pointed to the unmistakable gold-and-purple pamphlets on the desk. "Excuse me, but those are from the All Species' Library—"

"Not mine." A sequin-backed hand swept the little pile to the floor. "Station puts that junk everywhere. Next!"

Still no one. Evan didn't bother retrieving a pamphlet; he'd brought his own. "Then would you direct me to the Departures Area, please? I need pass—"

The same hand thrust outward and to the left. "Next!"

He picked up his carryall. "Thank you for your assistance."

Evan found an unoccupied table and sat, carryall between his feet. He sighed, tired beyond worry. Lost again. If there was intelligent purpose to the interior layout of this place, he'd yet to spot it. Unless it was to keep potential customers circling back through the same area of shops.

He pulled a little holocube from his pocket, thumbing through till he found what he wanted, then raised it to eye level. Away went his surroundings, that mass of shabby curved metal and garish signs. Here was home, where he'd grown up, where he returned when he could. In this image, Great Gran's study, with its windows overlooking the ocean and the comfy chairs set in front, just right for stargazing or conversation. He could almost smell the sea.

Great Gran was curled in one chair, mug in hand, talking to him. She'd concluded, since his last promotion, that he'd be too busy to respond properly from work. She should leave him messages instead. Long, detailed messages; Great Gran relished the opportunity to say whatever she wanted to him without interruption.

As Keeper of the Gooseberry Lore, the official list, with occasional pertinent anecdotes, of all those legally possessed of a last name passed in an unbroken line—if not always by genetics—from its origin on the birthplace of humanity, Earth itself? Much of what Great Gran had to say concerned his responsibility as the current most eligible Gooseberry of his generation. There were other Gooseberrys, but Evan was not only her direct descendant, but heir apparent to the Lore if he'd only agree.

As the mere thought of tending the Lore filled him with utter dread, Evan paid dutiful attention to Great Gran's plethora of adoptable orphans, handsome potential partners, and latest reproduction-for-solos tech. Not that he was in any sense ready—being a diplomat was his true calling and he'd only just started. Besides, he worked with aliens. Explain the whole Gooseberry name thing to them? Not remotely on the allowed topics list. Still, one far distant day Evan intended to produce the next Gooseberry and make Great Gran happy.

In this message, his future wasn't the topic. Great Gran gleefully listed the hazards of offworld travel according to his Aunt Melan Gooseberry, who'd recently returned from such a journey and hadn't enjoyed a moment. It was too noisy here to try and listen; Evan knew every word by heart anyway. It was Great Gran's face he wanted to see, every rich dark curve and line familiar. Especially when she reached the part about space pirates and smiled.

She'd the best smile of any Gooseberry. It started around her uptilted brown eyes, crinkling the edges, then flew across her cheeks to spread her lips in a smile so large and startlingly bright, his younger cousins believed she had lights installed in her teeth.

She might. Certainly the giant cloud of hair framing her face changed color with her mood and the seasons, and Great Gran was not above tucking auto-glitter among the coils.

There'd been an abundance of glitter when he'd met— Evan sighed again. He shut off the cube and tucked it safely into his pocket. He wasn't getting to them or the Library sitting here.

It was then he spotted the line of Urgians moving purposefully down the corridor, each clutching a very familiar pamphlet in an upraised overt.

His *snake-tentacle-snake* fear response disappeared beneath a wave of new hope.

Grabbing his bag, Evan Gooseberry hurried in pursuit.

"You. There."

"Thank you." Evan Gooseberry looked along the arm and hand of the ship's steward, refusing to focus on the dirt-grayed sleeve flecked with rust stains—the *Dimmont III* was a working freighter, not a liner—or on the Human skull tattooed on the back of the Snoprian's hand—taste differed—only to realize she indicated the topmost of three bunks. A Popeakan might fit in the meager space below the bulkhead; he wasn't at all sure he would. "May I req—"

"No requests. Humans stay in here or take another ship." A toothy grin. "No refunds either."

"I'll stay," Evan said hastily. The Urgians had led him into the cold and noise of a smaller than most loading area, but when he'd tried to follow them up the ramp into their ship, he'd been stopped by the crew and informed they'd no humanoid-suitable accommodations. Unless he'd be willing to be put in cryo for the trip.

He'd declined. There'd been two other starships in that section listing their next port as the Library—more precisely, he'd spotted the worn pamphlets affixed to their entries and assumed the best. The first of those awaited repairs.

Leaving the *Dimmont III*. To his relief, there'd been room for him and the quoted, one-way only, fare was unexpectedly reasonable.

Now he knew why.

Still with that predatory grin, the crewbeing turned to those coming into the stateroom behind him. "You and you. There and there. Lift's in twenty. Stow your gear or lose an eye." She was still chuckling as she went down the corridor.

Stateroom was perhaps wishful thinking. The back two-thirds of the rectangular room was walled in bunk beds and cupboards—storage for their belongings, Evan assumed. To reach them, you edged around a slim table and its benches, all bolted to the metal floor. The bottom bunks on either side were dark and filled with blanketed lumps, passengers—of whatever species—already aboard. The second bunk to the right contained a netted mass of Rands, the cluster of individuals shifting and crooning quietly to themselves, though one had rebelliously stuck a footpad through the mesh, and was that a pamphlet poking out from underneath?

It'd only be three shipdays and -nights, Evan assured himself, gripping his carryall. The *Dimmont III* wasn't luxurious or fast or even Human, being crewed by Snoprians. Of itself, that wasn't a problem. The species was theta-class humanoid, one of the few often mistaken for Human, if you missed the vestigial feathers capping their heads, but Snopria had a higher gravity than Humans found comfortable. The *Dimmont III* had reduced it, slightly, for their passengers. *Still felt as though he carried weights.* Maybe he'd make friends—

A shoulder pushed his, hard. "Get a move on, dregs, 'r get outta m'way!"

—or not. The latecomers were a pair of Human males, spacers by their garb and tans, hard of face and tone. The speaker was thin, with cold blue eyes in a face bearing a bubbled scar from eyebrow to chin. His partner was heavier built and bearded, a rarity among those who worked the lanes, yellow wiry strands caught up in tight beaded braids.

Maybe he shouldn't judge, but the pair seemed unlikely to have the All Species' Library of Linguistics and Culture as their ultimate destination. Both, by Evan's estimation, were the sort his friend Rudy wouldn't let near his ship, the *Largas Loyal,* let alone employ, and if he met either in an alleyway, he'd count himself lucky to get out again whole.

So Evan moved as he was told, though he paused first to smile a pleasant greeting: the pause to show he wasn't to be pushed and the smile because he intended to be civil regardless.

After all, he was a diplomat. Grumpy, tired spacers of any species, even of criminal bent, couldn't be worse than a roomful of grumpy, tired bureaucrats. Tourists, on the other hand? Smiling now to himself, Evan climbed the ladder to his bunk, rolled inside, then squirmed until he could pull in his carryall.

This wasn't so bad. He could touch the ceiling, if not straighten his arm while doing so. *Cozy.* The bedding was recycled plas, the pad beneath lumpy, but, by the nose-stinging smell, all recently disinfected. There was a stowage cupboard within reach if he laid on his side and stretched, though if he wanted access to his things without climbing—

Doors were slapping closed. *He'd best hurry.*

Evan stuck his head out to see what was left. The scarred spacer grinned up at him. "That 'un's yours."

Of course it was. Sighing to himself, Evan shifted back against the wall and opened his carryall. There was a net at the head of the bunk, intended for whatever you'd want at hand.

A *thud* followed by a shouted curse made him peer over the edge.

Scar and Beard were claiming the bottom bunks. As

their first victim struggled and cursed from a roll of blankets, the spacers prepared to dump out the occupant of the other, directly beneath him. Evan tensed, torn between a heroic leap into what wasn't his business and the safer if slow approach of climbing down the ladder into it. Ignoring the situation didn't occur to him until later.

Before he could decide, the two halted in comic unison, facing the business end of a—a plain, nonthreatening rod. "I'd take your assigned spots," with a suggestive wave. The voice, female and Human, was composed and calm.

To Evan's surprise, the pair shrugged as though giving up. Then Beard gestured at the now-empty bunk. "Whaddabout—"

With a shake, the rod expanded to twice its length and *hissed*. Evan's stomach clenched at the sound—*SNAKE*—

Scar yanked his partner back, but the rod grazed the tip of Beard's finger. He screamed, hunching over his hand. They staggered, one helping the other, to the end of the stateroom where they stood, Scar glaring in dire promise at whomever lay in the bottom bunk while his partner continued to whimper in pain.

"Next time don't be late. Lift's imminent," the voice told them. "Jumpy Lyn, get back in your bunk."

The blanket lifted, and four eyes looked out cautiously, then the Ervickian, late wis-morph from what Evan could see, freed itself and rose. It, Jumpy Lyn, wore what appeared to be a purple Human sweater, stained and stretched, with a hole reinforced with peeling tape mid-torso to allow access to its second mouth, likely source of the stains. It settled itself on the bunk, pulled the blanket overtop, and muttered dark things about Humans.

"Take the top," Scar ordered.

"I can't climb with this." Beard held out a trembling hand, the finger swollen and starting to blister.

Evan felt a queasy sympathy. What had that rod been?

The other spacer snorted. "Got two hands, don't yer?"

As the two went to their assigned bunks, Scar noticed Evan and scowled. "You got sommat to say, dregs?"

"I do." Evan couldn't resist. "Sleep well."

The quiet chuckle from below didn't help. The spacer's eyes narrowed in threat. Evan eased back into what now felt a haven.

He busied himself unpacking a few essentials. His notebook and stylo went in the net; the cap to protect against clingers over his tight curls—the pests had been number eleven on Auntie Melan's list; the container of water and emergency rations; his light and temp air supply—the *Dimmont III* wasn't a new ship, *not that he'd dwell on possible calamity, but being prepared was never wrong*, according to the travel guides and Great Gran, who'd surely voiced that opinion to his flustered aunt.

About to close his carryall and wiggle out to stow it in the cupboard, Evan hesitated. He reached inside, fingering what sat in the midst of his belongings. Did he dare leave it in the bag, or would it be safer in the net?

It was only then he realized Beard, who'd managed to climb up to the other top bunk, could see across the room. Was watching him now, by the glint of eyes in the shadow.

Decision made, Evan closed the carryall and tucked it behind him, against the wall. Leaving very little room to move, but, he thought with satisfaction, not even a catastrophic loss of gravity would set it loose.

He yawned, ready to take his own advice and sleep, only to realize a new problem.

How was he to remove his boots?

2: Library Morning

WE had planned for every biological necessity, in my estimation providing sufficient choice in transport, seating, lighting, atmosphere, and access nodes to handle any sort of being who came to the Library. Well-tested choices at that; I'd enjoyed my many varied selves.

Paul oversaw the precious growing collection, datasets constantly refreshed by sources that would multiply as the Group checked clearances and motivations. We didn't need what was readily available, though we'd the usual links to those. Our clients—the ones who mattered most to us—were after what they couldn't find elsewhere.

As was I. The Web of Ersh had contained six: Ersh, Eldest and First, Lesy, Ansky, Mixs, Skalet, and me, Youngest by millennia, *as they'd regularly remind me*. While the others had traveled, listening, watching, and above all, remembering, I'd stayed home.

Other than a few excursions with Lesy to the Portula Colony, set to drift alongside the Jeopardy Nebula. *The colony had had such a wonderful pool—*

The point was, through Ersh, Senior Assimilator, we'd shared the memories in one another's flesh, informed of changes in what we called "ephemeral" species. It made it possible, at whim or need, to cycle into each species and blend in with the current culture.

Our camouflage, not our purpose.

For the Web of Ersh recorded in our flesh the accomplishments of ephemeral species, determined those would never be lost, the species themselves going extinct with distressing regularity.

Along with keeping nonextinct intelligent species safe from another incursion by the non-intelligent version of my own, the Web of Esen continued what Ersh had begun. To remember the lost.

Other than Skalet, only Paul, of my Web if not our flesh, knew. In our early years together, he'd ask me to show him the beauty of an Ompu, or to sing with the haunting voice of a Jarsh, seeming to take delight in what no one else ever would again.

Then he stopped asking. If Paul had realized the time would come when what was Human would be extinct and lost, except to me and mine, he didn't say, nor would I ask.

The other reason to collect data, to help me—and Skalet—blend unobtrusively in any form and so keep our existence secret, appeared sufficient.

Besides, Paul and I had a new, vital purpose: to share knowledge in order to prevent ignorance-based conflict and, hopefully, stave off premature extinctions. Hence the All Species' Library of Linguistics and Culture. Our hope? That before tensions grew out of control, someone would come to us and ask the right question.

A question I was more than happy to modify and interpret, as required.

Ersh would not approve.

Skalet did, which troubled me. She shouldn't have, other than to value what she could assimilate from me, and I had to agree with Paul. He suspected her Kraal-self enjoyed being the first to know about pending conflicts, perhaps to take what advantage she could. Making it necessary to assess which such information to share with her, as if being her Senior Assimilator while Youngest wasn't complicated enough.

"Family," I grumbled to myself.

"I thought we were going to lunch," Celi protested, skipping to keep up with me.

Not to myself, then. "We're keeping you out of the Garden," I whispered back, ears flat in disapproval.

I'd brought the Anata through the field portal without a problem, the entrance into the Library necessarily coded to be more lenient about alien tissue, a trifling accommodation we hadn't felt like sharing with the Botharans. After all, the Garden was for our clients. And me, but mostly for our clients, to provide a calming refuge.

Over the past half year, our clients had come to us out of curiosity or scholarship, even some to challenge the Library's claim to being the largest repository of cross-species' information in the Commonwealth. Especially the weird stuff.

Yet to arrive? Those who faced a crisis they couldn't understand, be it because of lack of knowledge, or the wrong sense organs. Paul and I knew they were out there. We'd seen it for ourselves. The Tumblers, robbed of their children by those who couldn't comprehend their language or biology. The Feneden and Iftsen, the former unable to believe the other existed. Ganthor, their instincts abused and twisted by those seeking to use force first, understand later—

"Lunch?"

And wasn't understanding to start here? Poor Celi. I relaxed my jaw in a grin. "Lunch. C'mon."

Only one place in the Library supplied food, though in the interests of not having researchers expire from dehydration there were beverage dispensers in each zone a prudent distance from its access node. You could make your tech slime-proof, but life found a way to spill.

I led my unwanted guest along the still-empty corridor, with its smooth white curves, then stopped at the door, also curved.

To most Botharans, the Library represented a pinnacle of exotic architecture, alien yet efficient and, above all, envied. Unsurprising given the most urban area on this planet remained stuck in that stage of Human planet settlement I referred to as "rock and tree" when Paul couldn't hear me.

In contrast, the Library's exterior was smooth and white, its arms embracing the low hills of what had been the Ragem family farm, plus a few others, as well as plunging below ground to form a modest two-floor basement.

The construction material was a mix of dirt and minerals dug from what would be the basement, subjected to a process to produce a slop our offworld contractor called "dynamic slurry." Extruded from the right machines, also from offworld, and flung over a deceptively flimsy-looking framework, the slurry quickly set into its stipulated shape, the result proof against the harshest environments.

In other words, the Library was an oversized Commonwealth Survey emergency survival shelter. Human tech. Capable of absorbing solar energy, or geothermal if you preferred, with any portion of the exterior walls varying from opaque to translucent on command.

Being an honest person, Paul looked uncomfortable whenever the Botharans sent another aircar full of design students overhead. One day he'd give in and tell them.

Wouldn't hurt. While it'd cost the Library its standing as wildly creative, I applauded anything that kept our neighbors believing we operated on a tight budget, albeit a large one.

We couldn't risk anyone outside my Web becoming aware of the extent of our resources. Ersh had grasped the importance of local economies before most present-day species had one. She'd taken the acquisition of wealth as a tenet of survival—and a pleasant hobby akin to collecting small utensils, not that she'd admit it. I could, if I wanted, buy this planet without making a dent.

Not that I'd want to—Web-beings didn't view physical objects the same way as ephemerals. It might be the lack of hands—what mattered was that excessive wealth attracted attention, dangerous attention. Ersh, ever-vigilant, had spent centuries burying and disguising the Web's resources.

Where Paul and I spent the most? Other than the tariffs for my Garden, fees to the coffers of government, and making payments toward the landing field, plus taxes to the joy of all? Inside the Library, hiring only Botharans, using only Botharan materials. My Lanivarian-self had traveled to Grandine, the planetary capital, to lure the finest general contractor on this world to build the Library. Duggs Pouncey had been too busy for us until she'd noticed the varied habitat zones in our proposal, reluctant to commit until we'd offered her final authority on structural issues, and only truly willing once she'd heard about local sources where possible.

She hadn't left the Library since, proudly and profanely informing us this was the project of a lifetime and when were we expanding?

"Lunch?"

I put my paw on the control, waited that essential reverent moment despite the rumble from Celi's empty revis . . .

Then opened the door to the Library.

Inside was a world of light and color, movement and noise, all with a ripe undertone of smelly alien feet to make my Lanivarian-self inclined to drool, but that'd hardly be polite. While there were elegant, hushed main entrances to public buildings across known space, this, to my unending pride, wasn't one of them.

After all, as I'd told Paul, in a climate where it did rain, and yes, did snow—we'd made paths, but who'd stick to them—racks for soggy outerwear and boots were essential, and after a space journey of however long, plus the slightly longer than envisioned transit ride through the hills, everyone wanted *in* without delay, meaning each train unloaded in thirty-being stampedes.

Precluding Skalet's vision of tediously thorough checkpoints, body cavity searches, and the sampling of genetic material whether permitted or not.

Well, we did the last part, but more discreetly, having outerwear and boots lined up and waiting on those handy racks. As Ersh taught us, *you couldn't cycle into a form unless you'd tasted it first.*

No one, I thought contentedly, would notice another alien here, even one who'd supposedly left days ago.

The bedlam was more organized than the participants knew. Textures flowing across the floor looked like art, but were actually preference passages, designed to separate those who liked shaggy and soft underfoot from those who'd trip on anything less than mirror flat, and variations between. Past that, the walkways presented other subtle and less so choices as you moved deeper into the Library. We'd had a curious Ket wander into the habitat zone meant for Iftsen; the feel changed her mind immediately.

Aquatics and non-oxy breathers entered with the rest, doubtless resigned to having to stay in their species-appropriate suits, grav carts, or bags over the shoulders of hired help. *I did enjoy their expressions when they learned they could safely strip.*

Leaving their protective gear, and genetic information, in handy racks.

Why, there was an Oieta now, poling along in a very snappy exo-suit—

Someone stepped on my tail. "Ow," I exclaimed, the word becoming a snarl.

"Sorry, Esen," Celi said weakly, flaps a distressed pink. "Getting a little desperate here."

To risk stepping on my tail he must be, Anatae wary of any form that, while civilized, was not herbivorous and could, in a famine because those happened all the time, forget who not to bite.

I threw an arm around what passed for his shoulders. "Let's take care of that right now," I promised.

Having more practice than anyone, I slipped us through the eddies of incoming clients; this early, there were none outgoing to complicate the flow. I leaped over a prickly strip of passage that didn't bother Celi at all, then helped him avoid one to attract the more cold-blooded among us. *Some liked it hot.*

He twisted to look over his shoulder and down, showing off a nonarticulated yet robust spine, then back to me. "What's with the floor?"

So few ever asked. "Later," I told him, having spotted an excellent reason to move faster.

Lionel Kearn was among the new arrivals.

Lionel and I had history. He'd been among the first Humans I'd encountered, at the time being Paul's immediate superior on the Survey ship *Rigus,* then its acting captain. Mind you, I wasn't supposed to encounter Humans on my first assignment from Ersh, who'd selected Kraos as safely pre-contact and uncomplicated. No one having told the Commonwealth, they'd sent their eager First Contact Team to a planet that not only wasn't pre-contact, to my dismay, but firmly intended to stay that way. The Kraosians murdered, then buried any alien visitors. They prepared to do the same to the Humans.

Ersh sent me to observe and do nothing.

I couldn't. I broke Paul Ragem out of a Kraosian dungeon and made the rest up as I went. While I did save the Humans, Ersh was not impressed. I'd revealed my nature to Paul, who became my first friend—and the only being outside the Web of Ersh to learn our secret.

As first assignments went, at least mine had been memorable.

Trusting Paul to keep that secret, I ran home to Ersh and all could have been fine, give or take another century before Ersh sent me out again—except for Death.

You see, the Web of Ersh existed because—*not that she ever admitted it*—Ersh grew lonely, having become the first of our kind to think, rather than simply respond to appetite. Instead of spending excess mass to travel in space, or shed it, the moment came when she kept it. Let herself grow.

Let herself split.

It wasn't as simple as that, web-flesh being full of memory and the essential "who" of us. Ersh chose what to share, what to keep to herself, and *though she'd never admitted that either,* what she excised from herself. She valiantly resisted the instinct to gobble up her other bit and Lesy was "born."

Ersh might have developed a belated conscience, but she'd all the emotional capacity of an asteroid. Lesy was—gentle. Creative. A dreamer. Ersh, once over the shock, tried again every so often, budding off Ansky, Mixs, and Skalet—all of whom were more Ersh-like than not.

My arrival being a surprise, there was no presorting of me. As Ersh often said, *and no guessing what I'd do next.*

Death was the original, base version of a Web-being. Sans intellect, sans feeling, at first nothing more than a living hunger in pursuit of the sweetest flesh of all—ours—while cracking starships and habitat domes and generally being everything we were not.

It didn't take long for such behavior to attract attention of the worst sort.

Kearn, already nervous about Paul Ragem's mysterious friend—*I'd blown up in his office, but it hadn't been my fault*—seized upon the evidence and leaped to the stunningly inconvenient conclusion that Death was a monster named Esen-alit-Quar and the Enemy.

Paul, associated with me, became his enemy, too.

Many underestimated Lionel Kearn. Granted, in person, Lionel came across as a humorless, easily offended wisp of a scholar with the management skills of a Queeb. However, he was also brilliant, obsessive, and determined to end me for the good of all. Even as Death, ironically, was ended by me, with Paul's help, Lionel came close to an unfortunate success.

To escape, we'd faked Paul's death and I faked mine—though I didn't fool Paul as I'd intended. *I rarely could.*

Unconvinced, Lionel spent the next fifty standard years crisscrossing known space after his Enemy, wearing down his opponents with charts and facts, infecting followers with his paranoia.

Meanwhile, Paul and I, reunited and under new names—and, in my case, a new shape as the Lishcyn Esolesy Ki—lived happily on Minas XII, running Cameron & Ki Imports. Paul took a temp-partner, Char Largas, and to my delight they produced offspring. I enjoyed the twins' growth to adulthood, gaining yet another personal reason to keep watch in case another Death crossed into this part of space.

Paul, though I didn't know it till later, organized his Group to watch over me and keep an eye on Lionel Kearn.

I'd pitied Lionel, trapped in a life ruled by pointless fear, almost as much as I resented what he'd done to Paul. My friend had sacrificed his own family and friends, letting them believe he'd died in order to hide me. To be all I had, for I believed myself the last of my kind.

Until Skalet showed up, not dead and thoroughly

aggrieved I'd some of Ersh she didn't. She used poor Lionel and anyone else she could influence to flush us from hiding, not that I knew it was her then. In the process, innocents died, Paul was tortured—though not by Skalet— and two species almost went to war.

Lionel Kearn had stopped it. With a little help. I'd risked revealing myself to him, tired of being his Enemy, and then, on impulse, sent him a message with the key to resolving the crisis. I even gave him my name. He hadn't believed in me at first. It was a measure of his character that he sought the truth in his own way.

When Skalet finally revealed herself to me, it hadn't been a warm family reunion. She poisoned Paul, damaged me, then tried to rob Ersh's tomb.

As families do, Skalet and I resolved our differences; being what we are, we did it in dust and blood. She would be of the Web of Esen, I its Senior Assimilator, and I would never give her what she'd only thought she wanted: Ersh's knowledge of how our kind moved through space.

The poison I couldn't forgive, but Skalet had to live with me, the Youngest, in charge, making us even.

I got over her suddenly not being dead; it made me impatient with Paul's family, who hadn't.

Lionel had been there, when I'd faced off on Picco's Moon with my web-kin. Had, with Rudy and Paul, witnessed our sharing of flesh—not something any of the Humans found comfortable, adaptable as they were.

Lionel had shown Skalet kindness, surprising us both. *Now, here he was.*

The problem? He'd promised to come months ago, to share his considerable expertise and help curate the collection, only to change his mind abruptly, without giving a reason. Paul had refused to speculate, saying only we shouldn't think ill of Lionel.

I didn't. Instead of panting my stress, I walked faster, pulling Celi along.

Not every Human could deal with what we were. Rudy had known, then struggled to comprehend; as a result he'd come within a breath of killing Skalet.

I wasn't ready to find out if Lionel had faced all the strangeness of me he could handle, that day on the moon.

Perception

HE'D been wrong.

About so much, for so long, he'd come to doubt everything, a feeling Lionel Kearn embraced, given how poorly he'd done when certain.

He took another step with the beings from the transport, not the only Human, but two arms and legs were hardly the norm. Under other circumstances, he'd have been fascinated. Such variety in one place, most sure to be fellow scholars—

Was he wrong now? The familiar litany played through his head, but there was nothing he hadn't checked, no parameter unconfirmed. It was time—

"Welcome to the All Species' Library of Linguistics and Culture, Hom Kearn."

And too late if he was, Lionel thought with relief. "Thank you," he replied, tilting his head courteously to the greeter. This elderly male Octarian wasn't *her*. He'd learned enough about Esen and her kind to be sure. Though she could be someone—anyone else here—he kept his attention where it belonged. "I believe the Director is expecting me."

"Indeed, he is. Follow me, please."

Lionel was ushered into a simple office, lit by sunlight pouring through one wall. From the train, he'd recognized the construction with a jolt, then wry humor. None of the shelters he'd used in his career had polished wood floors or a view of a farmhouse and barn on a hill. The desk was a plain table with a built-in comp access node, prudently dark and inactive. A cluster of brightly colored rings caught his eye. Ganthor snout clips?

"Lionel!" Paul Ragem Cameron came around from behind his desk, offering his hand with a smile.

The honest warmth in that smile brought forth his own. "Paul." The former member of his alien specialist team—*another life*—looked well, mature and fit, happy. The almost daunting intelligence remained, the avid curiosity that had made Paul Ragem stand out from the very first day. "It's good to see you," Lionel said, and knew it was true.

Their hands met, Paul bringing up his other hand to hold Lionel's firmly. "I can't wait to show you all of it, Lionel. It's better than we dreamed it could be—will be better still." Those perceptive gray eyes searched his, and the warm smile faded. "You aren't here for a tour."

"I look forward to one, believe me, but no."

A nod. "Come. Have a seat." There were a pair of chairs by the curve of wall, a homely pot of tea and cups waiting between on a raised tray. Paul poured for them both, after his questioning look got a nod, then sat back. "We're private."

Meaning there were safeguards in place against snoops or eavesdroppers. Given Esen and Paul's connections to S'kal-ru and hers, likely more advanced tech than any Lionel had available. He took his cup, unsurprised his hand shook slightly. Devices dropped into pockets, clinging to a hair on your head, hell, you could drink a tracer in your tea and never know it. "You should scan me," he cautioned.

Paul smiled again, almost to himself. "Already have." A nod to the door. "Built into the frame."

Relieved, Lionel steadied the cup, took a sip, steadied himself, too. "Thank you. I'm—reassured."

"So this is serious." Paul frowned. "I'll call Esen."

"No. No," more gently as that frown deepened. "This isn't about our—our friend." Lionel still found it hard to say her name aloud, as if it would betray a trust too precious to risk. "This concerns you."

"Me?" His host sat back, brow rising. "Go on."

"First. As you asked, I completed the removal of your problem. The Hurn."

A startled laugh, "Gods, Lionel, you make it sound like an execution."

The solution had been proposed by Lionel's contact within the Group and once captain, Rudy Lefebvre. To Rudy, the comp security expert from the Dump on Minas XII—hired to safeguard the Library's system—had crossed an unforgivable line. Not when he'd used his access to steal data for Hurn benefit, because no one in their right mind had ever trusted Diale.

But the Hurn had dared kidnap Bess, Esen as Human. While she hadn't felt in any danger, from what he'd heard, Rudy wanted Diale gone.

"Nothing of the sort," Lionel managed a chuckle. "Diale's accepted a lucrative contract elsewhere, one that will require his full attention and resources. He's prepared to pay a penalty to extricate himself from your affairs as well as the Library's. You should hear from him soon."

"I'm not going to ask how. Thank you." Something dark flickered in those eyes, gone in the next instant, implying another not ready to forgive the Hurn. "You said that was 'first.'"

"Ah, yes." Lionel took refuge in his tea, studying the whorls. "Bear with me, please. Why Botharis?" He looked up. "Why your real name?"

Paul gave a charming little shrug. "Esen."

He'd guessed as much. "She wanted you to have your life back." As Paul Cameron, he'd had no past, only the future. As Paul Ragem, once more on home soil? "How has it been?"

Paul took a breath and then let it out slowly, cheeks puffed. "About as well as I'd expected. Some of the family are coming around. The rest?" His lips twisted. "Let's say it's a work in progress."

Nowhere had Paul's reputation been more tarnished than here, where he should have been revered and cherished, as he had been. *I'd done it.* Lionel remembered as if it were yesterday. He'd interviewed every relative, however distant, in person. Tracked down every friend, classmate, or lover in his pursuit of any clue as to why Paul Ragem turned on his own kind to side with a monster. Spread his false belief like poison, until the Ragems abandoned their homes and farms, moving to the other side of the world.

Worst of all, Paul's mother had died believing her son dead.

"That's why I stayed away," Lionel admitted. He'd practiced what to say; that didn't make it easier. "When I learned the Library would be here, here on Botharis, I thought—I knew—if I came, my presence would bring it all back. Raise doubts. Make it—" He stopped.

"Peace, Lionel," *and, oh, that dreadful compassion.* "You did what you thought was right at the time. I don't blame you."

"But there's still doubt, isn't there? To this day. Because of me." Lionel put down his cup, too agitated to trust his hands. "To end it, you'd have to tell them the truth, about the Monster and what happened. About—her. And you can't."

"Won't."

The weight of that word. By rights, the foundations of this building should shake, cups shatter on the floor, and every being that drew breath find themselves unable to inhale.

"Lionel." Paul leaned forward, eyes intent. "Listen to me. My family and former friends have their own issues and, frankly, for a good chunk of them, it's more about why I haven't hired my cousins to work here, than whatever happened offworld. I swear they don't look up at night. A couple think the world's flat. My mother was the first of her generation to leave home and attend university overseas. Still the only Ragem, other than me, to leave Botharis for space." The start of a smile. "One of many reasons I'm glad to see you. Esen will be, too. She's been worried seeing her true nature offended your sensibilities. That business on Picco's Moon?"

"What?" Lionel blinked. Watching two blue teardrops sprout mouths to neatly snap exactly the same amount of flesh from one another was nothing compared to being present for the carnage of "settling" order within an Ervickian crèche, and *don't get him started on the Heezle.*

"Surely—why, I considered it a privilege, a profound privilege, to witness the establishment of her Web. Esen told you she's worried about me?"

"She didn't have to." A full smile appeared. "I know the signs."

"Well. We can't have that." Lionel gave himself an inward shake. *Later.* "I've come to warn you, in person. Someone's been making inquiries about you. About Paul Ragem."

Still looking amused, Paul straightened, holding out his arms. "Here I am. I've nothing to hide. I take it you know who this 'someone' is?"

"I do." A name the Group had flagged for good reason, the sole surprise being she'd resurfaced where there was such a price on her head. "Janet Chase."

Once captain of the *Vegas Lass,* part of the Largas Freight fleet, from all accounts a capable ship's officer and, from some, personally interested in the handsome then co-owner of their client, Cameron & Ki Exports. Until Chase revealed her true nature: a career criminal and mercenary for hire, working for the Tly to disrupt trade and obtain weapons for their war on Inhaven.

Lionel watched the good humor drain from Paul's face. "What does she want? Do you know?" The slow, careful way he drew in his arms was like watching a spring coil.

He hadn't been wrong to come. "Only that it concerns your father." A shock, he saw it in Paul's eyes; Lionel hurried on because there was worse. "I went to see him myself, before coming here, but he's—"

Stefan Gahanni's repair shop on Senigal III had been a blasted ruin, *not where he wanted to start.*

"Paul, your father's missing."

3: Chow Morning

WHEN we'd drawn up our plans for the Library, I'd noticed something missing. *Food*. Paul hadn't agreed, adamant that any multispecies' capable restaurants would be built at the landing field. While we waited for those who ran the Hamlet of Hillsview, our nearest community and delighted recipient of the frankly ridiculous tax put on the Library, to realize we were Here To Stay, and their hamlet would indeed Have to Change, and a properly planned shipcity could grow around the landing field without causing the End of Days—I'd been to Council Meetings and dramatic capitals were the norm— I'd put my paw down, adamant if I was to work at my best, I'd need snacks on site.

Not that I'd phrased it that way. Knowing Paul too well for the paws-down approach, I'd argued we could have clients arrive who'd neglected to eat beforehand or been spacesick—something my Lanivarian-self certainly knew about—and whatever the reason, we couldn't very well have them faint or expire inside the Library for lack of nutrients.

Paul agreed. I'd visions of a lovely café leading out to the Garden. What arrived was a wall-sized auto-dispenser made by Anywhere Chow Inc., guaranteed to satisfy any and all dietary needs at the push of a button, provided you filled it properly. Ours came with a grouchy installer named Lambo Reomattatii who'd grudgingly confessed—after installing the auto-dispenser with bolts better suited to bridge construction—that a Chow could only be operated by an expert.

Lambo had demonstrated. Sure enough, no one else could load the machine, let alone coax anything edible from it. Those handling claws moved in a blur, all eyes intent on the indicators, somehow producing the requested food item. Or at least close, Lambo less adept with the request part.

A month later, the Anywhere Chow Inc. head office, perhaps under the impression we were holding their valued installer hostage, called to insist we return Lambo at once. Paul insisted, politely, they provide a replacement operator for the Chow or we'd return the machine, too.

An operator? Their response hadn't been polite at all, particularly in its suggestion about Human limitations. After all, their product was so easy to use, a weanling Heezle could do it!

I cycled into a weanling Heezle to test their claim, we made a vid showing the Chow spitting liquid protein over everyone in the room, and, after a brief negotiation, Lambo's continued service was included in the rental.

Unfortunately.

Despite their resemblance to an armored assault servo, the Carasians you met in public were courteous, well-spoken individuals who—most of the time—got along famously with almost any other species. Everyone knew you simply kept a prudent eye on door widths and moved breakables.

Not so our Lambo, a being surly and combative by nature, with, as Rudy put it, a fuse shorter than an Ervickian who'd sat on a tack. Duggs Pouncey built a wide sturdy counter between client and Carasian, reducing the number of complaints immensely, but dealing with Lambo took a certain fortitude.

Celi arrived at the counter beside me. "This is lunch?" the Anata asked, clearly disappointed and perhaps mistaking the motionless black metallic lump on the other side for part of the auto-dispenser.

Others had. "It's me, Lambo," I said, standing firm even as the lump rattled and spun about, great claws snapping in midair—missing Celi's nostril flaps, the Anata jumping behind me.

Carapace and claws pitted and worn, the Carasian was due for a molt. The species could delay the onset of their next—after all, who'd want to be soft and vulnerable in front of a predator—but given how size conveyed status, they typically couldn't wait to shed their old covering and expand. Lambo? Overdue, not that I'd say so. *Though it might help his temperament.*

A row of black beady eyes, each on its stalk, surveyed me with doubt. "Which you?"

The question had worried me until I realized Lambo either could not—or would not—recognize individuals of any other species. "It's Esen."

"Huh. The curator." The claw lowered. "Whaddya want now?" Someone, probably Duggs, had convinced Lambo to put on an apron a while ago. The shreds were still tied to the base of his lower handling claws and no one, as yet, dared suggest the creature needed help removing it.

Reassured, and hungry, Celi eased from behind me. "Rostra sprouts."

The claw smacked the front of the dispenser, adding another dent to the growing number. "This look like fresh veg to you?"

It looked like a Kraal weapons console, in my opinion, but I kept my ears pricked and friendly. "Stewed rostra sprouts will be fine."

"Huh." Lambo lurched around, proceeding to tap various of the buttons and controls with that blur of speed.

We could have reviewed a slowed vid and deciphered the pattern. Paul refused, having a touching belief the Carasian wanted to work in food service.

Some did. Males tended to latch onto any skill that could become a business. Lust, not entrepreneurship, females of the species seeking stability and comfort in their breeding pools. Meaning a pool, literally, and if Lambo eyed the Garden as a perfect spot for one, I'd be agreeable—if the females, who became obligate predators in their later, fertile years, could be restrained from eating our clients.

There was a slight complication, one I'd yet to find a way to share with Paul.

Despite *his* avowed pronoun, Lambo was female.

Something I'd discovered while Carasian myself and snooping around the Chow after hours to see if I could make it work. The trace left behind shouted female, with the warning splash of territoriality you'd expect from any not yet ready to retire in the company of peers and willing male.

There was no reason a female Carasian shouldn't operate a clunky food dispenser for a constantly changing alien clientele in a library. There was just no reason one would.

The intellect of any female Carasian was off the charts, operating at levels embarrassingly beyond everyone else's. Ersh and Mixs had relished the form, if not the urgent sex-with-debate drive of their age-equivalent. Or Ersh hadn't shared their enjoyment, for which I was grateful.

I enjoyed its physical prowess, being young enough to be spared the compulsion to research and explore the universe beyond my normal curiosity for some time to come.

Lambo's male pronoun made some sense, there being those—particularly Humans—who worried they might not be able to tell when that otherwise pleasant Carasian colleague in the physics department added rapacious appetite to her impressive skillset. Really, it was easy enough. If she tried to eat you, it was time to leave.

I hadn't found out why Lambo went to so much trouble to stay in the Library, *but I would.* In the meantime, we had food.

Sort of.

"Here." A handling claw plopped a bowl on the counter, its contents kept from flying by the dispenser's thin film overtop. "Eat."

Celi and I bent over the bowl. "What is it?" he whispered to me.

The purple goo wasn't stewed rostra sprouts, that much was plain. "Lambo, is there anything we should know about this?" I gestured at the bowl.

"Yeah." A cold beady eye regarded me. "I don't do dishes."

"Understood," I said brightly, delighted by the opening. I shoved the bowl into Celi's reluctant grip. Lambo's unpredictable offerings hadn't harmed any beings yet; I suspected our gruff Carasian knew very well what digestive system was on this side of the counter, and the requisite chemistry. "About the dishes . . ."

Once used, Lambo refused to touch them. A sign at one end of the counter encouraged clients to "Pile Here," and they did, however disgusting the result. Every night, the Botharan maintenance worker who'd lost the draw would waste hours picking apart the sticky, smelly mess, feeding it into the maw of the Chow's recycler so there'd be new dishes for the next day.

Another pair of eyes joined the first. An ominous rumble began in the cavernous body.

I took it as encouragement. "This fine being, Celivliet Del, needs a job."

The Anata, hurriedly emptying the bowl into his revis, stared at me, nostril flaps dilating white with horror. "I do? I do?"

"Yes. Everyone here works," I made sure to speak clearly, hoping to reach inside that impenetrable carapace. "Unless you want to go home."

"I can do dishes!" Bowl in hand, Celi ducked under the counter's gate before I could stop him, dodged the casual swipe of a great claw, and inserted the dish into the right slot. "See? I want to stay!"

Eyestalks bent, but otherwise Lambo gave no outward objection to having someone on his side of the counter.

Now to talk the Carasian into allowing a box in the corner for an Anata den—*possibly more of a challenge,* I had to admit.

"Curator."

My ears tilted back in acknowledgment of that rich terrifying voice, giving me time to smooth the irritated wrinkle from my snout before I looked around.

Skalet—S'kal-ru, this the Kraal version of my surviving kin—stood in the entrance to the Chow. She was tall, with muscles wrapped like taut wire around her limbs, and her lean features bore the red-and-black tattoos marking her affiliations, those bonds to a House that were life and currency among this version of Human. She kept her head bald, the better for wearing a helmet, and was incapable of standing at less than parade attention.

She wore weapons, a couple as part of her black-and-silver uniform, the rest hidden. Not that she needed them. The regrettable dapples on the tender skin of my snout had been put there when her fist shattered the bone, a teaching opportunity not to be wasted.

Family.

"Have you come for a snack?" I inquired, keeping my tail aligned in that "I don't fear you" position, though my Lanivarian-self had excellent instincts and wanted that tail curled firmly between my legs.

"Kearn's here."

Yes, and I was here to avoid him, which Skalet probably guessed and wouldn't help matters. "About time," I replied. "I'll finish up with—"

"He brought news for Paul."

Skalet didn't run errands or deliver messages. She did, when it suited her, deliver warnings and this sounded like one, even if I couldn't begin to guess why. Flattening my ears, I went out the door, leaving Celi to Lambo's tender care.

Feeling, more than seeing, Skalet turn to fall in behind.

Perception

B Y his final shipday aboard the *Dimmont III*, Evan had come to a firm decision about his future, should he have one. At his first opportunity he would begin an emergency travel fund. Not that he hoped ever again to drop everything, claim a family emergency—which no matter how he tried to fool himself had been an outright lie and Great Gran Gooseberry would box his ears when he inevitably confessed—then take passage on the first available starship. Even if it was to seek help.

Anything to avoid another trip like this.

He'd written notes, studied those he'd brought. Recited the soothing litanies from his auto-therapist—while overwhelmingly glad small spaces and bad company weren't among his phobias. When the lights went out, he'd turned to face the bulkhead and gaze into the recordings stored in his holocube, thankful his Great Gran—and all the family, really—were so helpfully long-winded.

The only ones Evan hadn't stored to rewatch were Lucius Whelan's. They'd been introduced at Great Gran's last birthday celebration, the connection—friend of a cousin's something—tenuous but the intention obvious. The result? Evan felt himself flush. Unpleasant. Oh, Lucius had been smart, funny, and, yes, gorgeous. He'd even an interest in the non-Human, if working for a firm specializing in Ganthor merc contracts counted, and by the messages he'd sent since, had developed a serious interest in Evan Gooseberry.

Messages with uncomfortably personal content. He'd stopped opening them after the first. He'd have blocked Lucius entirely, but Great Gran had been so happy that day and for all Evan knew, maybe this was normal in a courtship. It wasn't as though he'd much experience—

Yet part of him was quite sure it wasn't. The part that thought, often, about someone else. Compared to Paul Ragem, Lucius Whelan was a shallow, self-centered bully, with all the compassion of a sponge. A dried-out, dead-on-the-beach, smelly sponge.

Satisfied, Evan resumed rubbing his calves, having let out his breath in order to reach them. He'd learned the importance of this step the first time he'd tried to climb down the ladder after being sandwiched in his bunk for hours. Falling most of the way to the deck had entertained the others; he'd been lucky not to break his neck.

Best not to break anything, he told himself, unfolding to gasp for breath, then bending to rub harder. Any injury would be like meat tossed to a school of adolescent Gigamouths.

His stomach growled at the thought. The rations he'd brought with him had been yesterday's breakfast, lunch, and supper. The lights were still dimmed for ship's night, the Ervickian below snoring through both mouths, but the crew responsible for tossing in food packets should be here too soon. *This time,* he vowed, *he'd be at the table before the door opened and get his share.* Before they took it.

Moving gingerly, Evan eased over the side of his cot, found a rung with his foot, and made his way down to the next.

A viselike hand closed around his ankle. "Wake me, will ya?" The hand *pulled.*

Instead of retreating, as he had before, Evan gritted his teeth and pushed down with all his strength, with the pull. Scar, failing to let go in time, came tumbling from his bunk and Evan landed on what wasn't floor, answered by a pained grunt and furious stream of curses.

He staggered to put the table between them.

Scar surged to his feet in pursuit, the glint of a blade showing.

"Lights!" They squinted in the sudden glare. The Human female came out of her bunk, looking none-too-pleased. "Shut it down, you two."

Evan sat on the bench nearest the door and folded his hands neatly on the table.

"He attacked me," Scar claimed. "You saw!"

A flash of uncanny violet as her eyes found then dismissed Evan. Tory was her name; he'd heard it during their low murmurings. The others—except the Rands, still clustered in their net—were hers.

Tory looked at Scar. "What I see is needless trouble. We're off ship today. Unless you *want* the grounders involved?" The top of her head barely reached his shoulder.

Nonetheless, Evan thought, she towered over him. Scar and his companion were dangerous bullies, the Ervickian disgusting—and a thief—but she was lethal.

"Let's be civil for a change," Tory announced, sitting across from Evan at the long table. "Shipmates' last meal and all that. Right, Evan?"

She knew his name. Blood gone cold, he didn't dare glance at his bunk, but he'd left his carryall there, had to, in order to use the accommodation across the corridor. He'd brought his valuables, they were in the bag inside his shirt, but his name—

Name, undergarments, didn't matter what they'd seen. The ordeal was almost over. "I'm agreeable," he replied, surprised his voice worked.

Scar banged a fist under Beard's bunk. "Get up."

The Ervickian slipped around the big Human, choosing to sit beside Evan.

This close, the startling violet of Tory's eyes proved to be a ring of tech replacing her irises. It made her steady regard uncomfortable to meet, especially when he'd no idea what more she could see, but Evan, well accustomed to the assessing stares of senior embassy staff, had no trouble regarding her back.

Her lips quirked. "You're more interesting than you look."

Gods, he hoped not.

Before he had to figure out a reply to that, Beard sat on Evan's other side, sliding over to squeeze him against the Ervickian. Scar smiled coldly. "Hungry?"

Not anymore. Knowing better than to admit it, Evan made himself smile. "I'm looking forward to breakfast." And leaving his "shipmates" behind, that most of all.

There was a sharp rap on the door, then it slid open. By the way his stubby feathers shot upright, the crewbeing was surprised by the group around the table. Evan had the uncharitable thought he'd expected bending or bloodshed, with himself the object. The Snoprian set the food packs on the table in a tidy stack instead of tossing them. "Fins down in two. At the alert, grab your own gear. No one's carrying for you." The door closed before Evan could ask a question.

At Tory's look, Beard spun one of the packs to Evan. There followed a moment of, well, it wasn't peace, not with Jumpy Lyn sloppily pouring the contents of its pack into the gaping maw centered on her chest, but focus.

Evan ate mechanically, without tasting. *Just as well.* The sort of bargain rations a freighter like this offered was fuel, not food. When done, he copied the others and rolled the packaging into a ball to tuck into a pocket, then went to stand up.

A heavy hand on his shoulder kept him in place.

He looked at Tory. "What do you want?"

His awareness of who was in charge here pleased her, he could tell. "You can satisfy my curiosity, Evan Gooseberry. What is it you keep in your shirt?"

Surely they could have robbed him at any time. Killed him, most likely, and explained it as a clumsy fall. That she asked, like this, before they parted ways? Might be curiosity. They were all bored.

Or she wanted to discover if he was worth following through the shipcity, to attack later.

He'd no choice. Evan pulled out his bag, all but Tory leaning forward with greedy expressions, the Ervickian drooling.

Opening it, he pulled out his most prized possession, the gift he hoped would be enough.

Evan set the little bust of Teganersha-ki, the ancient

Dokeci leader, on the table, cupping his fingers around it possessively.

"That's it?!" Scar grabbed the bag and turned it inside out. He gave it a frustrated shake.

Fingers dug into his shoulder. "Where's the rest?"

"There's nothing—" He was shoved violently against the wall. Jumpy Lyn's hands grubbed through his pockets, his clothing, leaving bits from her breakfast. Evan endured, keeping still, his eyes on Tory.

She'd picked up the bust, turning it over in her hands with a frown. "I've seen the real thing. This is a cheap replica." The frown aimed at him. "What's so important about it?"

"You wouldn't—" Evan pushed the Ervickian aside, "—understand."

She tossed the bust to Scar. "Scan it."

Evan didn't protest, holding still and quiet, waiting. The spacer produced a small black object Evan assumed was a scanner, not that he was familiar with the tech other than the embassy-issue one they'd used to try and find what was scurrying in the kitchen, then used to see if those trapped in a mass of falling metal were still alive—

His spine stiffened. He'd lived through that fateful day. He'd survive these petty criminals and be on his way. *Do what he'd come to do.*

"Not'n. A piece o'junk." Deliberately, Scar dropped the bust on the table. It tumbled to a stop, the baleful three-eyed gaze of the dictator who'd have ripped Scar apart with her bare arms aimed at the ceiling.

Without looking at any of them, Evan picked up his treasure and put it in the bag, along with the tiny bits of glitter jarred loose. After resealing the bag, he restored it to his hiding place, only then lifting his eyes to Tory's. "It was a gift from my teacher," he said, his voice strange to his own ears. "A reminder to follow my dreams, no matter how difficult the journey."

"A dream? Here?" the spacer laughed, spittle dotting his beard.

Tory didn't. There was that not-a-smile quirk of her lips again and he wasn't sure, this time, if it was mockery or something else. "Said you were interesting, Evan. Wasn't wrong." A flick of her fingers sent Jumpy Lyn scrambling out of his way. "You heard. Two till we're down."

Before she could change her mind, Evan was climbing the ladder to his bunk, chased by raucous laughter.

Only when he was safe did the trembling start.

The next two hours were going to be the longest he'd lived.

4: Library Morning; Kitchen Noon

THINGS would have gone much better if I'd avoided the Rands and their Ergonomic Multiplexing Oscillator, Patent Pending in two systems, entirely. In hindsight. *Never the view of the moment.*

The entanglement started when Skalet proposed we cut across the Line. It wasn't so much any urgency to reach Paul and Lionel to uncover whatever she found threatening, as it was my web-kin's thorough distrust of any gathering of unrelated beings who weren't surrounded by vigilant armed Kraal troops, ideally with those arms out and ready. The fresh-off-the-train crush in the main lobby made her uncomfortable.

The Line wasn't much better, a seething clot circulating in the opening past the boot and exo-suit racks, but at least those here had their purpose, in Skalet's view, waiting their turn at the Assessment Counter.

These were the clients who brought stuff.

We hadn't expected anyone to bring physical things, didn't want anyone to, and in the beginning cherished the ever-shrinking hope that making the process a nuisance would discourage repeat offenders. To our mutual chagrin, much of the stuff presented to the Library in trade did qualify as "new information we couldn't get any other way," so we had to keep accepting it in trade. Under that broad heading fell certain inventions, materials, new children's toys, styles in hats—*not fudge, just as well*—overall, an eclectic clutter none of which had intrinsic value and nothing we planned to keep. Paul developed a system to record all relevant data for the collection; the next logical step was to send the objects home with their owners.

But no. That wasn't "trading" and almost no one proved willing to carry out what they'd struggled to get here in the first place. The Library's first basement level having filled, Paul predicted we'd reach a crisis by the middle of our second year of operation and have to pay to ship it offworld.

Scholars.

Fortunately, the majority of objects were small enough to slip into a pocket or hold in one's appendage. We'd neglected to add luggage to our contract with the local company operating the transit system from the landing field, more concerned about overnight guests than knick-knacks. A saving strategy now. I shuddered to think what would arrive if we'd arranged for freight.

My first inkling of the Rands' offering came when Skalet stepped fastidiously clear of their cluster, feeling the same about communal organisms as she did about scuff marks on her polished boots. As I was right on her shiny heels, this put my next step inside the Rands.

Who panicked. The Ergonomic Multiplexing Oscillator harbored in the cluster turned on—turning out to be a wildly inappropriate sex toy to bring to a library—and I cycled.

Finding myself *oh so happy . . .* and *oh so glad . . .* because to be *within* and *one of* was the best possible feeling, though there was a smidge of *confusion, who? . . .* I answered with . . . *I love you all so much . . .*

Which would be when the net engulfed us.

"You can't just grab a—the clients."

The voice was *one* and *annoying.* Or was it annoyed?

One . . . I drifted back and forth, cilia reaching for . . . *more . . .* and not finding. Being *one.* Lacking a voice, I wept salty tears and tangled . . .

"Be glad I did. She'd have been absorbed by now."

COLD . . . that voice and *one* . . . *but not. Lonely, too?*
Absorb . . . I reached outward, *seeking* . . .

My universe *shook!*

"Don't you dare, Youngest." Another shake, letting me know I was inside *something* . . . *one* and *alone*. The voice went on, "I've told you what to do," so *COLD*. "There isn't much time."

"Es?"

This voice made me *oh so happy* . . . I wept salty tears because I had no voice to say so and was . . . *alone* and *one*.

"Paul, don't—" Annoyed no longer. Alarmed.

"You heard Skalet." Now the voice that made me *oh so happy* . . . was hard and made me . . . *oh afraid* . . . and *oh alone/afraid/alone* . . . "If she won't help, it's the only way."

And my world went up in flame.

My tail wouldn't budge, so I left it between my legs where it could stay forever, as far as I was concerned.

Being more embarrassed than I'd ever been before.

"Accidents happen, Old Blob."

I lifted my lip clear of a scornful fang.

"Fine, yes, it was Skalet's fault. But she did help save you."

Both fangs, with a definitive wrinkle to my snout. Ignoring the clear and present threat, Paul leaned forward to touch his nose to mine. The eye I could still see had lost several lashes, the eyebrow above scorched as well, which is what happens when you set a boxful of Rand on fire, Rands known for the flammable nature of their oily skins. It was even an expression used by Humans: "went up like a cluster of Rands," proof of Ersh's contention that the most dire events could and would be turned into humor by those not personally involved.

Fingers rubbed behind the ear I'd flattened, and I growled deep in my throat. Paul, predictably, smiled. "Feeling better?"

There was no resisting my determined friend, short of

churlish behavior he didn't deserve. "Give me a century," I grumbled.

He took my head in his hands, no smile now. "Was that as close as I think it was?"

"I don't know. Maybe."

It was the truth and terrifying, as well as embarrassing. I'd never been a Rand before, though the form was in Ersh-memory. Lesy, not Ersh, had risked it for the Web. She'd found her way back, but how she'd remembered her true self—how long it had taken—those details were oddly blurred, as though felt through cloth and not almost experienced, the way assimilated memory should be. "Did you have to set me on fire?" I complained.

It not being worth complaining to Skalet, who could have roused me at any point by cycling into web-form, but we'd sworn never to show our true selves before aliens again. While I took that more as a preference, to break when necessary, Skalet?

Would willingly die first—or kill first. Either way, to her a rule was a rule.

"It was the fastest way."

Paul knew, that meant. Much longer as a Rand, whose individual mental capacity made a Quebit seem a genius, and I might have forgotten what I was. That I was Esen, and not a mindless appetite. That under threat I wasn't to instinctively release my hold on a strange form, become perfect and blue and deadly—and *take* the nearest living mass.

Which had, in this case, been provided by the bag of duras leaves Paul had tossed over burning me in time for my instincts to assimilate it.

Skalet had risked Paul, I thought grimly. Gambled I'd still have the sense to differentiate between my dearest friend and a plant, or hadn't cared, preferring I receive the lesson.

Learned. *There'd be a conversation about this.*

"Hello, Esen."

Later. I shook off the last of my ill feelings, my tail finally swinging free, to greet Lionel Kearn.

Who was smiling happily at me with such delight in his

eyes, I was fairly certain he hadn't noticed his sleeve was smoking a bit.

Well, so much for worrying what this particular Human thought of Web-beings.

I'd an undeclared Anata living in the Chow, a Carasian female with ulterior motives, and had yet to shake off the sheer terror of having almost lost myself.

Lionel's unwelcome news put it all in perspective. "Chase." I managed to snarl the name.

"Why does she continue to exist?" Skalet asked reasonably.

I couldn't disagree.

We'd adjourned to the farmhouse, the Library too distracting a place, though I saw the regret in Lionel's eyes as we'd left. My Garden changed his mood to puzzled, but then he'd never seen my greenhouse on Minas XII.

He'd been to the Ragem farmhouse before, under less happy circumstances. I watched Lionel hesitate at the door until Paul said something quiet and intense to him, my friend being the forgiving sort and a good example. I paid attention, having Skalet in my Web, who was not.

Skalet and Lionel had their history, too. When he'd believed me a monster, she'd manipulated and spied on him without compunction; when he'd accepted me, she'd judged his knowledge potentially useful. Never trust, not Skalet. She'd come away from their last meeting *impressed*. Poor Lionel.

The parlor was my bedroom, full of grass beds for my Lishcyn-self, flat raised platforms for this me, and a hammock for a range of others, so we'd settled in the kitchen with its massive antique-to-Humans table, hand-hewn by the first Ragems to push up sleeves and get dirty in the name of world-building and furniture. The table I liked, especially once Paul showed me where he'd lain underneath to carve fanciful aliens in the wood.

There were plenty of chairs and stools to choose from, most stacked in corners and all well-worn. Easy to imagine them crowded around the table, easier still to pretend I could hear Paul, newly back from yet another First Contact mission, regaling his breathless audience with stories of the oh-so-strange and amazing. Rudy had sat here, had listened to his inspiring, favorite cousin.

He'd followed Paul and the rumors of Paul and the hurt of losing Paul into space, desperate for the truth and afraid of it.

Rudy was happy, now. Faith restored, not that it had ever been lost. Cousin restored, too.

Plus me. *Clearly a bonus.*

Alas, the rest of the chairs and stools gathered dust, waiting for Paul's family to return. Lionel realized it, his face going gray.

Though the sun was still high, it felt like night. Maybe that was why I offered, "There's wine."

Heads shook. Human heads. I could have been one, and felt the draw to fit in, but being an apparent ten years of age was a challenge among the species at the best of times, which this wasn't. To reinforce my maturity, I'd resisted the temptation to jump up on the table, sitting on a stool. The tail made a chair problematic anyway.

"Chase exists because she was no longer a threat," Paul said tersely, eyes flashing as he replied to Skalet.

"She is now." A pale eyebrow rose. "Or do you believe your father died by accident?" Calmly said, in Skalet's rich, low voice.

Nonetheless, I shivered.

Lionel looked aghast. "We can't know he's dead. There was no body."

Her little shrug encompassed the myriad ways to be rid of a corpse. "This Human, Janet Chase. The destruction of the shop on Senigal III. It isn't coincidence."

"No." Paul rubbed the edge of the table with the palm of his left hand, the slow movement a habit when thinking. "But it makes no sense. Stefan Gahanni's part in my life ended before I was born."

I'd heard some of the story. Paul's parents had met when Stefan came on board the *Thebes,* fins down on Senigal III, to repair her drives. Shortly thereafter, the *Thebes'* navigator, Veya Ragem, arranged a temp contract for Stefan, off they flew, and everything was joyful fun and frolic until they discovered Stefan wasn't suited for space. He was queasy in free fall, and chronically spacesick under ship's gravity, something my Lanivarian-self could empathize with completely. Veya, having no interest—or future—in a grounder lifestyle, the pair parted ways. She gave birth to Paul and landed long enough to leave him with her family on Botharis.

Veya didn't abandon her son, she gave him a home, one she returned to as often as possible. Paul, as he grew, came to understand her choice hadn't only been because her talents as a navigator were in high demand, earning her a post within the Commonwealth's Survey fleet. Veya's education had been paid for by her family, a debt she repaid many times over.

On her visits, she'd stay with Paul, full of tales of aliens and their worlds, expanding the mind of her brilliant only child until what else could he want, but the stars for himself?

We'd heard rumors Veya's career in Survey faltered following the news of Paul's death—possibly that she'd been driven out by the ensuing scandal. Eighteen years ago, Paul had come across a cold, official report stating that Veya Ragem had been one of the dozen casualties on the ill-fated *Smokebat,* the freighter struck not once but twice by unmapped orbital debris.

Looking at Paul now, I wondered what I didn't know about his parents. He'd told me stories of his father's family, of grandparents on Hendrick, but if he'd had no contact with Stefan, were the stories true, or a child's wistful thinking? More puzzling, to me at least, if his father couldn't travel to Botharis, why hadn't my ever-curious friend made the trip to Senigal III to meet the other half of his heritage? It wasn't as if he were unaware. Hadn't Paul brought Zoltan Duda, a distant relative of Stefan's third contracted partner, into his Group?

Humans, Ersh would say, *could make any relationship complicated.*

"Where is Chase now?" Paul asked Lionel.

"Isn't your father more important?" I interrupted. "Surely we have to find him."

Skalet's laugh seemed almost affectionate, *unless you'd heard it for five hundred years and were familiar with that mocking note*. "Youngest, do you hear yourself?"

Paul's frown was instant. "Esen means well."

"She always does."

Not in any sense a compliment. "I didn't mean we'd have to—" become trackers and hunt the jungles, assuming Senigal III had some, a notion this form found immediately appealing, "—find him ourselves. Lionel said Chase made inquiries about Stefan. If she was after something specific, wouldn't he know what it was?" If he wasn't dead and now a disappeared corpse, a fruitless discussion I didn't want resumed. "We've resources," I stated with confidence, waggling my toes in the air. "Let's use them."

Lionel nodded. "I've the names of the officers investigating the explosion and left a request with the Gahannis warning them about Chase—and to contact me if she shows up. I hope you don't think that presumptuous?" To Paul.

Astonished, I stared at him, jaw agape, then managed a faint, "There's more family?" I turned that stare on my friend, "You didn't tell me?" With reproach.

Paul made a weary gesture. *Don't ask,* that was, so I closed my lips. *Another conversation for later*. "Thank you, Lionel. It sounds like everything's covered, then."

"Waiting for results is . . . tedious." Skalet touched the table with a fingertip. "I could end this concern."

My web-kin, being her version of generous. At a loss for why, I narrowed my eyes. I had her memories; granted I stayed as far from the details as possible, and only nibbled what I must to recoup my own shared flesh, but I was regrettably familiar with what Skalet experienced.

If not the workings of her mind.

"I'd prefer your focus be on the Library," Paul said, as if they discussed work assignments, not assassination.

"As you wish." Skalet withdrew her hand, a truly disturbing amount of satisfaction in her expression.

Ersh save us. She thought he'd given her permission to overhaul the Library security system, presently consisting of turning off the lights and closing doors we didn't lock.

When I opened my mouth to protest, I caught the look Paul gave me.

It was *trust me.*

Skalet was the one we mustn't trust. When she turned to address Lionel, I lifted a lip to express that opinion.

Paul responded with the tiniest nod, as if I needed a reminder he knew, firsthand, the sheer paranoia Skalet brought to everything she did.

Chase. Because of her?

The doors were going to be locked.

Being a solitary and desperate Rand-in-a-box at the time, I'd missed any telling nuances to Lionel Kearn and Skalet's reunion. My predicament, let alone the subsequent setting-of-me-on-fire, also meant I'd missed any non-nuanced, blatant reactions to one another.

Timing.

During the kitchen discussion, I'd tried to read my web-kin's expression for clues as to how much peril Lionel faced as another alien who knew about us. *My fault, that.* The tattoos covering much of her face didn't help, not that my odds were good. Skalet had practiced keeping expression from her face and voice for most of her life. Unless it was disdain at me. Or anger. Frequently, amused scorn. Outrage, on occasion—

But every so often, when she looked at Lionel, I glimpsed something else, something disturbing. At first, I didn't understand, never having seen the muscles around her eyes and mouth relax. *What did it mean?*

I drew on my memories of Paul's familiar face, running through his expressions at various moments in our time together. Only one was remotely similar: when he'd sung lullabies to Luara and Tomas in their beds. These years later, I'd still spot it after he'd heard from either twin, as if for some odd reason those brief hellos with blurts of news made him remember lullabies, too.

Which couldn't be it, the Web of Ersh—even my birth-mother, Ansky—devoid of parental instincts, so what was Skalet feeling?

Not something to ask her. I couldn't risk so much as an informative bite. If, hard as it was to imagine, her reaction to Lionel was unconscious?

Bringing it to her attention would do the Human no favors at all.

Salad . . .

I kept an ear on the discussion—presently revolving around drastic action against perfectly functional doors and why didn't we have scanners?—and sniffed tactfully, Humans lacking my superb sense of smell and prone to sensitivity about their own aroma.

Not salad . . . digesting greens. And not supposed to be here.

"All worth considering." Paul rose to his feet. "Thank you, Lionel. Skalet, I'll have Duggs provide the building schematics. Es and I have to get back to work now."

"The Pouncey Human?" Skalet asked, showing her displeasure. "She has never listened to me."

And loudly compared my arrogant web-kin to a farm animal. Something I hadn't shared with Skalet for Duggs Pouncey's health.

"I'm happy to participate," Lionel offered. He spread his hands. "I've some experience with emerg—with buildings of construction akin to the Library's."

Skalet actually appeared mollified. "I would value your contribution. If the Pouncey Human is instructed to be reasonable."

Paul's lips twitched, but he didn't smile. "I'm sure Duggs will understand the importance of protecting the Library. Esen? Are you—" a pause, as if he'd wanted to ask if I'd recovered, then realized who else was listening, "—ready to get to work?"

"Of course." I pricked my large lovely ears in the eager "ready to race you" posture that usually made my partner rethink whatever he'd planned for me to do. Partly because I wanted to avoid seeing any more Rands for a while.

But mostly because I discovered where the *digesting greens* scent originated. Celi was peering in through the open kitchen window; seeing my attention, the Anata began waving vigorously.

Gray eyes full of suspicion met mine. Before Paul could turn around, I jumped from my stool with a dramatic flourish of my tail—not something done in polite Lanivarian company, but you worked with what you had. "Let's go!" I headed for the hallway.

"There's one small matter," Lionel said, spoiling an excellent retreat. "I hadn't planned on staying longer than to give my news. Could you recommend a hotel?"

"Nonsense. You'll stay here." Skalet's emphatic statement surprised the rest of us.

Which was nonsense, since I wasn't sharing and Paul's little room in the loft was his private space. Plus I doubted it could fit a second cot.

And I'd yet to see it, so why should Lionel?

Lionel looked around the empty kitchen, then at Paul. The blood drained from his face, leaving it older and sad. "I can't. There are—I don't think it's right, me staying here."

Something told me I didn't want to find out if Skalet would offer him a berth on her ship. "We've a room with a bed in it at the Library." A still-empty storeroom in the second level of the basement, the "bed" a cot with a mattress roll Paul used when working through the night, but those were, I knew, unimportant details. "I'll show you. After—" I raised my voice, "—I see to the pest in the Garden."

Everyone turned at the answering rustle outside the window. A length of vine, stripped of its leaves, nodded in the opening.

"Big pest," Lionel commented, looking anxious.

He'd no idea.

Inception

BELIEF is not enough.

This I have learned to my dismay. We climb in hope, the hope of leaving the Ever Dark, of achieving the Rise that is the culmination of life.

I can hear them, my kindred. Their claws. Their anxious, driven breaths.

Can they hear mine?

Our tongues make no sound. I know, like mine, theirs rasp stone with each small advance upward. Together, we sample and taste. Sample and taste. Sample and taste.

It is not hunger we satisfy, but the cold tenet of survival. This is our needful offering.

We are countless. Or few. In the Ever Dark, beyond the Womb, it is not possible to know. I am not alone, which is a comfort.

Though the time must come when I am.

5: Garden Afternoon; Chow Afternoon

"**I** had to find you!" Celi panted as if he'd been running. To beat me here, he probably had.

"Sit down. Don't do that!" I added sharply.

He lowered the hook that had been sneaking toward the nearest greenery. "Sorry, Esen."

I sighed. It wasn't as if there was much left of my Startipped Lilies. "Oh, go ahead. But only here."

Not waiting for me to change my mind, the Anata quickly harvested a couple of hookfuls before shoving them into a suspiciously full-looking revis. "Thank you."

I curled my tail over my useful toes. "Now, what's this about?" Not that I couldn't guess. *The surly Carasian, without a doubt.*

"It's that Carasian! Do you know what she's doing?"

"'She?'" I echoed.

Celi's nasal flaps waved derisively. "Please. Anyone can smell it."

"So what is—" I chose the neutral, "—Lambo doing that has you upset?"

"Stealing the precious artifacts!"

We'd "precious artifacts"? Not what I'd call the offerings, given their typical lack of quality, though I wouldn't stoop to "gemmies," shipcity slang for what beings brought to trade at the All Species' Library of Linguistics and Culture. Much as Paul loathed the term, it had stuck and spread, with "ooh, have you brought your gemmies?" now fighting words in some bars. I didn't mind, privately considering any new knowledge to sparkle like fine gemstones, or taste like fudge, but I appreciated the higher tone he wanted to set.

Then again, those in the Line professed to care deeply for their items, at least until we'd taken them off their appendages. Theft, though? I checked the nearest shadow. Noon. A bit quick for conclusive detective work, particularly in the Chow, especially by an overstuffed Anatae scholar who'd been living in the Garden until two hours ago.

Ersh knew I shouldn't ask, but curiosity claimed me. "This is a serious accusation, Celivliet Del. Explain yourself."

"I found our Trident Cuspid under the counter."

Whatever a "Trident Cuspid" was, I hadn't been the one to log it, but we'd a rotating staff of three, Paul, myself, and Henri Steves on loan from the family's business, THS Trailside Treasures and Oddities. We'd tried to entice Henri to take payment in items, a clever scheme to keep them from our basement that could potentially create a useful market for "Alien Gemmies" on Botharis. She'd refused, proving to have better taste than we'd hoped.

The Anatae's Trident Cuspid could have dropped from the grav cart on the way to the storeroom. Stopping at the Chow for snacks did happen, *being necessary*. As did items tumbling from an overloaded cart, not something to bring up at the moment.

"Go on."

"I found more precious artifacts." Celi clutched his revis as if protecting the contents presently under digestion. "Jammed together. Some were broken! Ruined!"

Oh, dear. "Your—artifact?"

A trembling hand produced what looked like the business end of a medstapler. "This is all that remains intact."

Because it *was* the business end of a medstapler, Human manufacture. Taking it from Celi, I saw the original device had been cut in half, then glued to—*might be the top of a candy dispenser*—something pink and round. Lest the name be in doubt, a three-pronged fork had been lovingly scratched on one side, with a nice image of a Human tooth on the other.

Making so much clear. "Celi, who in your group was responsible for procuring this—" gemmie on my tongue, I managed, "—precious artifact?"

"Full credit to Osmaku Del, our august Head of Off-World Inquiry. She acquired the Trident Cuspid at great expense. We were—surprised—when it wasn't accepted. This is why I remained," flaps an earnest rose. "I continue to long for the answer to our question, only to be found within the Library."

They'd been sold a lie to trade for a truth. If the Anatae's question was truly vital, the situation had all the tragic irony of a Pabstian play, without the redemption of the published afterword to soothe the audience.

This time, maybe it would. "What you can trade me, Celivliet Del, is the ident of the person who sold this to Osmaku Del." I held up the medstapler.

"You? But, Esen." A hook indicated a freshly denuded branch. "You're the gardener."

"Yes, I am." I almost smiled, then remembered this being didn't care for the sight of my fangs. "It's just not all I am."

I'd a name.

Celivliet Del had his answer. The Anatae had come to ask why they'd failed to attract an embassy—and trade—from the Efue. I was able to tell him, in the guise of a Library databurst. The Anatae had made the first mistake, interpreting an Efue's request for Nogo Tea as an error in translation—because the stuff had no taste at all—cheerfully substituting Blackened Seoberry, a local delicacy they hoped would find favor, and tea was tea, really. But no. Nogo was an important tonic for the Efue who found it delicious, while Seoberry was a nerve toxin.

The Efue then made the second mistake, assuming the substitution was an attempt on the life of their trade delegation, or at least, terrible manners.

For the Efue at home there wasn't much difference. They'd wanted a reason to stop the embarrassingly profitable trade in *Zilpahre* between their systems. The potent Efue recreational drug was legally restricted to non-reproductive adults who no longer held important jobs, drove machinery, or needed to converse intelligibly with others. When they learned the Anatae gave it to their children, in pretty shiny packages no less, the outcry was instant.

Mistake upon mistake. Zilpahre had become the favorite treat of young Anatae, and a boon to parents, nutritious as well as sweet. That government complained bitterly the Efue were deliberating ruining their children's holidays out of spite and who didn't like Seoberry Tea?

Yet another reminder that intelligent beings of good intent could totally fail to comprehend differences in biology. As Ersh would say, *all gooey bits must be the same as mine.* Well, not that she'd ever used those words, but she'd stressed the concept.

Armed with this new information, supplied in every language in current use by either species and with sample warning labels because clarity saved lives, I'd every confidence Celivliet Del would be able to restore civil dialogue. I liked to think there'd be a glimmer of mutual respect restored as well, though I suspected the Efue would continue to think the Anatae remarkably reckless in their parenting, and the latter think the former incapable of telling a good tea from mouthwash.

Celi, torn between giddy and a solemn sense of mission, hadn't stopped burping. Until he calmed, his digestion would suffer, so I'd let him return to his den under my fystia. He'd leave tomorrow. Score a win for the Library.

I'd have been happy, if it weren't for what Celi had left in my version of a lap. According to the Anata, I'd a Carasian hoarding what should have been removed from the Library or tossed in a recycler.

And I'd a name. The Botharan running a scam on our clients?

Kevin Ragem. One of Paul's cousins.

Aware of no law or regulation against selling homemade gemmies to naïve aliens—though I took a very dim view of attempting to defraud the Library—I chose to tackle my Carasian problem first. As a bonus to delaying more bad news for Paul about his family? I'd get a snack.

That had been the plan.

Beady black eyes regarded me steadily. "Last time you wanted stewed rostra sprouts."

"Those were for Celi," I protested.

"You ordered them." A claw spun the bowl in my direction. "You got them. Stewed sprouts. Eat or leave me alone."

Poison to a Lanivarian, something Lambo knew full well. Bringing me to the sudden and highly uncomfortable realization I was being teased. By someone much smarter than I was.

Likely for months.

I took the bowl, removed the cover, and delicately lapped the contents, there being no spoon in sight. It was, in fact, a lightly spiced meat dish I ordered regularly, if never before looking exactly like stewed sprouts.

Lambo rumbled in discontent as he turned away. *Game over.*

We were alone, however briefly. As alone as an open space alongside a busy corridor could be, so I put aside the bowl and leaned forward. "Why are you here?"

An eyestalk bent my way. "Been chewing on your plants again?"

"I really want to know. Why here?"

"Here?" A second eyestalk joined the first. "Because I was dumb enough to agree to run the Chow and be pestered by you."

Lambo's gruff persona was impenetrable. *Well, there was the direct approach.* Taking the requisite steps back, I eyed the counter, took a quick breath, then sprang. Four powerful limbs and a supple spine gave my Lanivarian-self the ability to leap a considerable height from a standing start—the species had several expressions to describe this celebrated skill, my favorite being "soars skyward to land with grace."

Not that I did. The soaring worked, clearing the counter and bowl, until I met the rise of a claw that might have been a wall for all the chance I had to evade it midair.

Batted aside, I skidded along the floor to hit the wall.

While alarming to experience, I'd been batted gently, only my dignity in pain as I wobbled to my feet. There'd be a bruise or two, but that claw could've snapped me in half.

I was, however, where I wanted to be. Before Lambo could react again, I stuck my snout under the counter. Then sneezed. *Did no one clean under here?* I continued, despite the alarming clatter and thudding of gigantic feet, until I reached the edge of the gemmie pile.

Something grabbed my tail. *Pulled!*

I slid into the light, grinning toothily up at my captor as I waved a gemmie in each paw. "Aha!"

"THIEF!" The bellow flattened my ears.

A familiar "Esen-alit-Quar!" raised them again. I switched my grin to Paul, the Human leaning over the counter looking—perturbed. Yes, that was the look.

I couldn't blame him. Lambo continued to bellow in outrage, there were other faces now peering over the counter, none Human and all curious, and my poor tail remained in the Carasian's claw.

"Just stopped for a snack!" I shouted as Lambo pulled me along the floor like a cleaning rag.

The other faces disappeared in a flash.

Paul held up his hand. "Peace, both of you."

The Carasian halted, eyestalks on my friend—his employer—except for three bent to glare at me. I smiled up. "Tail?"

A sigh from my friend. "If you please, Lambo."

The claw opened. I tucked my tail out of reach and made my exit through the now-open counter gate.

The Carasian followed right behind, claws snapping. "Give them back!"

"Peace, I said!" Paul glanced at what I held out to him. "What are those?"

"Mine!" With that, and a threatening rattle, the giant lurched to a stop.

I won't say I dodged behind Paul, but I did move closer. "You can have them back. Whatever they are," I added, not entirely sure myself. The object in my left paw looked like a blend between a mixer blade and a teapot, while the right? All I could tell was it had started with a fistful of colored stylos and a stretchy band, there'd been some melting, and—

"When?" in a more reasonable tone.

"I remember that." Frowning, Paul touched the melted stylos. "An Oduyae offered this last week. Why do you have it, Lambo?"

"It was a gift."

If so, it hadn't been treated well. Like the Trident Cluster of the Anatae, these objects looked as though they'd been crumpled in a claw and thrown. Or thrown then crumpled. That they weren't completely pulverized had more to do, I judged, with the ragged condition of Lambo's claws than any lack of desire to see them in pieces. *Really time for that molt.*

But why?

"There are dozens more under there, all broken. You've been searching inside them," I exclaimed.

Eyestalks milled with convincing confusion. "For what?"

Having no idea, I looked to Paul, who appeared as puzzled or more. "They were all 'gifts?'"

"Left on my counter." A handling claw chimed. "Aren't dirty dishes." Another chime. "Presented for my gracious service."

Not gifts, then. Tips. As "gracious service" from Lambo didn't merely strain credulity but sent it whimpering away in embarrassment, in reality a good number of the rejected must be dumping their failed gemmies in the Chow before leaving in a huff, or the species-appropriate equivalent. Including the Anatae's Head of Inquiry.

I supposed we should be thankful Lambo didn't view it that way, or there'd have been crumpled and tossed body parts.

Next time, I won't jump to conclusions. At Paul's nod,

I held out Lambo's property, but before those claws—capable of precise fine movements—made contact, I pulled back a little. "Why break them?"

"They're junk." Pitted black claws snatched them from my hand. Lambo hurried behind his counter, dropping the gate with a crash and a grim rumble. "But they're my junk."

Who could argue with that?

Perception

THE air was warm and scented with growing things, the sky above the sort of blue that made Humans smile inside—except for a line of growing clouds that promised rain—and Evan Gooseberry refused to take another step down the ramp. This couldn't be the right place.

The *Dimmont III* had landed in a field. A farm field. In the middle of other fields and hills. Hills empty of anything but plants.

Yes, it was a paved farm field, with a distant pair of low buildings that didn't, if he squinted, look like barns, or what he imagined barns looked like, being an urban person. And, yes, over there was a stationish sort of thing with a shiny rail leading from it into those plant-infested hills—but this was not civilization.

To prove his point, tents and temp stands sprawled along the side of the field nearest the station. He could hear the loud music and voices from here. *A festival?*

Evan clutched his carryall to his chest. "This can't be it."

"Oh, but it is." A too-helpful shove sent him down a couple of steps. When Evan turned to protest, the crew-being grinned, showing too many teeth. "Ship lifts in thirty. Be outta the way or fry. Your choice. Or pay for return passage."

He'd no funds left. If they'd laughed at the small amount in his carryall, it hadn't stopped them taking it.

Still, he'd paid to be delivered to the Library. Reaching for his pamphlet, Evan steeled himself, prepared to argue. *Because this couldn't be right—*

Tory walked past him, chuckling at whatever showed on his face. "There's a train."

—but was.

Instead of leaving his unpleasant shipmates behind, Evan found himself walking across the pavement between them and the cluster of Rands, mutely thankful to be ignored. It was a proper landing field, not that he'd set foot on one before, but you could get a glimpse from an aircar—if you tore your feasting eyes from the wonders of the strange and splendid alien Port City ahead for an instant—so he was grudgingly convinced of that much.

It was the splendid shipcity that was missing, built from ranks of starships tethered in place, separated by lanes with lights and markings for the tugs to ferry those ships to and from the landing field. The Port City, with its All Sapients' District, would nestle welcomingly near the ships, solid buildings ready to provide comfort and rest to space-weary travelers. Some were the capitals of their worlds, such as beautiful Kateen on Urgia Prime, his first posting.

And there'd be food—

Evan's stomach growled. This field was empty but for the *Dimmont III*, fresh scorch marks indicating there had been other ships, but none had lingered on the ground. Why would they?

There was nothing here. If he'd wanted to be on a First Contact Team, he'd have applied for a First Contact Team. If he'd wanted to be anything other than a diplomat, Great Gran would have approved, but he'd stuck with it through thick and thin and parental argument and here he was.

For now. The future of his beloved career would depend on many things outside his control. Being here, that was.

The Rand cluster pulled ahead as their little group neared the first of the tents, as if eager to sample the offerings. The shelters were arranged as though tossed from above, each crowding the other. An aisle snaked through the confusion, beings shuffling shoulder-to-whatever body part, and Evan decided he'd go around even if it did take longer—

Tory slipped her arm through his as if they were old friends. "Ready to check out the local wares, Evan?"

This wasn't the ship. "Not with you," he said firmly, extricating his arm. With a sharp look, he dared Scar and Beard to try something in such a public place, then Evan stepped forward into the crowd.

His heart pounded as though he'd seen a *SPIDER!* though that *FEAR* had subsided significantly, and he was doing so well lately he'd left his auto-therapist at home without a thought.

If he'd brought something of such value, they'd have stolen it.

Didn't matter now. He'd separated himself from the criminals—not that he trusted they'd leave him alone, but Evan knew how to walk among the non-Human and those were the majority here. He bowed and gave way to the cluster of Rands, stepped around the sloshing pillar of a Heezle, and minded his manners. He smiled at a furious squeal from behind. Someone hadn't been as careful.

Humans of every age and shape worked in the tents, each with tables covered with articles for sale, local produce, and other oddments. There were those selling food and drink, each with a placard inviting species to leave comments, presumably displayed to reassure those coming after that someone of their kind had partaken and survived. Some offered entertainment as well—the source of the music—and one of the pipe bands wasn't bad at all.

The last tent was the liveliest. Seeing the line of beings waiting their turn to enter, Evan slowed to take a look, first checking over his shoulder. No sign of his former shipmates. Emboldened, he eased closer to the entrance and looked inside.

A gallery, he decided. Though puzzled why art consisting of cobbled-together tech and toys would attract such attention, there was no denying the demand. Evan watched as an Oieta and a Ket argued over who'd been first to touch what appeared to be a toaster with plas flowers growing from it, only to lose the item of their desire to a sneaky Queeb who snatched it up and rushed to the sales table.

"Amazes me every time."

The Human, female and about his grandmother's age, wore a smock with an abundance of pockets over her shirt and pants, the fabric dotted with glue and paint. Evan returned her smile. "Hello. Are you the artist?"

"Art? Hells, no. I stick things together for my son. He couldn't keep up otherwise." A nod to the dark-haired male behind the table. "Clever lad, my Kevin."

Kevin lifted his head, as though hearing his name, and smiled.

Evan felt a stab of recognition, but no, Kevin was much younger, and his eyes were blue, not gray. Still, something about the face. "I mean no offense," he said hastily, though by her tone she'd take none, "but why are these so popular?"

"Everyone needs shiny new info to swap at the Library. This lot?" She grinned. "Fresh off their ships and anxious to impress. It's not hard to encourage them to take a true rarity. A one-of-a-kind precious artifact."

His mind locked on the word "Library." This *was* the right place, however unlikely it seemed at the moment.

"We call'm gemmies," his informant went on cheerfully. "Combo of 'gem' and 'gummies.'" She produced a bag of soft candy. "Have one?"

"No, thank you." Evan felt sick. Without doubt, those at the All Species' Library of Linguistics and Culture would recognize a gemmie and dismiss any who brought one. This was fraud. Worse, fraud perpetrated on those like himself, desperate for an answer, who might well have the right facts or tidbit to offer but would defer to the experience of those here. People like this Kevin and his mother.

Evan wanted to sink into himself. He'd brought nothing better, had he? *Why had he thought what was precious only to him would matter?*

She turned to speak to someone else, and he let himself be pushed back by incoming customers.

Because he'd hoped it would matter to Paul, that's why. That he'd be granted special privileges based on what—a few hours spent together, half a year and most of a quadrant ago? A tumultuous few hours, granted, during which Paul and Rudy, but most of all the latter's young niece Bess, had helped him save the Pink Popeakan from the Hurns, then orchestrate the successful attachment of then-Senior Political Officer Simone Argyl Feen to Pre-!~!-la Acci-!~!-ari, producing the new Popeakan Ambassador to the Commonwealth and Human species, C'Ril Pre-!~!-la Acci-!~!-ari Feen.

None of them would forget that day. Paul had written on this very pamphlet, inviting Evan to visit the All Species' Library of Linguistics and Culture, being director and co-owner.

Evan breathed a little easier. When it came down to it, he probably did have something novel to add to the Library. The Gooseberry Lore was in the care of his Great Gran, but surely it was his legacy to share if he wished, despite what she'd say.

Thinking what she'd say, Evan shuddered and put his hand over the lump in his shirt. *Better still, this could work.*

He followed the sound of an announcer's voice to the train station, hurrying to jump on board the final car. There were three, each holding the equivalent of ten adult Humans. Evan squeezed in between four Urgians, feeling quite at home.

A pleasant-faced Human leaned in the still-open door, and beckoned to Evan. "Sorry, Hom. No luggage."

Evan tightened his grip on the carryall, only now noticing his was the only luggage in the car. With a sigh, he prepared to get off. Spotting a pair of too-familiar faces approaching, he stopped. "What am I to do?" he blurted, not expecting an answer.

The Human smiled. "Don't worry. I can take that for you, Hom. We've secure storage. You can pick it up when you come back tonight to meet your ship."

Why would he—with a sinking feeling, Evan realized when he'd read *no overnight accommodations* and assumed it only applied to the Library itself, he'd been terribly wrong. He'd no ship to return to—and no place to stay. He'd been so intent on finding answers, to be sent to the embassy at once, of course, if he did, that he hadn't thought beyond that.

Other than to daydream about saving the Elves with one pithy yet stunning fact, after which the embassy sent a ship to bring him home in triumph. With a new desk waiting and maybe a window—

One problem at a time. Evan handed over his carryall. "Thank you." He moved inside, watching Scar and Beard start to run.

The door closed, and the car began to move. The spacers halted on the field, glaring after him.

Evan knew better than to wave.

6: Response Room
Afternoon

THERE was only one way for clients to reach the Library: our transit system, itself comprised of four trains of three cars, a capacity based solely on how many beings could fit inside the main lobby without stepping on one another. With notice, any of those cars could be swapped out for non-oxy breathers, but so far they'd all arrived in exo-suits regardless, it being natural not to bet your survival on an untested service, especially when free. I'd suggested to Paul that if we charged, some would risk it. He'd yet to agree.

The schedule was based on the availability of our Botharan operators, neither Paul nor I willing to rely on servos. Promising the hamlet's residents first choice of employment opportunities, we found ourselves with a group of retired farmers who enjoyed driving through the countryside and had sufficient experience with machines and livestock to take transporting aliens in stride. They were upstanding, reliable beings outside of the calving season, the cornish harvest, or the Hamlet of Hillsview's Fall Harvest Festival, during which times they responded to obligations older and stronger than ours. "Retired," it turned out, was more "taking it a little easier between the real work."

Paul had chuckled when I pointed this out, saying we could use the downtime ourselves. The Library thus operated with the framework of seasonal change and what lived, not against it, which pleased me and, I thought, pleased our neighbors, too.

That said, when the train operators did work for us, they delivered clients at hourly intervals from dawn till noon, then began returning those clients to the landing field till dusk. There not being room for more than six ships on the field at once, others waited in orbit—with varied degrees of patience—for their turn.

As a result, our clients had time limits—which panicked more than a few. *In no way was it ideal.*

I did what I could. Until they could develop a Port City, as agreed, with hotels and restaurants, I'd suggested the Hamlet of Hillsview take an interim step: a shipcity of modest size. Let the ships park, in other words. They'd written back to say they'd Consider The Issue once done with Fall Harvest Festival grant applications, renovations to the fountain in the square—which had sputtered all summer then turned green—and the lengthy list of hoped-for improvements to their library. In the interim, they suggested we use the perfectly adequate shipcity on the outskirts of Grandine, the planetary capital; itself on the eastern shore of Lowesland.

To which I'd wanted to reply: fine, we'll move to the other side of the planet.

Not that we would. This gently rolling landscape held Paul's beginning, and I'd come to love it, too. Recalcitrant council and all. To be fair, no one in the hamlet believed the present mad rush of offworlders to visit *our* Library would last. To them, this was our "Rainbow Moment," as the expression went; I supposed what ephemerals found ephemeral seemed extremely chancy indeed. While we could have told them this was only the trial first year and wait till we used more than a few pamphlets to spread the word?

Paul worried the prospect of even more aliens would send the hamlet into complete paralysis. I disagreed. My bet was paralysis would come when they learned we'd plans for an orbital station.

Which other planets had, being safer for everyone than letting ships plop themselves overhead willy-nilly, and I'd a smidge of hope we'd ultimately filter the truly silly requests before they breached atmosphere and wasted our time—*Paul had doubts they'd see it that way.*

The second last train of the day disgorged its passengers at the Library entrance as I went about my favorite task, putting aside, for the moment, Paul's troublesome cousin.

Time to verify the information we gave in return, against that in my flesh.

Ally Orman didn't know *what* I was, other than the Library's curator, arbitrator of fact from fancy, and one of her two bosses.

I was also the dapple-snouted Lanivarian she'd initially mistaken for a scruff, the pet canid common on this world. In her defense, at the time I'd been using my front teeth to free an annoying hunk of vegetation from between the pads of my foot, with the muffled moist snarling that entailed, thus not presenting myself as the intelligent, civilized being I was.

As relationships go, ours had definitely started on the wrong foot. She'd apologized, Paul had smoothed over the moment as he always did, and we settled in to work together, Ally being responsible for the physical format of what we dispensed to our clients.

From the way she'd stare at me at unguarded moments, I was reasonably sure she still wasn't quite convinced. *Might not help that when I caught her stare, I'd let my tongue loll and would swing my handsome tail in slow sweeps.*

She'd blush.

Paul wasn't amused. I was. Ally was a good person who lacked experience with my kind, that was all. As the first Lanivarian to reach Botharis, I'd fully expected to be confused for the local four-footed variety, albeit a warped version, and had anticipated some innocent fun, but it disturbed Paul too much. He remembered when I'd disguised myself as a serlet on Kraos, a dark time indeed.

Most of all, I thought, *my friend needed to believe I felt safe here.*

Owing him that, and everything, I refrained from being a scruff on purpose. What other people assumed? *Not my problem.*

Today, the past resurfacing thanks to Janet Chase, Paul's father, and—oh, yes—Lionel, I shrugged on my lab coat, with its convenient slit for my tail, and composed my snout with dignity instead of showing Ally a cheery fang. "I'm here. How are we doing?"

"Hello, Esen." She waved at a busy tabletop. "Quite the mix, I'm afraid."

Bright-eyed and energetic, Ally Orman was taller than Paul and outmassed him by a considerable amount, her shoulders and chest thick with muscle. She'd been a world-class swimmer before settling in the hamlet, a curious choice, given there wasn't a swimmable body of water within a day's ground travel. She'd told us it was to prove she was serious about her retirement from the sport. *Humans were so odd.*

Now she worked here, in the Library's Response Room. Situated safely distant from clients, and along the same corridor as Paul's office, it could offer the same lovely view of the farmhouse and hills beyond through its wall if Ally ever set it for transparent. She'd left a broad slit along the top to admit light and glimpse sky, presumably to know whether to grab her raincoat before heading out the door. It worked now, the exterior dotted with thick raindrops as the afternoon showers arrived on time.

Our staff, in whatever conveyance they preferred, went home along the original farm lane that followed Ragem Creek to the Hamlet of Hillsview. The creek was sleepy in this warm season, but it would rise over its banks in spring.

I swam myself then, in a lithe form that loved the wild free run of water over rock, careful to go unseen but not too worried. While tricky to explain the presence of a Rrabi'sk, being long-extinct, the original settlers had brought with them dire stories of scaly toothed swimmers who rode the floodwaters, useful through generations to keep children from drowning. Close enough.

My adding to the mystique was, therefore, a public service.

Ally had opaqued the rest of the wall to make room for a built-in workstation with cupboards below. Another wall held shelves of art supplies, with the best fabricator we could fit taking up the third. The fourth wall held the rack for coats, a cupboard I knew held cookies, among other things, and Ally's access node. The busy table in the center of the room was for me.

"Have a seat." Ally set a basket in front of my usual spot. "These are the latest."

The ever-changing variety within the basket's contents gave me particular delight, each time a demonstration of how very good Ally was at what she did. This basketful included an assortment of datacrystals, postcards showing the entrance to the Library, a statuette of a six-legged pony with huge googly eyes I found disturbing—being in no memory of mine or Ersh—and a bag of common pebbles.

Responses. Not the Library's answer, in these special instances, but mine. *Not that anyone but Paul or I would know.* Ally received instructions, created each using her skills and imagination, then gave them to me, as curator, for a final check.

All in the interest of clarity.

Clients who added to the Library's collection, be it the image of a Rand sex toy or a documentation of significant grammatical shift, were shown to a species' appropriate access node and allowed to ask a question. One addition, one query, leading—hopefully—to an answer that let them trundle away satisfied. Most questions could have been answered as readily anywhere and those clients weren't my concern. They received their answer as a datacrystal with an embedded date and the Library's verification code.

For those who activated the collection's unique datasets? The verification was me. I'd confirm the information we were about to share—the answer—against the memories in my flesh, preserving the Library's reputation for accuracy. On to the datacrystal and away you go.

The rest? Oh, that's where the alerts came in, triggered by a preset algorithm we'd developed and tested before opening the doors. *Esen, pay attention* was the gist, and I did.

The commonest alert flagged if a client was likely to misunderstand the answer. Words were fallible. Some species did better without them. *When in doubt, ask me.* What I had before me, and whatever was mid-process on Ally's workstations and burbling to itself in the fabricator, were responses customized for such clients.

Another signaled a question the Library couldn't answer. I would input the required information so that it could.

If there was a question I couldn't answer?

Well, that would be an exciting day, if and when it arrived. My plan was to soar off into the cosmos with my trusty companion in search of the unknown, preferably wearing capes. Paul, being my trusty companion, had been with me on such adventures in the past, though without capes. As our adventures had proved thus far to be uncomfortable, tedious, and occasionally life-threatening, he'd insisted we confine future actions to the Library. *Still, a blob could hope.*

What we waited for most of all? The alert warning us of serious implications, whether because of *who* asked, or *what,* or both. Our purpose.

I would do my best to interpret the *why* behind those questions. Any question could be innocent. A chef after biologically-safe substitute ingredients. An architect wanting details of a forgotten-by-others material. A historian desiring the opposing point of view for a pivotal battle. A linguist seeking the source of a phrase or myth. A musician who'd heard rumors of a song lost to time. A spacer after a more profitable trade route.

If the "why" was simply to find another piece to add to their puzzle, inert alone, useful with others, I allowed the answer to be shared as it was. It was no concern of ours.

If the "why" fell into the category of species confused about one another? Anatae wondering what they were doing wrong. Ganthor paralyzed by the inability of Tumblers to answer their calls. Feneden about to eliminate the Iftsen because they didn't believe they were real.

An ephemeral species about to be extinguished because their attackers didn't know a truth that mattered.

Those were our concern. Species approaching a fatal

crisis due to ignorance, an ignorance we had the power—the obligation—to change. To help them ask the *right* question, and to understand the answer.

Oh, Ersh wouldn't approve of that at all.

I didn't dream, but Humans did. Paul confessed to me he had nightmares where we'd receive an alert about serious implications—would have a client with the right question and intentions—and we'd fail, having no answer to give.

Telling him species went extinct all the time hadn't helped.

But it was true, and before the Library, the universe of diverse life-forms hadn't collapsed on itself for the simple fact that most ignorance wasn't serious, falling into the category of "who thinks what" is obscene, delightful, insulting, attractive, and so forth. Saving beings from social and biological missteps was another area in which I was uniquely equipped to resolve, having been all of the varied "whos" in question. *While making my own assortment of missteps.*

I started with the datacrystals, labeled and secure, putting each in turn into the reader. Every so often, I'd glance at the nonsensical pony. It would look back with those huge googly eyes.

Ally busied herself with the fabricator, glancing at me once in a while.

Why had she made a six-legged googly-eyed pony?

Refusing to ask, I kept going. There was nothing in the lot—or the clients' questions—to suggest major turmoil brewing or even a petty spat, so I gave each my seal of "checked and safely boring" by putting each crystal between my large back molars and biting with enough pressure to leave a mark. The trace of spittle was for Skalet's doorframe scanners, proof to my web-kin that I did work.

My Lanivarian-self having superb peripheral vision, I noticed Ally's too-casual stance by the supply shelves as my paw reached for what would be next. Stretching past the pony, I collected the postcards, twitching an ear at her tiny sigh. *Something interesting, was it?*

Postcards before pony. There were two. The first had been punctured with a needle so that when held to a light, as I did, a faint pattern of holes could be seen. Barely. *Interesting.* Perhaps sight wasn't the approach.

My paws, or hands, had well-callused knuckles despite my diligent filing; appearances, after all, but while travel on all fours was considered regressive, there were times I couldn't resist a good run.

I stretched out a finger to sweep its sensitive pad over the card. The pattern came to life: a complexity of varied heights, with a texture provided by the direction the needle had gone through the fibers. I half-closed my eyes to concentrate. Could be a flower. Or a shell.

I'd need to cycle into the form to be sure, not something I could do in front of Ally or in air for that matter, but it wouldn't be necessary. This response was for the Oieta art student, presently swimming in the aquatic zone of the Library while her Soft Companion, an Engullan, waited in the dry. The student had asked how she could better appreciate the works of Margis Krips, the foremost Ket hoobit maker of the past century, that being her professor's assignment.

Art appreciation was an interspecies' minefield, one I loathed with a passion, being as even Paul had to admit "tasteless in any form." *In my callow youth,* I reminded myself. Hopefully I'd develop an aesthetic of my own in a millennium or so.

The initial answer provided by the Library had been the opinion of someone else, hardly helpful for a student with a hopeless assignment.

To appreciate this postcard required the sense an Oieta lacked: touch, coupled with the ability to translate touch into image. Moreover, the card was composed of dried pressed plant material—a Botharan specialty—meaning it could only be touched while dry, an environment no Oietae, even an art professor, could survive. I waved the card. "Nice response, Ally."

"Thank you. To understand it, our client must consult with someone biologically capable of communicating with her, an Oieta, who is also capable of feeling this card." Ally paused meaningfully. "Those are the requirements to appreciate the tactile art of Ket."

"Question answered. Either our student should request a more species-suited assignment," I concluded,
grinning. "Or collaborate with a non-Oieta."

Ally smiled back, her brown eyes shining. "Exactly."

Pony next—

"Esen. You here?" A head popped in the door, topped
with light brown curls.

"Come in, Henri," Ally greeted. "I'll put on tea."

Curls danced as the other Human shook her head.
Blue eyes found me. "I've someone waiting in the Line
who says they know Paul."

"I'm not Paul," I told her distractedly. *I'd a pony to
question.*

"Yes, of course you're not, but when I said the director
was busy for the rest of the day, they asked for Bess instead." She gave a helpless shrug. "No one knew who that
was. Do you?"

It was the name of my Human-self, not a form I
planned to be on this too-Human world. I swallowed an
anxious whine.

"I'll come." Standing, I held out the pony, giving Ally
my best pleading puppy expression. "I could take this
one. To work on."

She knew, and I knew, and probably everyone remotely connected to the Library knew the point of this
behind-the-scenes Response Room was that I didn't.
Take things, that is. Once approved, responses sped from
here to the waiting client by automated messenger, it being impossible to debate with a servo tube unless you'd
the mental acuity of a drunk Mobera, in which case you
wouldn't be waiting for anything, but that wasn't why.

Well, it was, if I were honest. On opening day I'd insisted on delivering responses in person, to provide full,
meaningful explanations and helpful tips. By my fourth
delivery, the last train of the day had left the Library,
leaving us with a plethora of incompatible houseguests.
From that moment on, Paul insisted on the non-Esen
system.

"Go ahead." Ally chuckled. "I made it for you."

I blinked. "You did?" The pony didn't appear edible,

but I gave one of the googly eyes a cautious lick. No, not edible at all. "Why?"

She lifted her hand in that shooing gesture most of the Humans in my life used eventually. "Go with Henri, Esen. Paul can explain later." When she turned back to her work, her shoulders were shaking with repressed laughter.

Also something most did.

Pony in hand, one curiosity foiled for now, I followed Henri intending to solve the other: who knew the name of my Human-self.

And, more worrisome, who'd use it here.

I ran through the short list of those who knew "Bess" as I walked. Lionel Kearn, who wouldn't use it here. Rudy, our old friend, Paul's cousin, and presently captain of the *Largas Loyal,* wouldn't either. On impulse I'd given it to Z'ndraa, a Grigari musician on Prumbin, but he'd called me Not-Small-Bess anyway. Skalet had used it in front of the crew of the *Octos Ra,* but as they were affiliates and subordinates, they'd cut out their tongues before betraying her confidence. While smiling. Kraal were peculiar like that.

Would Chase? Rudy'd introduced me to her as his niece, Gloria, but Joel Largas, Chase's former employer, knew I was Bess. No. He'd never let it slip, especially not to Chase.

She'd betrayed him, too.

Machine memory. I didn't—dared not discount what might be out there. About Paul. About me—what I was. If someone knew the questions to ask . . .

I almost stopped, pony in hand, to suggest we collect S'kal-ru on the way but didn't. When it came to my web-kin?

Some worries were best not shared.

"Is something wrong, Esen?" Henri frowned at me. "You're growling."

No surprise, given my thoughts. "Sorry."

"I can fetch Paul, if you wish. He's downstairs with

Hom Kearn. I hadn't thought this important enough to interrupt them—Gooseberry seems harmless, if insistent."

Evan?

"I should have asked the name right away, Henri," I
told her, feeling all manner of a fool. "Don't worry. I can
handle this."

If not stop my tail trying to wag.

Perception

"THIS is—" *unexpected, wonderful, more than he deserved.* Lionel Kearn settled for, "—fine. Thank you."

"I wish we'd better to offer." Paul looked around the small room. He'd already gathered the bedding, promising fresh, and offered a proper change of clothing for tomorrow, leaving coveralls folded on a stool. "It's where I crash when working late—especially in winter."

"I'm sure I'll be comfortable." To demonstrate, Lionel sat on the cot and patted the mattress.

"If it looks familiar, it is. We've a Commonwealth surplus store in the capital."

Lionel looked down in surprise. "Goodness, I haven't—I think the last time I slept on a service cot would have been Ungar Tierce. Remember?" He chuckled. "Twenty-three nights, waiting for the Wombas to follow our invitation."

"I remember twenty-three days of leaving that trail." The other shook his head, grin turned rueful. "Tomas believed you were punishing us—not that he could figure out for what."

Lionel stood. "You didn't." With confidence. "You'd researched the Womba before we arrived. I could tell."

"Because I didn't complain about urinating on fifteen rocks each day?"

"Twenty." He'd placed them himself, in the proper alignment. "There were twenty trail markers, Paul."

"At the start, yes," with a chuckle. "But we'd run out by fifteen, so Tomas and I removed five and spread the rest out. You didn't notice?"

Clearly not. "But—" Lionel frowned. "The Womba still came."

"And we made first contact with a new species." Paul's eyes shone, and the two gazed at one another in a moment of perfect understanding.

It had been so simple then. Lionel sighed to himself. Pee for the locals, share a ceremonial supper, obtain permission to record—everything, for you didn't know where the breakthrough in language or understanding would be. Or where the breakdown might happen. "This Library," he asked abruptly. "Have you had any—special requests?"

A thoughtful look. Paul knew what he'd hesitated to say. Had the Library fulfilled its purpose yet? "A few," the other replied. "According to Esen, none would have escalated beyond trade disagreements without us. The only peril we've helped avert so far was to discourage an Iedemad named Tallo from opening a salt spa on Iftsen Secundus."

"A salt spa?" Lionel sputtered. "You know the chemistry of their atmosphere. The fumes alone would kill any patrons, not to mention the risk of explosion. What was this Tallo thinking?"

A wry smile. "That's what we wanted to know. Tallo bought the spa franchise from someone who hadn't bothered to stipulate physical constraints—or didn't care. Fortunately, the Iedemad had some doubts and decided to ask the Library first."

"Still, a close call. You reported this reckless 'someone,' surely."

"No." Eyes flashed. "We don't act beyond these walls, Lionel. That's the deal."

Esen had wanted to, he guessed, and Paul pulled her back. "You keep her safe," he acknowledged warmly. "It can't be easy."

A wry, then grateful look. "No." That abrupt cheerful grin. "I can say the 'someone' in question tried to sell another spa franchise to an undercover patroller and is now out of any business for the next ten years or so."

Not coincidence, Lionel thought. Paul had a network of those who could ensure such things, a network developed over the decades of hiding from him. Those in it ranged from individuals who'd no idea who paid their wages to those who'd met this Human, listened to him, and fallen under his spell. A leader was what his former subordinate had become, his compassion weathered into an unconscious nobility, that ardent curiosity now wisdom.

He could be dangerous. Not what Paul had ever wanted to become, Lionel knew that, being a gentle soul. But Esen had needed that side of her friend before now.

She might again. "A moment, Paul," before the other could open the door. "Rudy—he shared Skalet's opinion about Chase."

Bedding hugged to his chest, Paul Ragem suddenly looked too young. "Janet is after what's best for her. That won't have changed. I've never considered her a threat to Esen or to me. Whatever she's up to now—it's about credits." His expression changed, as if hearing what he'd just said.

And there he was, Lionel thought with a pang almost like grief.

The dangerous Paul Ragem.

7: Sorting Line Afternoon

HENRI didn't talk or waste time, cutting through three habitat zones rather than take the walkways. Normally, I enjoyed the diversion provided by nipping in and out of the varied environments—except the freeze-your-nose-hairs of the polar zone—but I followed behind Henri, automatically supplying the species' appropriate "excuse us" to any we rudely interrupted.

She didn't go to the counter at the head of the Line, instead veering to bring us into the main lobby along the elevated walkway. It was a feature we'd added at the last minute, Paul realizing we'd nowhere for aerial species to escape the footed, but now I appreciated the view it provided.

Henri pointed. "There he is."

I'd know that cap of deliciously springy tight curls anywhere.

There was no stopping my tail.

Evan Gooseberry had come to the Library.

Henri resumed her seat behind the Assessment Counter, her ever-expressive face a mix of emotions. Curiosity appeared to win as I pulled up a stool to join her.

Across from us stood a slightly built young male Human, about 40 years of age. Pale freckles dotted his thin hooked nose. Uptilted green eyes regarded us anxiously, their long pale lashes striking against his very dark skin. Add the light brown mass of dense curls I'd recognized from afar and Evan hadn't changed a bit.

I had. Profoundly. Evan had met Bess, the Human me, last year on Urgia Prime. While he'd seen my giant Crougk-self, he'd no inkling we were one and the same. *Small mercies.*

So as much as I'd have preferred to touch noses in a warm greeting, I kept my demeanor professional. "Hello. I'm Esen-alit-Quar, Library Curator. How may I assist you?"

"That's not a Lanivarian name."

Of course it wasn't. Ansky had picked it, for whatever reason, but the only other person to ever comment had been Paul Ragem. I showed an appreciative fang, then moved on briskly. "And your name?"

"I gave it to this fem." He didn't quite bow at Henri but came close.

"This is Evan Gooseberry, Esen. The one who asked for the Director."

There was an impatient *toot . . . toot* from back in the Line. Henri lobbed a bag of candy over the first few heads, then shrugged at me. "Thielex's come again. Should keep her quiet for a while."

Ah. The musical prodigy from Baelexen, "prodigy" a term with unique meaning for Lexen, a species with a deep appreciation for the way mutation or painful accident could permanently bend their respiratory tubes. She'd asked on her initial visit about a Human instrument called a kazoo; I looked forward to whatever she was after now.

"Excuse me, but I asked for Paul Ragem some time ago. What's the delay?"

Evan might look the same, other than wearing rumpled casual clothes able to offend lesser olfactory senses than I presently possessed, but he wasn't acting like the same shy, polite person I'd known.

Travel could do that, I told myself. "I'm here now. How may I assist you, Hom Gooseberry?"

He stared pointedly at the pony in my paw. "I don't

mean to be rude," he said, in the tone Humans used before being exactly that. "But you're a bit young to take seriously. A curator? No. I want to speak with Paul or Bess."

Knew his Lanivarians, did he? Fine. I wrinkled my snout and half lowered my ears; *offended but refusing to lower myself, that was.* "You're entitled to your opinion, Hom Gooseberry. We have another train about to arrive. If you insist only the director can help you, I ask you to step aside and let the next client up."

The next client, an Ervickian, grunted approval.

Something flickered in Evan's eyes, a look I recognized. *Fear.* But of what? He'd several, to my knowledge, all barriers to his hoped-for career as a diplomat, all battled with impressive courage.

This wasn't quite the same. He was simply breathing more quickly. Sweating, too. I'd mentioned the train. Did he fear who might be on it?

Had I missed a memo? Lionel. Then Evan. Now . . . ? This morning, I'd worried about harboring an Anata. I stood and beckoned impatiently. "Come with me, please."

Henri sent me a worried look.

"We'll wait in Paul's office," I told her, trusting she'd know what to do.

Find Paul and tell him to meet us there.

I'd hoped to delay any discussion until my capable friend arrived, but the instant Evan entered the office, he turned on me. "Where's Bess?"

Oh, dear. I was, as Rudy put it, a terrible liar in any form. It didn't help that was the moment I spotted the forlorn pile of Moody-Mood Bracelets left on Paul's desk. As Bess, on Minas XII, I loved playing with the things; he must have ordered them for the family reunion. Gifts for children we'd yet to meet.

Flustered, I blurted, "There's no Bess. Not here. I thought you wanted to speak to the director. Tea?" I finished urgently, having sniffed the air to check Paul had made a pot this morning. Whether it remained drinkable—

"So Paul is coming."

I certainly hoped so. "Have a seat, please."

Evan collapsed more than sat in the chair. He let out a sigh, rubbed his hand over his face, then looked at me with a wan, very Evan, smile. "Please accept my apologies, Huntress. I'm—it's been a difficult journey, but that's no excuse."

"Space travel." My shudder of sympathy wasn't entirely feigned.

His eyes lit up. "Yes, it's harder for you. I admit, I was surprised to find—you're a long way—" he stopped, then went on, "—I'm making it worse, aren't I?"

I sat in the other chair. It was only then I realized I still clutched the blue google-eyed pony in one paw. With what dignity I could muster, I set the ridiculous thing beside the teapot. "I assume you've come to the Library with a request, Hom Gooseberry." Given he had our pamphlet crushed in one hand.

"Yes. Yes, I have. An urgent one." To my bewilderment, Evan put away the pamphlet and began fumbling at the buttons of his shirt. He glanced up. "I read the requirements. I've brought an item to trade."

In his shirt? "We do prefer—"

Evan scrambled to his feet, shirt askew, eyes widening. I turned my head, hoping for Paul.

Facing Skalet.

She looked displeased, an intimidating expression for her at the best of times, and as a Kraal? Suffice to say I understood Evan's instinctive leap to a position in which he could run, and even more his decision to stay perfectly still.

Family.

I stood as well. "This is Evan, a friend of Paul's." And mine, a message I added with one slow sweep of my tail. "Evan, this is—"

"Security." One pale eyebrow rose, challenging me to argue.

Which I wouldn't. "Ah, yes. Thank you for coming, but there's no problem here. Evan was about to show me the item he's brought to be assessed."

The other eyebrow joined the first in silent, undeniable demand.

"It's—" Evan hunched. "It's not much."

This form had no eyebrows worth raising. "I'll be the judge of that, Evan," I said firmly.

He reached in his shirt and brought out—

"Ersh—!"

Before Skalet could utter more than that betraying gasp of a word, could do more than lunge forward, only to stop, trembling, I jumped in. "What a delightful rendering of Teganersha-ki."

Ersh as a Dokeci. As *the* Dokeci, the infamous and famous individual who'd united a planet under one rule, hers.

My eyes locked on the ugly little bust, held in Human hands, seeing *Ersh* stare back with her trio of dead eyes, the greatest of us, the *Oldest* and First of us—

In *HUMAN* hands—

And in that instant I felt the same sickening betrayal as Skalet must—the same *RAGE*—

What saved poor Evan Gooseberry was another hand, closing over those eyes. Another voice, calm and sure, saying these words: "Evan. I'm glad you've come."

Paul. Standing here, close enough to touch—to *assimilate*—

Skalet glared down at him, the skin of her face drawn into a death's mask, tattoos stark against pallor—

I, *Ersh save me*, fought the urge to rip and tear—not with these teeth, but with my own—

Paul froze in place.

Later I'd replay the moment—feeling every sodden lurch of my Lanivarian heart, hearing each harsh breath Skalet dragged into her Human lungs, both so close to losing control—and I'd know the full extent of the risk Paul had taken. Not only for himself and his fellow Human. For us. For our ability to live with *them*.

In the moment, I felt and listened. It was all I dared do.

A soft, "Easy, Fangface."

My friend, aware something was wrong if not what or why, took a slow step back, drawing Evan with him, their hands clasped around Ersh.

Not Ersh, I tried to tell myself. *Why couldn't I believe it?* Because . . .

There was more here than a little bust.

Web-flesh!

Another step, with thoroughly unreasonable calm. Another as Paul moved Evan with him, as if they began a dance, pulling him away from us.

In dreadful synchrony, Skalet and I turned our heads to follow.

A final graceful move and Paul Ragem stood between us and Evan, who looked anxiously over his shoulder and thought—*Ersh, I couldn't begin to guess.*

Gray eyes met mine, telling me what to do.

I grabbed Skalet by the hand and pulled her with me out of there.

Later, I'd be amazed she let me.

Perception

THEY hadn't held hands, they'd held his bust of Teganersha-ki, and he'd no clue why the little thing had upset Esen and the terrifying Kraal the way it had, but Evan Gooseberry found himself breathless because . . .

. . . he might have fantasized, a bit, regarding the holding of hands.

They weren't now. He stood forgotten in the middle of the room, Paul at the windowlike wall, staring out at the rain. There was upset in the curve of those shoulders; hands flexed as if they wanted to be fists but didn't dare. Even if Evan could think of anything to say, his mouth was too dry for words.

He looked down at the bust in his hand. Three eyes looked back, and there was an answer in their beady gaze if only he could decipher it.

"Bess isn't here."

Startled, he looked up. "Why?" Then blushed. "I mean—I thought she'd be wherever you—are." *What was wrong with him?* "Bess, that is."

The corners of Paul's generous mouth deepened, softening what had been a grim line. "This isn't the world for her," he said. "But you, Evan. What brings you to the Library?"

You.

For a horrified moment, Evan thought he'd said that aloud and wanted the Kraal back or the floor to open beneath his feet and swallow him whole. Because you didn't say things like that, not to someone like this, not when it was fantasy . . .

When Paul appeared still waiting for an answer, he let out a relieved breath. "I'm working at—" his voice failed, and he tried again, managing a cracked, "—the embassy on Dokeci-Na."

"What's wrong?"

He touched his throat, whispered, "Thirs-ty." And was, desperately so, the tension of whatever the hell had or hadn't happened with Esen—he knew the face of a Lanivarian about to attack, and that Kraal?—causing a veritable storm of reactions. The dry mouth, the tremors in his legs, the contrary urge to sneeze as his eyes watered.

Reaction to the past three days—that, too—not that he could afford any of it.

He wiped his eyes surreptitiously as Paul went to a wall dispenser, returning with a tall glass of water. Nodding his thanks, Evan sipped slowly, needing the respite to compose himself as much as the liquid.

Paul waited, his face unreadable.

Done, Evan put the glass by the blue pony, then walked to the table serving as a desk. A pretty set of what he guessed to be Odarian trunk rings caught the light, perhaps a gift for a youngster. He put the bust down on the opposite end. "This was to be my offering in trade." He didn't lift his fingertips from it. "I fear it's unacceptable." As for the Gooseberry Lore?

During his walk from the entrance through the main lobby he'd seen enough of this amazing place and those coming to use it to realize how laughably inadequate the family list was—no matter how important to Great Gran.

Paul came to the table. "May I?" He picked up the bust and regarded it, turning it this way and that.

Not seeing it, Evan thought. He had to say something. "I'd a teacher who knew I wanted to work on Dokeci-Na. Who knew I'd—difficulties with their appearance."

Having *SNAKE arms!* Worst of all, they'd erupt without warning in . . . *SKIN SPOTS!*

He collected himself. "This was to encourage me. A

symbol of what I could achieve, if I could overcome my, my problem." He tried to stand taller. "I did. More or less." Groups were—hard to bear.

"Congratulations, Evan." Paul held it out. "Here. You should keep this," warmly.

He took it. "But—" then blurted desperately, "I don't suppose you'd consider the Lore of the Gooseberrys in trade?"

"The—?" There was the smile he'd remembered, wide and full of gentle humor. "I'll ask you to explain later, Evan." The smile faded. "You can ask as many questions as you wish. Don't worry about that. First, I need to know what just happened in here. What can you tell me? Take your time."

Because this was important. Evan could see it. Beneath the calm courtesy, Paul held a powerful emotion in check and whether anger or fear, it wasn't directed at him.

At Esen?

"I arrived an hour ago and went to the Assessment Counter. I—I admit I took advantage of our previous acquaintance and insisted on seeing you. I should have let the person in charge see what I'd brought."

"You're our friend, Evan, invited here. Go on."

Just like that. Encouraged, Evan forged ahead. "Fem Steves brought the curator—Esen—and I, well, I was really quite rude to her. But—she's very young for such responsibility. Isn't she?"

"Not always." Paul's eyes were hooded in concentration. "Why did Esen bring you here? To wait for me?"

That hadn't been why, had it? Not if he'd read her expression as well as she'd read his. "When the curator reminded me the next train was due to arrive, she saw I was afraid. I think Esen wanted to protect me."

A sharp look. "From what? Who's on that train?"

8: Garden Afternoon;
Nebula Aside

WE ran together, hand in paw. No one saw us, and it wasn't until we stepped through the portal into the rain that Skalet pulled free.

She stayed beside me, for some unfathomable reason, as I rushed through the Garden. There were paths here. I'd made them, ensuring they flowed through lovely spaces and curious spots, to encourage thought and calm.

We didn't use them. We stepped over mounds of moss to walk through a tall dense hedge of Red-tipped Conchie, planted so rows overlapped to make a hidden entrance. A second deceitful passage, this lined with Cully Grass with plumes touching over our heads, then down the steps to our meeting place.

Stone, here.

Quiet but for the drumming of rain.

Ours.

The Web of Ersh had met atop her wind-scoured mountain on Picco's Moon, each in our preferred form. I remembered being afraid then, knowing what was to happen.

Today, I felt only the burning *need* for it.

Skalet took her place, leaving her uniform neatly folded on the stone.

Tossing my smock aside, I took mine. Our eyes met.

"What would you have me know, Youngest?" Skalet's beautiful voice trembled. Perhaps her rage lingered. Perhaps something else. Her bare, scarred arms thrust out to the sides. "We've lost Ersh and the others. Being what we are, the pain cannot be diminished or forgotten."

"Nor should it be," I said.

Her arms dropped. "Then what? If you think to punish me, remember you were as near to ending that Human as I was. To giving in to what we are. For what? A representation of Ersh. A poor one at that. It makes no sense." Softer. Troubled. "No sense."

"That's not all it is."

An Alini Dove cooed from the maze of branches above us; pairs sang a romantic harmony in the rain. While I waited for Skalet, I tilted my ears to catch a reply, but none came.

"I don't understand."

"You will."

I cycled into the blue teardrop perfection of web-form . . . losing sight, sound, taste, smell, and touch, sensing Skalet do the same . . .

. . . gaining more . . . the echoing beats of gravity from Botharis and her twin moons, the spin of her sun, everywhere the whirl of atoms and the tides of magnetism and . . .

Tasting what was us, but not here. That infinitesimal trace . . . feeling Skalet's confusion, tasting the same but unable to grasp its source . . .

I sorted what she'd need to know from what I would keep.

Share . . . releasing the irresistible demand into the air between us, offering my flesh . . .

Enduring as Skalet's jagged teeth bit, tearing pieces of me away . . .

My turn would be next, the return of mass exquisitely precise, and quite likely full of Kraal moments I wouldn't enjoy assimilating in the least.

No matter. What Skalet consumed came from when I'd been significantly younger, Ersh still very much alive, and held a memory about our web-kin I'd never shared before.

. . . she was going to hate it.

Picco's Moon, 82 Commonwealth Standard Years Ago

Ersh, Senior Assimilator and center of my personal universe, had firm ideas about what I should do with my time. These ideas doubtless stemmed from my being the most Recent of my kind and, to be honest, an unprecedented accident, but I hardly viewed them as fair. After all, was it my fault I'd been born instead of properly budded from Ersh's flesh as the rest of our Web?

I plopped another seedling into its pot and straightened it morosely. One such idea was this morning drudgery in the greenhouse.

My education was another.

Ersh had decided I was to receive the wealth of knowledge gained by our kind of the biology and cultures of more ephemeral races only after she herself had sorted that knowledge through her own flesh. *Doubtless leaving out the good bits.*

My toes snapped the seedling at the stem. I hastily shoved the remaining piece deeper into the soil. It might not wilt until after I'd left. Despite centuries of practice, I wasn't good with plants.

I wasn't good with anything.

I sighed heavily, my tail sliding between my legs. Enjoying the melancholy, I sighed again.

"Esen."

I straightened in haste, the movement sending the tray of transplanted seedlings flying off the table in a spectacular spray of dirt, tiny green stems, and pots—pots that shattered noisily on impact with the stone floor. Well, except for the one that arced through the air all the way to the wall, which produced more of a smash and slither.

"Esen-alit-Quar!"

At least she wouldn't notice the broken seedling, I consoled myself as I warily turned to face Ersh.

I was Esen-alit-Quar when in trouble, Esen for short, Es in a hurry or between friends, not that I felt warmed by friendship at this moment. Ersh's massive crystalline

Tumbler-self had an ominous tilt forward. I tried to unobtrusively tilt backward—not easy in my current form, that of the canidlike Lanivarian. This was my birth shape, the one I preferred for the value of its useful hands and still the easiest for me to hold.

For we were Web-beings, creatures of energy and matter and transitions between, able to spend some of our mass to bind our remaining molecules in a different, memorized form until choosing to release and return to the flawless teardrop of blue that was our heritage.

I was still working on that part.

"Hi, Esen." A dark eye peered around the side of Ersh. My jaw dropped in a grin. "Lesy! Welcome home!"

My web-kin didn't come out any farther. I wasn't surprised. We were six in the known universe: Ersh, Skalet, Mixs, Ansky—my birth mother, Lesy, and myself. Lesy and I shared one other characteristic. We both did our utmost to avoid facing Ersh when she was annoyed.

Ersh herself, likely taking my grin and greeting as signs I wasn't suitably grief-stricken about her dying seedlings—which wasn't entirely true, since being the one who'd have to clean up and repot fresh ones all afternoon, I felt significant anguish at my fate—chimed a note of distinct temper. Lesy's eye disappeared.

I spread my arms in appeasement, which helped hide pots. "You wanted me, Ersh?" this brightly, with a deliberate lift of my ears.

"Not on any level," she muttered, but not loudly enough to expect a reply. She did expect me to hear, being fully aware of the capabilities of my current ears. In more normal tones, "Lesy does. You're going with her, Youngest."

I blinked. "Going where?"

The immense greenhouse was the deepest portion of Ersh's house, that house a series of rooms quarried into the side of a cliff almost as old as she. The cliff was part of Picco's Moon, a world of rock and rock-based life, its surface stained by the lurid orange-and-purple reflection of Picco except during Eclipse. Lesy didn't come here unless summoned by Ersh; she kept to her windowless room when here, other than occasional conquests of the kitchen. She wouldn't go outside unless forced by Ersh.

Why? Because Picco's exact shade of orange, as she frequently reminded everyone but Ersh, drained her creativity.

As creativity was something Ersh insisted I avoid at all costs, I judged Lesy's claim as another concept I'd be taught when I was older. *If that ever happened.* Though I suspected this one fell within the category of what Skalet called "Lesy's idiotic prattle."

We were the closest of kin, together forming the Web of Ersh. *Didn't mean we were always kind to one another.*

"Go where?" I repeated, ears heading back down. A kitchen summons was likeliest. Lesy could clean up after herself. Well, she could, but rarely did. I'd take refuge in planting if necessary.

I hated wet paws.

One, then three dark eyes, each the size of my clenched fist, peered at me from behind the crystal form of Ersh, reflecting in gleaming facets until there might have been thirty. The glowing green ring encircling each signaled unusual excitement. Or a fever. Lesy's middle-aged Dokeci-self was prone to stress-related illness if she persisted in using it within significant gravity. Which she did. "Dokeci-Na, Youngest! The western continent. I'm holding my first exhibit in the capital!"

"Pardon?" Our kind might possess perfect recall; that didn't mean we couldn't confuse one another. Portula Colony was Lesy's preferred home. I'd been there before: a quiet, self-contained environment inhabited by, at most, forty self-absorbed artists. It wasn't Picco's Moon, but the next best thing for a young Web-being of uncertain parentage—so Ersh had proclaimed. *Boring.* Though there was, I recalled fondly, a remarkable pool. But Dokeci-Na?

An entire planet teeming with life—life that had evolved there? Life that wasn't rock?

There would be restaurants, I thought, charmed beyond reason. I tipped a questioning ear toward Ersh, hardly daring to believe my good fortune.

"After you finish here," Ersh said with remarkable restraint, considering, "pack and be ready. The shuttle's on its way. I need not remind you of the Prime Law or what I expect from your behavior offworld, Youngest."

"No, Ersh." Her expectations consisted of my staying out of sight and out of mind, which basically translated into "don't talk to ephemerals." One day I would, *if I lived that long.* Right now, I wasn't trained for such interaction. Wouldn't be a problem; Dokeci didn't believe anyone my age could hold a conversation.

But if behaving meant I'd get my first-ever visit to a world without opinionated crystal?

My tail swung wildly, knocking the surviving pots to the floor.

"Esen-alit-Quar!"

I possessed Lesy's memories of Portula Colony—those Ersh deemed fit for me to have, anyway. A private space station, it lay within view of the famous Jeopardy Nebula, said view the source of inspiration for the colony's artistically-minded population. Portula was the place Lesy currently favored when not on a mission for our Web. Since she went on fewer missions than any web-kin but me—for no reason Ersh deemed fit for me to know—Lesy had had time to become well established within her isolated home. We were to head there first, to finalize the shipping of her art, then accompany that art to Dokeci-Na.

The closer our transport drew to Portula Colony, however, the more worried Lesy became. *And not about her art.*

"You're sure you can maintain this form on the planet, Youngest?"

This being the fourteenth time she'd lifted the top of my crate and peered within to inquire, I wrapped my arms over my face and wiggled the now-black fingerlike tips at her.

"Don't do that!" she gasped. "That's—it's not done. Do you hear me, Esen-alit-Quar? That's very rude!"

If Lesy was trying to sound like Ersh, I didn't have the tubal pumps to tell her how infinitely far from the mark her soft, anxious complaint registered. I did lower my arms and sent an apologetic ripple of pink through my skin. "Sorry, Lesy," I added aloud, though Dokeci relied more on appearance.

Hers? More flustered than ever, judging by the welts rising over her round face. "Don't call me that!"

We were alone, and she'd used my birthname first, but I'd learned over a century ago never to correct my elders. *Where they could hear me, at any rate.* "I'm sorry, Riosolesy-ki." My name in this form, Ses-ki, lacked respectful prefixes, a prejudice against callow youth I'd noticed crossed species' boundaries. "Are we there yet?" I tried to shift position.

"Don't do that!"

I was truly trying to behave, but this was one too many "don'ts." *Especially before we'd even arrived.* "You try sitting on—what am I sitting on?" My box, while padded on all sides, held more than overcompressed Esen. Lesy had slipped in a few packages at the last minute. None, she assured me, edible, or I'd have been rid of them during the preceding hours.

"Those are art supplies. Important secret art supplies."

I squirmed. "They feel like rocks."

The welts acquired a mottled red. A frown. "You peeked!"

"I sat," I corrected, shifting again. The Dokeci form consisted of a round head with a handsome rubbery beak and those three massive eyes. The head sat on a thick neck from which the five long flexible arms sprang like a collar above a pair of sturdy hips. The rest of the body was a boneless abdomen that swung like a pendulum between the triple-jointed legs. Mine, though compact and firm, now had distinct sore points. This form wasn't designed for sitting, let alone being pressed against rocks, artistic or otherwise. "Can't I come out?"

"We're almost there," my web-kin promised, slamming the lid down.

I put my arms over my face and wiggled my fingertips.

Free at last. *In more ways than one.* I stretched my arms, after carefully checking the placement of fragile objects, kicked myself from the floor, and let myself drift back down in a slow spin. Not quite null-gee, but close enough for fun. Portula's operators balanced the physiological preference of older Dokeci with the practicality of keeping paint on brushes and out of the air scrubbers. The Dokeci were a species who lost significant musculature with age; to make it worse, their abdomens enlarged and sagged floorward. By the middle of their lifespan they depended on the strong limbs of younger kin.

Those, like Lesy, who wanted to remain independently active had a choice of donning support devices—none, she confided, in the least fashionable—or cheat by living on low-gravity stations like Portula. Personally, I'd have abandoned the form by her age, not that she'd asked my opinion. I'd noticed that about my Elders before now.

Spin done, I poked around Lesy's quarters. Nothing had changed. The pillows, carpet, and cupboards of supplies were in my memories along with the way to the station galley, its menu, short cuts to the common areas—including that remarkable pool—and, for some reason, the completely unremarkable aft shipping hold.

Where I didn't plan to waste my time. "Will we have time to use the pool?" I asked.

Lesy's topmost eye sent me a vague, preoccupied glance, the rest of her attention on the packages of rocks she was removing from my crate. "Yes, yes. Let me put these away first."

"I'll help." I bounded toward the crate, abdomen swinging.

Unfortunately, it was somewhat more difficult than I'd anticipated to lose all that wonderful momentum.

I crashed into both crate and web-kin.

We fell together in a slow-motion grapple of writhing arms and packages, packages that spilled out over the lovely finger-knotted carpets, packages that cooperatively rolled free of their wrappings to expose the deep glitter of gemstones.

I extricated myself from Lesy, whose skin flickered with alarmed pseudolightning and rising splots of violet. "Sorry," I said. *Already a habit.* I picked up the nearest stone, being helpful, only to stare at what I held in disbelief.

"Pretty, isn't it?"

Pretty was an understatement. The gem had a fiery inner glow that could come from only one source. *Biology.* "This," I scowled, "isn't a rock." It was a Tumbler excretion.

Or worse—I dropped it and wiped my fingertip vigorously on the carpet, the rest of my arms stretched as far away as possible. "It's not one of—"

"Waste not, want not."

Smuggling excretions was the only persistent non-Tumbler enterprise on Picco's Moon, an enterprise involving clandestine landings and distressingly noisy responses by those who claimed to be in charge—not that Tumblers noticed either, considering soft-fleshed beings to be, at best, implausible. Ersh herself took precautions to discourage prospectors, licensed or otherwise; namely she sent me out every few nights to collect any deposits made by wandering neighbors—not to mention the piles from those who visited Ersh for those month-long chimings over rare salts. I'd almost filled a deep cleft in the cliff over the years.

Ersh's own? Suffice to say I'd never asked nor wanted to know and viewed that ignorance as one of the bright spots of my short existence.

I rose from the floor, my own skin flaring with outrage. "You've been stealing from Ersh!?"

"There's no need to raise your voice." Lesy somehow managed to pout adorably without lips. "She lets me take the prettiest. For my creations. You know how highly Ersh values my art."

I was beginning to get the idea. Elder or not, Lesy was a worse liar than I was.

As for her art? I remembered innumerable lectures from Ersh. I wasn't to ask about Lesy's creations, or Lesy's dreams for that matter. When either topic arose during our rare meals together, those decidedly unweblike aspects of our web-kin's nature made Skalet twitch, Mixs grumble, and Ansky offer more food.

While they made me curious. And, I realized abruptly, Ersh wasn't here. That she'd inevitably find out wasn't something I need worry about now.

A great many of my decisions were made on that basis.

"What do you do with them?" I asked, unable to stop myself.

Her skin ridged and developed a faint flush of pink. "They're part of my newest creation. An entirely new art. Would you like to try? I'll teach you. What a wonderful idea, Esen!"

Where had that *come from?* My epidermis did its best to turn inside out. "Try?" I echoed weakly. "I really don't think we have time for—this isn't—"

Lesy was ignoring me. I was used to that. But what she was doing while ignoring me offered sufficient novelty that I closed my mouth and watched with all eyes.

Two hands opened cupboard doors, while the other three reached in to pull out, with blinding speed—Lesy could move when motivated—a bucket, several narrow white tubes, an assortment of hammers and pointed tools, and, last and requiring all five hands, what appeared to be a large nondescript mold of, yes, it was a face.

Ersh's face, to be exact. Even as a Dokecian of considerable age, features reversed and made of puce-toned plas, I'd know that expression anywhere. Lesy might have thrown molten plas over the Senior Assimilator while she was mid-argument with me.

Lesy must have mistaken my stunned silence for approval, for her blush deepened and she thrust the mold at me. "Beautiful, isn't it? It's the very same image they used in the Forty-fourth Dynasty coins. Not the same, really. Bigger." This with small spots of worry. Her arms twisted, rotating Ersh's frozen scowl. "Too big? It's 155% life-size. I like big eyes, but one never knows—"

"'Coins?'" I echoed.

"Some shields did survive, a statue or two. Coins were the main—you should know this."

"A certain person doesn't," I said testily, "share everything with me." While it was quite reasonable Ersh had lived within Dokeci society in a time known only through the earliest—that I did know—remains yet uncovered by that species' archaeologists, it went against everything I knew that the center of our Web, the being who ruled by caution above all, *who insisted I travel in a crate* . . . that she'd be . . . "She was famous?"

"Infamous," Lesy giggled. "Legendary. Teganersha-Ki. Rose to power on the severed arms of her enemies. United the western continent against the east and north. Brought in plumbing."

The plumbing I could believe. Ersh regularly cited the hallmarks of a successful technological society. Sanitation was top on her list. "Does—" There was no safe way to ask, so I went for blunt. "Does she know about this?" I flailed a finger at the face.

Lesy faded to a smooth, nonplussed beige.

While I flushed abashed purple. *Of course, Ersh knew.* There were no secrets from the sharing of memories held within our flesh. Well, there were plenty of secrets within Ersh's flesh, but only because she alone had the ability to pick and choose what to include per bite.

The rest of us? Doomed to reveal every memorized instant of our lives. However dull or personally mortifying.

I stared at Ersh's reversed face—presumably shortly to be coated in pulverized Ersh excretion with the result sold to the locals for use as pots or doorstops—and felt an unexpected twinge.

How often did we disappoint her?

As a Web-being, I had intimate access to the aesthetics of all more ephemeral species my kind had yet explored. That didn't mean I knew good art from bad—only how to fake it in the appropriate company. At the moment, I would have gladly traded all the memories in my flesh for a clue how to tell the three glittering heads on the shelf apart.

"Don't you want to take yours home, Youngest?" Lesy's skin was beginning to spot.

I tried not to look obvious as I examined the results of our labors. The molding process had reminded me of putting soil into pots, though wetter. The final finishing—that had been more challenging. Lesy's instructions consisted of "follow your dreams" as she herself used all five arms to quickly glue bits from a box to Ersh's thunderous face at seeming random. While singing, which I hadn't attempted.

Glue I could and did. *Not that I'd anything to follow.* Only Lesy claimed to remember dreams. The rest of us? Memories lasted, intact and detailed; whatever might visit our sleeping minds did not. After first learning of ephemeral nightmares, I'd decided that was fine with me.

Without guidance—and to be honest, some coordination issues with five arms—an embarrassing number of my small bits were also glued to carpet and furnishings. Lesy forgave my lack of control once I'd helped pulled off the pieces somehow glued to her skin. All three busts now stared back at me, looking as if they'd rolled down a garbage heap after dunking themselves in syrup. The leftmost one had only one eye exposed, giving it a baleful look. The centermost was blinded by strings of cheap plas beads. The right—I looked away, hoping in vain Ersh wouldn't taste the memory of her heads.

"Shouldn't I leave it here, Lesy?" I suggested. "This is a place of artists." *I had no shame.*

She almost glowed. "We'll do better than that. We'll put your first work of art on exhibit with mine!" Her arms swept up the leftmost lump as if it were precious. "I'm proud of you, Es."

Which made no sense. We had no possessions. There were no physical manifestations of a Web culture. We were, that was all. Was this Lesy's difference? A compulsion to make things without purpose or value?

Then what were dreams?

My troubling thoughts might have manifested in stripes on my skin for all my web-kin noticed. After tucking all three heads into a fresh shipping crate with great care—a procedure which required privacy for no reason I could imagine, but I was used to climbing into cupboards on command—Lesy grabbed the nearest of my arms. "I'll show you the rest." She towed me toward the door with frightening enthusiasm, her abdomen bouncing up and down. "My best work is in aft shipping already." She halted our forward motion with a quick grab by two arms at a convenient handhold. "I think it's my best. Oh, dear. What if it isn't? And where are you going?"

I'd have thought it obvious, since she'd let go of me in order to grab said handholds. I thus sailed onward, arms flailing as if that would help, tumbling in midair until the lower part of my anatomy met the corridor wall with a *smack* and I slid, slowly, to the floor. "Who knows?" I muttered.

"Know? I can't. Can I know my best?" Lesy could fuss without pause for breath. She hurried forward and took my arm again, hauling me to my feet. "Cureceo-ki says it's my best work. He'd know, wouldn't he?"

I blinked at her, something three eyes did quite well. "Who is Cureceo-ki?"

"You remember, Ses-ki!"

"No one told me," I stressed the second last word. In this alien environment, no Web-being would be more specific. *Or ought to be*, I thought, worried by Lesy's now-distraught posture. Upset, a Dokeci's forward-facing arms became rigid and unusable, aimed outward to fend off trouble. Which was me, in this instance. As she continued to hold onto me with an arm over her hip, the rest were fending off my abdomen. "Who is she?" I asked more gently. The pronoun was the accepted neutral, since the species had an astounding variety of reproductive forms. It took birth or an autopsy, Ersh had told me, to sort out who was pregnant.

"'He,'" Lesy insisted, either knowing more than I did about the individual in question—*presumably*—or imposing her own pronoun—*likely*. Since my arrival, those in the "family-way" made her uncomfortable, Skalet admitting the same reaction. "The museum's curator. Cureceo-ki personally arranged the exhibit." Her third eye widened, its aim somewhere behind me. "Oh, dear." The surface of her skin wrinkled, the crevices lime-green. "He looks upset. Hush."

"Greetings, Riosolesy-ki," the approaching Dokecian said, ignoring me. His skin was lumpy and dark, arms almost stiff. *Not a happy being.* "What's the delay? We've been waiting for the rest of the shipment."

Compared to Ersh's ability to obliterate my existence when preoccupied, this corpulent and aging being was an amateur. However, he did have species-mores on his side.

Dokeci my age were considered little more than obstacles to traffic. So I did my best to be inconspicuous, though I'd have preferred to bristle. With aquamarine highlights. *And a pithy comment or two.*

"Why the haste, Curator?" Lesy surprised me by protesting. "I've yet to pick which cloak I'll wear to the gala. You did promise a gala for the opening of my exhibit."

Trust personal adornment to stiffen her arms. Lesy loved anything she could add to her form's sake. Otherwise, in any form, her reaction to conflict was distress and flight. None of us, not even Ersh, would speak harshly to her. Unlike this curator.

So different was Lesy from our siblings, so frail and uncertain, that I often wondered if Ersh had somehow robbed her at birth—if birth was what you called sorting which parts of your own flesh would leave you and become opinionated.

Or had Ersh chosen to discard with Lesy's flesh every shred of weakness from her own?

Some curiosities I knew better than pursue.

"Some haste would be useful, my lovely Riosolesy-ki. There are precautions to be taken—much to complete!" Cureceo-ki's tone eased only slightly, but he held out a gracious arm, eye rings aglow. "I will take care of everything while you prepare yourself. I merely need—" His lower two eyes seemed to search Lesy for something. Sure enough, he asked sharply: "The rest of the supplies—for the demonstration. Where are they! Don't tell me you forgot them!"

If I'd been Lanivarian, my lip would have curled over a fang, rude or not. My fingers itched to wiggle at him.

But Lesy's skin swelled into a glorious mottling of amber and ultraviolet. *Triumph?* "We've created three new works for the exhibit! The crate's waiting in my room. You will take care of them, won't you?"

"But . . ." I'd never seen a Dokeci completely pale before. *Not attractive.* "What about the supplies?" Cureceo-ki squeaked. "Don't tell me you rui—used them all?"

"I don't think so." Lesy took a moment to think deeply. I could have answered for her; under the circumstances, I couldn't imagine why. "Why, yes. There's quite a few left."

The curator's skin flushed with smooth whorls of elated rose. "With more of your exquisite art, Riosolesy-ki. How splendid! Splendid! Come now, you must rest and prepare yourself while we finish our tasks. Your audience awaits."

I kept my third eye locked on the curator. Dokeci vision was extraordinary, quite reasonable in a species that relied on the morphing of skin to provide emotional context, though such cues could mislead, depending on the intentions and skill of the owner of that skin. Dokeci dialects were laced with wisdoms such as "wrinkles don't lie" and "never buy from a smoothie."

Needless to say, by this point, I didn't trust a patch of Cureceo-ki's hide.

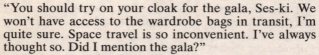

"You should try on your cloak for the gala, Ses-ki. We won't have access to the wardrobe bags in transit, I'm quite sure. Space travel is so inconvenient. I've always thought so. Did I mention the gala?"

With every other breath. "We know mine fits," I reminded her. "Are you sure we shouldn't go down to shipping and check on your work?"

"You may be fine." The pout was back. "I'm still in turmoil. Turmoil!"

I relented. What Lesy didn't mention was that whatever cloak she wore would have to hide the supports her more mature Dokeci-self would need on the planet. Here, on the station, she could enjoy swirling the fabric around. Her arms swept up the next option, a green gauzy mass that resembled a "cloak" only by virtue of being wrapped first about her neck. It gave her a striking resemblance to an overripe seed pod.

Cureceo-ki had taken the crates, including the one with Ersh's heads. If his arms were tighter around the crate containing the remaining excretions, that wasn't my business. *Ephemeral greed,* as Ersh would say, *was their curse, not ours.*

The door chime sounded. Lesy swirled her way to it, clearly thrilled to show her cloak to someone of better taste than her Youngest web-kin. But it was only a delivery. She turned back into the room, arms wrapped around a bouquet of flowers and a slim twisted bottle filled with a copper liquid. "Look, Ses-ki! Welcoming gifts from the gallery!"

"You haven't left yet," I pointed out.

Lesy ignored this, busy pouring the liquid into two glasses. She looked at me, her skin mottled pink, then returned the liquid from one of the glasses to the bottle. "When you're older," she clucked at me. She took a sip. "Wonderful vintage."

As I was at least 400 years more vintage than any living Dokeci, I opened my mouth to complain.

The glass slipped from Lesy's finger. She let out a surprised moan and her skin went flaccid, its color draining away. She slumped to the floor, the gauzy green cloak settling around her.

I desperately firmed my hold on my Dokeci-form as Lesy abandoned hers, cycling to that perfect teardrop of blue, her surface glistening with drops of moisture. *Poison.*

There wasn't much time. The Prime Law. *Never reveal web-form to aliens.* I lunged for the bouquet of flowers and tossed them at her. The leaves, stems, and flowers touched and became her, their living matter assimilated into web-mass. *It should be enough.*

It was. She was back as Riosolesy-ki, sprawled on top of her gauzy cloak, a copper stain spreading from the dropped glass.

I waited expectantly.

She didn't move.

Not good. It was impossible to poison a Web-being; our instinct to cycle was too quick for that. When Lesy returned to her Dokeci-self, her memory would have rebuilt everything about her form's sake, not unmetabolized drugs. A Web-being remembered broken bone, not any painkiller still in her blood.

My tubal pumps were protesting. I eased closer, careful to avoid the stain, and poked Lesy firmly in the abdomen. *Nothing.* I laid the first portion of one arm over her skin. Warmth, overlapped pulses, a rise and fall that signaled respiration.

I moved away, far away, finally huddling in the farthest corner from my web-kin's unconscious self.

I was alone.

I'd never been alone before.

How was I to know what to do?

Portula Colony was a cluster of spheres, the centermost and largest containing both gravity generators and living quarters, the outer being studios and communal space. The pool, with its view of the nebula, was at one end. At the other was a slowly growing tangle of warehouse pods. Most were for Lesy's previous creations—she was, if nothing else, productive. I shuddered at the image of corridors jammed with junk-coated Ersh heads.

But I had other concerns. Lesy was still unconscious. There was nothing to eat in her room. *Panic made me hungry.* Help for her and food for me could be summoned. There was also a criminal curator to be caught, preferably in the act.

All of which would be easy—for an adult. There was a com panel—visual, given Dokeci self-expression. There were neighbors. Probably five-armed station security patrolling the outer corridors, eyes vigilant.

And there was me, alone, trapped by this form. Young Dokeci became clever mimics before developing an understanding of language. Lesy's "idiotic prattle" about covered it. No adult on this station could believe a word I said. The sudden inexplicable appearance of a non-Dokecian on Portula would likely be noticed.

Ersh would not approve.

That left me one alternative. I went to the art supply cupboards. "I'll show you nonverbal," I muttered to myself, pulling out supplies.

"My work's been stolen?? Are you sure?"

I could only gaze, mute, at my web-kin. I'd never seen Lesy happier.

I wasn't alone. The station manager rumpled in confused distress. "You authorized the shipping request, Riosolesy-ki," she repeated, as if this might help, "but the destination wasn't the gallery on Dokeci-Na. I'm deeply sorry, Riosolesy-ki. The entire affair appears to have been a hoax. The gallery hasn't—there's no exhibition of your work scheduled. Cureceo-ki falsified her credentials. You were sedated." *A neat sidestep around "nearly murdered,"* I decided. "Altogether an elaborate, well-planned theft, I fear. Portula Station will, of course, pursue a full investigation."

"Oh, I couldn't possibly press charges." Lesy sparkled. "No need for an investigation. They loved my work. They had to have it. What artist could want more?"

I felt sorry for the perplexed station manager as Lesy almost pushed her out the door.

There was something less happy about my web-kin as she looked at me. "You've done it now, haven't you?" In a low voice. "I can't hide what happened."

"What do you think happened?" I asked innocently.

"You called for medics, security personnel. Set the station on alert! She'll have to know. She will know. This will be bad, Ses-ki." Lesy sank on a cushion, her skin mottled with distress, only to bounce up again. "What—?" She reached underneath and pulled out the head of the infamous Teganersha-Ki. "This isn't mine," she announced. She plucked at the gauzy green fabric covering most of the face "This is. What have you done to my cloak, Ses-ki?"

I took the head and put it over mine. "Help! Help! This is Riosolesy-ki. I think I've been poi—poi—poisoned!! Ahhhhharggghhhhh." My voice echoed within the cavity, coming out deeper and nicely desperate. I pulled off the head and grinned.

"That's—" One of the things I loved most about Lesy was her laugh in any form. Now, she dropped on her abdomen and rocked back and forth, her beaked mouthparts clicking together in a blur, her skin rising in welts of purple that drew the same response from my own.

Ersh might not like being imitated, but she'd have to admit I'd followed her rules.

Well, she didn't have to admit anything, but there could be a volume reduction in the inevitable lecture.

Once we'd both calmed, Lesy sighed. "My only regret, Youngest, is we won't be going to Dokeci-Na. I know you were counting on it. I'm sorry."

I shrugged with all five arms. "There's the pool."

Lesy smiled. "Wonderful idea. Just what we need. Let's go!" She surged to her feet.

It felt odd to feel the Elder. "What about your art?" Cureceo-ki might have been after Tumbler excretions, but the end result was the same. All of Lesy's "best"—or at least her newest—work was gone. "What if it's never found?"

My web-kin lifted her arms and spun around. "I will always have it in my tubal pumps." *Which made no sense.* Then she stopped and winked her uppermost eye at me. "Besides, each piece is marked. Long after the current owners pass into dust, I'll be able to find every single one."

"How?"

"My creations are part of me; I am part of them."

Was this more idiotic prattle?

Looking at my triumphant, ever-mysterious web-kin, I wondered suddenly if any of us took her as seriously as we should. "What do you mean?" I asked.

Lesy winked again. "A touch of blue, Youngest. That's all. Signed work is more precious, don't you think? Now, shall we go?"

I followed my Elder to the pool.

But I kept wondering . . .

Where was the first Ersh-head I'd made?

And why hadn't I seen blue paint in Lesy's cupboards?

Library Garden, Present-Day

It takes a while to weave the threads of another's living memories, their flesh, into your own. *Assimilation.* Information must be detached from personality, what you don't dare keep respectfully shed as drops of water. We sat where we'd stood, I, for one, glad of the rain.

Skalet knew what I did now. Lesy had used her own flesh as her signature. *Obvious in hindsight, if not to a younger me.* Since then, I'd put something of myself into the medallion Paul wore around his neck and felt the faint draw of it when we were together, no matter my form. A draw immensely greater to my web-form.

"I should have known it was Lesy's," I said at last, disgusted with myself. A lack of imagination that was. I'd seen one size of her Ersh-heads, so assumed. Paul wouldn't have.

"We don't know how she did it. Put her flesh on *things*. Made it last, enough to *taste*."

"I was in a cupboard." I shrugged, having regained shoulders.

She was right, *how* was a puzzle. Paul's medallion contained a miniature cryo-unit. My growing stash of Esen bits—definitely not something I shared with Skalet—was similarly preserved by freezing. Whatever Lesy had done wasn't at all the same. We'd need the bust to find out.

Skalet leaned forward, elbows—for she was again Kraal and dressed—on her knees, to stare down at the wet stone. "You didn't recognize the—her art?"

"Like you," I said heavily, "what I saw in Evan's hands was Ersh. What I'd tasted was—" *Web-flesh.*

Lesy's. Not that I'd recognized the individual from the strange corrupted trace.

"I thought you'd salvaged her work."

Skalet hadn't called it that when Lesy had been alive. To be fair, none of us had, our creative web-kin less interested in quality than quantity. "I've what was stored in the pods at Portula Colony." *Presently in orbit.* Lesy hadn't *signed* those, unless in a way I hadn't detected. In which case, I'd a distressing amount of *tasting* to do. "The busts were already gone. Sold or dumped on Dokeci-Na."

"Coated in Tumbler excretions." Her low laugh had nothing of humor in it. "Ersh knew?"

A loaded question. Ersh knew—had known—everything, including how Skalet herself had once schemed to establish a Kraal House of her own, though she hadn't used Ersh's crystalline excretions but duras plants stolen from Ersh's greenhouse. Duras being a robust source of oxygen and poison, as well as ever-useful as mass, Skalet had inserted them on every Kraal ship.

Her bizarre ambition to start an unweb-like dynasty appeared on hold. For now.

While Lesy liked what sparkled.

"That Lesy took hers? Yes." I'd kept to myself the thankless memory of Ersh's amusement. Not about Lesy diligently collecting her excrement, but over how she'd otherwise fuss over bodily functions, determined to keep whatever appendages she had clean.

Leaving any other mess for me. *Maybe I shouldn't have spared Skalet the details.*

I watched her long finger direct a glistening raindrop along a crease, the fabric of her uniform immune to moisture, flame, and quite likely blasterfire. "Then that's it." She looked up. "We know what happened and why. It won't happen again."

Was she telling me or asking? This less-than-certain version of my web-kin made the hairs on my neck prickle. *Or was it that I didn't know the answer?*

"We'll be prepared," I agreed, more to reassure myself. It didn't help my fur lay plastered to my skin. This me detested *wet,* which wanted a good long shake and warmed towels. *First things first.* "Before we go back, we need an explanation for the others." For Evan in particular. Paul knew our nature. He'd understand. Eventually. There'd be some discussion, doubtless including *why didn't you tell me about this before* and *how could you put a client in danger of being eaten—*

"We need no such thing, Youngest. Explain to Humans? Ridiculous!" Skalet rose to her feet. "What we must do, at once, is determine how that Human came in possession of Lesy's work and why he brought it here, to us. Then," ominously, "we can take action."

Back to normal. I stood, the muscles under my skin quivering in a thwarted battle with my fur. Skalet was right—though let her interrogate Evan? "I'll look after it," I promised. "Evan knows me. We met in Kateen."

"Which you?" with justifiable suspicion. I hadn't shared our little adventure on Urgia Prime, an omission now plainly apparent to my paranoid web-kin. "Don't tell me you went to that festival as Bess." She glared at me. "Esen-alit-Quar, don't tell me this is another of your *friends!*" As if I'd brought home a fungus between my toes.

Then I won't—wasn't going to help. It was for me to know how I felt about Evan Gooseberry. For me to protect him. Skalet would use his fears against him given any provocation.

"I will tell you he's a courageous, intelligent Human, who's earned my trust and Paul's. And while we stand here discussing my—" they weren't *faults,* despite her opinion "—interests, Paul's with Evan and you know he'll ask the right questions." *Time to deflect.* I lifted my lip, "Isn't Lionel with Duggs, waiting for you to consult on Library security?"

Her eyes narrowed. "Are you being clever, Youngest?"

"Strategic," I countered, one of her favorite words. "We've resources. We should use them."

"You said that about Chase."

"Was I wrong?"

Skalet pressed her lips into a thin line, still glaring. *Never would admit I was right.* "Good," I said cheerfully.

Then dropped to all fours to shake from nose to tail. *Finally.*

Inception

*B*ELIEF *endures.*
 I have no other choice. Without belief, there can be no hope, and hope is all that moves me. Draws breath. Sets claw to crack. Tongue to rock. I believe there is Light. I will Rise and find it. I will leave the Ever Dark and present my offering.

Sample and taste. Sample and taste.

It's colder. Upward is all we know, and before the climb we say to one another it will be better. Believe it will. We have no other choice.

Colder is not better, but there is only up, after all.

I no longer hear other breaths, other claws.

Sample and taste.

I believe I am alone.

9: Alarm Afternoon

A dry smock was no substitute for one of humanity's finest inventions, a warmed fluffy towel, especially when one's fur was thoroughly soaked and shaking off the excess *wet* while indoors, however imperative the urge, was frowned upon by those who didn't have fur. Species prejudice, that was.

Discovering a catastrophe underway in the Library—as indicated by the alarm running up and down the tonal range along with annoying flashes of light—I swallowed my snarl, donned the smock, and prepared to be helpful.

Once I found out what the catastrophe was.

Beings were dashing in every direction, Skalet disappearing into their midst with a disturbingly cheerful look on her face, but I couldn't see anything obviously wrong. As a Lanivarian, I'd be able to smell two-thirds of the conceivable reasons for an alarm, from smoke to species who could emit noxious gases when upset. I supposed an air lock malfunction in a non-oxy habitat zone could be involved, but those had auto-containment.

Without this ongoing painful racket. Ears flattened, I headed for the lobby. Someone had to appear calm and in control.

What this wasn't? A prank. Scholars could be tricky, especially Ervickians, but we'd thought of that. Or rather, I'd experimented with all the false ways I could set off an alarm and Paul, seeing the result, had instituted changes.

Other than the building cracking apart, or a raging out-of-control fire? Only staff could activate the wailing with lights, and wouldn't do so idly, faced with the ensuing mix of panic, annoyance, and apathy. Species tended to differ. Humans were the worst for ignoring warnings.

Such random musings brought me to the lobby.

The empty lobby.

That was new. Why would staff direct clients away from the Library's main exit during an emergency? I sincerely hoped they weren't trampling my Garden instead.

Then I spotted the shadow crouched like an enormous shelled vulture on the elevated walkway, great claws hanging over the edge.

"Lambo?" Hopefully he'd remembered to put the Chow into standby. The last time we'd tested the alarm he hadn't, and the dispenser kept shooting out bowls of initially frozen Joffre Sorbet.

Maintenance had filed a protest.

But why perch up there?

My move to find out brought me through a whiff of familiar scent. *Paul.* He'd passed by here. Recently.

With Evan.

Following my nose brought me to the coat rack. No, behind it. *Curious, indeed.* "Paul? What are you—"

"Es," an urgent whisper, though with the alarm blaring only my excellent hearing caught it. "Over here!"

Directions I didn't need, Evan anxious and sweaty; not to say wet Lanivarian didn't have its own overwhelming odor. *I hated* wet. I sniffed my way around the half wall—the smells from the various coats were entrancing, but this wasn't the time—to join my Human friends.

Who were also crouched. "Why is everyone crouching?" I demanded, dropping to all fours beside Paul in my own version. I spotted the alarm remote in his hand. *He'd done this?* "What's going on?"

"Shhh."

Huh. Crouching was useful if you were being harassed by angry Skenkrans. I twisted my head to aim an eye up. The air above was Skenkran-free, though flashes of disorienting color splashed everywhere. After several minutes of this, ears ringing to make it worse, I began to doubt this was the ideal approach to public warnings.

Paul activated the remote.

The abrupt silence and restored light was a shock itself. Before I could point this out, Paul was on the move, still crouching. He pressed Evan's shoulder to hold him still, then took off, running along the wall.

There being no Lanivarians around to be outraged—the species had significant issues around its recent evolutionary past—I rolled my hands into paws and ran in pursuit.

Paul not having suggested otherwise.

The end of the coat rack wall coincided with the start of a curved planter, the sides of which were high enough to dissuade casual grazing by our clients, though I'd caught the Anatae scholars athletically forming a living ladder, with poor Celi on the bottom, in an attempt to reach the greenery. Another planter curved on the opposite side of the gentle ramp from the main doors, together encouraging clients to where they could deposit mucky footwear, etc.

Paul stopped before going past the planter, sinking lower. I slipped up beside him and dropped to my stomach.

He glanced down, face set, and shook his head once, hard. *Go back,* that was.

I grinned at him, tongue hanging out the side. *Make me,* that was.

Which he couldn't. With a *we'll talk later* glint in his eye, Paul turned back to watch for whatever he was watching for, almost vibrating with tension.

Eyes weren't as useful as ears. Mine, freed of the alarm's din, heard it first. The train. The one that had spooked Evan Gooseberry. I reached out a paw to press against Paul's ankle, feeling a hand on my neck in a brief acknowledgment.

The alarm. Clearing the lobby. It made sense, if trouble was expected through the front door, as, I supposed, did a grumpy Carasian in an apron hanging like doom from the elevated walkway. Not a team player, our Lambo, but Paul had an uncanny ability to talk other beings into what they'd not expected.

What that was in this instance, other than hanging like doom, I couldn't imagine.

I wanted to know where Skalet was. *Or maybe I didn't.* My web-kin considered herself a precision instrument; a minimalist adept with needles and poison, or a knife in a hurry. That didn't preclude terrifying escalation. If she thought there was a threat about to exit the now-stopping train?

She'd blow it up. Or have it blasted from orbit. Or—it would be bloody and wasteful and now I really wanted to know where she was and what she was doing.

I must have whined under my breath. Paul's fingers fastened on my scruff, then gave me a steadying little shake.

The trio of doors slid open automatically, a courtesy to smooth entry I suddenly viewed as the hazard Skalet did, because beings poured through in the usual flood of personal quests and "get there first," and how were we to spot a problem?

"They were on the *Dimmont III.*" Evan pointed to the fresh cluster of Rands who were first through, giving Paul an apologetic shrug for disobeying orders so matched to mine I'd have laughed.

If not cringing from the Rands. The problem with web-memory was its perfection. Seeing the happy cluster, the *loneliness* of being detached stabbed through me. I took refuge in knowing Ersh would approve of yet another life lesson achieved. *Biology has power over us in any form, Esen.*

The number arriving on the last train of the day varied. We'd seen it packed. A miscue between Grandine's shipcity and an approaching liner had sent us the entire inbound shift of asteroid miners—the system's one space endeavor of note. They'd arrived crammed in each car like pickled prawlies, setting a new record. Fortunately, we'd decent weather, so I took the miners to the hill beside the farmhouse, provided blankets and beer, and waited while they picnicked. The unbridled air and sunshine proved intoxicating on their own, another fortunate aspect as we ran out of beer hours before the aircars from Grandine arrived to pick them up. A few hadn't wanted to leave.

The train could be empty, too. Humans weren't the only beings to dislike being the last to arrive, though Skenkran enjoyed making an entrance.

The Rands didn't care about the stark absence of greeters or other clients, heading with determination for the Assessment Counter. Repeat visitors, then. Hopefully not with another sex toy.

The rest did that comic reset in which the first through the doors stopped abruptly, perhaps daunted by the empty space available, those behind forced to stop as well or crash into them. Most crashed, scholars prone to internal focus, but as the majority of our clients were also non-aggressive, cooperative sorts, a round of species-specific apologies began as they sorted themselves out and started moving inside again.

"I don't see them."

I bent my head around. "Who?"

Before Evan could answer, there was a second mass halt and almost collision, this time because someone noticed the looming Carasian. Not even internally focused scholars missed those outstretched open claws.

"You're sure?" Paul asked. At Evan's nod, he rose to his feet, straightening his jacket with an absent hand. "We're up, Fangface. Let's calm things down before the non-oxy car unloads."

I rose with him, ears perked. "Who?" *"What" being rude.*

"Mixed," was the tantalizing answer, the Human a stride ahead, his body language morphing in that step from *ready-for-trouble* to *warm-welcome* with underlying *reliable-competence-trust-me-with-your-lives* he did so well it crossed species.

Though I usually indulged in a moment's speechless admiration, I elected to start the calming with someone closer and grabbed Evan's sleeve. Besides, I could feel that faint *draw*. Ersh—Lesy's bust—must be in his shirt. I wasn't letting it, or him, out of my sight. But first, "Who were you expecting on the train?"

He stared over my head, still scanning the crowd. "Criminals. Human ones. I shared a stateroom with them on the way here—not that I'm a criminal," he added fervently, facing me.

I gave him a reassuring pat with my free hand. "We know, Evan. Did you get their names?"

"No. Well, I tried not to." A rueful sigh. "Tory's one. She's the scariest. I called the others—to myself—Scar and Beard. Jumpy Lyn—there was an Ervickian, too."

No need to ask if Evan thought Jumpy Lyn was a criminal. The species was known for its flexible interpretation of the moral codes of others. They weren't violent, but as opportunists with quick digits? *Lock up the portables* was a prudent host response.

Seeing he wasn't about to flee, I let go, then gestured to those gathering around Paul as if he were a magnet of sanity—with the bonus of being farther from Lambo. "We don't ask what our clients do for a living, Evan," I said gently. *Much to Skalet's dislike.* "What matters here is their question."

At that, he changed. Stood straighter. Settled, in some odd way, into his skin. That anxious expression was replaced by a determined one, almost stern, and I knew this Evan Gooseberry, too. This Evan had overcome his fear. Had put his career and dreams aside, himself in danger, to help an alien.

Now, he'd come to us, traveling in a starship with criminals, and all at once I'd a sick feeling we'd wasted time we didn't have—

And that nothing was as important as why.

"Evan, what did you come here to ask the Library?"

Oh, the anguish in those eyes.

"How do I save them?"

Perception

THE room was windowless, dark, and unfurnished. No architects' plans or schematics revealed its existence, for this small space had been inserted during the slurry pour as an internal bubble. A boil. The hatch into it had been carved afterward.

The technology, after that.

Input feeds covered all but the space on the floor needed to stand, their dim light trapped by pale skin and paler eyes. Tattoos slid, shadows, as Skalet's attention flicked from display to display, seeking. Uncomfortable truths had brought her here. *Necessity.*

Her sharing had been more recent memories, not this place. She'd kept away, using remotes, loath to be exposed too soon.

Ersh would have taken a larger bite, would have insisted on every memory since their last sharing, on knowing everything. The Youngest's restraint was *convenient.*

As for her sharing? The Youngest was . . . *remarkable.*

A galling admission, but necessary if she was to, what, *be part of this?* The Nonsense, the All Species' Library of Linguistics and Culture. The Library. Pandering to ephemeral lack of recall, granting sops to their fleeting harried existence.

Prevent extinctions?

Ersh, Greatest of them all, had caused them.

To later develop a conscience, imposed on her Web.

Skalet couldn't disagree. Mass destruction, and the attention it caused, was . . . *inefficient*.

As was resisting this phase of Esen-alit-Quar. She'd tried once. No longer. However *annoying,* it would pass in an instant, as the Web experienced time. They would continue together, web-kin, after this building was dust, this world barren, this *turmoil*—done.

Safe from Humans.

Where had that *come from?*

Skalet made herself stop and retrace her thoughts with trained precision. Examine and test. She'd learned to be wary of habit or assumption, those dangerous skews to clarity. Perfect inner discipline. That was the ultimate goal, one the Youngest not only failed to appreciate, but challenged at every opportunity.

As she challenged the obvious, time and again. Refusing to admit Paul Antoni Ragem Cameron was perilous. *Look what he'd done already.* Building a life together.

Despite his being so short.

And so very *fragile.* Her eyes found the feed with Paul in the midst of strangers, playing the ever-gracious host. Dark hair tumbling, that deceptively attractive face and easy manner, all hiding a bone-deep, insatiable curiosity about *everything*—

Dangerous!

Without thought, her long fingers found knife hilts, caressed hidden needles and wire; in no sense did Esen's *care* for this Human keep him alive.

His, for her, did. However *inconceivable.*

Skalet looked for the other Human, Lionel Kearn. He was with the difficult one, Pouncey. Reassuring, his determination to seize on this task they shared.

Pleasant, to look upon his thin, aesthetic features again, high-browed and intense. An individual of wisdom and discretion, who refused to waste time on social pursuits; the passion for knowledge burned in him like a flame.

Admirable.

As a fine tool should be.

Skalet returned to her survey. What was here went immediately to remotes in orbit overhead, relayed to her warship, the *Trium Pa,* tucked behind the larger of the

Botharan moons to monitor traffic; regardless of what the planetary government or Esen believed, her mobility and access to resources were not, nor would ever be . . . *negotiable*.

The alarm, and the direction of staff, had flushed "clients" into areas they'd not been before, causing pockets of confusion. *Useful.* She'd replayed Paul's questioning, heard the description of those Gooseberry feared were on the train.

It could be nothing. Petty thugs. The weak, like this Gooseberry, were tasty fodder for such. She frowned, finding the Youngest consoling the fool. The weak were Esen's *hobby.* Hopefully, she'd remember to acquire the perverted statue.

It could be nothing, but she'd make no assumptions.

Skalet continued, methodically skimming the Library; she'd sensors everywhere.

Ah.

A gesture filled every display with the same scene. Theta-class life-forms, Iftsen the species. They waddled along the walkway in their exo-suits, the air of this world lacking the chemical soup of their own, heading for their habitat zone.

Suits rounder in girth than they should be, with helmets opaqued unnecessarily. Skalet sucked in a triumphant breath.

"Clever."

If not clever enough.

10: Chow Afternoon

LEAVING our new arrivals in Paul's capable hands—regardless of his request for my aid, no one really wanted to be greeted by a *wet* Lanivarian and we'd excellent staff who'd mostly kept their calm somewhere in the Library—I hustled poor Evan along. We'd moments, if that, before those evacuated from the lobby decided the emergency was over and rushed back regardless of staff. Some clients would be confused; most aggravated. There could be gas eruptions and other expressive behavior. A few might seize the opportunity to blend with those incoming and pretend they'd just arrived, but Paul would know.

I had to get Evan to the closest access node. "This way." I supposed I should have let him catch his breath, but this was too important. "Who needs saving?"

"The Elves."

Or maybe it wasn't. I stopped in my tracks. "'Elves'?"

He looked exhausted and deadly serious. "It's what Dokeci call them. I wasn't given any other name. We—embassy staff—aren't permitted to talk about them. It's under wraps because the Elves are a previously unrecorded sentience."

A new species!? A tremulous thrill coursed along my veins, as it would in any form with circulation. If that made me a shallow being unworthy of friendship or the keys to the Library or any fudge in future?

I couldn't help it!

Until I remembered the last time I'd felt this way. The Feneden. Chase had brought that name and news, and I'd believed, deliriously happy, until Ersh-memory was stimulated to surface and I was forced to relive her predation on the species, down to their *taste*. Ersh had been at the root of the Feneden's terrible manners toward others, being their cultural shared nightmare. The Shifter Monster.

No wonder I dreaded those upwelling memories. It was usually something like that. Few were safe. Every one changed me and my perceptions, rarely for the better.

Elves, I said to myself and waited for an echo. *Dokeci Elves.* Nothing, but I'd be more reassured once I *tasted* one. Not an intention to share just yet.

I kept pulling Evan along with me. "Not far," I panted. The closest access to the Library collection was on the wall in the Chow, not that others knew. Paul had it installed under the guise of an oversized com panel in case Lambo wanted to communicate; it being more likely the Library would spontaneously declare itself a life-form and demand vacation time, the access was really there because eventually we'd need instant access to data on, say, poisoning symptoms.

The Chow was empty. Presumably Lambo would return to work shortly, though I'd a suspicion the Carasian found looming highly entertaining and might keep it up till ordered by Paul to stop. I was pleased to find no bowls of melting fish products in sight. In fact, as I led Evan behind the counter, the place was spotless—

—other than a fragrant pile of leafy branches in the far back corner, surrounding by soil and debris. A peaceful, rhythmic snore emanated from its heart. Evan kept an eye on the pile, perhaps worried what could sleep through the alarm.

Worry wasn't what I felt. I'd left Celivliet Del burping peacefully under my fystia shrubs, shrubs now *here* and wilting before my eyes. The growl working up my throat died.

Only one being in the Library could uproot entire shrubs, with Anata, and carry them here. Lambo.

Poor Celi. Faced with such formidable kindness, I

doubted he'd dared admit he was leaving tomorrow after all and wouldn't stay to tidy the Chow. We'd have to intervene. There'd be bellowing.

Elves first. Something I never imagined thinking. "Over here, Evan." I keyed in my code. The flat black of the com panel flashed red, then the interface for the collection appeared. "Ask your question." The logical starting point, despite the unlikelihood of a useful response.

The Human gave me a stunned look. "You want me to just—say the words? Out loud? Now?"

His reaction was familiar. *Save me from academics.* I'd told Paul we should have installed something flashier, perhaps with a drumroll or the parting of curtains. "The collection is interactive," I explained patiently. "That allows our clients to request information in the way most natural for their biology. Humans," I added pointedly, "talk."

Evan regarded me narrowly. I merely waited. "And you're the curator," he said at last, in a tone suggesting he'd had time to reconsider several life choices, especially the one bringing him here, and regret them all.

I wasn't that *young.* Well, I was, but it was hardly the point.

"Want to save your Elves?" I unrolled a finger, pointing at the panel. "Up to you."

Perception

YEARS of physical work had honed Duggs Pouncey into the person sitting across from him at the planning board, hands scarred and callused, brown skin weathered. Gray streaked her short black hair, but nothing dimmed a vitality able to fill a room. Lionel'd rarely met someone surrounded by the evidence of their skill, yet everything about the plans she presented, the Library around them, informed him of hers. And more. Duggs was meticulous. Thorough. Innovative, yet prudent.

All attributes Skalet should appreciate. To him, they'd an uncanny resemblance, pigmentation aside. Duggs was almost as tall, if not so lean, having the build of someone who, while strong and active, enjoyed the rewards of life. Yet there was—Lionel couldn't put his finger on it. Was it the gleam of concentration in Duggs' eyes as she considered his suggestions? Or how at times she'd be so still, he couldn't tell if she breathed.

Or not. With an exaggerated huff, Duggs tilted back her chair and frowned. "What's your deal, Lionel?" A finger lifted, made a circle. "You walk off the train, the Director says give you total access. Why?"

Lionel raised an eyebrow. "I'm here to help. I've some knowledge of security systems."

A grunt he took as complimentary until her finger stabbed at him. "And that alarm nonsense. Because of you?"

"I—" About to protest it had nothing whatsoever to do with him, Paul having forewarned him the alarm was to flush out criminals possibly arriving on the next train, Lionel paused to consider. Had trouble trailed him as well as this Evan Gooseberry, whom Paul called a friend—not a claim he bestowed lightly.

No. He'd been careful. "When Skalet joins us—" She'd given him permission to use that name in front of non-Kraal.

"That Kraal—" Duggs pretended to spit. "We don't need her."

"It's you who are redundant," Skalet said from the doorway, her tone raising the hairs on Lionel's neck. "Come, Lionel."

"Oh, so you say we're done, do you? Well, then." Duggs Pouncey drove her fist into the node on the table, killing the display with a shower of sparks.

Telling Lionel why Paul had asked him to attend this meeting. It wasn't for his opinion on the impact of a sequenced security enhancement on incoming clients, however useful. First contact was a process, one that could take months to bring disparate species into a working alignment.

Like Duggs and Skalet. Powerful personalities who—at this moment—detested one another.

Defuse the confrontation. Lionel remained seated and put his fingertips together. "I'm glad you're here, Skalet. We've made some excellent progress, thanks to Duggs."

Who'd been about to spit out something they'd all regret, from the twist of her lips.

Did Skalet hesitate? If so, it was for a millisecond at most. "My apologies for the interruption," that rich lovely voice now improbably smooth. "To you both." Duggs' scowl deepened; Skalet lowered her head in a brief acknowledgment. "While the alarm was a test, there's been a sudden development and I require Hom Kearn. If you would spare him for a short period, Head Contractor Pouncey?"

Duggs growled in her throat, eyes hot with anger.

Take control. Lionel stood at once. "Thank you, Duggs.

We'll reschedule as soon as convenient for all. A pleasure," sincerely.

The contractor raised a cynical eyebrow before she conceded the situation with a gruff, "Go on, then."

Refuse to escalate. That being the only safe option, considering who he was with, Lionel didn't say another word. Which was easy, because he found himself challenged to keep up with Skalet's longer strides as she took them into the labyrinth of the Library. He'd had a quick glance at the building layout, enough to grasp they were heading for the non-oxy breather habitat zones. The walkways between zones met at air locks, prudent when one species' pleasant mix was another's poison, and an emergency here wasn't a good thing.

This wasn't, however, an emergency. Skalet revealed nothing without intent, so the hint of a smile playing across her lips meant—yes, that was satisfaction.

"Who is it?" he asked quietly. At her glance, he added, "You've found the threat."

"Possibly." The smile became a dire promise.

Lionel was certain neither Paul nor Esen would want Skalet acting on her own, regardless of why. She was ruthless; he'd encountered her first as a Tumbler, the blood of their enemies dulling the glitter of her crystalline form. Next, she'd been this shape, Kraal, battling others of that kind, wounded as a result. He'd held her afterward, her Human blood on his hands.

There shouldn't be blood here. Mustn't be. He believed in the concept of this place, Paul and Esen's Library. In the right of those here to peace. In protecting that peace. "I strongly recommend containment only," he broached, pleased his voice didn't shake. "Questions can be asked."

A low chuckle. "Why, Lionel. What you must think of me."

She didn't, he noticed, dispute his assessment.

The walkway ended in a rudimentary air lock, a short

stretch of hall between closed transparent doors with racks along one wall for exo-suits. "What do you see, Lionel?"

Obediently, he stared inside. Beyond the second door, the atmosphere roiled with a thick green fog, a corrosive one by the warning placard by the controls. "I don't see anyone."

"They are inside this zone."

He didn't ask how she knew. "The rack's empty."

"Indeed." Without warning, Skalet slipped out of her uniform, folded it neatly, and handed it to him.

Lionel saw, not flesh, but a work of art, sculpted in hard pale marble. Nothing soft, nothing weak, here. This was a warrior's scarred lean frame, blood vessels crawling like ropes over muscle and bone. *Menace given grace.*

He took the uniform and bowed as she had earlier. Her head rose, as though surprised, but all she said was, "Wait here."

Going through the door, she closed it behind her, hit the control, then *melted.*

He didn't see her perfect blue teardrop; the change was too quick for that. Even as the atmosphere within the air lock filled with thick green vapor, an Iftsen, Moberan by the frilled face, stood there.

The Moberan turned and waddled through the other door, into the zone, to deal with whomever thought to hide.

While he would wait, holding her uniform, Lionel decided, feeling the *rightness* in his heart, however long it took.

Or however long he lived.

11: Chow Afternoon

CERTAIN notions zipped across multiple species' lines; prime examples being those space technologies that worked, insulated plumbing, and how not to be eaten while dressed as a vegetable in a parade.

Forms of entertainment rarely made it intact. Take the playing of bagpipes, the Human version. The Grigari, while justly famed for the breadth of their musical acumen, considered the act actionable assault. Panacians, for their part, swarmed to the sound and—though they'd not admit it—found the resultant excitement of their typhanae a delightful impairment of higher function while it lasted.

Ganthor, predictably, drooled for joy.

As for literature? For those able to read another species, in the author's original, texts were simply a collection of words—or in the case of the Ycls' splendid odes, intriguing and powerful pheromones—lacking physiological context. *Then there were Quebits . . .*

Suffice to say, laudable efforts were made, and on the odd occasion a context didn't matter, something worthwhile could be gleaned by the intrepid.

Or the point missed entirely. "Elves." I shook my head in the Human gesture, ears flapping.

Sitting on the counter, Evan put out his hands, palm up. "Now we know why the Dokeci used it."

The Library's collection had provided one unexpectedly

clear answer. A Human family, visiting the March-Ne Art Gallery in Sandlamar Province, famed for its precontact Lishcyn ceramics among other alien artifacts, dropped their youngest offspring's worn and beloved copy of *The Everywhere Elves* behind an exhibit of pots. It was a picture book, a format having stood the test of time and space in part because you could chew the corners while reflecting on what you'd learned. The plot was straightforward: readers hunted within a concatenation of tightly packed, vaguely related images to spot the cheerful "elves" hiding in cups, saucers, and so forth. The elves were depicted in bright reds and yellows, to make it easier. If you had Human vision, that is.

If you were a three-eyed Dokeci with vision as your primary means of communication, as was the art gallery director who stumbled across the book and assumed—*there's always assumption*—the book was an artwork of tremendous value left by an anonymous donor for the gallery, said director wrinkling with such depths of gratitude he'd needed resuscitation?

If you were this, or any Dokeci, the elves appeared to leap from the pages, the embodiment of happy surprise. From an infinity of possible interpretations, the art scholars of the day wrapped their arms around on the book they declared depicted the hopelessness of life, alleviated solely by the bright little Elves of Joy, wherever they might be found.

Moving forward to Dokecian authorities designating a species as "Elves" implied—I'd no idea. *Yet.*

The collection offered nothing further of use. *My turn.* "There must be more, Evan. Tell me everything you know about Elves on Dokeci-Na."

He rubbed his eyes, sighed, then looked down at me. "Can't we wait for Paul?"

No, because Paul would immediately guess my plan and make that *face at me.* I pricked up my ears. "Paul's busy, and we've no time to waste," I assured him, both being true.

Since the last train to the landing field would leave in three hours. Realistically, I supposed we'd have to wait until tomorrow. I needed to pack. Arrange passage.

Tomorrow could also be optimistic but, *nothing ventured—*

Evan pointed a thumb over his shoulder at the quiescent food dispenser. "Could we at least eat first, Esen? I'm starving."

While a few days from that extreme, the Human did, now that I paid attention, appear slightly gaunt around the edges. As had Celi, still snoring.

Well, then. "Come with me."

Feed Evan, learn everything he knew, pack without Paul noticing, go meet some Elves.

I loved having a plan fall into place.

Later, I'd miss that feeling.

Inception

I believe.
*   I must, for the Ever Dark is behind me and down.*
Light must be what this is. This pressure.
*   The urge comes over me. They say it will, and we hope*
it will. Now, I only know I must answer. My claws dig not
at the earth and stone, but at what covers. What hinders.
What must be gone.
*   My flesh sunders, weaker than earth and stone.*
*   Light enters.*
*   BURNS!*
*   I wail and cower. I believe now I have failed.*
*   For why else would it BURN?*

12: Farmhouse Afternoon

HUMANS were far from the only otherwise-intelligent species with members who longed for a simpler time. Most defined this as before technology you couldn't fix with a hammer, aliens dropped in without an invitation, and definitely before the woeful lack of appreciation for work done with your hands or equivalent appendage.

Or, as Ersh put it, *the time when futures were short, ignorance rampant, and the only thing cheaper than life was death*. Mind you, Ersh also marked the onset of civilization by reliable civic waste disposal, so she'd her prejudices, too.

That said, sometimes you had to look back to go forward.

Botharis had been settled by Humans who'd thought more like Ersh. They'd followed the usual pattern: plan to recreate the lifestyle they'd enjoyed on their home-worlds, bigger, better, and shinier, only to slam up against the brutal truth. They were a finite community on an alien planet and forget city building. The first generations would be lucky to survive.

There were options, of course. Go home. Bind yourselves to neighbors, like the Kraal, who could supply what you lacked, for a price you'd regret later.

Or, as on Botharis?

You worked with what you had. Knowledge from a simpler time, coupled with careful alliances and sheer bloody determination. Fourteen generations later, give or take a couple, the Botharans were justifiably proud of themselves—regardless of what my Lishcyn-self thought of their fashion sense. They'd a widespread network of rural communities who knew how to live with the land and didn't need any newfangled tech to do it, thank you, though no one wanted to go back too far; a small but robust industrial base beginning to produce exports, and a peaceful population who'd grown up within a culture of stubborn "get it done." Botharans didn't resist invasion. They ignored it, too busy to bother.

It made them a distinct nuisance to govern, as the Kraal knew well, having come and gone from this world several times.

Botharans, particularly rural ones, were stubbornly practical, too. Why tear down a building when it was still useful? I suspected a factor to be the Human longing to keep a "simpler time" of their own in plain sight. The result was a landscape peppered with buildings of logs, mud plaster, and stone that refused to fall down unless you made them.

Such as the Ragem family farmhouse, barn, and that now-abandoned outbuilding in the back corner of a field through which grew what Botharans called an oak tree, really more a giant fern with a thick woody stalk, but you couldn't cut it down now because a great-great-great Ragem had begun the tradition of carving initials in the bark, and that was that.

It was clear Evan Gooseberry had never been in a farmhouse before, especially not the Botharan "well-used and rustic" version. I watched him sidestep to avoid the braided rug on the front porch, admittedly worn by a few generations of Ragems but clean other than the rust spots, edge his way, hands raised, past the bucket of dirt-covered gardening tools I'd brought in to keep from the afternoon rain, and once inside, upon passing the open door to what Paul called my "lair," start sneezing.

At a guess, our tender Evan hadn't been exposed in childhood to any loose organics, let alone the dried sweet grass and feathers belonging to my very comfortable beds.

"What is this place?" he demanded, a tissue pressed to his nose.

"Our home." I couldn't help myself. "Don't worry. We installed indoor plumbing."

I almost felt guilty at his shocked expression. *Almost.* Not a bad lesson, to know what shouldn't be taken for granted. "There's food in the kitchen," I assured him.

Which would have been fine, except when we entered the kitchen, he spotted the tiny brown *mousel* running across the table—

I'd missed one.

—and spun around to push by me, heading for the Library and civilization.

"Oh, no, you don't!"

Evan's green eyes locked on the plate. On it was Paul's favorite sandwich, made before he'd left for the Library this morning and not to be touched by anyone else. Namely me.

This was an emergency. Until the sandwich, Evan had been darting worried looks everywhere, tensed to bolt again. I could have told him there wouldn't be another mousel sighting while I was around. *The tasty little bites avoided this me.* Somehow, I didn't think he'd enjoy the explanation.

"What is it?"

I eyed the tower of carbohydrates and protein, unsure of the nomenclature, and settled for, "Paul's lunch."

A startled flash of those eyes, then he grabbed the sandwich in both hands and took a huge bite. He made a moaning sound I took for bliss, given how his eyes half closed. *That hungry, was he?* I already didn't like the criminals who'd made Evan afraid and prompted the alarm. Now I wanted *them* hungry.

He'd need fluids. I put a tumbler of water in reach, then went to put the kettle on what looked like the farmhouse's original wood-burning stove but was, thanks to Paul, safer for paws to operate. A sensor detected the arrival of a full kettle of water on the marked spot, the heat activated below, and all would whistle a summons when ready.

Now to wait. I sighed to myself, well aware consumption of this food item prevented a Human from any conversational gambits beyond nods, head shakes, and grunts. I could have started packing; even for me, that seemed premature without knowing more than "Mysterious Elves at Risk on Dokeci-Na."

On the other hand, the sandwich also prevented a Human from interrupting me. I pulled up my stool and regarded Evan fondly. Not that he'd have any notion why. *Oh, well.* "Your name sounds familiar, Evan. Are you the one Paul met on Urgia Prime?"

A nod.

"He said you'd saved the Popeakans."

A self-deprecating shrug.

"He also said you were very brave."

Another unreadable look—or was it *hope?*—then a repeat of the shrug.

How fun! Summoned by the kettle, I chose the tea I'd observed Paul had with this sandwich on the assumption he'd know best, then put the mug in front of Evan. He nodded his thanks, which is when I said, "It's been quite a while since Paul's copulated."

Evan erupted, partially chewed sandwich bits flying across the table and floor, sure to attract mousels later. Done, he gasped and sputtered, taking the napkin I offered with a furious swipe of his hand.

No problem reading his expression now.

I may have gone too far.

Still, an informative reaction. I put on my most innocent look, the one Paul distrusted on sight. "Do try the tea."

Perception

PAUL Ragem rarely showed anger, but he did now as he
stepped inside his own office. "This had better be—"

"Important?" Skalet finished when Paul's lips closed
tight. She waved the business end of a rod Lionel hoped
was a stunner at the two sitting in the comfortable chairs
on either side of the small table. "You be the judge."

The anger became something darker, then vanished,
the other Human's face assuming an even more chilling
focus. "Indeed. Our unwanted guests."

Human and male, both. They'd bolted from the habitat zone, falling over one another in their clumsy padded
suits, and Lionel would have been amused if they hadn't
also been armed with what weren't stunners. The whirl-
ing clouds of one atmosphere chasing out another had
hidden most of what happened next. He'd rushed into the
air lock the instant the door unlocked, too soon, really,
the acrid leftovers burning his throat and eyes, only to
find Skalet—again Kraal—standing over the facedown
pair, their weapons in her hands.

Weapons she'd handed him in exchange for her uniform. Lionel still held the ugly things—merc-style blasters, well-scorched from use—having no idea where to put
them. He'd settled for holding them behind his back,
sweating profusely as he'd followed Skalet and their captives here.

Fortunately, the halls had emptied. Good timing, or her planning. *Both were likely.*

It seemed reckless when Paul crossed in front of Skalet to stand before their "guests," but with an easy movement, she returned her weapon to its hiding place. Something in that silent acceptance made the one with the scarred face swallow whatever bluster he'd been about to utter. Despite their outward toughness, both stared up at Paul with the beginnings of fear.

Fear that became astonishment as Paul reached forward to pluck the little statue from the table between the two, then walk to his desk to set it down with care. Lionel watched him touch the nose of the six-legged blue pony with googly eyes, then shake his head at it.

The Humans exchanged derisive looks.

Go ahead, Lionel encouraged them silently. *Underestimate him.* At a guess, the pony had to do with Esen. Paul's priorities remained unshakable.

After a long moment with his back to them, Paul turned, leaning against his desk. "Palarander Todd and Sly Nides, late of Hixtar Station. Management's put quite the price on your heads. Theft. Assault."

Skalet's lips quirked in appreciation, and Lionel realized Paul had used the pony and that moment to check their idents. *The door scanner.*

But these two knew the game. They sat in grim silence.

"None of which matter here," Paul continued. "Everyone's welcome to use the Library. You did come with information to trade?"

His tone was almost cordial, but Skalet's gaze didn't leave them. *Did they know their fate rested on their answer?*

Todd and Nides frowned in unison. Skalet they understood, doing their best to pretend she wasn't there, those hunched shoulders telling the tale. Paul was the puzzle. Nides, the bearded one, finally tried a cool smile. "That's right. We're Library customers, we are. Don't know why the rough stuff." He chose to glare at Lionel.

"Perhaps because of these," Lionel hinted, and eased his hands from behind his back, bringing the blasters into view.

"Hey!" Nides looked ready to grab them. "Those are—"

"Shut it." Todd interrupted. "Botharis has no regs against carrying," he said confidently. "And, yeah, we're customers. What kinda information?"

"And what do we get for it?" from his partner.

"Lionel, you can put those here." Paul indicated his desk. "Don't worry, Homs. They'll be returned when you leave."

Skalet stirred. "If."

"Ah, yes. There is that."

Even knowing Paul didn't mean the threat, his tone sent a shiver down Lionel's back. He put down the weapons, absently noting the rings were gone from the desk.

Those seated appeared convinced. Todd lowered his head, scar in shadow. "What d'you wanna know?"

"Where is Janet Chase?"

Lionel couldn't help his start. *Chase—on Botharis?*

"Don't know any Chase," from Nides, visibly relaxing.

"Tory, then," Paul said. "Where is she?"

"Knew that mealymouth would squeal first chance—"

"Shut it." Todd's eyes glinted. "Tory went her own way and good riddance. She's trouble, that'un."

Skalet laughed.

They shrank back in their seats.

"Where?" Paul repeated.

"We don't know," Nides replied.

"You disguised yourselves to penetrate the Library and hide." Skalet's glorious voice could cut like a knife. "Why? What were you to do for her?"

Todd pressed his lips together, the scar livid on his face.

"We were to lay low," Nides said. "We'd another suit—" He shut his mouth at the hard look from his partner, but it was enough.

"An exit strategy," with grim satisfaction.

Paul pushed away from his desk, gray eyes flashing. "She's already here."

13: Kitchen Afternoon

"I'M not hungry."

This being the second time Evan had expressed in a sullen tone what I knew to be an untruth, I gave in, taking his plate to the counter. There was a sink, but I hadn't lived this long to get my paws wet on purpose.

There were gloves—which didn't matter. I'd struck a nerve while teasing him. Removing the food from sight was the start of my apology.

The rest could wait, and possibly involve telling Paul how Evan reacted—there being the need to explain why crumbs and bits of his sandwich coated the kitchen—though it was also possible I shouldn't. Unless I was mistaken, Paul's last kiss had been from Skalet, to deliver the antidote to the poison she'd administered to him in the first place; he hadn't enjoyed the experience.

Pairings were so complicated. I'd snuck Ycl mating pheromones once, winding up a miserable condensate until Ansky helped me cleanse.

Complicated we didn't need.

"To business, then," I ordered in my most official voice, standing where there weren't crumbs. "Tell me about the Elves."

"I have to tell someone," he muttered confusingly. He sat a moment, hands wrapped around the mug, then looked up. "Let me start at the beginning. I started work at the Commonwealth Embassy, in March-Ne, three

standard months ago. On Dokeci-Na. It was understood—
Paul knows—"

So did I, as Bess. This me showed an encouraging
fang. "You've phobias. Paul told me." I went on, because
it was how I felt, too. "He was impressed how you coped
in order to do your duty. It must be difficult," I finished.
An admirable being, Evan Gooseberry. Even if he had
wasted Paul's sandwich.

"It can be." Almost a smile. "The appearance of a
Dokeci triggers my two worst fears. Knowing that, I've
been preparing for years for this post and—it's going well.
I can be in a room with one. Converse. Do my work. I'm
still—I'm not comfortable out on the streets or in groups,
so my seniors assigned me responsibility for Human visitors."

I sat again. "Boring?"

The smile appeared, shaving off years. "The official
term, Esen, is routine. The same routine, day after day.
By the second week, I could do it in my sleep." His face
grew serious. "Until someone from Burtles-Mautil Intersystem Holdings showed up at my desk with a problem."

He went on to explain.

Perception

EVAN looked up, his face composed in the expression—dutifully practiced in a mirror each morning—he believed merged professionalism with approachability. His friends at the embassy could have told him that expression changed the instant he laid eyes on the next to need help, official or otherwise, but hadn't the heart to say so. They did, however, agree his charmingly shy smile and twinkly eyes made him look cute as a button and, besides, that friendly open face did wonders to defuse those inbound with a complaint—it being difficult to remember you are angry when someone's so earnestly delighted you've arrived at their desk.

The Human standing front of Evan this morning, however, barely appeared to notice his existence. "I demand to see the ambassador."

Which wasn't going to happen, that being why the staff at reception had directed this individual down the hall to the Office of Local Human Affairs. Meaning Evan.

"I'm Polit Officer Gooseberry. Please have a seat, Hom—Burtles." The ident dropped on Evan's access screen, along with a note he hastily scanned stating Hyma Burtles of Burtles-Mautil Intersystem Holdings to be the acting project manager of a "significant build" for the

Dokeci—no details available; a respected pillar of Commonwealth business activities here for over a decade—no details available; and was to be handled as a B6.

Damn. Bs were Persons of Demonstrated Influence, and handling them usually went to senior staff. At minimum, you didn't upset a B. The 6, though?

Made whatever brought Burtles here into a "pass it off" problem, the five-armed Dokeci considering the number six suspicious at best and never to be regarded directly. *Some slang translated across species very well indeed.*

"Please," Evan repeated, gesturing to the chair.

Burtles took the seat, though obviously reluctant to commit his valuable time to an underling. Well dressed, he was older, big framed yet trim, with a weathered, no-nonsense face that almost shouted he spent more time on job sites than behind a desk. "Whisky, neat."

Ah, the joys of dealing with a B. "Of course." Evan keyed in the request. "Now, what can I do for you today, Hom Burtles?"

"What clearance do you have?"

"Level Four." He'd achieved Two, and was proud of it, but there was nothing gained by getting into why he sat at this desk, instead of upstairs. *Four should be well over what this job required.*

Bushy gray eyebrows rose in acknowledgment. "Fair enough, Polit Gooseberry. I—" He paused.

"As requested." Dorton Freeny, juniormost and so assigned to be the embassy's runner, bowed politely and then offered a tray bearing a glass half full of amber liquid to their visitor. As he left, he rolled his eyes at Evan in sympathy.

Had he been that young?

Once the door closed, Burtles lifted the glass in a large callused hand, downed the contents in a gulp, then put the glass on Evan's desk with a clatter. "I need an exit, Polit Gooseberry."

"I see." Emergency transport clearance, with any/all dealings with the Dokeci officially terminated. Protocols were clear. Switching off his system to emphasize his discretion, Evan reached for a pad of paper and his stylo. "How soon?"

"Immediate." Burtles let out a whiskey-scented breath. "Not just me. I want my whole crew off this blighted planet. Can you do that?"

"It can be done," Evan said, careful not to commit. Evacuating one's kind from a trouble spot was a time-honored role for an embassy and essential, in the case of natural disaster, war, disease, or—on occasion—misunderstandings with the locals regarding who was edible and who was not. But this was Dokeci-Na, a world whose inhabitants were among the most civil and peace-loving of species. There were no trouble spots here. No conflicts.

Unless brought here. Making the person before him the likely source of the problem. With no tactful way to phrase the question, he didn't bother. "Hom Burtles, what have you done to upset the Dokeci?"

"Nothing. I assure you, they're pleased with our work. Ecstatic." The words said one thing; the harsh tone—the grim set of Burtles' face—said the opposite. "We've done everything they asked. A miracle of engineering."

As if this were the worst possible outcome.

"Then I don't understand—"

"They used us to do their dirty work!" Burtles slammed his palm down on Evan's desk, jarring the glass. "To steal their precious city. Oh, it was all a secret. The great charity of the Dokeci. All supposed to save the Elves."

Elves? Evan blinked. "I beg your pardon?"

"To exterminate the Elves, that's what it's for, and we won't be part of murder." Sweat had broken out on the other's forehead. "We can't be. My name. Our names. Help us." He sank back, hand covering his mouth, eyes pleading.

Security could be summoned in multiple ways: a coded phrase, the button near his right foot, pulling open a drawer with a rightward bias.

Not for this, Evan decided. His visitor was distraught. Why? "Hom Burtles. I need you to calm yourself." Or security would arrive regardless.

A mute nod.

"You've made a very serious accusation about our hosts." Even if the word "elves" made no sense whatsoever. "You must realize we require proof this is—ah—"

The hand dropped. "Real, you mean?" Burtles barked

a humorless laugh. "What do you know of the S'Remmer System?"

Evan didn't bother taking the relevant notebook from his drawer. "It's a Dokeci Protectorate and the site of their next colony." Mature Dokeci struggled with gravity; to remain physically active without personal supports such as grav belts, they moved into space. Most retired there. *Anywhere with a view.* Their culture assigned great value to creativity inspired by spectacular natural phenomena. Before his time, their Portula Colony had overlooked the Jeopardy Nebula. There were now hundreds of similar establishments, scattered throughout Dokeci space. "I've heard the rings around S'Remmer Prime are remarkable." The ads were everywhere.

Burtles grunted. "They are. And about to get more so. The Dokeci surveyors discovered the third moon's ready to break apart." He leaned forward. "That's when they noticed it was inhabited." He paused meaningfully.

Though he tried, Evan couldn't help himself. "By . . . Elves."

A firm nod. "Pre-space sentients. Oh, they weren't easy to spot—wasn't till the Dokeci landed to install sensors that they realized what they were seeing. The surface had become a wasteland. Nothing should have survived, but the Elves had built cities—shelters really—" hands described a stack in midair, "—able to hold in atmosphere." Hands opened palm up. "They appeared to all be broken and empty. At first, the Dokeci thought the species already extinct."

This was—Evan realized he was holding his breath and made himself relax. "I take it they weren't?"

"One was intact. The Dokeci found life signs. They hired my company to move it here."

Evan blinked. "'Move it?'"

"And those inside." Burtles shrugged. "We've done bigger salvage jobs. The Dokeci prepped their valley. Removed substrate, put in an exclusion zone to protect both ecosystems. Then we arrived with everything we could grab."

Elves, now a mystery project of this magnitude? Distraught was one thing, but transplanting the last survivors of an unknown species like some potted rose?

Last week, he'd spoken with a Human mother convinced the Dokeci had switched one of their newborn for hers, showing him the "unusually long fingers" of the baby in her arms. Who looked happy, normal, and very Human—if perhaps not as similar to the mother's contracted partner as might be predicted.

Before that, there'd been the tiresome Human artist who accused the Dokeci of ruining his career by exhibiting his work alongside Sendojii-ki's. The latter being very well regarded, especially here in the capital, it certainly wasn't the Dokeci's fault no one bought a single piece of the Human's. In Evan's informed and tactfully unshared opinion, it had more to do with the Dokeci's current distaste for oblique angles in visual media. You had to keep up.

Elves? Time this came to an end. "Hom Burtles, part of our mandate from the Commonwealth is to be aware of events on this planet." Not openly spying, that being rude, but a significant part of each junior staffer's duties was to sift through public reports and documents. Evan pointedly put down his stylo. "I assure you we'd have noticed something on the scale of what you suggest."

"I'm sure you did. The new reservoir in the Riota-si Valley? Ring any bells?"

Evan stiffened. *All of them.* A major water redirection project embassy staff had flagged as "unusually swift" in its passage through the maze of Dokeci authorities. They'd assumed the speed was because of some urgent, not-shared-with-other-species problem.

Elves, Evan repeated to himself. *Tell that to senior staff.*

What was he thinking—they'd probably tuned into the monitors to listen by now; "murder" and "extinction" were solid attention grabbers. *And today had started so well.*

"The Dokeci didn't hide what we were doing," Burtles continued. "Only why."

Evan roused himself. "The Commonwealth would have assisted any evacuation—"

"You aren't hearing me. It wasn't an evacuation. The Dokeci lied. They told us we were saving the last of the Elves. What they wanted was to snatch the last intact example of the Elves' shelter-cities before the moon cracked apart. To put a one-of-a-kind work of art on display, here. A monument to a dead race."

A chill ran down Evan's spine. By all he'd learned of the species and current culture, viewing such an exhibit would be tantamount to a religious experience. There'd be tours. Status changes would be witnessed in its presence—

No. He knew the Dokeci moral code, too, dating back to the time of Teganersha-ki, and refused to believe they'd risk one life—even alien—for art. "You told me these Elves were alive."

"They were when I left this morning. From what I saw—" Burtles' fingertips sank deep into the cushioned arms of his chair, "—they won't be for long."

"Enough riddles," Evan ordered sharply. "Explain yourself at once."

"We did as ordered." Words poured out in a torrent. "Brought the shelter-city here and everything seemed fine, I swear it. The Elves—I've seen them, you know— they appeared all right. Shocked, but settling in. Brave beings. Then this morning, without warning or explanation, Dokeci arrived in enviro-suits. They started pumping a poison—some gas—around the city. The Elves fled inside and sealed the openings. I protested—we all did— but the Dokeci wouldn't listen. They politely ordered us to leave." Burtles' eyes were haunted. "But we were part of it. Responsible. If Elves go extinct, it's going to be blamed on us as much as the Dokeci, unless you get us away from here."

"The embassy will facilitate your exit, Hom Burtles."

Evan leaped to his feet, startled to find his door open and Senior Political Officer Aka M'Lean, second only to the ambassador in authority, standing there flanked by security. By their too-neutral expressions, all three were unimpressed by his handling of the situation.

"Please go with these staffers," Polit M'Lean continued, his tone a firm blend of reassuring calm and they'll-drag-you-if-they-must promise. "They'll take idents for anyone else who wants our assistance to exit Dokeci-Na."

Burtles stood, but hesitated. "What of the Elves?"

Though small in stature, with gray wispy hair prone to fall over his forehead—when not blowing wildly in the slightest breeze—Polit M'Lean's cool hazel gaze left no doubt who commanded the room and those in it. "Your concern for them does you credit, Hom Burtles," he replied. "Despite all else."

Evan tensed. *What had he missed?*

His visitor frowned. "What's that supposed to mean?"

"We're in contact at the highest level with the Dokeci directly involved in the resettlement. The—Elves—are not being harmed. What you witnessed earlier today concerned citizens acting promptly and properly to eradicate a dangerous pest." Polit M'Lean's voice chilled appreciably. "An alien organism your company brought from the moon—a potential threat to this planet's biosphere. While the Dokeci won't bring charges? I assure you, Hom Burtles, the Commonwealth—"

"What the hells?! We did no such thing. What pest?! We have procedures—those—" Burtles launched into a string of impassioned curses.

Security came to alert. They were unfamiliar in their armor; Lynelle Owell and Lisam Horner sat in on the political office game nights, stuffing themselves on Freeny's savory biscuits and Evan's beer, and kindly let Evan win a hand on rare occasions.

The pair took an intimidating step forward, and Burtles shouted, "You can't believe them over us. We're Human!"

Evan winced inwardly. Polit M'Lean's professional demeanor remained unchanged, but he thought the corner of a hazel eye twitched and, at a guess, Burtles-Mautil Intersystem Holdings was going to find navigating Human bureaucracy a torturous nightmare for some time to come.

"The Dokeci have requested we ensure not only yourselves, but all of your equipment be fumigated," the senior officer said almost absently. "The Commonwealth takes the transport of noxious pests extremely seriously, Hom Burtles. This will be done immediately. With your cooperation or without."

Had Burtles brought *something* into the embassy?

Was it crawling under his shirt!? Evan barely stopped himself from checking.

"But—we didn't—" For the first time, Burtles looked uncertain. "What I saw—those poor creatures—"

Polit M'Lean knew to the heartbeat when to soften his tone. "Accidents happen, Hom Burtles, as do misunderstandings. I trust this will turn out to be a valuable lesson for both our species. While privacy during such a stressful situation is to be desired, with our assistance the Dokeci will be better able to preserve the health and peace of these unfortunate beings as they recover."

In other words, Evan translated with admiration, *now that we know what the Dokeci are hiding in their valley, they'll have to share.*

"I'm authorized to inform you, Hom Burtles, if you and your people adhere strictly to your confidentiality agreement, you'll receive your full contracted payment from the Dokeci." Polit M'Lean's smile had something of appetite to it. "I'm sure it will help with the fines."

Burtles gave Evan a helpless, dazed look.

He didn't quite smile back. "Thank you for coming to the Office of Local Human Affairs, Hom Burtles."

And that, Evan thought, *was that.*

Except it wasn't.

At home that night, though exhausted, Evan couldn't sleep. His skin prickled painfully from three stints in the fresher stall, in case the "pest" had been something transferable; though logically if it could jump from Burtles, Polit M'Lean would have insisted the guest chair be sanitized along with the rugs.

The prickles weren't what had him staring at the ceiling, oblivious to the evening breeze wafting through the screens, or the nigh-deafening chorus of webbed Purple Wobblies.

A new species.

Here. In reach.

He'd elected embassy work over a First Contact Team because he knew himself, too well. The strange, the novel—any such could trigger debilitating *FEAR!* He was fine—he managed—when he could predict what he'd face next. Prepare. Habituate. The unknown had never been what he dreaded; it was failing others who needed him, exactly when they did. You didn't go to a new world *knowing* you were the weak link. You just . . . didn't.

The dream of meeting a new species, of finding a way to communicate—he had it still. Felt the rush. Who'd have thought he might have a chance here?

Elves.

Evan flopped over and over, unable to settle and knowing it wasn't the tantalizing prospect or the prickles—

He buried his face in his pillow, still seeing the look on Burtles' face. Hear his voice. The conviction in it. The project manager had believed what he'd said, that the Dokeci were trying to eliminate the Elves.

M'Lean called it a misunderstanding.

In the dark, this late, Evan could recite a list of other "misunderstandings." The course work for a diplomat was as terrifyingly replete with examples of "what went wrong" as a med student's was of planetary plagues. You couldn't assume the best of intentions, not from your own kind and never with a species whose definition of the term had nothing to do with your own.

Could the Dokeci want to eradicate the Elves? Why— because *they* were the pests? In that case—

He raised his head to breathe and cool his flushed face.

—why bring them here?

What if . . . what if they hadn't known *what* the Elves were until it was too late. Haste. Urgency. Impulse. The Dokeci were capable of those, too.

Evan sat up and wrapped his arms around his knees. After a moment, he stretched out and grabbed the holocube by the bed, staring into it. Time shift. Cost. Translight com systems didn't always deliver.

Thumbing the cube to active, he spoke. "Great Gran Gooseberry."

The black inside the cube brightened, then dimmed. Disappointed, Evan went to turn it off.

"Evan? You should be asleep."

She always knew his time. He bent to rest his forehead against the cube, closing his eyes. "I'm having a little trouble with that."

"Let me set the auto."

He listened to her footsteps, caught the sound of sails flapping, then their snap into position. "I'm sorry to interrupt your sailing—"

"Tush. Talk to me, lad."

"There's—I think my seniors could be making a mistake. A serious one."

"Then you tell them."

Imagining that conversation, Evan's stomach lurched in protest. "I've nothing to say, Great Gran. I'm worried, that's all. They're making decisions, and we don't have all the facts."

"Then you go and get them. Isn't that your job, Evan?"

"It is. I—" Great Gran didn't know about his being assigned to Human Affairs; he hadn't had the heart to tell her. "I missed the chance." The embassy would send a small mission to the Riota-si Valley tomorrow. By rank—and qualifications—he should be going, but the assignment had gone to a colleague, Trili Bersin.

Because everyone knew Evan Gooseberry had *difficulty* being around Dokeci. At times, he grew exhausted, arguing with their kindness. It was easier to accept it than resist and struggle.

"Evan Gooseberry. What is it you always say to me, when things aren't going well for you?"

Yet only struggle moved him forward.

He raised his head, staring into the dark. "That it's up to me, Great Gran. No one else." *And he'd won before.* Had brought himself not only to *look* at a Popeakan, a species able to flare his *SPIDER FEAR* into full panic-mode, but to hold one in his arms in order to help ril survive.

"So what are you going to do about this sleep-stealing worry of yours, Evan?"

"Find out if I'm right or not. Tomorrow." He'd go to the embassy early and insist on joining the mission. Senior Polit M'Lean might be kind, but surely he'd prefer Evan, with his knowledge and clearance. "Thanks, Great Gran."

"Remember we're all proud of you. Get some sleep now."

"Love to everyone," he told her.

A mistake. Evan knew at once, for she chuckled warmly and said, "Oh, and shall I pass that along to your Lucius? Poor fellow has been wondering if you've got his messages?"

Let him. Which wasn't the approach to take with Great Gran. Nor was he willing to discuss those messages with her tonight—if ever.

Wincing inwardly, Evan made himself say the words. "I've found someone else. And no, before you ask, I can't talk about him yet. It's too—soon." *Gods, there was an understatement.* Blushing, he pretended to yawn, loudly. "Happy sailing, Great Gran." And thumbed off the cube.

Evan listened to the Wobblies' chorus. No, he couldn't sleep, not yet. He got up and found his com link. "Trili, this is Evan. You awake?"

"What do you think? I'm going in that death trap tomorrow."

"About that." Trili was his friend, his closest on Dokeci-Na. Evan knew she detested flying, especially in the embassy aircar, whose pilot took such pleasure in using swoops and sidelong dips to ensure each passenger had an excellent view of the ground.

"If this is about borrowing your auto-therapist, Evan Gooseberry, you can forget it. I don't need a voice in my ear."

"No. It's—I realize this mission is a chance for first contact." If his heart pounded at the thought, Trili's would, too. "I don't want to take that from you."

"Take it, please! Are you kidding? I get to stay on the ground. M'Lean will be thrilled. There's just—Evan?" She paused, then said uneasily, "There's a meeting with Dokeci onsite. An unspecified number. Are you ready for that?"

She knew him. They'd arrived in the same restaffing and had shared a room until they could afford accommodations of their own. They still cooked for one another on days off, he slightly less prone to burning supper, Trili making superb desserts. Great Gran, of course, had been very excited.

"I'll have to be ready," he told her. "I've a bad feeling about this business with the Elves. I'm afraid we're missing something. Something critical."

"Well, you can't take feelings to M'Lean," she responded, in complete understanding. "You go, Evan. We'll work out the details in the morning." A chuckle. "And thanks. Now I'll be able to sleep. See you tomorrow."

He ended the link, satisfied with his decision, and climbed back into bed.

His chance was here. To struggle forward, to manage his *fear* and be with the Dokeci, doing the job he'd trained to do.

And learn the truth about the Elves.

Evan fell asleep.

Trili Bersin had been more than happy to switch places; in fact, she'd planted a big wet kiss on Evan's cheek. Polit M'Lean had been—bemused, covered his outward reaction, but then he was well aware Evan wasn't good with large numbers of Dokeci yet, or even two at once—having *BONELESS ARMS* and abrupt *SPOTS ON THE SKIN—*

Evan took a breath and let it out slowly. He'd had a thorough session with his auto-therapist that morning instead of breakfast. *Arms and spots were nothing to fear.* He felt steady; knew he looked it. *Besides, he wasn't alone.*

Owell and Horner were coming, along with himself and Polit M'Lean, the unusual presence of armed security on Dokeci-Na in case there were any Humans left from Burtles-Mautil Intersystem Holdings to be forcibly fumigated. The pair hadn't stopped smiling; not much happened around an embassy on such a peace-loving, established world.

M'Lean handed Evan the diplomatic pouch when he boarded the embassy aircar. "Our briefing notes,

Gooseberry." An assessing look. "When you're done, I'd like your thoughts."

Evan gave a short, professional nod, resisting the urge to hug the pouch to his chest.

They'd a twenty-minute flight—straight there, presumably straight back. Once seated, Evan wasted no time gawking at the scenery. The notes were contained on a portable node, bio-locked. Acutely aware of M'Lean sitting across from him, he didn't hesitate, breathing gently over the screen, then keying in today's code.

It unlocked, pages scrolling by too quickly to read until he realized he'd clenched his fingers around the side with the controls. He glanced up.

His senior was gazing outside.

Relieved, Evan reset the rate and began to read.

The matter was as Polit M'Lean had described to Burtles. The Dokeci had acted with atypical haste because they'd run out of time, S'Remmer Prime's moon fragmenting in spectacular fashion shortly after the last ship left.

The decision to uproot the shelter-city—

Struck by the term, Evan paused the scroll to cue up images.

The first was one of the so-called Elves. To his vast relief, the being was theta-class and humanoid, with paired arms and legs.

He'd done his utmost not to anticipate *tentacles* or *spiderish jointed limbs,* but you never knew, did you—he took that steadying breath. *Those were body parts, and nothing to fear.*

The raised hand had four supple digits, set in opposing pairs. The head was devoid of hair, which could be choice or biology. The face was attractive, in Human terms; wider at the forehead, with huge brown round-pupiled eyes above high cheekbones, a long, almost beaklike nose, and a lipped mouth that might pass for Human when pursed, but otherwise appeared to wrap around the cheeks, almost meeting the small, pointed ears.

The flawless skin of this individual was as richly dark as his own, at least on the face. The neck was circled by lighter stripes implying the body could be striped as well, but the Elf—he made himself use the word—was dressed in layers of reddish woven material, loose around the torso, snug around the limbs. What they'd brought?

Could be clothing provided by the Dokeci.

Evan went to the second image, of the moon surface. The lack of scale frustrated any attempt to grasp what he was seeing, so he moved to the next.

This was a "shelter-city?" Evan stared down at a complex structure: a low central core that spread out in short, symmetrical wings, each ending as a tower. There were five wings and so five towers, a design with strong appeal to fundamental Dokeci sensibilities. The outer surface had no apparent openings. As there wouldn't be, if this was to contain what atmosphere remained. Practical.

And beautiful. Deeply incised textures formed elegant, intricate whorls and spirals down the towers, spreading out over the base. The Elves' shelter-city was as much sculpture as architecture. *Burtles wasn't wrong,* Evan judged, *to suspect the Dokeci of a smidge of art avarice.*

He flipped back to the previous image and felt a pang as he suddenly grasped what it showed. What had appeared to be jagged ridges were the shards of other cities, cracked wide, their walls tumbled to litter the landscape. The inner structure was lost in the broken jumble, but he thought there might be floors and arches. Had they burst from within, or been smashed by meteors, or—

Whatever had destroyed them, the Elves' shelter-cities were an impressive response to an extinction-level crisis, unlike anything he'd seen or heard of before.

Pre-space tech?

Not his expertise, but the question should be asked. Would be.

Evan glanced outside, dismayed to see they'd reached the foothills of the Riota-si Easterly Range. He started to skim more than read. The shelter-city had been encased in transport foam . . . a stabilizing force field . . . there'd been anti-gravs installed beneath—

Beneath? Evan went back and read more carefully. Scans by the company had detected cavities below the city. Assuming those were part of the structure, they'd tunneled down, then across, sealing with foam and fields. When done, they'd captured half a tower's height in sub-lunar material.

After that, it was apparently straightforward to attach linked star drives and bring the enclosed city, still full of Elves, via translight to land it, intact, on another world.

He would never, Evan promised himself, *take engineers lightly again.*

He flipped past doubtless vital details about environment systems and gravity compensation, but the Elves having arrived alive, "how" was redundant to the situation on Dokeci-Na. The key word was *compatible;* as theta-class the Elves should have been able to leave their now-unwrapped shelter-city, breathe the air, then move into the new homes the Dokeci would build for them, and live happily ever after.

Evan slowed to read the page flagged in red for Human readers.

The Elves withdrew inside their city during the day. The Dokeci roamed the perimeter in threes, ready to answer questions or deal with emergencies, filled with quiet triumph.

Until *something* had burst through the ground beneath their abdomens, swarmed up their bodies, and sunk a venomous fang into the tender flesh between arms.

All three had convulsed; two had died almost instantly. The third had lasted until meds arrived but couldn't be saved.

Evan closed his eyes until his breathing settled, then opened them to continue.

They hadn't told Burtles-Mautil, because what had attacked the three was alien to Dokeci-Na. They hadn't needed a pathologist's report—the small, shelled *things* were found with their victims, bodies twisted in death. Before the Elves emerged at dusk, the Dokeci had discovered more, burrowing up from beneath the shelter-city, and realized the grim truth.

The Elves weren't the only survivors rescued from the moon.

The next page concerned the urgent actions being

taken to contain the pest and keep it from attacking more Dokeci, including ordering the Humans to vacate immediately.

There was, oddly, nothing more about the Elves.

Closing the notes, Evan looked up to meet M'Lean's cool gaze. "I—I don't know what to say."

The other nodded. "It's a mess. We'll deal with the Human side, but the Dokeci have a problem on their arms. What's next, Polit Gooseberry?"

"We obtain our own data," Evan said without hesitation. "But the Dokeci won't let our techs on site without a *Fleullen-ni*." The literal meaning was *agreed prudence,* a signed statement of what constituted good behavior, binding on both sides. "That's what we're here to accomplish, isn't it?"

"With a bit of luck, yes." M'Lean looked out the screen. "Gods. There it is."

Evan turned.

The Riota-si Valley had been carved by glaciation. Its smooth sides cupped a scoured plain, itself sculpted in turn by a twisting river, now dry. Little hook-shaped lakes remained, flanking its course like forgotten punctuation. Otherwise, it was barren, windswept, and as close to a dying moon, he supposed, as the Dokeci could find on their world.

There was a trenchlike scar along the sides and around the valley. The exclusion zone Burtles mentioned, at a guess.

The shelter-city rose like a castle—or what Evan imagined a castle might be—in the middle of the valley, its arms spread, towers shading the ground below. That ground was churned and flattened by machine, not nature; scaffolds and cranes stood abandoned on all sides, no longer necessary.

The rays of an alien sun teased out the textured surface of the city and what did those inside think, to be bathed by the light of a new star?

One of so many questions he yearned to ask the Elves. Another, do you sleep?

"They've spraying again." M'Lean observed as they descended.

Owell listened to her com and nodded. "Nontoxic. Harmless to Humans and theta-class in general."

It didn't look harmless. The sinister yellow cloud rolled along the ground, emitted by a pair of ground vehicles. The embassy aircar was low enough now Evan could see the Dokeci in sight were encased in that species' version of an enviro-suit, a wide bag with supple sleeves for each of the five arms, topped with a clear hood to allow vision as well as to expose sufficient skin for others to read.

Should make them easier to be around—maybe—

Discipline, honed to habit, grabbed the words and rearranged them.

—I own my fear; my fear is not rational. Whatever they wear or do, these beings are as they should be. I own my fear—

"Evan?"

With a tiny shudder of released concentration, Evan looked squarely at his senior. "I won't let you down."

M'Lean studied his face, then smiled with abrupt warmth. "I have no concerns there. Now, let's go over the protocols."

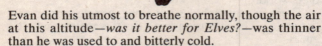

Evan did his utmost to breathe normally, though the air at this altitude—*was it better for Elves?*—was thinner than he was used to and bitterly cold.

They'd known the conditions and dressed for them as best they could. His coat and boots were embassy-issue, warm, if new and stiff. Hats were problematic around the Dokeci, but for once his thick cap of hair was an advantage. M'Lean's thin locks fluttered across his scalp like grass.

Commonwealth tradition held that diplomats didn't wear gloves, Humans ever-willing to engage in skin-to-whatever contact.

With the usual precautions. They'd dipped their hands and wrists in thermal lotion before leaving the aircar; diplomacy shouldn't mean losing fingertips to frostbite.

The cloud had settled rather than dispersed, blanketing the earth around the shelter-city in yellow dust. Poison above; danger lurking below.

Evan found himself walking on his toes as they approached the Dokeci dome.

The dome might have been plucked from space, too, a dimpled globe shedding rainbows in the sunlight. A more prosaic awning with a wind barrier to one side stood in front. By the raised benches for Human posteriors, this would be where they'd meet with the Dokeci officials in charge. *Hopefully not more than two.*

He'd manage regardless.

There were other signs Humans had worked here, and recently. A crane had Burtles-Mautil on the side. A handful of portable shelters stood around a forlorn patio with its heat lamps now off. All were coated in yellow.

No one could fault Dokeci thoroughness.

As juniormost on this mission, Evan was encouraged not only to stare with wide-eyed innocence in every direction and in places others might not want, but also to make recordings according to the time-honored Commonwealth tradition of "if they don't say no, go ahead." You could always apologize later.

He aimed the recorder, and most of his attention, on the shelter-city. There were openings on ground level, ringed in thickened loops like petrified rope. Each was plugged by what looked from this distance exactly like the blunt tip of a bottle stopper, albeit twice his height. There were, to his disappointment, no Elves in sight.

Evan eased a bit closer.

There were suited Dokeci in the dark shadows between the city's arms. They looked to be drilling into the ground at the base—

"Polit Gooseberry." Lisam Horner beckoned toward the awning. "They're ready."

Then the screaming started.

"You can't be serious. This is a normal behavior?"

Ekwueme-ki, lead individual for the Riota-si Valley Project—while they all knew what was happening here, such names, Evan knew, had a way of sticking past their usefulness—flushed pale mauve in acknowledgment. Her—the neuter pronoun for the species—pendulous body was supported within a grav ring, set so Ekwueme-ki hovered eyes-to-eyes with a now-standing Senior Political Officer Aka M'Lean.

If the Dokeci hoped this would lend sincerity to her words, it failed. There was nothing normal, in Evan's trained opinion and that of his senior's, about the continuous screaming from the shelter-city.

An arm swept through the air. "It is not normal. They prefer to avoid sunlight. This is an outpouring of grief," Ekwueme-ki said, raising her voice to be heard. "The *Rasnir-as* attack our poor guests as well, to terrible result. Witness." Another arm indicated the city.

The four Humans turned as one.

Evan raised and activated his recorder by reflex; his conscious thought totally consumed. The Elves were coming out.

A plug had been retracted from an opening. The screaming grew louder, sharper. *Angry* was his impression, though he changed his mind at once. Figures appeared. Though too far to discern features or expressions, what they were doing couldn't have been clearer.

They came out in pairs, between them supporting a wrapped bundle the size, shape, and terrible limpness of a corpse. They kept coming, scuffing through the yellow powdered soil, accompanied by that primal, collective *SCREAM.* Evan counted, unable to stop himself. Four, six, eight, ten.

One alone and unburdened, and when that Elf, taller than the rest, stepped into the daylight, the scream stopped.

The silence was almost worse.

Evan watched, they all did, from security to the suited Dokeci with their drills, as the Elves laid their burdens in a row on the clean ground, then stood back and bowed low. The lone Elf came forward, arms raised in supplication. To a deity?

To their hosts?

It could be to the unfamiliar sun, Evan thought in frustration. Guessing was the worst possible approach to this.

A great deal of the training for First Contact was to re-move that so-Human impulse to empathize and believe you understood because you cared.

They all cared. The Dokeci, too.

It was never enough.

The Elf lowered its arms—they'd no information on gender and he wouldn't *guess*—the others stood, and they walked slowly back inside.

And there it was. That *impulse.* There was something hopeless, something achingly resigned in what he saw, and Evan wasn't ready to dismiss it.

Besides, he told himself. By the odds alone, once in a million encounters with the alien and unknown, a Hu-man heart had to get it right.

"Oh, this is terrible, terrible," Ekwueme-ki exclaimed as the plug closed the opening. Her skin sported black welts. *Dismay.* Three arms signaled urgently, and Dokeci hurried forward on grav sleds to retrieve what could be offerings.

But weren't. Whatever they'd witnessed, those bundles weren't a gift to the Dokeci. They were a plea. "Polit M'Lean," Evan began, speaking in a low voice. They were together, had moved closer unconsciously while watching. "The Elves need help."

"I agree," with such harshness Evan turned in sur-prise. But M'Lean was already speaking to someone else. "Leader Ekwueme-ki, with your consent, the Common-wealth wishes to offer assistance. Please allow us to sign the Fleullen-ni at once, then grant us access to a speci-men of Rasnir-as, the cause of so much suffering." M'Lean's tone was resolute. "However unwittingly," be-cause you never admitted guilt to another species, "Hu-mans helped bring them here. We urge you to let us be part of the solution."

The flight back to the embassy felt longer, as if the mun-dane world had shifted away while they weren't looking. Owell and Horner shed their gear, becoming Lynelle and Lisam again, but they looked as weary and grim as he felt and sat without a word, so Evan let them be.

Polit M'Lean sat up front, alone. He murmured into his com link, made notes, set who knew what in motion, determined to bring the might of the Commonwealth—being the local embassy staff and, if lucky, a Survey ship might be close—to bear. The priority was to rid Dokeci-Na of the pest.

They'd a bag containing most of a dead rasnir-as under the back seat. M'Lean requested an intact living specimen for analysis, to help determine, he confided in Evan, if Burtles-Mautil Holdings—Humans—had brought the things from yet another world. In which case, where else might they have been spread?

A nightmare about that was entirely likely.

The Dokeci, though uncomfortable, said they'd do what they could, the Humans having signed the Fleullen-ni and now officially part of the investigation.

To Evan's intense relief, they were not offered one of the dead Elves, nor did M'Lean request it, though until they'd an on-site autopsy, they were forced to trust Ekwueme-ki's assurance their bodies showed the same damage suffered by the Dokeci. Bitten. Presumably poisoned.

Troubled, thoughtful, Evan sat alone. He'd rewatched his recording, the sound muted, over and over till, if he closed his eyes, he'd see every detail.

Were M'Lean and Ekwueme-ki right? The actions of the Elves could be interpreted as an attempt to communicate their losses with the only ones who might save them, the Dokeci. Who'd saved them already. Who could seem, to primitive society, to have godlike powers.

The Elves might be primitive. He didn't know. Wasn't sure how it mattered.

What did? What dried his mouth and kept him silent? *What if they were wrong.*

14: Kitchen Afternoon

THE youthful sparkle of Evan's eyes was gone, replaced by fiery resolve. "The embassy resources had nothing. I—I claimed a family emergency and left Dokeci-Na that night. I knew I had to hurry. M'Lean won't agree to breaching the Elves' city, or any drastic action, without more information—especially from our own experts—but the Dokeci? If there are more fatalities?" He rolled his shoulders as if they ached. "I hope I'm wrong, Esen. I probably am. But I have to be sure. That's why I came to the Library."

Which, in my opinion, was adult and most responsible of Evan, if you didn't count a reckless willingness to throw away his cherished career to satisfy his personal moral code. I'd my own regrettable tendencies, of course. His description of the Elves, of their shelter-city, were so tantalizingly *new* I had to remind myself of the seriousness of the situation. *It's not all about you,* was how Skalet would put it.

Still. *New species! New me!*

Once I could assimilate their genetic material. A wee bite of something left lying about would do; Web-beings weren't fussy. Except for Lesy, but then Ersh presorted—the point being I'd a perfect opportunity in front of me if only Evan had brushed against one. He might have collected skin cells. Even better, a hair follicle; he'd said

Elves were hairless, few noticed the wealth of little sensory hairs along the arms of most humanoids.

"So you didn't get to meet one," I grumbled, possibly projecting my own disappointment.

"No." Evan sipped a fresh cup of tea, the other vanishing as he'd lost himself in the story. I'd slipped the sandwich plate back on the table, pleased to see him take bites; I doubted he tasted any of it. "The Dokeci told us the Elves have stopped communicating with them." He winced. "Other than the screams. The bodies."

Unpleasant business, that. I liked it no better as a Lanivarian, despite being a species who howled their grief. The bodies themselves were . . . problematic. Queeb held no reverence for anyone's deceased and—historically— ate their own. Rumor held they'd never stopped, merely taken the practice somewhere without squeamish alien observers. *There was no end of variations, really.* In my informed opinion, these Dokeci—for in this case we did appear to have a separated group, most probably engineers—were overly quick to assume the presentation of corpses was a plea.

The Elves might have been sharing.

These Dokeci's communication skills with another, more familiar species didn't impress me either. "They should have told their Human employees about the attacks," I said. "They deserved the truth."

"Maybe." He looked at me, face grim. "Any other species would have blamed Burtles and his crew for those deaths. They avoided an interspecies' incident."

"They avoided sharing the Elves," I grumbled, but Evan was correct. Revenge, petty or otherwise, wasn't in the Dokeci mind-set. *Penance for failure to predict a problem,* however, was; I suspected several individual Dokeci were about to lose their status, including this Ekwueme-ki. If they hadn't already.

Families would fragment.

A paralyzing scramble to prevent exactly that would be underway as we sat here. Dokeci facing loss of status would go to any lengths to dilute the decision-making process, involving as many as possible, explaining why Ekwueme-ki had invited the Humans in the first place.

The charitable view held all involved would have their say in what would be a very important choice.

Other Dokeci, knowing better, would avoid becoming entangled with equal determination. The notion was to muddy accountability and spread blame. Ersh-memory supplied the phrase: *the more arms hold a burden, the easier to slip yours away.* A tactic I'd noticed employed with enthusiasm in the Hamlet of Hillsview council.

Both were true. The system worked for the Dokeci, at its best preventing, at the worst delaying, completely rash decisions.

My friend here would learn all this and more, granted he still had a job. Poor Evan. His talent for getting into trouble rivaled mine. *Not that I did so as often,* I assured myself, choosing to ignore recent events.

What mattered to us now? Unless things changed dramatically, any Dokeci action dealing with the Elves should grind to a sputtering halt.

Leaving the Human embassy staff—who, depending on their awareness of Dokeci and personal ambition, never to be discounted in the species, could seize initiative. *Oh, dear.*

The Human with me shifted impatiently. "I have to access the Library again, Esen." He looked around, then back to me, not hiding his doubt. "Can it be done from here?"

Yes, but he didn't need to know that. Evan Gooseberry also didn't need to know the Library couldn't help him any more than it had.

Yet. "Paul will let us know when the Library settles," I said vaguely. "Finish your lunch."

He pushed the plate away, gently but firmly.

Stubborn Human. Fortunately, I'd no shame. "What did you say the Dokeci called the pests?"

"Rasnir-as."

His pronunciation wasn't bad, stuck as he was with the limitations of a Human mouth. "The 'devils-that-stab,'" I translated glibly. "More commonly? Devil Darts."

"How—the embassy bank—I couldn't find the meaning." Evan looked decidedly put out.

"All Species' Library of Linguistics and Culture." I grinned at him. "Curator, remember?"

Though this memory was mine, not as yet added to the collection.

As a Dokeci, Lesy—Riosolesy-ki—exhibited a peculiar form of courage. She loved their scarier stories, so long as I'd sit with her to listen and we could hide under blankets. Among the darker figures in those stories were the Rasnir-as, mysterious unseen devils who'd sneak up on youth who weren't being useful to their elders and stab them in their pendulous nethers with darts.

The youths, that is, though elders had far more hanging down there.

A youth myself, I took exception to the bit where those darts were dipped in concentrated enzymes derived from the otherwise innocuous Purple Wobblies, supposedly so the victim would be digested from the inside out over several excruciating days. These weren't the cautionary tales of, say Humans; adult Dokeci hardly acknowledged their young existed, let alone told them stories.

Pure "grumpy elder" wish fulfillment, that's what it was. I should know, living with Ersh. The stories I could—

Which wasn't the point either. "Devil Darts are terrifying villains who appear in the Dokeci version of Human campfire stories," I explained to Evan.

Who looked baffled. "Campfire?"

About to explain, I stopped myself. As Paul would explain to me, *there could be such a thing as too much information.*

"Mythical monsters," I abbreviated. "Except that these are real."

He swallowed hard, as though his lunch no longer sat well. "I didn't get a good look—didn't want one. It fit in a bag." Evan held his hands apart, not more than the width of his body.

Size didn't matter. As Ersh would say, *every living thing had others to eat it.*

Except Web-beings, who ate one another. I supposed being our own sole predator was at least tidy.

But what it said about the chasm between everything biological and us, who were closer to cosmic radiation and stellar dust than wonderful, messy, interconnected life? Who measured time in epochs instead of breaths?

Who, having once assimilated living *thinking* tissue, were forever forced to rely on it, or become mindless once more—

I wasn't Ersh, to enjoy a cold philosophical debate about who and what we were, compared to ephemerals. I was only Esen-alit-Quar, who had a friend.

Paul, first and best.

And, maybe one day, this worried Human before me.

Who wasn't, to my chagrin, easily distracted. *Like Paul.* "We need to go, Esen. I've more questions than time—I trust you've a translight com? To reach Polit M'Lean—if I find out he's wrong, that is—" Evan's face was so delightfully transparent, I could see his concern shift from the Elves to his own future, then back again, with a determined, "Or not. There must be answers. I don't even know why the Darts who bit the Dokeci died."

"Happens all the time," I assured him. One being's meat, another being's poison was a truism of interplanetary travel and a significant problem for restaurants. I put my paws on the table. "I've a question for you, Evan Gooseberry," I told him. "Nothing you've said explains why you think the Dokeci and your superiors are wrong about the Elves."

"They told me."

A tendency of my Lishcyn-self was to circle around a point as long as possible; now I fully appreciated how Paul felt when I did. *If not how he resisted the urge to yell at me for it.* "Go on."

"Not that they *told* me," Evan said, which didn't help. "I—I know what paralyzing fear is, Esen. What it looks like. How beings show it. When the Elves' home was falling apart under them—they found a way to survive. Despite the most rudimentary communication with the Dokeci, the Elves understood they were being rescued and cooperated, pulling their population deep inside the shelter-city, letting the Dokeci send in instruments and equipment to keep them alive. They come to Dokeci-Na and, at first, willingly walked outside on a different planet. Interacted. Learned some comspeak. They're— their actions—" he qualified carefully, winning my approval, "—were pragmatic and even positive until the

Devil Darts attacked the Dokeci. When the Dokeci died, the Elves fled into their city and sealed all the doors."

But it hadn't been only the Dokeci who'd died, I thought. Devil Darts had, too. "Wait. That wasn't all that happened, Evan. You told me Burtles claimed the Dokeci were 'pumping poison.' You saw it for yourself. Be precise."

Lives could depend on it.

This was an intelligent being, who appreciated what I asked and why. Evan took his time and concentrated before he spoke. "According to the briefing, the Dokeci took three steps after the attacks. They donned enviro-suits when approaching the Elves' city. The Elves had seen these before and weren't alarmed. The Dokeci created a circular perimeter at a distance from the city to keep any Darts from escaping by sinking warn-offs below the soil—do you know what those are?"

I nodded. Tech to send pulses of high frequency sound outward, at levels that dissuaded a high percentage of organisms possessed of nervous systems to turn around. Quickly.

"They demonstrated a warn-off to the Elves first. When they didn't react, the Dokeci went ahead."

I growled. "A lack of response isn't agreement."

"The Dokeci acknowledged that, but what choice did they have? They faced a deadly threat and worse, the first dead Elf was brought out of the city. The Dokeci took this to mean the Devil Darts had been driven beneath the city and were attacking its inhabitants." Evan tapped the table three times. "Latest and last was the spray we saw being reapplied to the ground around the city. Hom Burtles assumed it was poison. We were told—" with self-conscious clarity, "—it was a passive restraint, a glue to prevent another Devil Dart from breaking through. The Dokeci offered to apply it within the city." A sober look.

Ah. "That's when the Elves sealed themselves away."

"That's when they panicked," Evan corrected. "According to Polit M'Lean, Ekwueme-ki said the Elves who'd been doing their calm best to understand the Dokeci grabbed one another, then turned and ran. Within moments, every opening into the city was plugged.

Since then, they scream and only come out to bring their dead. That," he finished with profound sadness, "is fear."

Maybe.

While I wasn't ready to fall in with Evan's view of events, I did agree with his doubt. Something wasn't right.

Plus, time to meet some Elves!

I stood on my tail, so it wouldn't wag. "Evan," I began in my best, serious tone. "I know exactly what to do."

He looked up at me with sudden hope. "What?"

"Field trip."

Hope shifted to a wary confusion I found quite familiar. *Did Humans practice it?* "I don't see how—"

"Under extraordinary circumstances, the collection can be accessed off-site. By myself. Leave all the details to me," I offered loftily. I, in turn, would leave them to my web-kin, who enjoyed reminding me she had starships at her disposal. "We'll . . ."

What was that?

I cocked my large ears for what had disturbed me. It came again, louder. A *rustle-sssslide* from overhead. Evan and I looked up at the same time.

"How big does a mousel get?"

"Not that big," I answered, only half paying attention. The sounds came from Paul's room, in the loft.

I'd have smelled him arriving.

Unless it wasn't him. I sniffed deeply. Among the delights of the kitchen was an abundance of odors, some I enjoyed more than Paul, and vice versa; more came on the still-damp breeze through the window screen. There were, under all that, the aromas of our life here.

Then there was Evan, with his distinct *ripe* of anxious, tired, and not-very-clean Human. Clouds of it. Enough to mask anyone else. I frowned distractedly at him. "Stay here."

I dropped to all fours, ignoring his scandalized gasp—yes, Lanivarians didn't *do* such things—and padded noiselessly into the hallway.

The farmhouse was divided into four rooms on this level: in order of size, the kitchen, my quarters, the accommodation—which was as properly modern and comfortable as money could buy, given the amount of hair I shed in several forms—and the cramped corner space the Ragems fondly named the "pantry." The pantry did contain shelves for food and hooks for coats, but mostly it was where a steep narrow staircase led into the stone-walled basement I refused to enter, and a steeper, narrower staircase led up to the loft and Paul's private place.

Where I didn't go.

That being the definition of "private" he'd patiently drilled into whatever head I had.

Paul would share living quarters, just not his own. He'd move into his partner's of the time. When he'd contracted with Char Largas and they'd raised their twins together, it had been with that understanding. Though Char would also disappear onto her starship regularly, so the twins would come to me.

I missed babysitting. Though it was one of those odd Human activities where the sitting part, when they were very young, was mostly running after them. They were also very fast. Faster than me. Then came the blissful phase with sitting, Luara and Tomas sharing my generous Lishcyn lap for a story or treat. Which ended too soon, and I was back to running after—only by then they had friends and weren't interested in me—

I swallowed a whine and focused on olfaction.

Two had used Paul's stairs, so recently their scent had warmth as well as shape. An Ervickian and—

Lowering my head, I let myself *SNARL* silently, lips rippling over my fangs.

Janet Chase.

I put a paw on the first step, so consumed with fury I completely forgot my promise to Paul never to enter his private place—

Which is how a Carasian was able to sneak up on me in the pantry.

15: Loft Afternoon

A Carasian shouldn't have fit through the farmhouse door, let alone inside our little pantry, but the claw presently around my midsection was proof otherwise. Stealth not a species' trait, curiosity might have overwhelmed me—

But *Chase* was in Paul's private place! I had to get up there. *Stop her!*

"Put me down!" I whispered, or tried to, it being hard enough to breathe while held in a claw. My paws and feet swam wildly through air and I couldn't even twist to look Lambo Reomattatii in the eyestalks—the wear on the claw distinctive, proving I was in the clutches of an employee. I panted to dump heat though exploding might be my only choice.

CLANG!

I flew up the stairwell. Having flung me aside, Lambo whirled on his attacker and before the echo of our antique metal frying pan hitting hardened shell faded, I'd bounded to the top, heading for the open door. I heard a roar and clatter from below, and hoped Evan kept running.

No Carasian could fit up the stairs behind me, a conviction that lasted until I heard the cracking protest of centuries-old wood and realized motivation could be a factor I hadn't considered.

I burst into the loft, shouldering aside a cowering

Ervickian, intent on the figure standing steps ahead. Hunter-focus shrank my senses to this Human female, this *INTRUDER,* my lips had never been so far back, and I might have gone for her throat without a thought—

Someone grabbed my tail! *AGAIN!* I curled on myself with that useful Lanivarian suppleness to *BITE* whomever dared—

"Es!"

I closed my teeth on my tongue instead of Paul's hand, blood filling my mouth.

He let go, staring past me at Chase. Seeing he looked more bewildered than angry, I shook myself from head to abused tail, a signal that relaxed both muscle and instinct, then rose to my feet and turned.

She hadn't aged well. An uncharitable thought I enjoyed greatly and would keep to myself.

Chase was small, for a Human. She'd lost whatever softness she'd possessed in the days when she'd captained the *Vegas Lass* for Largas Freight and been a *not-by-me* welcome guest at our home. She'd made no secret of her lust for Paul Cameron, though I admitted—grudgingly— she'd been decently polite about it in public.

Less so alone. I'd overheard her speaking against me to Paul, trying to undermine our friendship. *That nothing could?*

Didn't stop the growl deep in my throat.

She'd also proved to be a criminal, working with the nastier sorts from Inhaven to divert trade items, then conspiring to kidnap us. Reprehensible, yes. But most importantly? *She'd tried to undermine our friendship.*

"Hello, Paul," calm and cool. "You must be the new friend, Esen-alit-Quar."

On no level did I enjoy hearing my name fall from her mouth, but Chase didn't know *this* me. Before matters grew dangerously complex, I snapped, "Who are you?"

"This," Paul said tightly, "is a criminal named Janet Chase. Who should be in prison."

Her insolent shrug rippled the fine black mesh covering otherwise shabby, worn coveralls and boots. It had a hood, presently draped over her shoulders, and whether the mesh was holo-camouflage or full anti-scan tech, it was far too expensive to be here, on her, in our loft.

She'd another backer. But what would Chase or anyone else want in Paul's quarters?

The sanctum I hadn't seen till now was a disaster. His clothes littered the floor, the mattress was in shreds, and the walls were bare wood, empty of art. Much as I wanted to blame Chase for it all, surely I'd have heard this much destruction.

"You. Stay where you are," Paul snapped.

I'd forgotten her accomplice. Leaving Chase to him, I spun around only to see the Ervickian run back in the loft, escape foiled.

As if to explain, there was a loud rattle from the staircase, followed by a plaintive, "I'm stuck."

If Lambo was down there, how had Paul—I didn't wait to find out. "And who are you?" I demanded, nothing loath to establish my ignorance.

"Jumpy Lyn." Four eyes blinked at me. Late wismorph, I judged, old enough to be responsible to a crèche for its misdeeds, had it sired one. I had to doubt. Ervickians weren't picky, but Jumpy Lyn appeared a disgrace even by their standards. The sweater draped over its body had been purple and made for a Human. Bits of filthy tape hung like little tongues below the opening for its second mouth and its breath?

Had I not arrived in this form, I'd have cycled into something unable to smell.

"What's the game this time?"

Chase smiled at Paul, her augmented eyes glittering like ice. *We'd never learned what they could see—or transmit*, I thought suddenly.

Then wished I hadn't. Paul's privacy was already spoiled, not that I saw any reason he'd care. The loft was smaller than I'd realized, and along its length the sloped ceiling met walls only waist-high. There were windows in the walls to either end, neither large; both, to my discomfort, were obscured by cobwebs. *Dusting not a priority, then.*

I was the messier one. Paul was meticulous. *This wasn't like him.*

A discussion for another time and place, if he were willing. Although having been here once, surely I'd be allowed back—if only to dust—thoughts I put aside when Chase replied.

"You tell me, Paul Cameron. Oh, wait. Now it's Paul Ragem. Or is it both?"

"The constable's on the way," he said, not smiling. "If you've something to say to me, do it now."

"No, no, Tory!" Jumpy Lyn cried. "Mustn't say! Mustn't say!" At a glance from Chase, both mouths snapped shut.

She shook her head. "See what I have to put up with these days? Good help is so hard to find. What do I have to say to you, Paul?" The female walked forward with a swing of her hips. "Wherever shall we start?"

Really? I snorted, and she sent me a look of pure bile. "You're a trespasser and probably a thief," I informed her. "When the authorities arrive, you will be searched, thoroughly." Not that Constable Malcolm Lefebvre deserved that task, but he'd do it for Paul. The peace-loving former patroller was Rudy's uncle and, from what I'd heard of his past? Tough enough to deal with three Chases. *If they didn't run.*

"There's nothing here to steal," she assured me, then turned her attention back to Paul. "So, where's her logbook?"

My friend frowned, seeming as puzzled as I felt. "What are you talking about?"

From the stairwell, "The *Sidereal Pathfinder* logs!" the Carasian bellowed. "I'll pay more than she can!"

Paul glanced at me, brows raised.

I moved my snout left to right in denial. My memories held an abundance of examples of that name; none of them made any sense here. "You can explain to the constable," I told Chase.

The Ervickian erupted again. "No, no! Mustn't!"

"For once my colleague is correct." Chase pulled a weapon from her pocket—a blaster sized to her palm—aiming it midway between Paul and me. While a little late to remember Skalet's exhortation to *always disarm your opponent first,* I did take some comfort in knowing Chase wouldn't shoot Paul for several reasons, including pent-up lust, and couldn't kill me, though cycling now would be A Bad Idea.

Plus, an angry Carasian plugged the only exit, and the authorities were on their way.

If they were. I hadn't seen Paul call Malcolm, had I? *Bluffing was,* I sighed to myself, *a distinct possibility.*

"Get me the logbook, and we'll be gone."

"Com'ere and I'll gut you!" bellowed Lambo. "Grasis' Sucking Scum!" A hollow *BOOM* resounded.

True to its name, Jumpy Lyn leaped in the air, coming down to hug itself, crooning with anxiety. I felt my own and hoped the old farmhouse was as sturdy as the Hamlet of Hillsview Preservation Committee claimed, however much I doubted they'd anticipated testing-by-Carasian.

"What logbook?" Paul snapped. "What's 'pathfinder'? Make sense!"

Was that a flash of sympathy? Before I could be sure, Chase's lips spread in an unpleasant smile. "You sound like your father. A shame about his shop. I'd hate to see the same thing happen to your precious Library."

The threat sent my temperature soaring, and I dumped heat. I'd have preferred to explode, but the reflex was usually more trouble than it was worth—other than the temporary relief from stress.

Besides, I'd much rather be larger. *Much larger and with teeth.*

I looked down at the miserable Ervickian, and for a terrible moment all I saw was *available mass.*

A hand, cool against my overheated side. "Easy," Paul breathed more than spoke.

I shuddered, sane again.

Aloud, to Chase. "We're done here." Turning his back on her and her weapon, he led the way to the door. I followed, the fur on my back rising.

Instead of firing, Chase spoke. "The *Sidereal Path-finder* was Survey—a secret research ship sent into deep space twenty years ago. Her navigator was Veya Ragem."

Paul's mother?

He stopped, so I did. I watched the muscles along his jaw work, but he didn't turn around. "Veya Ragem is dead."

"I can tell you why. For a price."

We knew why, I thought, at first confused. There'd been an accident, the sort that happened all the time, space being the ultimate predator of the tech-dependent.

That wasn't what Chase implied. And from the sudden pallor and unfamiliar lines of Paul's face, blasting us might have been kinder, making it my turn to touch him, to ground him within our friendship.

He gave me a tiny, grateful nod before drawing a steadying breath. We turned to face our adversary once more.

"The *Sidereal Pathfinder*'s logs went missing," a voice boomed up the stairs. "Veya Ragem was accused of their theft and dishonorably discharged from Survey."

"You can shut up any time," Chase shouted, furious.

So it was true, then.

Paul hadn't been the only Ragem with secrets.

Inception

THEY believe.

I hear claws and breaths as they pass. Another wave leaving the Ever Dark, drawn by hope. I cannot bring myself to move with them.

Believing what I do.

That there is no hope, no up, no Rise.

Only the BURN. The betrayal of pain. I fear to go higher.

I cannot move. My offering is in vain.

Yet . . .

I do not Fall. We were told to fail is to Fall. Why do I not let go and accept?

I believe this is the end for me.

16: Loft Afternoon

ERSH would say *the real truth is in our flesh,* dismissing the fallible memory of ephemeral beings. Including written records, which she considered even less reliable, given the varied motives of their authors. *But she'd never known someone like Paul.*

An honorable being, brilliant and kind, doing his best to reclaim the life and people he remembered—as well as his kind could—suddenly finding both changed. I couldn't imagine the pain of not trusting what I was, what I knew.

The grief I could see in his eyes, before he collected himself. "We're taking this downstairs," he announced.

Chase waved her weapon as if making a point.

Paul stepped too close, holding out his hand. Before I could do anything at all, she'd slapped the blaster into his palm.

While a positive development, we still had a problem. "We can't go down," I pointed out. "Lambo's stuck on the stairs."

"Stuck!" the Carasian shouted.

Paul's lips quirked in that way I knew meant a secret, then he reached up and knocked on an exposed wooden rafter.

The ceiling cracked without a sound. A third of what had been rustic planks and plaster lowered smoothly to meet the floor, becoming a wide, carpeted staircase. I peered up, seeing a perfectly clear sky. "It's stopped raining." With selfish relief.

Chase and Jumpy Lyn looked up with greedy eyes. "So that's where you live," the Human murmured.

He did? I whined as I turned to my friend. Privacy was one thing. *What was this?*

Paul had the grace to blush. "You first, Fangface," he said, waving me up the stairs. I took them in two quick bounds, guessing I didn't have much time before they followed.

I stood on what appeared from the ground or sky to be the peaked, shingled roof of the Ragem family farmhouse, mossy on the north side. The Hamlet of Hillsview Preservation Committee would not be pleased to know Paul had had it removed.

In its place was this. The floor was carpeted—to muffle sound, I guessed, not for comfort. The walls and ceiling were invisible to the eye, the former not, I discovered, to the touch. The view was breathtaking. At night, there'd be stars from horizon to horizon. Now, as the clouds broke apart, I could see the hills and fields, the outbuilding with its oak, the gleam of Ragem Creek as it wandered the valley.

Over there, our Library, nestled in its Garden of unBotharan colors and shapes. An easi-rest faced that view, a small cabinet in reach.

There was nothing else.

It needed nothing else, I thought, then smiled to myself. *Except Paul.*

He came up the stairs with Janet Chase and Jumpy Lyn, meeting my look with a resigned shrug.

The Ervickian moved to the center of the room, crooning unhappily at being so exposed. Chase gazed around briefly, eyes touching on the furniture.

I stepped between, in case she planned to attack Paul's comfy place as she had his mattress. I'd need to bring him some straw for the night.

Or he could sleep with me. He had before, most recently when my Lishcyn-self had come down with a virus and been huddled in mucus-laden self-pity. I'd been about to cycle and rid myself of the microbes, but Paul arrived with soup and it seemed unnecessarily rude to send him away again.

"Where is she?" Chase demanded abruptly, spinning on her heel to face Paul. "Your scaly lump of a partner, Esolesy Ki." A thumb over her shoulder in my direction. "Or has your taste gone to fur these days?"

Paul laughed with such honest spontaneity I relaxed my jaw in an answering grin. "Esen-alit-Quar is the Library's Curator and a close friend. Esolesy Ki, not that you deserve to know, remains my friend and our partner. She's busy elsewhere." He looked over Chase at me.

Meaning Esolesy Ki the Lishcyn should make an appearance while Chase was around, to keep her guessing. Though Esen was my preference, I switched forms every so often. To explain why Esen and Esolesy weren't seen together, we'd relied on the ill-repute of Lishcyn stomachs and implied a violent sensitivity to Lanivarian dander. Not that my lovely pelt produced any such irritant, but both species were represented on Botharis by a sample size of, well, me. Our helpful staff went to great lengths to be sure "we" stayed safely apart.

To be Esolesy for Chase wouldn't be a problem.

In hindsight, never helpful, I should have guessed two mes would be the problem.

"Trapped here. Trapped high," the Ervickian moaned.

Neither of us trusted it—the species tended to the dramatic at the best of times. That there weren't more Ervickian actors had more to do with their eating habits than innate talent, but Paul gave Jumpy Lyn a compassionate look nonetheless. "We'll go."

I wanted to ask how. I wanted to ask about this room and what he gained from it, if his clothes were below and what had been his bed—not to mention the accommodation was on the ground floor. *Not in front of others.*

Most certainly not in front of Janet Chase, who'd a detestable smugness about her as if learning Paul's secrets let her possess some of him after all.

His eyes met mine, full of understanding and frank apology.

Then my so-mysterious friend said a word. "Exit."

An area of the wall at the back of the farmhouse shimmered, shaping a door-sized rectangle. Paul went to it and put his palm flat in the middle. Though nothing appeared to change, outside air ruffled my fur, bringing with it the rich scents of outside and picnics and *remember when we didn't have secrets.*

I wanted to whine. If this door opened onto another staircase, it meant Paul not only sought a private place—which I'd long known and accepted as his right—but a way to avoid me as he came and went from it.

If true, it was a hurt the likes of which I'd never experienced before. My tail tried to slip between my legs, my body heat rose, and maybe I was a coward, but I didn't want to find out. *I couldn't.* I eased toward the stairs to the loft, desperate to escape. "Lambo will need help," I explained, my voice nowhere near as firm as I'd intended.

Paul knew. How, I couldn't imagine, but he ignored Chase and Jumpy Lyn, speaking directly to me, his expression the gentle one I loved. "It's an emergency lift. I haven't tried it, but the techs assure me it will hold us both."

Any us. I saw that on his face, too, and had to stop my tail wagging. We'd been trapped before, Paul and I, and while I'd hoped it wouldn't happen again, trusting our new home?

He hadn't hoped or trusted. He'd prepared this, and who knew what else. For us. Our safety.

If we'd been alone, I'd have licked his nose. By the smile in his eyes, he knew that, too.

"So we're to test it for you?" Chase did not look happy. This moment kept getting better.

"Esen will go with you," Paul commanded.

I wrinkled my snout to show my blood-stained fangs, on the off chance she'd forgotten our first encounter and how nearly those fangs came to meeting in her flesh. *Not that I'd taste her willingly,* I thought with an inner shudder.

Not something Chase needed to know.

Perception

RIGHTLY concerned by the *SNAPSNAP* of claws behind him, Evan dropped the heavy pan and dashed down the hallway—leaping over the disgustingly stained rug—and out the door through which he'd arrived.

Evan kept running, having momentum not to be wasted and the lane sloped gently down toward the Library, speeding his pace. In fact, he might have run all the way to the Library, having determined to get help, if it hadn't been for the mousel.

When the malignant speck of brown darted across his path, Evan leaped and twisted away, instead of sensibly jumping over it. He came down with his legs in a tangle, landing on his back hard enough to drive the breath from his already gasping lungs.

Sprinting and, to be honest, any form of sweaty fitness hadn't seemed important to his career as a diplomat. *He'd have to amend that*, he thought, rather dizzy and unable to move. He stared at the sky, pleasantly full of sun-kissed clouds, and decided, since there were no sounds of clattering pursuit, he should stay like this a while longer.

Until he felt *something* slip up his pant leg. A squirmy, *SOFT* SOMETHING!

Evan was on his feet in an instant, hopping in wild circles. *Something* brown bounced on the ground and squeaked in outrage.

Puffed up, it scurried *toward* him.

So he ran.

And ran—paying attention to nothing but the ground and what might be on it—until an unfamiliar pain in his side brought him to a staggering stop.

Hands on his knees, heaving for air and quite certain he couldn't run another step, Evan looked warily around, embarrassed to have fled from something smaller than his hand, but relieved, too. *No mousels.*

No Library!

His relief vanished under waves of self-disgust. In blindly fleeing the mousel, he'd managed to turn himself around and run most of the way back to the farmhouse, instead of toward help.

Great Gran Gooseberry could cite a wealth of anecdotes from The Lore involving Gooseberrys of the past who'd taken desperate chances for some cause or other because they'd left themselves no other choice, and he'd best be smarter or—*unspeakable horror and blame!*—fail to produce the next new Gooseberry.

Esen was in the farmhouse with an enraged Carasian. In his present state, he'd take too long to reach the Library and be too late bringing help.

Out of choices, Evan found himself suddenly sympathetic to his antecedents. He'd have to be that help.

So in he went.

🖐

Evan walked on the revolting carpet because it deadened his footsteps. Rather than pick up his pan, he elected a longer weapon, pulling one of the filthy implements—a shovel—from its fellows in the bucket, moving very slowly, sweating until it cleared without a sound. Shovel in hand, the business end over his shoulder but angled to clear the odd low-hanging lights, the Human edged forward.

A subdued rattle made him freeze in place.

Nothing.

What now?

No doubt there were tried and tested official diplomatic protocols for those skulking through a house infested by a Carasian, along with other hazardous activities; he'd neglected to find them, that was all. On his return to the embassy, Evan vowed as he eased into the small room, not only would he sprint daily, he'd ask Lisam and Lynelle for lessons. The security pair might tease him, but anything was better than this—this *fumbling inadequacy.*

He'd a shovel. What he thought was a shovel, anyway. Without the slightest idea how to use it.

Admittedly, he'd once chased a thief through a crowd, but in hindsight he hadn't caught anyone, being himself kidnapped by Bess. Evan held in a wistful sigh, wishing he had Bess with him right now. The fearless child would skulk through this farmhouse with calm confidence.

"Who's there?" The voice was low and deep—and anxious. "I know you're there. Grasis' Sucking Scum! You won't get away with this. Authority's com'n!"

"Well, that's a relief," Evan proclaimed and started to put down the shovel.

At the thunderous *BOOM* shaking the walls, he picked it up again. "It's all right," he said hastily. "I'm—" not the authorities, and "a diplomat" hardly seemed likely to appease the Carasian. "I'm Evan. Evan Gooseberry. Don't be afraid."

"WHO'S AFRAID!?"

A forlorn chunk of plaster tumbled down the staircase, landing near his feet.

Ready to jump back, Evan eased to where he could peek up the stairs, squinting to see through air filled with motes of settling plaster dust. It looked as though someone had rammed a dented, black freightcar into an opening too small for it by half, a freightcar now firmly wedged into what remained of the walls to either side.

This Carasian wasn't chasing anyone, at least for the moment.

"Please accept my apologies." Evan put down the shovel. "Are you injured?" He couldn't tell. Part of the massive body was *inside* the right-hand wall; presumably those claws were, too. The top and bottom chitinous plates of the being's head pulsed slightly, but with a steady rhythm, which Evan took for a positive sign, though the edges had already scraped away layers of colored paper and were into the plaster. Despite Esen's claim it would take explosives to renovate this sturdy old building, he had to wonder—

An eyestalk wobbled into view. "I'm stuck, you fool."

That he was. The giant's efforts to free himself had made it worse. Evan bent to take a look. As he feared, the Carasian's thick legs had broken through the stairs. Splinters of wood that would have impaled anything softer had shattered against armor plate. That didn't mean he'd escaped harm. Fresh gouges crisscrossed existing ones, and it'd take a molt to remove the damage.

Still, this was the being who'd grabbed poor Esen in one enormous claw, then dangled her, paws running in midair. Who might have done worse, if not for his frying pan—

Where was Esen? What if, after he'd run from the house, the Carasian had pursued her up these stairs?

She couldn't come down again.

So, still upstairs. But had Esen found the source of the noise? Or—he licked dry, dusty lips, had the source found her? What should he do now? Shout to let her know he was here, or keep quiet in case she was hiding?

Briefing notes. He needed notes. Did security have—

"Hey, Gooseberd," the Carasian rumbled suspiciously. "Whatcha up to back there? Huh?"

He'd no choice. "Esen!" he shouted at the top of his lungs. "It's Evan. I'm down here!"

A disgusted rattle. "Seventeen Sandy Hells, Human. They're long gone."

He'd ask about "they" later. "To get the authorities?"

"How should I know?" Another rattle. "We didn't discuss it." With considerable sarcasm.

Evan supposed he'd be testy also, if their places were reversed. First things first, then. Botharis was a Human planet; it wasn't part of the Commonwealth, but as the Commonwealth's—therefore Human—representative on the spot, he was responsible for interspecies' relations.

Can't leave the poor thing like this. "I'm coming up. Hold still."

Before the startled Carasian could do more than grunt,

Evan was climbing. He'd liked climbing the cliffs near home, until Great Gran caught him at it and made him watch gruesome vids of falls. Who knew she'd been prepared to avert such recklessness in the Gooseberry line?

This climb was easier, the carapace roughened with wear and speckled with finger-sized scars. *Why? Where had the Carasian been?*

Where he was being the more crucial at the moment, Evan focused on his task. He stopped short of the head. "Please retract your eyes, Hom."

The body beneath him shuddered with violent effort, not to help, but to shake him off. Wood creaked and cracked, plaster rose in choking clouds, and Evan clung to what he could until the Carasian went still again. He spat out dust before saying, as patiently as possible, "I can't see past you, so I have to get to the stairs above. I really don't think anyone can help until your situation is properly assessed."

Evan took the ensuing silence for permission and reached for the head, trying to avoid the eyestalks.

A claw larger than his body appeared above him, coated in dust that only added to its menace. He froze in place, gripping the Carasian with both hands. "I won't tell any—"

The claw closed terrifyingly near to his face, the tips meeting. Past the tips, the ridges were so worn, there was a considerable gap. "Hurry up, then."

Evan collected himself, and his nerve, then took hold of the claw. The Carasian lifted him up and over with ease. Given the circumstances, he forgave being shaken off like lint once clear of the creature, even if he did drop painfully to the stairs.

A row of dusty black eyeballs regarded him, the stalks of a couple badly twisted, and Evan thought he detected a certain wild desperation in that gaze.

Little wonder. From this end, matters were worse. The Carasian was entombed, his right side and claws deep in one wall, his left not so deeply in the other but with that handling claw punched through a bit higher, giving a nasty twist to the whole.

They'd have to tear the farmhouse apart, if they could, and even then—

"We'll have you out of here in no time," Evan said firmly, on the tried and true tenet that under no circumstances did you upset a Carasian. Especially one with a claw in reach. Most especially one whose continued struggles could conceivably cause the staircase and associated structure to collapse around them both.

He sat on a stair, deliberately in reach. "So, tell me about yourself."

Eyestalks whirled in confusion. "What?"

"If Esen isn't here, help's on the way." Of that he was convinced. The Lanivarian struck him as a being who cared for others. *Then there was Paul*—Evan switched thoughts immediately, feeling his face grow warm. "We just have to wait." He casually brushed dust from his sleeve. "I work on Dokeci-Na—or did." He always seemed to have to qualify that. "I'm here to consult the Library. You work there, don't you? As—a cook?" The unlikely apron he'd seen on the Carasian in the lobby was now a shredded rag pinned by a splinter the size of his wrist to a stair.

The eyes had settled, a disquieting but attentive fix on his face. "I operate the food dispenser. My name's Lambo Reomattatii."

Progress. The Carasian understood the seriousness of his predicament; that didn't protect them from instinct and reflexes evolved to do battle. "It looks like a very complicated device."

"It's not." A grunt, almost amused. "I'm a drive engineer."

Making the intellect within those dented head plates a remarkable one indeed. "Then why did you grab Esen?" Evan asked, too worried to care about the abrupt change in the Carasian's speech patterns.

"I was to stop her going upstairs." Eyestalks bent up. "Someone dangerous was there." They lowered to gaze at him. "Then you hit me." With approval.

"'Dangerous'?" Evan echoed, barely managing not to squeak. "Is Esen all right?"

"The director arrived," with satisfaction. "He did as you did. Climbed up and over me and, from what I overheard, he and Esen dealt with the intruders. They've left. But—" Lambo subsided with a creak of wood. "I told the director I only pretended to be stuck."

Evan stared at him. "So they might not send help."

A sigh like rain on a 'brella. "They might not. The director is sensible. He'll take the intruders to the Library first and contain the threat. He'll expect me to return to the Chow. Perhaps I will be missed. Perhaps not for some time."

"Then we—eek!" Evan squeaked as the staircase beneath them lurched! He grabbed the claw Lambo offered for support, his heart pounding. The movement stopped. "We can't wait."

"I concur. You must leave at once, Evan Gooseberry," Lambo said all too calmly. "Go! Hurry! Bring back assistance." His claw opened. Moved closer.

"No!" Evan scrambled backward on hands and feet up the next stairs, stopping out of reach. "You have to molt, Lambo. Now!"

The Carasian became a statue, gray-black and streaked with debris.

"You're due," Evan insisted. "Past due." The new chitin would be pliable—for a short time, but they didn't have more. "You can climb out yourself. Of yourself, I mean."

"I won't," Lambo said very quietly. "If I do, I won't be the same."

He'd never heard of a Carasian afraid to molt before. Cautious about doing so on beaches, where there could be sand fleas able to burrow through the temporarily soft carapace, but this? Of course, there was the too-obvious reason. "What," he said half-jokingly, "You'll be a mature female and eat me?"

When Lambo didn't answer, Evan felt the blood drain from his face. "Oh. You will."

"It must happen," quietly, surely. "Soon. If not this molt, then my next. I shall grow and become superb—but there is a cost. I lose this." The great claw moved gently between them. "I'm not ready, Evan, to assume the proud mantle of my sex. I haven't accomplished what I intend. I haven't found what I seek. I cannot continue the search myself if I'm—" The claw *SNAPPED* near his foot with nightmarish speed.

Somehow, Evan managed not to pull it back. Lambo's new chitin was compressed inside that hard outer case, like a spring. "If the stairs collapse," he reasoned quickly, "or you're damaged when they try to get you out, you could—" *no tactful way to say it,* "—crack and molt anyway. Isn't it better to do it now, when it's the two of us? I promise to run," he added, with emphasis.

"You sound as though you know us, Human." An intimidating *rattle.* "How can you?"

He'd read a great deal? Carasians being fascinating and, for a change, a species that didn't trigger any of his *FEARS*—which was why he'd decided to work with the Dokeci, who did. Only struggle moved you forward— Great Gran understood. Evan focused. "I'll tell you later. Please, Lambo. Trust me."

"Prove what you know. Come close," in a voice so deep, dust danced in the air. Lambo's eyestalks parted, and two needle-tipped jaws emerged.

Reading about this ritual didn't help a bit. Evan rose slowly, getting his balance. That ominous waiting claw didn't help either. If he failed, Lambo would toss him down the stairs and he'd have no choice but to run for help. He'd be too late.

Nothing to worry about, Evan told himself, trembling to his core. Basic diplomacy. Respect the customs of others—even if they could kill you. He stepped down. One stair, two, until he stood in the Carasian's shadow, his face between those threatening jaws.

The tips pressed his cheeks, once, as lightly as a butterfly wing. Tears of joy—and probably relief, but mostly an incredible, undeniable warmth—filled his eyes.

The jaws retracted, and Lambo gently pushed him back with that great claw. "Very well, Evan Gooseberry," the giant said. "I will do as you suggest."

He blinked, feeling moisture track down his face, knowing he'd never forget this moment. "How can I help?" There'd been something about peeling, the need for a starting point—a crack. *Why hadn't he kept the shovel, or the pan?*

Lambo's eyes retracted, her head plates slamming close. "Get as far from me as you can," she ordered, her voice muffled.

The great claw rose, then swiveled the wrong way on a joint with a horrible *tearing* protest, but it kept moving, opening to grip the front of her head—

Evan turned and ran up the stairs. He staggered into the room above, behind him a *CRACK-CRUNCH!!* which would have been disturbing—but the Carasian's impassioned *HOWL* wiped everything but flight from his brain.

17: Greenhouse Afternoon

OUR design for the All Species' Library of Linguistics and Culture hadn't included provision for Chase or her cronies. Perhaps we'd been, as Skalet put it, "foolishly optimistic"; nonetheless, we'd refused to add a dungeon just to make her happy.

However handy it might be now.

We'd abandoned Evan Gooseberry and Lambo, taking a secret lift to a secret hanger implausibly *above* the secret hidden room—where a roof appeared to be—to pile into a sleek aircar and zip to, yes, my Garden.

Through a Kraal field that didn't turn us into harmless ash, implying either collusion with a certain Web-being, or a devious work-around that shouldn't exist.

And who knew that secluded patio so dear to Paul's heart and plans was a landing pad, too? Certainly not me.

Unsettling described it. Three hours ago, I'd planned to put tables on it for his family, complete with the sacrifice of flowers. Just as well they hadn't come, I decided, considering how our day was going.

Now we gathered in the greenhouse, steps from the aircar and patio-now-landing pad. I'd have indulged in some self-pity at the intrusion if Paul hadn't suffered a far deeper indignity.

Still, this was *my* space. The Garden spread over fifty rolling acres, in Botharan terms, cupping the Library within one edge. Paths for clients so far accessed only a quarter. Even with the largest specimens we could import, it would take a Human lifetime for every part to grow together in the natural-as-possible scheme I'd set out—and at no point could what grew here be neglected. The more "effortless" the Garden, the harder the work behind it, and this sturdy, practical greenhouse was the heart of it all.

That it was usually warm and mostly dry and always fragrant in here, through the varied local seasons, was simply good planning on my part.

If the Library was the current Botharan ideal of exotic, alien architecture, my greenhouse was the opposite. Built in Paul's great-great grandparents' time, Skaletmemory remembered a glittering conservatory—the jewel of Grandine's brand new park—built as a nostalgic tribute to the original settlers.

In other words, a place to exhibit those fabled plants Humans hadn't been able to grow here—no matter how they'd tried—so future generations could see, smell, but please, not touch, what they were missing.

Generations later, tastes and needs having changed along with agricultural accomplishments, the Botharans found themselves with a conservatory full of plants no longer relevant and in fact slightly embarrassing. Why admire a "rose" when the modified native version was twice as lovely? Needless to say, what Humans called "roses" wasn't the same plant on any two planets; roses on Yelldyn 732 migrated on spiny little feet and were not plants at all—

The conservatory went from beloved landmark to forgotten to, after decades of neglect, so much scrap. Duggs found most of it in a twisted pile, waiting to be recycled, and I'd had the pieces brought here. The original plans were on record, letting Duggs replicate whatever was missing.

Thick metalwork arched overhead, supporting real glass between clawlike clamps. Ventilation was achieved by twisting ornate handles that turned panels along whatever side brought a breeze. It glistened in sunlight like an enormous gem left among the surrounding trees and ferns, filled with urgent seedlings and the earthy smell of compost.

When it rained, seams leaked and the entire structure attracted lightning, hence the rods and wires to the ground. At the height of summer, the inside sizzled; in winter's chill, clouds of condensation, with occasional icicles, formed. Colonies of tiny Botharan bats slept in the lofty twinned peaks of the roof—and how they got in and out with the vents closed I'd yet to discover—and while we'd gone with a perfectly modern floor and plumbing, I'd yet to keep out mousels.

I loved it.

And shared it. During the Garden's formative months, there'd been a succession of ground crews and hired specialists to do the major preparation and planting. Now a rotating staff of interns mulched, tidied, and observed, it being more useful for all concerned, and safer for the plants, to have them ask me about anything alien. At the moment, I'd fourteen graduate students from the four universities of the Botharan capital, Grandine, interested in alien flora, plus the first apprentice from "down the valley" who didn't cringe at what I'd done with the place. All were free to wander in and out of the greenhouse as required.

Unless I'd hung the flag.

It was a paw towel Paul had given me, printed with red shrimp things. Smiling shrimp things. With Humanish teeth. After much use, it was more rag than towel, but I refused to part with it. I'd hang this distinctive if improbable flag on its hook by the greenhouse entrance to warn others when I was communing with the plants and under no circumstances to be disturbed.

Not a lie—*appropriate phrasing*, as Ersh would say. Assimilating plant mass into more of my own was arguably a communion of a sort and I'd a healthy crop of duras in pots throughout the greenhouse for that purpose.

Being safely unaware of the truth, I imagined some of those who worked for me snickered behind my back. I didn't care. Others took the appearance of the flag as their signal to read on a bench or visit the Chow between breaks.

Also, not my concern. I tested my flag's effectiveness often enough to catch any new arrivals inclined to peek inside.

It hung outside now.

We'd moved inside, to a clean stretch of counter. On it, Paul had spread a portable access screen and was busy doing something with it. He'd summoned Skalet, that much I knew.

I watched our guests.

Chase behaved, standing peacefully where she'd been told, in my dim view a sign she was pleased by the direction of events. I'd have been pleased by how Jumpy Lyn clung to the Human like a shadow, the pungent aroma of its digesting meal hovering around them like a cloud, except it seemed more a demonstration of Chase's imperturbability.

Unless she'd no sense of smell.

My Lanivarian-self possessed a predatory fixed stare I liked to think was intimidating and Rudy, when I'd tried it on him, kindly said it made me look hungry. Which I usually was, so I wasn't entirely convinced, but right now, I'd that remembered urge to *BITE* behind my stare. It made Jumpy Lyn anxious, adding to its odor, but Chase?

I might not have existed. Her augmented gaze never left Paul. A convenient stack of recently emptied compost bags were in reach under the counter and I'd have happily put one over her head.

But Paul didn't appear concerned. His fingers raked back a tumbled lock of hair absently, his focus on whatever showed on the screen.

I was concerned, enough for us both. What could be in this mysterious logbook worth all this? *If it existed*, I cautioned myself, well aware we'd only Chase's word. A being devious to the core.

Witness how she'd snuck into our farmhouse during the confusion caused by the Library's alarm, said alarm supposed to forestall any sneaking. Which I kindly didn't point out to Paul as he was already a smidge aggrieved on the whole matter.

It being news to Paul that his mother had been the navigator of this *Sidereal Pathfinder,* with Chase hinting her subsequent death hadn't been an accident?

My friend was more than a smidge upset about that.

Adding to my concerns? Our surly Carasian. Was he working alone—or did he answer to Chase?

Or Paul? That felt far more likely, if another puzzle. Not that it mattered. What did, above all, was Evan and his Elves, something I desperately needed to tell Paul, *now.*

Chase chose that instant to look at me. I showed her my fangs in frustration. Now *wasn't the time.*

Hearing familiar footsteps, I cocked an ear in welcome.

A welcome that lasted until I saw who'd arrived with Skalet.

Their names were Palarander Todd and Sly Nides, and I didn't need to smell them to know these were the two Humans who'd come with Chase and abused Evan.

Though to be honest I couldn't help but smell all of that—along with a puzzling hint of Iftsen.

Skalet had dressed them in Library maintenance coveralls and returned their weapons—or given them new ones—now slung at their hips. The pair, looking revoltingly smug, stood at attention behind my web-kin. All they needed were half-erased facial tattoos and they'd resemble those rare unfortunate Kraal who'd shamed their affiliations and eked out a living as muscle on some backwater world instead of dying as they should.

I'd caught the dismay, fleeting but stark, on Chase's face, and could almost forgive Skalet.

Almost. "You can't be serious," I told her.

"I am always serious." But her thin lips curved. "These fine, capable Humans recognized a superior opportunity when it was—presented."

At a guess, they'd adequate survival skills and recognized the only choice left.

"They're your responsibility," Paul stated, unamused but, I thought, not surprised either.

The curve widened. "I assure you, they are aware of their commitment."

Both paled. The bearded one swallowed.

"In addition, I've acquired three Iftsen enviro-suits, modified to fit humanoids," Skalet went on, her voice smooth as heavy silk. *Explaining the scent.* Her drifting gaze alighted on Chase, as if by accident. "And quite the story."

"And who might you be?" Chase demanded tightly. "Other than a Kraal thug."

Paul closed and tucked away his access screen. "Library security, Janet."

The two hadn't met until this moment, though Skalet had my memories of Chase: those I'd deemed necessary, not the embarrassing ones. Now, Skalet closed the distance between them with two deceptive easy strides. Seizing Chase's chin, she tilted the Human's face to the light, then let go with a dismissive chuckle. "I hope you kept the originals."

"Of course not," with defiance. "It's too late, Kraal. I've seen your face and affiliations—and I'm not the only one. Hear me?"

Paul stilled, understanding.

I went cold, because he couldn't, not as I did. Paul knew we were ourselves, in whatever form. I, *this* Lanivarian and no other; Skalet, *this* Kraal, S'kal-ru, and no other.

What Paul didn't know?

Skalet's fierce, unweb-like determination to remain among Kraal, to continue S'kal-ru. After a singularly foolish, in Ersh's view, attempt to improve her station among them, Ersh had forbidden Skalet this form for two generations, but she'd found her way back or been unable to resist it. All along, she'd protected her identity—reborn, remade, reinvented, yet always, inevitably, *this* version. Stealth and cleverness were her preference, disguise and lies her tools, but when those failed?

Skalet was surgical in her finesse. Literally. *The pin, not the dagger, Youngest,* she'd tell me. *Pay attention.*

Did Chase know she'd just signed her own death warrant—and that of whomever else had seen? Face-to-face, the two were mirror images, Skalet cool and dangerous, Chase flushed with temper and, perhaps, the beginnings of fear.

"I do hear you, Janet Chase." Skalet said, after a calculated delay that raised the fur on my neck. "Though I prefer to use the name your parents did: Victory Johnsson. As for your pretty lenses? I rerouted their signal before you entered this building. From that moment, everything you witness goes only to me."

"That's impossible. No one—" Something in Skalet's smile made Chase—no, Johnsson, *a name free of our home and her betrayal*—shut her mouth on whatever she'd thought to say. She stood, trembling, fists clenched at her sides, those betraying eyes full of hate.

Paul stirred. "Do you have access to previous data?"

The smile turned to him. "Alas, no. I have access to her, however."

Cosmic Gods. A blatant offer, from a being who knew more ways to extract information from those unwilling than anyone should. Did my web-kin honestly believe Paul Ragem, upset or not, would take it?

Johnsson did. Jumpy Lyn belched fearfully, and the Human flinched.

My so-clever friend propped his hip on the counter, his expression almost bored. "Let's see if our guest will answer polite questions, shall we?" He turned to Johnsson. "Victory, it's time to cut your losses."

Believing she knew his limits—*though I could have enlightened her*—Johnsson might have bluffed. Not so, now. She gave a last searing look at Skalet, then deliberately relaxed. "Where do you want me to start?"

Perception

CLOTHES tripped him. They were strewn every-where, along with the stuffing from a mattress, and after the second step entangled in fabric, Evan forced himself to stop. He did so, hunched over and shaking, but who wouldn't?

Hearing what he could.

Reading hadn't prepared him for the violent urgency of a Carasian's molt, especially one so long deferred. Impacts echoed. More *crunching*—

The floor vibrated to another *BOOM!*

Evan looked through his bent arm toward the door-way, half-expecting to see pieces of black shell flying through the air. From the sounds, amplified by the stair-well, Lambo was self-destructing like the machine she resembled.

Except she was . . . *singing.*

Loudly. It wasn't melodic, and her loud voice hit minor keys that made him wince, which would have been fine because music was really a personal as well as species' choice, but hers?

Held a fearsome triumph.

Suggesting he'd best find a way out of this room, and quickly.

Evan ignored the windows, as they were too small and covered in *COBWEBS* and he'd enough on his mind at the moment to deal with the thought of *SPIDERS.*

He spun in a circle, searching the walls. The staircase—before Lambo—had been finished, but this part of the farmhouse was almost primitive.

Paul lived here?

Quaint, Evan thought staunchly. When not so disheveled—

"Hu-man?"

It wasn't as though she didn't know where he was. Evan faced the door, swallowed, then made himself answer. "I'm here. Are you—out?"

"I need you." A desperate, low rumble.

He took a single step, then froze. "Do you need me because you're hungry? Because I'd rather not, if you don't mind."

Another rumble. Hardly reassurance, but Evan decided it was the best he'd get. He eased to the open door—

—backing quickly as an enormous, glistening black claw, perfect in every way, waved above his head. "Don't eat me!" he shouted.

"I won't eat you or anyone else," Lambo replied, speaking very quickly. "But if you don't help me NOW! I'll harden where I am."

Evan dashed into the stairwell.

Old and new Lambo blended in a confusion of dull versus shiny new black. The new was mostly free—and enlarging before his eyes, the still-pliable chitin expanding to allow the Carasian a significant growth spurt. The head was, to Evan's vast relief, identical to the one pre-molt, eyestalks now pristine within flawless plates. Not a predator—not yet.

The giant lurched toward him, claws gripping the stairs. The feet were free, then. What was the—

That one claw remained inside the wall, somehow caught on the old shell.

"Pardon me." Evan didn't wait for an answer, clambering over the Carasian once more. His boots dimpled new shell and she uttered involuntary grunts. Distress, not pain, he guessed. This was the only time the adults were vulnerable, and it couldn't be pleasant. He'd worry about leaving footprints after saving her.

He reached the joint of the claw and grabbed it, but

though soft enough that his fingers sank in, beneath was as rigid as a metal girder. "Lambo. Stop pulling," he ordered. "Trust me."

What he held relaxed. "Good." There was a gap now, and hurriedly Evan stretched out along it, reaching inside. He winced as razor-edged shards cut his hands, but he didn't stop. *Couldn't.* He could feel the shell beginning to harden. Coughing as dust filled his mouth and nose, he wriggled to the wall, inserting his head within the remnants of the original claw. An edge sliced open his cheek—*almost there.*

His fingers closed on what had to be the new clawtip. Lost their grip—*why was it slippery?*—regained it. Refusing to worry what he might be doing to the tissue, Evan pulled back with all his strength.

POP!

He tumbled, caught by a gentle claw, seeing a red-streaked second claw lift into the air.

"Let's get outta here," Lambo rumbled. With a now-joyful *ROAR,* she thrust upward, squeezing herself along what was left of the stairwell and in through the door to the loft, holding Evan suspended in front like a flag.

After setting him down with care, Lambo collapsed on Paul's clothes. "Oh, my," she said weakly. "I don't ever want to do *that* again."

Collapsing was an excellent idea. Evan dropped where he was, sitting upright only because he'd been put against the mattress. "Agreed," he panted. "I hope I didn't—" *what did one say?* "—bend anything."

Eyestalks shifted this way and that, inspecting. She raised each claw into their regard, closing them slowly. The glisten was fading, replaced by a solid sheen. "I am truly magnificent," she announced with casual pride. Her eyestalks converged on him. "Thanks to you, Evan. I deeply regret your damage."

His? Wondering what she meant, Evan looked down at himself, shocked to see his hands and wrists wet with blood. More drops fell, and he raised now-shaking fingers, finding a hot slickness below his left eye. "Oh, this isn't good," he said, or thought he said.

Before everything went black.

18: Basement Afternoon

I was no stranger to the selfless courage of Humans. What Evan Gooseberry had done for Lambo was no more than Paul had done for me, many times.

Experience didn't make seeing the young diplomat unconscious on a cot, face and hands coated in medplas, any easier. "I should have gone back."

"And I shouldn't have left them, no matter what Lambo said." Paul ran a hand through his hair. "I let Johnsson—and her nonsense—distract me. None of that matters."

All of it did. But I agreed with my friend. What Johnsson had told us of the *Sidereal Pathfinder* and his mother—however troubling—was history. It could wait.

The Elves of Dokeci-Na? Might not have that luxury. While Duggs treated Evan's injuries—her calm "seen worse on the job site" attitude a comfort—I'd told Paul what little I knew.

Leaving out the part where I'd planned to go with Evan and meet this shiny new, if endangered, sentient species in person.

Since Paul had given me *that look* when I'd finished, it was possible I hadn't needed to bother.

"What do we do now?" I asked quietly. Because it wasn't up to me alone. Because we'd important responsibilities.

Most of all, because I trusted him.

"Now?" Paul rested his fingers on Evan's shoulder. "Whatever we can, Old Blob."

My ears rose in feigned surprise. "We?"

A dimple appeared. "You don't think I'd let you meet a new species without me, do you?"

I'd certainly hoped not.

Relaxing my jaw in a grin, I merely replied, "Field trip it is."

"Eat somewhere else, scum!" The claw, freshly immaculate in its black gleam, left a deep new dent in the Chow's abused food dispenser.

Clearly the molt hadn't helped the mood, though Lambo Reomattatii did look much better, other than the faint, now-permanent bootprints on his/her carapace. Bigger, if not yet her full size and ultimate shape.

Fortunately, or there'd be nothing of Evan to mend.

For now, the only threat to safety or machine posed by this Carasian was temper. *That I could deal with*, I decided, perhaps optimistically, but you didn't grow up as I had without learning to appease those furious at you. "You don't have to go back to work—right away," I qualified hastily as the being whirled to glare at me. "Or you can. I'm here to apologize. What happened to you and Evan was my fault. I'm sorry."

Lambo's raised claws lowered, slightly. "You shouldn't have rushed into danger."

"You're absolutely right." *At least not when someone was watching.*

They sank a notch lower. "You were stupid."

I preferred charmingly impulsive, but whatever worked. "Yes, I was."

To the floor. "Stupid Celi abandoned the Chow. Ungrateful wretch. When I find him—" a menacing rumble.

The change of topic took me by surprise, but I chose not to complain about the withered remains of my poor fystia. Celi had enjoyed a good nap in them, at least. "You mustn't threaten a—"

"And you abandon Evan. Again! Grasis' Sucking Scum," in a melancholy mumble.

Ah. Neither I nor Celi was the object of this particular tantrum. "Evan needs to rest, undisturbed. That's important for Humans."

Especially one who'd been through a tough few days and nights before lacerating hands and face. Lambo's bellowing, accompanied by the wanton destruction of a good part of the wall around the window facing the Library, had alerted Garden staff. They'd come looking for us, dealing with a Carasian trapped in a loft not remotely in their job descriptions.

By the time we'd arrived, it was over. Lambo had lowered Evan in a sheet. She'd then jumped down, the species agile for something so massive, ruining the Botharan rosebushes planted by Paul's great-great-grandfather, but Evan was intact, if alarmingly still.

Duggs had sealed his deepest wound, a cut on Evan's face, and pronounced the rest "not worth mentioning." Then again, our head contractor was scarred from head to toe. If Evan needed his lovely skin repaired properly, the Library would take care of it. We would.

I put my paws on the counter, regarding Lambo. "Evan helped you because it's his nature. He's—" I wanted to say *a good person*, but the Human expression didn't translate well into Carasian mores. "He acts responsibly and with courage."

A subdued rattle. "Yes."

Despite Lambo's past conduct, I believed I faced a being who did the same. "You came with Paul to the farmhouse, in case Johnsson was here."

Eyestalks whirled. Tension, not denial. *I'd thought so.* "When you saw me about to run into her, you tried to stop me."

A claw snapped. "I did stop you."

I conceded the point. "But when you followed me up the stairs, I don't think you were trying to catch me anymore—you were trying to get to Johnsson yourself. Why?"

An unnerving focus. "The female talked to you, didn't

she?" Gone were the surly tone and shipcity dregs' dialect; her posture altered, too, subtly different. Confidence, rather than bluster. "A trade, then, Esen-alit-Quar. Information, for information." A delicate *snap*. "Or do you need the director's permission to share?"

If she only knew . . . I kept my voice even. "Paul sent me here to do just that. The female's name is Victory Johnsson. She told us the *Sidereal Pathfinder* was destroyed during a test of a revolutionary new star drive. That ship's crew, including Veya Ragem, escaped in lifepods, all but those working in her engine room. The data from the ship's final tests was lost. All that remained were the navigator's logs."

"Which, by protocol, Ragem kept with her." Another *snap*.

"You said she stole them," I countered. "That she left Survey in disgrace." A service Paul believed she'd left for good years earlier. *Secrets upon secrets.*

"I said she was accused and dishonorably discharged," Lambo corrected. "The accusation couldn't be proved. By what I've learned—and I will not share my sources—Ragem claimed she handled the ship's logs properly, handing them to the appropriate superior officers as she stepped from her lifepod. They denied receiving them."

Johnsson hadn't known that—or told us. "They lied."

"A working hypothesis." Eyestalks glinted. "A thorough search of her pod and the rescue ship failed to locate the logs. There was sufficient doubt that Ragem was discharged without further penalty."

Other than her future. "Johnsson believes Veya Ragem kept them. That she died when her ship was destroyed by someone after the *Sidereal Pathfinder* logs." My voice held a growl; I'd seen Paul's face.

Worse, if possible, I knew he mourned more than his mother. The *Smokebat* had been lost with all hands. Like most such small freighters, like most of Largas Freight's fleet, the ship would have been home as well as employment for an extended family. Veya would have been the exception. Knowing Paul, he had to be asking himself if they'd died because of her.

"If that were true, and the logs lost with Veya Ragem

or taken by some unknown entity, why has this Johnsson come to the Library? And why now?" Lambo laid a gleaming handling claw on the counter, making a point.

Or for my admiration. Post-molt Carasians were prone to vanity, deservedly so; they never looked better than those first hours, and this one had been shabby for a very long time.

I was letting myself be distracted. "If," I stressed, "Veya ever had the logs. We don't know that." *And if it were true, how could I tell Paul?*

"We do not." The claw waved in the air. "But we can work from that assumption. This Johnsson has, has she not?"

I didn't like any of it, but as Ersh often reminded me, *The universe doesn't care what you like.* "Yes. She'd have come before if there was reason to believe the logs were on Botharis. To come now? The only thing new is the Library. Maybe Johnsson thinks it holds some new clue to finding them. She could have asked before tearing apart Paul's room," I finished sourly. *Rotten manners, that was.*

"What you have gathered here is unique and valuable. I must concur."

Aha! So much for Paul's secret access panel. Lambo wasn't here to operate the food dispenser at all.

Which was hardly news, so my momentary triumph faded. "There's nothing about the *Sidereal Pathfinder* or a secret drive in the collection."

There was a plethora of entries about "secret this, thats, and other things" but that was simply because some clients insisted what they brought for us was, indeed, secret. That it wasn't the moment we received it didn't appear to matter, so long as we kept the word with their information. *There were times ephemerals perplexed even me.*

Lambo gave a low chuckle, amused for some reason. It occurred to me we were getting along a little too well, all of a sudden. I remembered Ersh's warning about females of this species: *they've minds like floating ice—it's not the little they let you understand you need to worry about. It's the depths.*

The chuckle was followed by, "I mean no offense, Curator—"

For her first time using my title, I suspected a distinct tang of *irony* to the word.

"—but I'm a drive engineer. An extremely good one. How I search is not how you would."

"Fair enough," I acknowledged, thinking of the broken gemmies under the counter. *Depths to avoid.* "Any results?"

Her head plates dipped from side to side, a shrug. "Not yet. Nor have I found the rest of the *Sidereal Pathfinder*'s crew. By all accounts, each has vanished."

Well, that was disturbing. Another tidbit Johnsson hadn't known—or shared. Mind you, I'd serious doubts about her veracity be she Chase or Johnsson, and no trust for this new "willing" version. I grimaced inwardly. Skalet insisted the Human repeat her story for Esolesy Ki, presumably so I could compare details and catch any falsehood. Since Johnsson was too smart for that, I concluded the unpleasant assignment was my web-kin entertaining herself at my expense—a favorite hobby—and would have refused. Alas, Paul thought it a good idea, too.

I supposed it was, if it reinforced to Johnsson that Esen and Esolesy Ki were distinct individuals with only Paul and the Library in common.

"What good are the logs alone?"

I'd time to compare my reflection in an assortment of black eyeballs before Lambo answered. "With the prototype drive and its inventor lost with the ship, the navigation logs would offer the only clues. Did the drive work at all? If it did, how well? Knowing the *Sidereal Pathfinder*'s route could answer those and other questions."

"Questions only someone like yourself would know to ask."

"Exactly."

I hadn't paid much attention to starships, other than to value good maintenance in something that could crack open and spill you into space without warning. *Too many trips as a Quebit, that.*

Ersh-memory remained stubbornly silent on the topic. It made sense, for a being evolved to *be* a starship, if the achingly wondrous ability to swim through oceans of unseen light and delicious energies could be compared—

An ability I'd forbidden myself, and Skalet, more importantly, for excellent reason. That said, for the first time I realized I'd no idea *how* what we could do related to what star drives accomplished. Had Ersh steered us away from such learning, by instinct or design? Let Skalet have strategy, Mixs architecture, Ansky relationships—as complex if messier, and Lesy her art? Me—the undecided and difficult, fed scraps from the rest?

She'd been capable of it.

Or was it simpler? Had she chosen to forget? After all, Ersh had learned to hunt starships, dropping into normal space, following them with unmatchable speed and stealth, all to rip them open and *taste* what screamed inside—

"You're drooling on my counter."

Embarrassed, I rubbed the spot with my sleeve. "Why are you interested? In this star drive." *Not the drool.* "Twenty years ago—whatever was new then isn't now." Had it been a century, I could see it. The excited discovery of what they'd let lapse was a trait of most cultures.

"The *Sidereal Pathfinder*'s drive is rumored to be of a type never seen before—or since."

Making my case. "Because it didn't work?" I hazarded.

A claw snapped. "That, too, is information worth having."

To a drive engineer, maybe. To Victory Johnsson?

Unless they were one and the same, Lambo the one looking through her eyes, a regrettable thought given the proximity of those restored, larger claws to my neck. Johnsson hadn't named her employer or partner; more self-protection than honor at a guess. Turning her over to Skalet's lack of mercy remained an option we'd prefer not to use.

"I didn't hire the Human or her scum. I do my own hunting," the creature replied, either uncannily aware of my inner fussing or, more likely, deducing it would be my next logical assumption. *Logical Esen, there was a concept.* "I am reduced to hypothesizing her motives, in the lack of more complete information." Suggestively.

My turn, that meant. "Before coming here, Johnsson went to Senigal III to find Stefan Gahanni, the individual male with whom Veya Ragem contracted to father Paul." Carasians were passionate beings, but as they'd evolved to have sex in tidal pools, shedding the results into the sea to return if they survived? The direct lines of Human reproduction made them uneasy. "When she couldn't find him, she came here." A shop—and livelihood—she'd destroyed to cover the signs of her search.

"Why seek Paul's father?"

"Johnsson's sources," *more distressing unknowns* "discovered Veya paid Stefan a visit."

Rudy had told us, late one night and after too many beers, how, upon learning of her son's supposed death, Paul's mother had abandoned her Survey ship and risked her career to return home. How, while on Botharis, she'd been interviewed by none other than Lionel Kearn, who'd told her and anyone else he could find that Paul had been in league with a monster and died a traitor.

How, the very next day, without a word or warning, Veya Ragem had headed back to deep space. She'd found ships that would take her farther and farther out.

She hadn't come home again.

That we knew. There was no official record to prove Veya had ever returned to Senigal III either, but there wouldn't be, if she wanted to keep attention from Stefan.

Secret Survey research. The *Sidereal Pathfinder.* How different her actions looked now, warped by that lens.

Lambo rattled, coming to attention. "This visit by Veya Ragem was after her ship was lost?"

"Yes." I wanted, suddenly and badly, to find Paul. To ask him what he thought of all this, what it might mean. He'd been close to his mother. She'd been his inspiration. Paul would tell me her stories, remembering them all with the clarity only an impressionable, brilliant child would. As I'd listened, what had impressed me was Veya's own curiosity. Whenever her ship was fins down, she'd leave it and explore. She'd rent transportation and go beyond the confines of shipcity and tourist haunts, seeking those places other spacers didn't go. She'd even learn phrases in alien languages to teach her son.

Was there something in what she'd done, I thought abruptly. A pattern only Paul would understand?

That was it, wasn't it. "Johnsson wasn't searching Paul's room for the logs," I thought aloud, forgetting I wasn't alone. "She came here for him."

High-tech eyeballs. Iftsen suits. Weapons.

And I'd left Paul alone.

Inception

BELIEF can be shattered.

If the world can be, for that is what I feel. A convulsion of the solid. A tidal force of what is not, bearing me . . . where?

I cry out. We all do, for others are swept up with me, against me, and it is dark and LIGHT and dark and LIGHT.

Up?

It's true, we go up, the only direction that offers hope, and their cries, my cry becomes a gasp of effort as my claws dig and grasp—

Nothing.

There is nothing to grasp, nothing for claws to cling to or move.

I refuse to believe the impossible.

The world cannot be gone.

19: Library Afternoon

LAMBO came with me. There being no faster way to clear a hallway than a charging Carasian, I didn't waste breath arguing. So long as she kept up.

On all fours, *motivated,* very few could. Looking back, it's possible I should have tried the com panel before careening with a Carasian through our alarm-weary clients and staff, but hindsight was only useful if situations repeated themselves.

This one mustn't.

I'd been such a fool. Johnsson, *behave?* My hackles had tried to rise in warning, but no—

I jumped the cluster of Rands, ears back at the language.

—I'd been civilized.

No more.

I slowed only once, to lunge up and slap a paw on the door lock to the admin corridor, leaping forward as it opened. Lambo followed behind, sounding like pans rolling downhill. Paul's office was the third in sight, its door closed.

He'd asked Lionel to meet him there, to talk about matters sure to startle the other Human. Rather than involve local authorities in what now involved Paul's mother, Johnsson and the Ervickian were with Skalet and her hired thugs—*Johnsson's leftovers.*

And had anyone checked Jumpy Lyn's stomach? All it

took was an acid-proof bag. I'd noticed the riper-than-normal stench.

Now I understood it.

Paul's door. I stopped and rose, ears up, gesturing to Lambo to be quiet. Familiar figures moved in the distance, stopping, too. Henri Steves, following to see what was the matter. Ally. We weren't alone, I thought gratefully. Our friends—

—*mustn't be risked.* I touched Lambo's near claw, pointed my snout at the pair, then shook my head.

All but two eyestalks shifted to track them, the Carasian turning without a sound on those massive balloon feet.

My nose assured me Johnsson and Jumpy Lyn hadn't been in this hall. Yet. Paul's scent lingered, recent and heart-warming. Lionel's, too. An older trace of Skalet from . . . I looked toward the admin maintenance closet, surprised. Then again, my web-kin tended to lurk in dark corners.

And rarely where I needed her. A thought that would trouble me later, but my focus was Paul.

Having smelled everything potentially useful, I *listened.*
Wind?

The rustle of leaves?

What the combination meant, I couldn't guess.

I set my paw on the lock.

Perception

"I came to beg your forgiveness," Lionel pointed out, feeling oddly unsteady. "Leaving me in charge of all this—" he swung a finger in a grand loop, "—is not what I expected." *Or deserved.*

Amusement crinkled the tiny lines framing his eyes, but Paul's look held nothing but resolve. "I'll admit it's sudden, but I wouldn't ask if I didn't have full confidence in you."

Or if there'd been another in range with his qualifications, which included firsthand knowledge of Web-beings. Collecting himself, Lionel nodded. "I understand."

"Good. I've left instructions for the staff—your staff now—to continue our normal routine. Skalet'll take care of security, no doubt, but if you need other help, rely on Lambo—"

Lionel frowned. "I thought Lambo was implicated in this *Sidereal Pathfinder* business."

"He has an interest," Paul corrected. "For the moment, we should consider Lambo a resource, hopefully one with useful insights. Es is consulting with him now. Just—don't go to the Chow to eat. Use the farmhouse kitchen, or get Henri to show you how to order from the hamlet. Don't worry, Lionel. With any luck," now the amusement grew to include both eyes and a dimple, "your most demanding role while we're gone will be interpreting client requests and their answers. Sound familiar?"

It sounded—wonderful. Nevertheless, he had to be honest. "I wish I could come with you—to meet this new species." Despite its positive meaning to Dokeci, Lionel couldn't call them Elves. The word was too loaded with Human connotation and its use, by Humans? Unsafe, described it. He'd said as much to Paul.

Who now startled him by putting a friendly hand on his shoulder. "I wish you could, too."

They'd never been friends before. He'd been Paul's senior officer, his mentor, on the *Rigus'* First Contact Team. Then captain. Then—

Lionel dared return the gesture. Wanted, in this splendid moment, to say something, to express his gratitude, his regret, to—

No need, he realized, relaxing with a smile. They were—

An almost silent *WHOOMPH* of force dropped them to the floor, debris falling around them. "Stay down!" Paul ordered, but Lionel looked up with him.

They were—outside. Rather, the outside was in, the transparent wall of the office gone, dirt and roots littering the floor, leaves drifting through the air. Before Lionel could do more than tense, four figures cloaked in black mesh darted in, weapons raised.

When Paul lunged for his desk, those weapons fired.

20: Field Afternoon

PAUL'S office had become a porch, open to the fields beyond, and he wasn't here.

I ran within the strong plume of his scent, and Lionel's, and *STRANGERS'*—outside to where all vanished within the reek of metal and machine, then lifted my head and *HOWLED* in grief.

He wasn't here!

Heedless of anything else, I released my hold on this form, thinning my web-self over the ground, *assimilating* every bit of living tissue I touched into more web-mass until instinct, form-memory, told me I'd enough.

I cycled again. Drove forward on powerful legs, wings outstretched. Five steps, ten—if not for the steep slope to the creek, it would have been more and too many and I'd have slammed into the waiting train—

Air caught, *resisted* the essential amount. My first mighty beat broke feather tips against the ground, but the second thrust me high in the air and over the train.

Find him!

I met rising air, a gift of the afternoon's unsettled weather, and soared upward. Even as I gained altitude, I searched, tilting my head to bring this form's remarkable eyes to bear, scanning for my quarry.

There! A glint, artificial, fleeing.

Skyfolk, as this species was known, couldn't outfly an aircar. *I didn't need to*—

I remained where I was, as I was, long enough to be sure of the kidnappers' course, then snapped my wings closed and plummeted to the ground.

Wind screamed past me. I screamed with it, for I knew where they were going. To the landing field.

If they got Paul and Lionel offworld—

That, I warned the universe, *wasn't going to happen.*

Perception

LIONEL Kearn sat without moving, as he'd been ordered, hands secured by a lockbar across his wrists, and couldn't help wondering what he'd done wrong.

There had to be something. Had he led Chase here? Exposed Paul? Failed in a precaution with his inquiries or contacts, though it was hard to imagine how. He'd stopped trusting others years ago. Kept most of what he knew or surmised in his head. Didn't talk to anyone else.

The aircar bounced. The five up front, for they'd a waiting pilot, gave a variety of curses and grunts. He took careful note. They thought themselves disguised, hood-to-toe in black mesh, but to his ear they weren't all Human. Two sounded distinctly Snoprian—that pitch to the—

Lionel risked a sidelong glance at his seatmate. Paul remained slumped over his bound wrists, head at a painful-looking angle. They hadn't stunned him once, they'd done it three times, laughing as their victim spasmed, and if he'd a stunner right now—

Sit still, he reminded himself, *or be stunned, too.* They'd grabbed him even as Paul broke free, trying to reach his desk and sound the alarm. The first stun had hit, and if Lionel closed his eyes, he could still see Paul collapsing, hands outstretched. How the silly blue statue of a pony had fallen to the floor with him, bouncing.

How one of their captors had stepped on it before firing again—

They'd left him conscious to carry Paul, a pair taking over when there was no sign of pursuit. Lionel had kept up, running with them through the wet grass, determined not to be left behind.

Though until they'd ordered him to climb in the aircar and bound his hands, he'd been reasonably certain they'd kill him.

Here, alive, he was an ally. Skalet would come, of that he'd no doubt, if only to prevent her impulsive younger sister from needless risk. He would bide his time and do whatever he could.

Starting now, during this hasty flight. *Assessment.* Two Snoprians. In his opinion, the rest were likely were Human, one possibly female. Expensive, off-market tech. All capable and ruthless—professionals, if he had to judge. Not a wasted motion, other than their abuse of Paul—and that posed its own question: why?

Lionel would be the first to admit he wasn't an obvious threat. Paul might not appear to be, but he'd landed a solid blow or two while resisting. Payback, then? No. These wouldn't waste the effort, but a personal grudge?

That might be indulged.

If so, one or more of those here knew Paul Ragem. Or Paul Cameron.

Invalidating his earlier assumption, Lionel thought, mouth suddenly dry. The extra stuns might not have been punishment at all—or not only that—but a means to render Paul unconscious as long as possible. To keep him from recognizing someone in this aircar.

Chase? He couldn't be sure. The five were seated, of similar heights. It was possible.

The Group had watched her movements. How much had she been watching in return? Lionel would rather be paranoid than rely on the ignorance of those with bad intentions. He and Chase hadn't met, that he knew, but his trip to Senigal III, his visit with the Gahannis, hadn't been secretive. For that matter, it wouldn't be hard at all for Chase to learn he'd interviewed Veya Ragem, on Botharis, fifty-plus years ago. It was public record. The stuff of newsvids, in fact. At the time, he'd promoted it as widely as he could to gain attention for his search. The media had been more than obliging. Monsters, emptied starships, attacks on domes—there'd been a frenzy of coverage.

That connection to Veya? *They'd also wanted him,* Lionel suddenly realized, not in the least cheered to know why he wasn't lying dead on the grass. Whomever "they" might be.

A lost star drive—even a revolutionary one—wasn't reason enough for this. Ship design—be it for commerce or warfare—functioned within the common realities of physics. Vacuum and radiation. Distance and time. Regardless of species, design flowed from those same constraints. Standardization was not only desirable, it was inevitable, with change in the safest, smallest increments acceptable to all.

The Commonwealth and her associated systems were still bickering over a proposed modification to air lock shape, to accommodate a proposed modification in station hookups, which in turn would affect—needless to say, a resolution would be years in the making. By then, the air locks would likely need to be modified again.

In the meantime, air locks of any ship fit any station. And that was the goal.

Increase a ship's speed beyond its design parameters? It would drop you out in the wrong place or not at all . . .

. . . unless you developed a new, superior navigation system at the same time.

Was that it? Lionel's heart began to pound inside his chest. More ships were lost due to nav failures than any other cause, including space pirates. There hadn't been a significant improvement in nav systems since he'd stepped on his first starship, despite the efforts and research of thousands of species.

Maybe this wasn't about the *Sidereal Pathfinder*'s star drive at all.

But about her navigator.

21: Office Afternoon

SHEDDING excess mass as molecules of water, I reentered the Library through the violated wall as Esolesy Ki, the Lishcyn.

It being prudent not to confront Johnsson as a form possessed of flesh-tearing teeth.

Part of me was impressed I was thinking so clearly, considering even the calm disposition of this me was shaken to the core, and if I didn't fill my second through fifth stomachs soon, the latter could erupt with stress. *Plus clothes.* This me needed them before confronting anyone, or eating, but that part was simple. I kept extra outfits in cupboards throughout the Library, including Paul's office.

Crunching over soil that belonged outside, not here, did nothing to settle my stomachs. I paused only to pick up a shattered piece of blue ceramic. A reproachful googly eye gazed up at me, rolling back and forth.

I set the piece on Paul's desk. *Why a pony?*

And that did it. Sickened, upset, I couldn't help the defensive response of this me. All over my sturdy body, the flesh beneath each scale engorged, pushing them outward until they overlapped and locked. My natural armor, however inappropriate, *felt* comforting, even though it seriously stiffened my movements and I barely managed to shrug a nice silk caftan over my sloped shoulders before the doorway filled with eyes.

Not all were black and beady, though a row of Lambo's hovered over the anxious blue and green of Henri and Ally. "Fem Ki?"

"Where is Esen?" boomed the Carasian.

"What's happened here? Where's Paul?"

I held up a three-fingered hand for quiet, using the other to quickly brush the leaves from the node on Paul's desk. We'd an emergency code, at Skalet's insistence, and I tapped that in before looking up at the others. "Paul and Lionel have been taken by force," I said bluntly. "Henri and Ally. This might not be over. Please lock down the habitat zones and gather the remaining clients in the lobby. Lambo, keep everyone inside. Don't let the train leave."

Without so much as a glance at one another, the Humans nodded in my direction, then disappeared at a run. For Paul, I knew. And approved.

Where was Skalet? I started tapping the code again.

"What are you?" in a low, disturbed rumble.

Deliberately, I finished the code, then raised my head to meet the scrutiny of those many eyes, that brilliant mind within restless headplates, and it didn't matter, at that moment, what I was, or how much smaller—or how Esolesy Ki had a reputation as the soft touch if you needed time off or a favor, though she'd appreciate fudge. *What mattered?* Paul and Lionel.

I spread my arms at a low angle from my sides, my hands closed. Slowly I opened them, thick fingers wide, in the closest this me could come to the Carasian display for *I did not come for battle.* The qualifying *we'll grapple later* being understood. "I'm someone who needs your help. For Paul and Lionel."

Eyestalks milled briefly, then formed a decisive line.

"I'll stop the train." She turned.

"Lambo—"

An eyestalk bent back. "Yes?"

"The train—don't break it."

A wicked chuckle, then the sounds of clanking pans receded down the hall.

Where was Skalet?

I stared down at the access node as if it could tell me,

stomach churning. *We were running out of time.* She was the one with a ship in orbit, packed with highly trained soldiers ready to obey her slightest command. There were, she'd told me innumerable times, no comparable assets in this system—likely this part of space.

Assets I couldn't use without S'kal-ru.

Perception

EVAN opened his eyes.

Oh. He wasn't dead. *That was a relief.* Though if he wasn't, he must have fainted, which he hadn't done in some time and had hoped not to do again, especially in public. On the plus side, he'd had a wonderful dream about Paul and Esen, who talked about coming with him. A field trip, together—

They'd save the Elves!

Evan gave a deep, wistful sigh. *If only* . . . he paused, struck by an alarming thought. If it had been a dream, why had he only heard voices, not *seen* them?

Oh, dear. Had Paul and Esen been here while he was unconscious?

As if that weren't embarrassing enough, when he sat up, it became obvious someone had removed his clothes. Dirty clothes, covered in blood and plaster dust, and of course they'd had to come off before he was put on this clean cot, between fresh sheets—

Who'd seen him naked?

It wasn't *FEAR,* more a nasty whimpering bit of *anxious.* Clothes were protection. Clothes were his, in a very uncertain *not-his* universe, and he wanted them back—

Evan took a breath, then another, waiting until his heart rate eased closer to normal before looking around the room for his things.

This was someone else's room. There was a small

travel bag on a table and a jacket hanging on a hook. Otherwise, it didn't appear lived in at all.

An open box on the floor held his things. Beside that were his boots, wiped clean, and on a nearby stool a tidy folded pile of new clothing waited. The bust that had caused Esen and the scary Kraal such concern sat on top, eyes glinting at him.

Needing no more encouragement, Evan got up and dressed. His hands and wrists ached when moved, the right more than the left, but the medplas held and, if he were careful, he could ignore the discomfort. There was a tightness over his cheek he knew to leave alone.

Maybe he'd end up with a scar, like a space pirate.

He grinned despite the twinge of pain. Chasing one another around on the hot sand, shouting and waving stick blasters, had been the best game when he'd spent summers with his cousins. They'd drawn fearsome scars on one another—

Evan cautiously touched the covering on his cheek. *Good.* Not too big. Even better?

He had heard them. Paul and Esen were coming to Dokeci-Na. They'd save the Elves—or, he reminded himself—they'd determine once and for all if the Elves needed saving. Whatever happened, he'd have help of the best kind.

Best to leave fantasizing over stateroom assignments and those intense gray eyes for later.

The clothing was clean, if used. Work coveralls, with loops for tools and handy pockets. They fit his shoulders but sagged over his boots. He rolled up the sleeves to keep the fabric from catching on his bandages, feeling remarkably better. Rested. Fed.

Making it high time he found the accommodation.

Nothing here, this being a very plain room, without windows and only one door. Probably intended for storage, not sleeping. There wasn't even a com panel; *that he could see,* Evan corrected himself, remembering the trick Esen had used in the Chow. He'd his holocube, but the device wasn't a com link. Calls and messages could only pass within the immediate family's set.

Which Lucius Whelan wasn't. Evan suspected Lucius had talked one of his cousins into sharing theirs, most likely Justin, Aunt Melan's eldest and a hopeless romantic. Justin—everyone—wanted to make him happy. He just wished they'd ask him what would.

Family.

Finished straightening the sheets on the cot, Evan tucked the bust in one of the handy, oversized pockets of his coveralls, his holocube in another, picked up his box of dirty clothes, and went out the door.

To find himself in a very ordinary basement. A wide, brightly lit hall stretched in either direction, bending in the distance much as the building above—surely the Library, the walls being the same material, and Evan refusing to contemplate this as below the Carasian-battered farmhouse.

Behind the nearest door was a basic theta-class humanoid accommodation, a convenience for whomever slept down here.

Was it Paul?

He had to stop these, these *flashes* of whatever they were. Well, he knew what they were—and so did the Lanivarian—but he wasn't Lucius. In no way was it appropriate, Evan told himself sternly, to have such *interesting* thoughts about someone else or their sleeping arrangements without their permission, particularly in their basement. *Why, for all he knew, Paul had been the one to—*

"No. Not thinking that," Evan said aloud. Because if so, he'd been unconscious, and likely snoring, and missed the most wonderful opportunity of his life—not that he'd had any yet, but—

Thud.

It wasn't a loud *thud,* but it cleared Evan's mind of everything but being alone, in an unfamiliar basement, and if there was no one else down here, as it seemed?

Who'd made the noise?

Setting his box against one wall, Evan walked slowly toward the sound, a choice he made to forestall any phantom *thud-maker* from creeping up behind him.

He made it to the bend before the next *thud.* Pressing

himself flat to the wall, he eased sideways to the junction. *Quick or slow?* A quick look seemed the right choice, but he might not see enough and have to look again. A slower look could be riskier—no, what moved quickly caught the eye, didn't it?

Evan leaned forward, and very, *very* slowly, peeked around the bend.

Nothing. More pristine hallway and doors. Spotting those for a lift, he let out a pleased sigh.

And was heard.

Thudthudthud... THUD! THUD... THUD... THUD!

About to run the other way, Evan froze in place. The sounds were evenly spaced, a signal. A plea for help!

He rushed forward, following the *Thuds*. "I'm coming!" Someone could be trapped. Shelves fell on workers all the time, if not secured properly—

He reached the door. When it didn't move aside automatically, he slapped his palm on the lock. *How careless!*

The door didn't open fully, caught by something. The lights were off, which was strange, so Evan entered with careful steps. "Hello?" He didn't want to step on a hand or—

"Don't move."

Unmistakable, that voice, even as a whisper. The Kraal.

"I'm not moving," he whispered back.

"Make sure you don't. Evan. The shiny new friend. Of course, it's you," this last with sheer disgust.

He'd be insulted when he knew what was going on. "I'm here to help you."

"Of course, you are," no happier. "Fine, then. The control for the lights is to your left, head height. Wait!"

He froze at the command, his hand outstretched.

"Don't touch it with bare skin."

Moistening his lips, Evan turned his hand over, activating the control with the bandage. The lights came on.

His bandage was on fire! Hurriedly, he smothered the flames against his coveralls, thankful the material was fireproof. "What was—" The words died in his mouth as he saw what the light revealed.

The shelves were properly secured against the walls

and that was a good thing, because someone had wired dozens of heavy-looking canisters to them. More wire formed a mesh across the floor—some snaked a finger-breadth from his toes—and a device the size of his fist squatted in the center, telltale lights blinking in the finest terrifying tradition.

Evan knew a detonator and explosives when he saw them. Well, no, he didn't, other than from vids, but every-thing about the arrangement looked malignant.

They hadn't wired the Kraal. She was fastened upside-down to the door, explaining why it hadn't opened fully, thick sticky brown threads holding her against the metal. A booted foot was loose, explaining the *thuds*.

. . . trapped in a spiderweb . . .

He dismissed the words. "Tell me what to do."

"Put that *thing* you carry outside. It's—distracting."

Careful not to move his feet, Evan squatted and leaned back as far as he could. He set the little bust from his pocket on the floor, sliding it toward the lift. He stood. "Now what?"

"Now, Evan, I confess I find myself in what Esen would call a crisis of conscience. You answered my sum-mons. To improve my situation, *you* are what I most ur-gently require." Surely it wasn't *appetite* he heard in her voice.

Surely . . .

"Yet. Yet. Yet." Softly, as if debating with herself. "You are the Youngest's—friend."

Who? Maybe being head down so long had affected her thinking. "I'll go for help."

"It's too late for that." The threads adhered to her clothing and skin; puckered white blisters edged the strands on her face and neck, but her voice was as calm as though they discussed the weather. "Johnsson has accom-plices. By this time, they'll be in the Library."

Another crook? "'Johnsson?'" He felt a surge of righ-teous anger. This was a peaceful place of scholarship, not some shipcity alley or backwater station. "What about Chase?"

"Same person."

Who was also Tory. *He should have kept notes.* Evan closed his eyes, then opened them. "What is she after?"

She'd one eye clear of thread. It narrowed. "Paul."

And there was nothing he could do, nothing anyone— except—Evan looked at the Kraal who'd introduced herself as "Security." Even like this, she was the scariest being he'd ever met. "You can stop them."

"Yes."

"Then we get you free," he declared, looking around desperately, then back to her. "There has to be a way."

"Oh, yes. It amused Johnsson to point it out. There. The shelf to your right. The jug of cleaning solution. If you pour it over me, the threads will release."

He'd have to get to it first. Wires carpeted the floor. Contact with a finger-length loop of the same stuff had set his bandage on fire.

This time, move quickly, he told himself. "What about the detonator?"

A laugh, if short and cut off. "That's no detonator. It's something more interesting."

"Oh, good." He wiped his forehead. "So all this isn't going to explode."

"I didn't say that. The jug, Evan?" Her tone altered, lowered, sending a primal shiver down his spine. "Before I change my mind about you. MOVE!"

Evan crossed the wired floor as quickly as he could, taking long hops rather than strides. The thick soles of his boots were smoking when he reached the shelf. Grabbing the white jug in both hands, he hurried to the Kraal, and only his obsessive attention to his footing let him spot the label's stark warning. *Highly corrosive.* "Wait—this isn't a cleaning solution." He looked at her in dismay.

She knew. "It's that, Evan," almost gentle, "or forfeit what I've gained." With a more familiar sharpness, "I fully intend to share this experience, should we survive it. Move!"

He hop-stepped closer.

"Stop there," the Kraal ordered. "Listen to me, Evan. Once you throw it on me, run for the door and keep running."

He'd run enough today, Evan thought with abrupt certainty and before she could say another brave word, he stepped right up to her. His hands rock-steady, he removed the cuplike lid and poured liquid into it. Quickly, but with care, he dribbled acid along the largest thread, the one crisscrossing her torso and thighs. As the thread sizzled and dissolved, the pungent reek stung his eyes and nostrils. He coughed. Blinked tears that cleared his sight.

"What are you doing?"

"Hold still." Time slowed, or he moved through it differently. Pour, dribble. Pour dribble. The stuff splattered and hissed. *Burned* where a drop hit his skin, but he didn't flinch.

Nor did she.

Pour, dribble.

His feet grew hot, but the threads were fraying before his eyes. One more—

The Kraal came free with a convulsive twist, landing on her feet. She shoved him toward the door, and the jug flew through the air, acid splashing over wires and canisters. A new smell, as those dissolved and *sparked*—

Sprinklers activated, filling the air with a fog of fire-suppressant—

Evan stumbled. A powerful hand on his back kept him going, and it wasn't until they were both clear and in the hallway that he realized two things.

His boots had melted.

And the Kraal had the device in her free hand.

She cut away his boots with a knife she seemed to pluck from midair, then peeled the steaming remnants of the soles from his feet. When Evan bent anxiously to see, she pushed him back. Her hand stayed on his chest, pinning him to the wall. Pale piercing eyes searched his face. Thread and blisters crossed hers, tattoos adding shadows, but nothing hid her scowl. "Why?"

He gave a hapless shrug. "I—it was the right thing to do."

"You even talk like her." But it wasn't condemnation—not entirely. She released him and examined his feet. "Lucky," she pronounced, rising to hers. "You can still walk." A feral grin. "It's going to hurt."

"Paul." More than a name, the reason for all this, and Evan used it—his concern and brewing *anger*—to stand.

Her grin grew almost warm. "Indeed."

The smooth cool of the floor soothed initially, but she was right. Hot pain lanced up his ankles and legs as he took a tentative step. He clenched his jaw and focused on her. "May I have your name, Warrior?"

To his surprise, the Kraal touched the backs of her hands to her wounded cheeks, a gesture of profound respect. "I am S'kal-ru, Evan Gooseberry. Let us dismember our enemies together."

Please let that be a Kraal figure of speech. Moved nonetheless, Evan dipped his head in acknowledgment; unless Kraal and tattooed with compatible or greater affiliations, the cheek salute wasn't an option.

He allowed himself a moment of modest gratification. First a Carasian, now this? None of his friends on Dokeci-Na would believe the company he kept.

As for his family, well, Great Gran would approve, so long as the company he kept preserved the Gooseberry name.

Without breaking stride, S'kal-ru snatched up the bust and tossed it to Evan. "Here."

Not going to ask. He tucked his contentious treasure safely out of sight in his pocket, limping behind.

It was a freight lift, still smelling new. Evan entered behind S'kal-ru, who went to the control panel.

Standing hurt more than walking. As the lift rose, he eased his weight from one foot to the other, but the tiny spot where acid had landed on his hand was pure, unignorable agony and Evan found himself transfixed by the Kraal. Half her face was blistered. There were powdery white circles on the black of her uniform, the fabric resistant, but despite his care some acid had splattered on her neck, leaving a spray of angry red dots. How could she appear so—unaffected?

S'kal-ru turned to regard him, thin lips half smiling. Evan felt his face warm with embarrassment. "I'm sor—"

"Stop." Her hand flew up. Her head tilted slightly, as though listening, though to what he'd no idea.

Then her eyes met his.

Evan swallowed. *"Dismember our enemies"* it was.

22: Office Afternoon

SKALET, blistered and disheveled, arrived in what remained of Paul's office like a tidal force, a barefoot, limping Evan Gooseberry in her wake, and I'd have been overjoyed to relinquish matters into her capable deadly hands except for one thing.

This was her fault. I knew the instant I laid eyes on her. "You let yourself be captured!" I accused.

"It worked, didn't it?" my web-kin declared, eyes fierce and bright. "They made their move."

Speechless, I stabbed a finger at the field where a wall had been.

An eyebrow lifted. "Blunt, but effective."

Classic Skalet. I'd seen through her scheming, now she chose to bait me. Next would come how clever she'd been, and *Youngest, you should learn to temper your emotions.*

Overwhelmed by a particularly welcome dose of fury, I lumbered forward. A Lishcyn wasn't fast but, once in motion, inertia takes over. My web-kin actually backed a step as I attempted to stop. "They've taken Paul and Lionel!" I shouted, rocking on my heels to keep from bumping snout to nose. "Do you have a move for that?"

"Lionel?"

Her honest dismay cooled my temper when nothing else probably could. "Fix this," I ordered, stepping aside to let her go to Paul's desk.

Instead, Skalet shoved chairs and toppled the little

table, intent on the floor beneath. I glowered as she applied the palm of her hand to what looked like wood but wasn't.

Glowered with an added rumble of displeasure when what looked like floor popped up, revealing a small column of lights and controls. She glanced over her shoulder at me. "Don't fuss. You hide clothes in here."

This wasn't remotely the same. I didn't bother to argue. If what she'd pulled onto her lap, having sat cross-legged in front of the column, would save Paul and Lionel—while ending the menace of Johnsson-Chase and all others of her ilk—I could live with Skalet's high-handed embellishment of the Library.

Till we were done, I promised myself. *Then I'd have Duggs rip it out.*

She attached a com button to an unblistered part of her jaw. "*Septos Ank.* Down, now. Hostage protocol."

I couldn't hear the reply, but it would be instantaneous. Landing her scoutship—and troops—would discomfort a significant number of innocent beings in the process, no matter how "tactful" the Kraal attempted to be—and they'd try; Captain Cieter-ro was a sensible individual for her kind and knew better than to be overtly aggressive on a planet not yet over the last time Kraal had stomped through.

"It was a nonmilitary aircar," I informed her. "Heading was direct to the landing field. Full speed. They left over seven minutes ago."

And where were you? We'd discuss her tardy response time later. "Five attackers," I continued. "Johnsson and her three weren't with them, but you'd know that." Being able to spy through the Human's eyes was our sole advantage. "Where is she now?" The tension rounding Skalet's shoulders wouldn't have been noticed by anyone else. To me, it was alarming. "Where?"

"I don't know." Her hands clenched. "Somehow Johnsson blocked the feed."

If she'd sounded impressed—shown that too-Kraal respect for a worthy foe—I have excised her from my Web forever.

Instead, Skalet looked up, allowing what was almost

humiliation to cross her face. "I thought I could handle this my way, Es. I was wrong."

"No. You saved the Library!" Evan said, limping closer. He turned to glare at me. "I don't know who you think you are, but S'kal-ru is a hero!"

I blinked, not in any sense prepared for more alarms. "Saved the Library from what?"

"Irrelevant," Skalet replied, and to her it likely was. *Among my web-kin's virtues was the ability to abandon a failed plan.* Especially when she'd a new target. "Our sole concern now is retrieving Lionel and Paul. The *Trium Pa* is moving into orbit above. I suggest you inform the Botharans before they panic." With her reassuringly normal disdain for the Human government of this world.

Who wouldn't panic, despite a warship on their screens. They'd be unhappy, loud about it, and blame the Library. Justifiably. The last time I'd covered for one of Skalet's Kraal operations, my excuse had been a vague "expected delivery"—in hindsight, not the most well-thought of answers, the Kraal being weapons' dealers without peer with this world their favorite hiding spot during the previous conflict. Before Paul's time, but unwary mountaineers continued to stumble over caches of deadly things. We'd been not-so-politely told not to invite the Kraal to land again without clearance. *Too late for that—*

A hand covered in charred medplas gripped my scaled arm. "Before you do anything, S'kal-ru needs medical attention—"

"I'm all right, Evan. Paul and Lionel first."

He released my arm, and I blinked again. That soothing tone didn't belong to any version of Skalet I remembered. *What could possibly have happened between these two?*

Which reminded me. "You must be Evan Gooseberry, our client from Dokeci-Na." I curled a lip to expose a friendly tusk, the one with the opal inlay Paul'd said was particularly cute.

Where was he now?

I went on. "Esen's told me about you. I'm Esolesy Ki. The—" we'd struggled for a title that would impress staff while keeping this me safely out of major decision loops "—Assistant Curator. Previously Paul's partner in our export business. We're very close." In case our visiting diplomat missed the distress cues of my current face.

Evan's was expressive even for a Human. His bright green eyes softened at once, and the corners of his lips deepened, turning down. "We mustn't worry, Fem Ki," he said earnestly, being a kind being. "S'kal-ru will take care of everything."

She already had, I thought, nowhere near forgiving, and flipped a sarcastic ear at my web-kin.

"I will do my utmost."

Skalet, humble? *Stranger and stranger.*

"What's all this about?" Evan looked back and forth between us. "I hope it hasn't anything to do with Paul and Esen coming with me to Dokeci-Na, to help the Elves? They thought I was asleep," he confessed.

"'Elves'?" Skalet echoed, in that intimidating *why wasn't I briefed* tone.

It terrified fleet admirals.

I wasn't one and ignored her. "It has nothing to do with those plans, Evan. You encountered Victory Johnsson as Tory. She and other criminals are under the mistaken belief we've something worth stealing."

"They stole Paul," he pointed out.

"They did. And—"

"Wait!" In no pleased tone, but Skalet wasn't talking to us. "Repeat. Understood. Standby." She snaked to her full height and spun to face Evan. "Who *are* you?"

There were times her Kraal-self was distinctly inconvenient. "This is a friend of—"

"I know that," without taking her eyes from Evan. Her voice could have sliced flesh; from her scowl, actual slicing was an option. "What else are you, Evan Gooseberry? Because your ship is on the landing field and its captain has refused mine permission to land."

"My—what?" Poor Evan looked remarkably like a fish gasping for breath.

Skalet never had taken surprises—those she hadn't planned—well. "It's a private field," I objected, hoping to deflect some of Skalet's attention before worse happened than an accusation. "What kind of ship could—" I stopped and stared at Evan, too. *There was only one.*

"They've identified themselves as the Commonwealth Survey Vessel *Mistral*," Skalet replied, each word ice. "Under the direct command of Diplomat-at-Large Evan Gooseberry, On Urgent Assignment, given full consent and operational authority by the Botharan Government."

"I don't—I didn't—" His face was so full of confused astonishment I was torn between hugging him and giving him a shake.

"It's not his fault," I told Skalet, sure of that much.

An armed *official* starship, planted smack in the middle of the landing field to prevent any other ships from coming or going. They'd gone through proper channels, too—I'd have spared a moment to be miffed we hadn't been informed, but then the Botharan government probably hoped the ship—and diplomat—were here to check on us.

"Of course, it's his fault. He came here."

"I didn't tell anyone—" I watched the *yes, he had*, cross Evan's face. "But why? I don't understand."

Skalet's hand lifted sharply, and both the Human and I braced for her to slap him. She merely offered her com button. "Survey ships carry a security complement," she said, her tone again calm and expressionless. "Put them under my orders."

"But—"

"That's unnecessary—" *nor remotely feasible*, a point I conveyed to Skalet with a glare. "Please do contact the *Mistral*, Evan. Tell your captain you're with our Head of Security, and we have a hostage situation at the landing field. Humans are in danger."

I'd hit the right note. With a determined nod, looking every bit the dedicated diplomat—if you overlooked the bare feet, bandages, and maintenance coveralls—Evan took the button.

Then looked warily at Skalet. "How do I use it?"

Perception

"**D**ELIGHTED you've found a com link, Polit Gooseberry."

Evan suspected the person behind the boisterous voice in his ear of sarcasm. "It's been chaotic here, Captain Clendon," he said, hoping to cover all manner of protocol lapses at one go. The Lishcyn dipped her snout encouragingly, but he could have used Esen's friendly face right now. Still, it was up to him. "The kidnapping?"

"Nasty business, but we're here now. We've dispatched an aircar to fetch you and the local expert. Make sure your liaison comes, too, no matter what she says about flying."

"My . . . liaison, Captain?" He made frantic gestures to those in the room with him.

Skalet frowned but left in search. Esolesy Ki looked, if he read the signs correctly, about to burst out laughing. Certainly her scales had returned to normal, the little hairs between popping out. They were a fetching amber color and she was quite handsome, though rounder about the middle than the other Lishcyn he'd met. Possibly sexual dimorphism—possibly a sedentary lifestyle. Some things you didn't ask—

"Polit Trili Bersin," the voice replied, interrupting his distraction. "She insisted on taking the train—surely she's been in touch by now."

Well, of course she'd take the train.

"I've been in meetings," Evan declared. Diplomats were always in meetings. The embassy had meetings about meetings, when it came to it, and he'd often joked—with Trili, in fact—that after hours gatherings of senior staff at the pub really should be in the agenda, too.

"The aircar should be there shortly, Polit. We'll prepare here. Was there anything else?"

"Anything else—let me see." Evan waved frantically at Esolesy Ki, who shook her big head in that very Human gesture. "No, Captain. I'll be there shortly."

Not knowing how to end the connection, he pulled the button from his cheek and held it out. A thick finger came down and pressed the center. "That's off."

He sighed, a little, his feet throbbing. "Oh, my. Oh, my." She picked up a chair and set it down near him. "Here."

He sank into it without a word. *What was happening?* The shadow-filled field offered no answers, so he lowered his face into his hands. Really, that didn't help either, but he couldn't stop himself.

A gentle touch on his shoulder. "Evan, we'll find our friends. Frankly," with a tinge of amusement, "I'm happier having the authorities involved than S'kal-ru's followers. They tend to be overenthused."

"Overenthused" Kraal? He raised his head with a shudder. "Fem Ki, I didn't know about the ship or Bersin coming here. I swear I didn't."

"I know." She flashed a pleasant tusk at him. "Friend of yours?"

"Trili? Yes. And colleague. She handles the trade portfolios. She's—" He wasn't making sense. "I'm sorry. Trili's the only one who knew I was coming here, to consult the Library," he admitted. "She's seen my pamphlet. I couldn't let her think there really was an emergency at home." He grimaced. "Trili knows how to reach my Great Gran."

Great Gran insisting, as always, on a contact where he worked in case of planet-ending catastrophe or his birthday, Great Gran delighting in surprise gifts. He'd regretted supplying a female name almost at once, though Trili was delighted. Ever since, his ever-hopeful relative had been sending Trili her favorite chocolates; it was only a matter of time before Great Gran broached the weighty topic of the Gooseberry lineage and Evan's responsibilities as the current "last of . . ."

"Family. I understand," Esolesy Ki replied.

He'd the oddest feeling she did. And not the way a stranger would, or a colleague. This being knew things about him. "Esen-alit-Quar," he guess. "She's your friend—a close friend—too, isn't she?"

Both inlaid tusks shone. "We couldn't be closer," she replied. "That's why I'm not surprised you came to the rescue of Old Pricklepuss." Her head tilted as she regarded him with sudden seriousness. "I am surprised she let you."

Evan couldn't imagine being brave enough—or familiar enough—with S'kal-ru to use any nickname, let alone that one. "I insisted." He shifted and winced. At his hand. Very much at his feet.

The Lishcyn ambled to an inconspicuous cupboard, returning with a small med kit. "I'm not Duggs," she said mysteriously, "but I know how to use this." She brandished a medspray. "May I?"

His involuntary "Please!" was so emphatic a tusk showed again.

A quick application coated and soothed the burn on his hand. She indicated the scorch mark on the medplas above it. "What's this?"

"The room was full of hot wires," he explained. "Don't worry. The fire-suppressant came on."

"There was a fire?" Scales began to swell.

"Oh, no. Well, I didn't see one," Evan corrected. "Just sparks."

"'Just sparks.'" A muttered "everywhere she goes" he didn't think he was to hear as Esolesy moved the table in front of him. "Put your foot here for me," she said, "if you can." He did so, gasping when the spray touched the sole. She reared back. "I'm sorry—"

"No, no." He hadn't realized the *heat* until it ended. Evan waved at his foot, bringing up the other. "More. Please. It's—it's—wonderful." He blinked moisture from his eyes. "You've no idea. Please."

The Lishcyn resumed spraying. As the cool took away the last of his pain, Evan gasped again, this time with guilt. "S'kal-ru. She needs this."

"Don't worry. She has exceptional pain tolerance," with dry certainty. "It's an occupational requirement."

"For Library security?"

A tusk. "Apparently. You burned your feet on these wires?"

"My boots melted." Her stomach's reaction was audible through his torso, so he hurried on in his most comforting voice, "S'kal-ru cut them off before anything worse happened." He hoped. *Hadn't dared look*. "How are they?"

"Red. A few blisters. You should have the med-techs on the ship check, but I'm sure you'll be fine." Esolesy's brusque cheer sounded as forced as his comfort. "I'll send for some slippers before you try standing."

"No need," came a new voice. "I've brought a complete change of—" Polit Trili Bersin's smile vanished as she entered Paul's office, seeing the missing wall. "—Evan, what's going here?" Sharply. "Are you all right?"

"I found your liaison," S'kal-ru announced, stepping around his friend.

Not only that, but in the brief moments she'd been gone, the Kraal had changed into a fresh uniform, and applied a skin patch to cover the wounds on forehead, cheek, and neck—a patch that allowed the lines of her black- and-red tattoos to show, if dimly.

Evan did his best to smile confidently at his friend. "I'll brief you, Trili."

She'd a round pleasant face, usually set in lip-chewing concentration around the office. Past her initial shock, Trili composed her expression in the approved *approachable but on duty* calm, though Evan thought he caught a glint of *glad I'm not in charge* in her eyes with a definite *you'd better tell me all of it*.

"Is there somewhere not outside," his liaison asked crisply, "where Senior Polit Gooseberry can dress?"

"Orders are to expedite your return with whatever resources you require. Pie-for-brains," Trili added, punctuating each word with a light fist to his shoulder. "We were all worried—now look what you've done to yourself."

About to protest he hadn't done anything, Evan remembered the molting Carasian, added a confined Kraal, and conceded his guilt with a nod. "I still can't believe it. The ambassador sent a ship after me?"

"Not willingly." She handed him his boots, then grinned. "Took Polit M'Lean an entire day to convince Hansen your mission to the Library warranted pulling out all the stops."

He'd a mission? Overwhelmed, Evan focused on pulling his boot over soft, thankfully cushioned socks. Esolesy Ki had shown them to a workroom, presently quiet, probably fascinating, had he been able to pay attention. "The—Library. You told him?"

"Of course not." Trili crouched beside him, putting a hand on his knee. "Your lame excuse didn't fool M'Lean for a moment. You, the Library, what happened with the Popeakans? All on record. M'Lean had a pile of those pamphlets on his desk." She grimaced. "Which he threw in the air while yelling."

"Sorry."

"Oh, he wasn't yelling at me," she said, grinning. "Just at you. When he calmed down, he told me to tell you if you try something like this again, he'll—well, you don't want that."

"I won't do anything like this again," Evan assured her vehemently. "Ever."

"Right." Trili gave his knee a pat, then stood and dragged a seat to face him. "Quick brief, Evan. M'Lean doesn't like the situation any more than you do. To resolve it, he wants all the resources we can bring to bear on the Elves' problem, including your Library. He'll delay any action as long as he can. The Dokeci are stalling, which makes it easier, but there's no telling when that will change. Have you learned anything?" With hope.

"Not enough." Evan wasn't the least reassured to have their cool competent senior admit to an emotional judgment. *What next? A diplomat should act on impulse?* A slippery slope, that one. Look where he'd ended up.

"Evan?"

He blinked at Trili. "There was progress. The director and curator were coming back with me—to bring the Library's resources to the embassy—but that was before Paul was kidnapped. And Lionel."

Her eyes went wide. "Your Paul?"

Because you talked with your friends, the ones who understood you when family didn't. "He's not—" Shaking his head, Evan deliberately reached for his other boot. "What's important is we find them."

Trili nodded. "The *Mistral* has a security complement. We're here to take your orders, Polit." *Putting it on him, as she should.*

He stopped, boot in his hands, meeting her sympathetic eyes. *His orders?* He'd no training in security operations—

Neither did Senior Polit M'Lean. Who'd sent him a ship, not just Trili, a briefing, and clothes—however welcome and important those were. A ship full of experts.

To take his orders—

Esolesy Ki had told him where to start. *Help those in peril.* He shoved his foot into its boot, rising to his feet without hesitation, and if Evan was unaware of how his entire demeanor changed in that instant, how fire ignited his eyes and determination tightened his lips, Trili was not. She gave a curt nod and stood with him, waiting expectantly.

And Evan found he did know exactly what to say.

"Polit Bersin, contact the *Mistral*. The resources our mission requires have been taken. I expect them recovered, unharmed, and the felons apprehended."

"At once, Polit Gooseberry." She pulled out her com link, relaying his orders, then listened. "The aircar has arrived."

She hated flying.

Evan put aside his sympathy, giving his jacket a tug to remove the last wrinkle.

"Let's go."

23: Platform Dusk;
Lobby Evening

PAUL'S aircar was missing, a tempting explanation for the absence of Victory Johnsson, Jumpy Lyn, and the two thugs who'd pretended to change alliance while Skalet pretended to believe them. Given Johnsson's gift for misdirection, I'd cycled into my Lanivarian-self and sniffed the patio stones for myself. Finding all four familiar scents, I'd answered an instinct as old as Ersh and erased them with my own.

Lishcyn once more, I walked my web-kin through the Library. Those waiting in the lobby let us pass without interruption; I couldn't tell if the courtesy was because of Lambo, looming this time in front of the main doors, or because word had spread about Paul.

Then again, it could be Skalet.

Skalet, as S'kal-ru the Courier, was in full uniform, complete with weapons in plain sight. To increase the intimidation factor, she'd donned her distort-hood; the device made looking directly at her almost painful. She wore it when she felt inclined, or a threat. The hood also prevented the capture of a clear image, especially of the affiliations inked into her skin; those uniquely Kraal conceits that, admittedly, conveyed detailed information on status and the ever-changing connections between the Great Houses.

Unfortunately, the hood did nothing at close range to obscure her small, satisfied smile. "Look at all these clients. You have vital tasks to do here, Youngest."

Unfortunately, I'd remained what couldn't snarl. My Lishcyn-self also had trouble keeping up with her long, too-eager strides, having generous feet, but I did my best, skipping with a *thump* every few steps. We were heading to the main entrance, where a Commonwealth aircar waited.

Not for me.

"We've staff," I countered, in no mood to be appeased. I didn't like any of it, starting with being left behind, but I'd added her almost jolly attitude to the mix. *Never a good sign.* I lowered my voice as we passed Henri, who waved distractedly on her way elsewhere. "You escalated all this with your little stunt."

She stopped and turned to face me. "Stunt, you call it? I saved this Nonsense of yours. You should be happy, Youngest." A pale eyebrow lifted. "After all, I didn't use his mass."

After deliberately putting herself in a position to need it?

If it hadn't been Evan, if it had been Johnsson or her crew or perhaps Duggs Pouncey—would Skalet have chosen differently?

Small steps, as Paul would say. Thinking of him, I curled my lip in a peace offering. "I appreciate both." Somehow, I kept it polite. *Maturity, that was.* "I'll be happy when we find Paul and Lionel."

Her lips curved. "Lionel's no longer lost." She started walking again.

I hurried behind. "If this is something you should have told me—" I gave up. *As well ask a Carasian not to strut.* "What do you mean?"

"I'd slipped a tracer on him, of course, but the signal had been screened."

I tamped down my relief. "You have it now."

"We do."

"We" meaning her Kraal. However much Skalet decried my relationship with a Human, she was incapable of seeing anything reprehensible or dangerous in her intimate attachment to entire shiploads of the species. Warlike, armed individuals at that.

Under the circumstances, a flaw I chose to overlook. "And?"

"I've informed the Commonwealth ship that Lionel— and presumably Paul—are being held in the Parts and Repair Warehouse, east of the landing field. And offered our assistance."

I hoped Evan knew better than to take it.

Filling most of the train platform, the aircar was shiny clean and three times as large as any such craft on Botharis that didn't haul ore. There'd be smaller ones on the ship, so either the *Mistral*'s captain had seen an opportunity to display the advantages of the Commonwealth to the uncommitted, or to emphasize the importance of Acting Senior Polit Evan Gooseberry's mission.

Both, I decided.

Evan and his friend were climbing inside by the time we arrived, a timing that let Skalet gracefully add herself—staring down the startled crew. She didn't look back, but Evan did, gesturing me to come closer.

He looked gratifyingly in charge, from his bearing to the well-fitted jacket that was likely a little warm for this climate but, given it was probably lined with blaster-resist fibers, the most appropriate wear for the Diplomat-on-a-Mission. As a bonus, the pale yellow accentuated his dark skin and the cut was wonderfully modern.

My Lishcyn-self earnestly wished Paul owned such a jacket, as that was better than worrying about how dusk's growing shadows were clawing toward me. I'd forgotten my lantern in the rush, and this form's eyes were useless in dim light.

Beset by biology as well as rational concern, I struggled to curl a cheery lip at Evan and failed. "Good luck." Botharans were among the many Human groups encouraged by the thought chance could turn in their favor. *Ephemerals.*

"I wanted—" he looked over my head at the Library doors. "Where's Esen? I'd like to say good-bye."

"The curator has other responsibilities," I said, unhappy at the disappointment in his face, but unable to help it. "There are a number of upset clients," I added, because he'd care.

Evan nodded at once. "Please tell her I asked. And that I'll be putting in an urgent request for her time and expertise on Dokeci-Na. And Paul's." He mouthed the word *Elves.*

Because as Esen, I'd proposed a field trip.

My stomach lurched. *I'd done so as the wrong me.*

Hindsight frequently resulted in such revelations in my life, a fact of no use now. I stared at Evan's hopeful face, lost for what to say. The day might come when I could explain to him; at this moment, all I could think? *Was that I couldn't.*

Lish Na was a Dokeci protectorate, the Lishcyn in space—rarely—in the ships and by the tolerance of the Dokeci, who'd admired Lishcyn pottery almost as much as their new allies' prime location on the zenith of Dokeci space, long a source of concern. It had been quite a rude awakening to discover "stiff arms" did not, to Lishcyn, mean courage and fortitude against all odds but rather a state of abject defensive terror, especially in the dark.

On such points did alliances swing. The pottery fad faded and the Dokeci resigned themselves to maintaining part of their fleet in the Lishcyn system, no better off than before.

The Lishcyn, having gained access to space, powerful protectors, and offworld appreciation for their pots, embraced all things Dokeci. Hence the popular suffix "Ki" attached to Lishcyn names, and the extra sleeves on winterwear, which made excellent food storage pockets for excursions.

Esen the spacesick Lanivarian—a species never seen in Dokeci space and bearing a slight, but unmistakable resemblance to a common scavenger—was not the form to take. I had to go as Esolesy Ki, the patently harmless, well-thought-of poor relation in the Dokeci hierarchy.

"Esen may prattle about spaceflight," Skalet explained, appearing behind Evan's shoulder. "She can't handle it. Invite Esolesy Ki instead," she told him, looking straight at me. "She's every bit as useful as Esen and less prone to vomiting on your ship." My devious web-kin gave me her most charming smile. "Don't worry, Assistant Curator. I'll come as your security. I've been waiting to make a return visit."

No, she'd been waiting for an excuse to come along and make sure I took care of what mattered to our Web: Lesy's artwork.

"Regretfully, S'kal-ru, Survey ships aren't permitted to convey Kraal personnel. I can—" Evan blanched at her look, "—I will try to make an exception." He turned gratefully to me, the unarmed option. "Would you come then, Fem Ki? Between us, I'm sure we'll resolve this crisis."

While watching Skalet's head spin around as she registered she'd missed an entire "crisis" had its amusing side—my web-kin spending intense amounts of energy and time to not only know everything worth knowing first, but preferably to be the only one to know it— laughing would only elicit a deep cold rage. Especially as her attempt to gain access to the *Mistral* had failed. *She didn't make good choices then, in any sense.*

I settled for privately enjoying the moment, my face composed. "I'd be honored, Evan," I replied, clutching my lantern, then couldn't resist. I showed both tusks. "I trust you agree we should refrain from any exchanges of information until Paul and Lionel are secured."

"You're quite right," he replied. "Yes, of course."

Skalet's look to me then?

Sometimes, it was worth it.

I didn't wait to watch the *Mistral*'s aircar lift. We'd the day's final trainload of clients milling around in the lobby under the scowling gaze of our newly enlarged Carasian, minus the few locked in their habitat zones. The former would not be happy, the latter might not even have noticed, but the posted rules—and my weary preference— were strict: no overnight guests.

Celivliet Del being the exception, but I planned to

make sure the Anata boarded the train with the rest, despite Lambo's attempt to hoard her dish handler.

There being nothing I could do for Paul and Lionel—

The Cosmic Gods must have been laughing, because that was the moment Lambo bellowed, loud and clear, "CELI! DON'T LEAVE ME!"

I spotted the Anata trying to hide in the midst of a group of Queeb scholars who stared up at the Carasian in horror, then started to abandon poor Celi. I made my way toward the group, only to see Carwyn Sellkirk, our greeter and invaluable coordinator of intersystem passage—otherwise known as the transport wrangler—arrive first. He put an arm around the Anata and hustled him away.

In a fit of pique, Lambo slammed both great claws into the side of the walkway, chipping both. "Stop that!" I bellowed back. "We'll find someone else for the Chow."

The sly Carasian settled back with a pleased clatter—to the relief of all in the lobby.

"Esolesy! Over here." As Ally was running toward me, I elected to wait for her. She plunged to a halt, holding out a box, her face flushed with triumph. "What do you think?"

Unaware of any clients small enough to fit, nonetheless I looked in the box. It was full of brightly colored slips of Botharan paper—itself a novelty item we could have sold in a gift shop, but this was a place of knowledge, not commerce.

I was wearing Paul down on that one.

"Take a close look."

I obeyed, picking a slip up and holding it where my left eye, the best for reading, could focus. The font was attractive, something of interest to this me; the words were alarming. I looked up at the Human. "We're giving away questions?"

"Shh," she said, then grinned at me. "One each. So many lost their place in the queue or chance to input, Henri and I decided it was fair. Do you agree?"

It had the ring of those questions staff asked my Lishcyn-self in order to truthfully tell Paul later I'd been consulted, the answer to any and all being—"Yes," I said, forcing some enthusiasm. "This is fair. And quite clever. Well done, Ally."

I helped distribute the slips, along with Henri's two-for-one supper coupons at the Hamlet Haven, which confused more than a few but were graciously accepted nonetheless.

To be honest, those who'd been through today's false alarm and lockdown—not to mention Lambo's grimly enthused looming—were more grateful to be able to return to their ships. Their train would load shortly. If the situation at the landing field turned hot, as Rudy would say, the train would be ordered to stop on its track and wait for an all clear. In no way would these innocent scholars be put at risk.

So far, no one but staff knew there was a potential problem at the landing field, because when Lambo informed Rhonda Bozak, the operator, her train had to wait, she'd left to milk her herd of dairy elk because they most certainly could not.

As excuses for a delay went, this one was so normal, some of our repeat clients had reportedly laughed.

We'd other excuses, and perfect recall or not, I was growing confused which to use. I overheard Henri assuring a Grigari that we'd had a small fire in the basement. Ally and Quin, one of our greeters, told the Rands the food dispenser had acted up—at which everyone in hearing, who could hear, had given Lambo meaningful glares. I decided to stick with the tried and tested "maintenance issue" *with a hint of blocked plumbing* until Duggs—who'd arrived in the midst of all this—complained I was maligning her plumbing staff and where were the coveralls for the night shift?

Since I couldn't very well admit we'd given them away, I promised to look into it.

"And the lad?" Duggs asked, having cornered me. "How's he?"

"Evan? Thanks to you, very well."

She shrugged, uncomfortable with gratitude at the best of times, then gave me a searching look. "How're you?"

Afraid, tired, alone. I flashed a tusk. "Ready to call it a day," I admitted.

"Look, once the train loads, me and most of the staff are going to stick around—for news," she clarified. "We can handle what's left. Go home before it gets dark."

I'd hung my lantern from its belt. Thinking of the walk to the farmhouse, my fingers sought its comfort. "Are you sure?"

"Stick to the main floor," she advised. "Rest. We'll send someone to fetch you the moment we hear." A rare gentle smile. "Go, Esolesy. Paul would want you to look after yourself, too. You know that."

I gave a long, blubbery sigh.

And did.

Perception

THEY hadn't wanted assistance.
Humans never did.

They'd appreciated her tracker, however, using the information she'd provided to plan a tidy roundup with no casualties. Security personnel were moving into position around the Parts & Repair Warehouse, ready with stun grenades and sonic pops and other nonlethal nonsense.

How inefficient.

Skalet moved from shadow to shadow. It had been easy to fade from the preoccupied cluster of Commonwealth personnel, easier still to evade the Botharans. The landing field market had been ordered closed by the hamlet constable. To Botharans, that meant gathering in the drinking tent to complain about authority and drink—with the constable. *Foolish.*

Canvas flapped in the evening breeze. Metal clinked, rings on a pole. Wild things called from the distant hills and Skalet paused every so often to listen for what didn't belong.

She'd lied about a tracker on Lionel. *No matter.* Those who had taken the pair would have found one regardless, and where else could they go but here? The Youngest had seen their course. *Quartos Ank* confirmed an aircar touching down beyond the field at this end.

As well as the destination of another. Skalet's lips

pulled from her teeth in what was in no sense a smile. Ersh always had the Youngest clean up. *Why shouldn't she?*

Thirteen starships were fins down at the moment. The Survey ship towered over the rest, smug, round, and *inconvenient.* The other twelve waited for their passengers to arrive on the final train. Two were expensive private yachts, but the rest were the sort of transports you'd expect in a backwater like this.

The *Dimmont III* had set down at the very edge of the field, the side where the aircar had landed. Johnsson's ship. The *Trium Pa* had run her ident and stops, learned everything about the Snoprians and their passengers. When comp systems were pricked by Kraal, data bled. *Satisfactory.*

Paul Ragem valued her unique knowledge of the Kraal. He understood its danger, too, which was why what she gave to his precious collection couldn't be accessed through the Library itself. Only through him or the Youngest. He called it a priceless legacy.

Amusing.

Not yet full dark. Better, this confusion of twilight and shadow when Human eyes saw what they didn't and missed what was there. Skalet could roam this valley blind and know where she stepped. Here, the drainage ditch. Further along, the spill into a small pond—dry this time of year. She kept her head below any horizon, moving quickly.

They could not be allowed to reach their ship. Despite tales of space pirates, it was easier to destroy a ship than catch one without damage—and almost impossible to affect a rescue.

She would not fail.

The Youngest dared find fault. Allowing herself to be betrayed by Todd and Nides—*those fools*—then captured by Johnsson had been brilliant. In a surgical strike, without a hint of disturbance, she'd gained access to Johnsson's tech capabilities and discovered the means by which Johnsson had intended to destroy the Library.

All while learning her enemy. Driven by greed. Affected by spite. *Wasting what might have been a fine tactical mind . . .*

She worked best alone. Safest, alone.

Her Kraal were superior members of their kind. Loyal, but *ambitious*. Such served until an opportunity for greater glory presented itself. The Youngest couldn't appreciate the pleasure of that endless struggle. Never understood how S'kal-ru couldn't reach out from seeming weakness, only from strength. You didn't call for help.

You helped yourself—

Skalet activated her scope, reset to what she'd learned about Johnsson's mesh, lifting her weapon.

—and you became *the glory*.

24: Kitchen Night

I shone my lantern on the path ahead, startling flat leaf-shaped amphibians who jumped and tumbled out of my way. The light reflected tiny coinlike disks from the darkness of grass. Mousels, active in this, their time, and unafraid of me.

"No treats tonight," I told them. It wasn't so much I fed them as this tended to shed crumbs.

It wasn't the first time I'd toddled back to the farmhouse at day's end as Esolesy Ki, lantern in hand, talking to the locals.

Just the first time alone.

Good for the perspective. When I was with Paul, it didn't matter if I couldn't see past my fingertips. His presence gave me the courage biology hadn't.

Ersh would be horrified.

Maybe. There were times I tasted something in her memories, a name or place, that came with an unexpected warmth. I tried not to dwell on them, since most involved eating and often screaming, but still . . .

Thoughts not a comfort right now. I raised the lantern, sure I was almost home. Though if I defined home by where we slept, this wouldn't be home until Paul's loft was restored and I'd suggest some improvements—

I shut down my inner babble, the coping mechanism abruptly distracting, and raised the lantern higher still, giving it the little shake that sent the beam outward with enough brightness to cross a field, albeit in a slender beam.

It was a very good lantern.

The old barn, sides bleached white. It stood over the Library's main storage system, though that wasn't the only one. Branches and leaves, stark black, moved against the white.

Beneath them, tucked against one wall, rested Paul's aircar.

I turned, sending spears of light around me. No one. Nothing out of the ordinary.

Everything was! It didn't take Lishcyn nerves to sense it. They were back—whatever combination didn't matter— *they* were back. The ones who'd done violence to my web-kin, which she'd allowed but still upset me. The ones who'd wanted to destroy the Library and harm all those inside.

And it didn't matter if *they* had taken Paul and Lionel, or helped, or had nothing to do with that nastiness. *They* didn't belong here.

I stomped forward, instead of away, having no plan whatsoever beyond expressing my firm opinion—and possibly vomiting.

But when I reached the aircar, those inside were beyond listening.

The two Humans. Jumpy Lyn. They sat in the aircar, collapsed in the humiliating disarray of fresh corpses. At least the Ervickian had closed its mouths first, sealing in what was sure to be a stench. They wore mesh suits and I could see the handles of weapons, for what good they'd done.

What I couldn't see was Johnsson.

I turned my light toward the farmhouse, lowering it to the ground, and squinted mightily. These eyes couldn't tell if any lights were on inside.

Oh, to become something . . . different. To become a weapon.

Or flee, a sensible part of me suggested.

But I was more than this form or any other. *Paul had taught me that.* This was our home.

Holding my lantern to light my steps, I made my slow careful way to the back farmhouse door.

Refusing to think who might be waiting.

Perception

A hand closed over his wrist. Lifted but didn't leave; Lionel could feel the warmth of it. A fingertap. Taptap. Three more, then one.

Attention. That was the initial contact. The rest—*what did the rest mean?* He hadn't used hand signals in over fifty years, infrequently once promoted, but surely the sheer weight of practice—

They sat in a hole, or ditch. Tied back to back, mouths sealed with tape, and a thick, smothering cover over top. Dirt and moss below. Damp below that. He couldn't see, couldn't hear. Paul hadn't moved until now. He hadn't, other than to try and ease a cramp.

Tap. Taptap. Three more, then one. Another grip, and the hand was gone. *Think,* he ordered himself, frustrated.

There were only so many situations where a First Contact Team employed covert hand signals; all ones you did your utmost to avoid. In hiding. While being pursued and trying to hide.

Having failed both, capture. *That was it.* Paul's signal. It meant "rescue coming."

Or was it "be ready to escape?" Regardless, both offered hope and Lionel fought to keep his breathing slow and steady. He wriggled his hand, reached, and found Paul's arm. Squeezed once. *Understood.*

He wasn't as desk-bound as a few years ago; it had become habit to run each day. Lionel raised his knees and

did what he could to work his ankles in their bindings.
There was no knowing how Paul felt. At minimum, he'd
have a stun headache. Multiple hits could cause heart pal-
pations and dizziness. Their captors had half-carried him
here from the aircar.

Then he'd carry Paul, if he had to—

What was that?

The cover shifted! Lionel flared his nostrils, breathing
as hard and deeply as he could, ready to burst into action.
He felt Paul tense. This was it—

With a blast of fresh air, the cover was whisked away.
Bodies tumbled out of the dark into their hole, dropped
on them, still warm. *Still breathing,* Lionel realized when
one groaned. A fellow prisoner?

Unlikely.

He tried to kick, felt Paul do the same, but his legs
were pinned.

Something pulled the bodies away, then a thin beam
of light flickered over his face, touched his bonds, went
past his shoulder.

Then turned briefly back.

Skalet's smile was the best thing Lionel had ever seen.

25: Kitchen Night

THE farmhouse was dark. The dark of lurking monsters and pits of endless depth and the only reason I didn't turn on the lights when I entered the kitchen was simply because I wouldn't let go of my lantern and I couldn't let go of the door handle.

"Wine?"

I raised the lantern, illuminating the figure seated at the far end of the table. A bottle was cradled between her hands. The neck had been broken off, explaining the spill and the drips to the floor.

If not the eyeballs.

"You like that cheap red, with the bubbles. Right?"

"Chase." I made my hand release the door handle, though my scales were swollen tight. Her real name might be Victory Johnsson. To me that voice, with its quick little barb, was pure Janet Chase. "It's over."

"Maybeso." She raised the bottle, pouring toward her mouth, capturing some. The rest stained her cheeks and chin red. More red leaked from the gaping holes where her eyes had been and *were those worms crawling from inside?*

My hand had trembled—the light had. When I steadied, what I could see were the broken stubs of connectors. Her augmented eyeballs sat on the table cracked open like eggs; blood smeared their workings.

I took a step into the kitchen, not the least ready to put down my lantern. "What happened to your crew?"

"Dropped dead." The bottle swung to encompass the kitchen and beyond. "Things were going so well, too." With a smile made grotesque by wine and blood, Chase produced a blaster, leaving it on the table by the eyeballs. Given the size of target offered by my Lishcyn-self, she hardly needed to set it to wide dispersal, but the weapon was, I judged, just for show. "Why hasn't your Library blown up?"

As if honestly curious.

"Why would you want it to?" I countered, quite honestly upset. "You could have left, got away. Why try to kill all those people?"

"Not them." She tipped the bottle at me. "You. I needed to kill you. I warned my backers no one could take Paul Ragem without you following. You and—" the bottle waved, "—your friends. You've far too many. But it's you—" another salute, "—who inspire them. You're the threat."

I didn't feel like one. I found I'd sat down, my scales softening enough to allow my middle to bend. I set the lantern down but left my hand near it for comfort. "Why take Paul? He doesn't know anything about his mother's ship."

"Answer my question . . . Answer mine . . . first." Chase frowned and shook her head as if to clear it. "Why aren't you dead?"

It wasn't the wine. "You shouldn't have captured S'kal-ru," I said sadly. "I'm sorry."

Her head lifted. "That Kraal—?" Expressions fought to own her face. Rueful won. "Damn. An assassin. You keep . . . you keep interesting . . . company, Esolesy Ki."

An understatement. Any contact would have been sufficient. A needle's prick, perhaps, but I wouldn't put it past Skalet to soak her uniform in poison. She'd have chosen precisely the type and dosage for the desired result. *That Chase wasn't already dead?*

Given a choice, Skalet didn't waste a potential resource. Her original plan would have been to interrogate Chase—to offer the antidote for the truth. *She'd done it to Paul.*

Because of Paul—and Lionel—my web-kin had discarded her plan and this Human without a second thought. After all, she'd five more "resources" waiting at the landing field.

"Tell me, Janet," I urged. "About the *Sidereal Pathfinder* and Paul. While you—"

"You're afraid of the dark, Lishcyn. Die in it." She grabbed the bottle, pouring wine over her face and mouth. I watched the muscles of her throat as she swallowed convulsively. Didn't move as, emptied, the bottle flew in my general direction, smashing on the floor.

I asked, having no other comfort to offer, "Shall I get you another?"

"NO!" Her hand went unerringly to the blaster, closing on the handle, dragging it close. The other swept out, dashing the remnants of her eyes to the floor. "I don't—want—damn you to all the hells, Es. I don't want to die like this! I don't want to die with YOU!"

"Then don't." I leaned forward. "Think of Paul. Help him, Janet. Why is he in danger?"

Eye sockets aimed at me. "Paul . . ." wistful. Her body began to slump, her free hand fumbling at her chest—

Too late. I knew it, knew there was no point, but couldn't stop myself from shouting, "Tell me! Why is Paul in danger? Why now?!"

The echoes of my voice stopped, and I heard the last breath leave her lungs. Felt the dark pressing around me, cold and empty.

Her hand fell on the table, palm up, holding a disk.

Above it, hovering in lantern light, appeared an image. It was rendered in the cooler end of the light spectrum, framed in what might be script or decoration. Details I remembered later, too shocked by the subject itself: a starship—what remained of one—adrift in space.

I'd asked *why now*. Here was the answer.

Someone had found Veya Ragem's ship.

The *Sidereal Pathfinder*.

Perception

"**Y**OUR Kraal lied to us, Polit Gooseberry."

S'kal-ru would have a reason, a good one. However much Evan believed it, it wasn't the answer to give Kamaara, commander of the well-armed, highly trained Survey security detail standing around in the empty warehouse like so many lost cadets.

"She did, Commander." *M'Lean had put him in charge.* "I take full responsibility."

Kamaara gave a curt acknowledging nod, her face still clouded and grim, but perhaps slightly less so. "I suggest, Polit, a return to the ship before the residents notice we've rousted them for nothing."

"We'll continue the search from there." *Had that sounded like a question?* Evan coughed to clear his throat. "That's an order, Commander."

Her lips twisted as if on something sour. She lowered her voice. "Polit Gooseberry, if I may speak frankly?"

He'd prefer she didn't. *Another answer not to give.* "Of course."

"You're new to all this. With respect, I don't believe you fully grasp the mountain—not hill—the mountain of stinking hot dung about to fall on your head if you continue to deploy Commonwealth resources in grounder business. Polit."

About what he'd expected, if more colorful. Evan nodded. "Thank you, Commander. Allow me to be frank in return. These grounders are essential to my mission, and that mission, authorized by the Commonwealth's embassy on Dokeci-Na, is why you and the *Mistral* are here. We don't lift till they're found." His tone sharpened. "Is that clear?"

To his astonishment, her face cleared as she snapped to attention. "Perfectly, Polit. Let's go hunting." This last loud enough to garner pleased looks from her staff, who picked up their gear and moved forward.

This wasn't something to be happy about, but that was his admittedly biased opinion. Hadn't his friends at the embassy been glad to use their training? He'd puzzle over Kamaara's reaction later. Much later.

Electing to go around the field perimeter, avoiding tents, lights, and the train station, they moved out in a tight formation, with him in the middle. Evan was quite sure the security personnel thought they were going at a slow pace for his sake, but their steady distance-eating jog would have been sufficient challenge without burned feet.

He kept up, soon lost in a state of mindless misery. S'kal-ru, Paul, Lionel, let alone the Elves, all faded under the effort to put each now-flaming foot ahead of the next. Over and over.

So when they stopped, he didn't, plowing into those in front, careening backward. Hands took hold, strong but polite; Evan brushed them aside with an embarrassed mutter of, "I'm fine. My fault."

He abruptly realized they stood at the bottom of the *Mistral*'s ramp, her port open and welcoming above, and they were far from the only ones. The area was abuzz with activity. A grav stretcher was coming down. Uniformed security was everywhere, blending confusingly with his, and Commander Kamaara plunged into the mix, shouting at someone.

A silky soft whisper in his ear. "Evan."

He jumped, he couldn't help it, then wished he hadn't because the motion jarred his feet and he barely kept his groan between his teeth. "S—"

"Don't use that name. Skalet will do." Her arm went slipped beneath his and she took most of his weight. "You didn't have the med-techs look, did you? That's not brave. It's foolish."

Whatever it was didn't matter. He strained to see over the milling crowd. "Did you find them? Paul and Lionel? Are they safe?"

"Did you doubt me?"

He rubbed his forehead with a shaking hand. "You lied—"

A laugh so low he felt it in his bones. "I arranged."

What had the Lishcyn said? *That this was all her fault—*

If he'd dared, he'd have pulled free of her. "Does she know?" Evan demanded, his voice cracking. "Esen. We have to tell Esen."

Her careless shrug started them moving forward. "Plenty of time for that. Let's get you tended."

But when they reached the first med-tech, Evan found himself alone.

26: Kitchen Night;
Porch Night

I cleaned up.

Ersh would have expected it. Doubtless Skalet had.

I didn't mind. It wasn't as though I could curl up in my straw bed, sleep the night, then the next morning wake up and go, "Oh, look. Someone left a body in the kitchen."

Our home. Our kitchen. Places that would never be the same if Paul saw her. *Saw this.*

He'd be back and safe. Was likely on his way now. Or I would, as Chase so succinctly put it, follow and bring him back, safe. Those were the only permissible options, leaving me the task at hand.

I opaqued the windows—which in the farmhouse and to the Hamlet of Hillsview Preservation Committee meant pulling pieces of fabric together on their slide—and turned up the lights. *Not an improvement.*

The eyeballs and broken bottle went into the recycler, digested to their component molecules. Unsure what would happen if I tried that with the blaster, I stuck the weapon in a pot and shoved it in the back of a lower cupboard. Safety first.

Should I recycle the disk or not? Veya's ship was Paul's inheritance; it had proved to be a magnet for trouble. In the end, I put it in my mouth, rolling my forked tongue over it to clean off the remnants of wine and Human. *Maybe Paul would believe I found it.*

What to tell him troubled me. The Web of Esen held

two Web-beings and a Human. As Senior Assimilator, it was up to me to presort what I shared with the rest. Until this very moment, I hadn't considered it my responsibility to do so other than for Skalet.

I hadn't felt the centuries I'd lived before Paul until now either. To me, he was the Eldest, my teacher as well as friend. Did he remain all of those, if I decided what he was to know, and what not?

Would he trust me, ever again? Should he?

I spat the disk out, and dried it with a towel, tucking the thing in the cookie jar. "No lies," I vowed aloud. No cookies, either, and my stomachs protested.

They could wait. Removing my caftan, I hung it on a hook, then calmly released my hold on this form.

There were myriad ways to get rid of a corpse.

The cells of her body were dying, not dead, permitting me to assimilate them into web-mass. Before cycling again, I excised every last scrap of what had been Janet Chase, Victory Johnsson, or other name from my flesh, leaving a puddle on the floor.

I stepped over soaking wet clothing, avoiding her boots, and shook my paws with distaste. This me hated water.

Her clothes and boots went into the recycler.

Mop next. Gloves first.

Duras. I'd tasted it in Chase's flesh, a substance having no effect on mine. An extract from duras' sap was the quintessential Skalet poison. Adaptable in its timing. Sure in its result. The only antidote remained *within* Skalet's Kraal-self. She'd taken centuries in that form to develop its immunity, one only she could grant. A drop of her blood would have saved Chase. A moist kiss. I felt a little better, knowing there was nothing I could have done.

Could do? That remained to be seen. My impetuous— *how she'd hate to be called that*—web-kin had responded to a real threat as she always had. Her way. No doubt she'd expect me to be grateful. Because of Skalet, the Library stood, those within it alive.

Grateful I might have been, had I believed that result mattered to her in the slightest.

Family.

I cleaned and scrubbed until the least suspicious person on this planet would be convinced I was hiding something, the kitchen never before the recipient of this much attention. Well, that time I'd spilled—

I would tell Paul what had happened in another room altogether, before he saw the now-gleaming kitchen. Maybe even outside. Not near the barn, though. I'd left those nice informative corpses in his aircar, after all; the constable should like that. *Paul, not so much.*

Predictably, I came to the point where even I couldn't find more to clean—unless I was truly ridiculous about it and brought in a ladder to brush years of cobwebs from the rafter peak.

No news. Nothing.

Nothing didn't prove a problem, I assured myself, despite the number of times it had. Rescues were complicated. It was night. There were hills.

I should have gone.

Where there were individuals with weapons and who knew what other tech, on both sides? Where there were innocent bystanders, an additional trainload having set off a while ago—I'd heard the whistle—while I scrubbed the table? Starships. There were those as well, and they had crews and lights and—

I should have heard by now.

I grabbed a com link and chose the front porch, with its vantage point over the path and Library. No need for lights. This me had excellent night vision and, to my Lanivarian senses, the air itself was painted with scent and alive with sound. I curled up on the wide cushioned swing, rested the com link between my feet, and willed it to activate.

Nothing.

To while away the passing minutes, then slow march of hours, I called up memories of my time with Lesy, trying to estimate how many Ersh busts she could have made. After all, to Skalet, that was my reason for going to Dokeci-Na. Remembering the allure of web-flesh from the miniscule amount on Evan's bust, she wasn't wrong, simply—optimistic. Yes, I'd that essential to my Lanivarian-self, a workable search image allowing a heightened predatory fix on my intended prey. But I wasn't going as a Lanivarian, the busts weren't mousels hiding in tall grass—

And Paul and I could hardly search an entire planet. *Excuse us, have you a bust of Teganersha-ki handy? I want to—*

What? Lick the bottom?

Paul would find that funny.

Before he could, I'd have to reveal Lesy's careless use of her flesh, something I wasn't quite sure how to broach even to this Human.

Before that? Paul had to be safe. Come home.

With a sigh, I began doing the math on how many Tumbler excretions Lesy could have collected while engaged in Ersh bust creation.

Done with that, I began—

A throbbing *whoowhooo—OO* from outside interrupted my running tally—already depressingly long—of all the works of art Lesy had produced that Ersh had bothered to share with me. The hunting cry of the *wertowl* was a familiar sound this time of year; we'd a pair living in the barn, with mouths to feed.

The cry meant it was time to head home, according to Botharans, who called the bird "Midnight."

I whined and picked up the com link, a clawtip poised to activate it. With another, deeper whine, I put it down again.

Who could I call? The *Mistral,* and ask for Evan? He'd have been in touch if he could. For all I knew, the Commonwealth had locked him up for deserting his post at the embassy. Wake poor Constable Lefebvre? I could hear him now. *Leave it to the experts.*

Skalet? Our code was for emergencies of the life, death, exposure of Web secrets variety. *Not my feelings.*

I drew my tail over the tip of my nose and watched the dark.

Perception

THE Commonwealth Survey Ship *Mistral* was freshly commissioned and state-of-the-art, so new her corridors smelled like a showroom, and Lionel Kearn—former captain of not one but two such vessels back in the day—would have loved a tour.

Had one been offered.

They had, with firm politeness, offered him a med exam instead. Insisted really, and while he sat to wait his turn, sipping on a warm restorative drink—in a mug with the ship's logo, no less—Lionel was relieved to see they'd taken Paul first. He lay on a medtable under an array of sensors, being examined by three techs who murmured to one another.

The row of five, stripped to undergarments, seated against the wall to Lionel's left didn't say a word, nor did the five guards lined up facing them, stunners out and ready.

Everything was bright and clean and, yes, so new Lionel had the distinct impression they were the first patients to be treated here.

Begging the question why. *Why a Commonwealth ship? Why here and now?*

Paul had briefed him on Evan's claims and these "Elves." Tempting as it was, Lionel had difficulty thinking Evan's superiors would send such substantial support for an officer who'd, in essence, deserted his post and taken an alien diplomatic crisis entirely too personally.

Like someone else he knew . . .

Paul and Esen would believe it. It could even be true. But without corroborating evidence—or Evan himself—Lionel preferred another, colder hypothesis: the *Sidereal Pathfinder* logs. Something had rekindled that twenty-year-old mystery, and she'd been a Survey ship. He'd been Survey, too, and remained proud of the service's legendary past, of its mandate to be the first official Human presence to go forth, alone, and greet the new.

He knew its flaws, *having been one*. Officers trained to be self-sufficient, surviving because of it, became self-reliant and impatient with authority. Dismissive of it. *He had, believing himself right.* Within the sprawling hierarchy of the Commonwealth, little wonder Survey was an entity unto itself.

Their welcome aboard the *Mistral* did nothing to dissuade him. Conversation had been firmly, but politely, discouraged. They'd taken his name. Asked for his patience and after his needs. Assured him "this won't take long." Much as Lionel approved of caution, especially fins down in a foreign port, that wasn't what this was.

This was secrecy above the chain of command. This was need-to-know, and the *Mistral*'s captain? Didn't.

Hence confining them here, under the guise of care. Expose the minimum number of personnel. Gather unknowns in a single, well-watched area.

Conspicuously absent, a certain "Kraal." Lionel dipped his head to hide a smile. *Skalet was remarkable.* A force unto herself, really. She'd subdued the five as easily as he'd peel fruit. After removing his and Paul's bonds, and a quick inspection, she'd had their former captors help them go around the landing field, avoiding their ship, to bring them to this one.

He'd lost sight of her, among the *Mistral*'s security.

Before that?

In wonder, Lionel touched his cheek—

"Lionel?"

Paul! Aware those watching were armed and suspicious, Lionel rose slowly, gesturing to the medtable. He waited for a guard to nod before going to Paul's side.

Paul turned his head on the pillow in a listless movement, hair tumbling over unfocused eyes. His skin was an unhealthy gray, and Lionel shot an alarmed look at the nearby med-techs. "Is he all right?"

"You can ask me, you know," faint, but with reassuring humor.

A med-tech glanced at the display above the table. "Hom Ragem's condition is improving," she replied. She gazed down at Paul, brows lifting. "Not enough to leave this bed anytime soon."

Lionel's stomach clenched. The tech used Paul's real name, the name under which he'd served in Survey, the name Lionel had besmirched. Restored, yes, but those records—the information in them never went away.

What of the *Sidereal Pathfinder*'s? Veya Ragem's? Had they been expunged or buried under the highest clearances—or did they connect, now, to Paul?

Let alone the fact that First Contact Specialist Paul Ragem had been pronounced dead fifty-one years ago.

Paul's look sharpened, a warning in them, and Lionel collected himself. The moment his friend had been put on this table and scanned, his identity had been revealed. They'd deal with any repercussions if—when—they arose.

"Then you're in the right place," he asserted warmly.

"No, I'm not." Firm gentle hands thwarted Paul's attempt to sit. He lay back without a struggle. "I have to go home," he continued, his tone now the persuasive one Lionel knew well. "My family will be worried."

Esen. *Who, despite being the next best thing to immortal, didn't take waiting well at all.*

"I'm sure they've been notified," Lionel began.

This time, Paul moved too quickly to be stopped, sitting up, his feet over the side. The head med-tech lifted her hand to prevent reaction from others in the room, lowering it when her patient didn't try to stand.

Paul's focus was on Lionel. "You haven't called her?"

Hurt and accusation in the question. Worse, disappointment, and Lionel felt himself flush.

"We've no exterior coms here," the med-tech replied for him. "As your friend says, I'm sure those concerned have been told you're safe—"

"Right." The prisoner half-rose, ignoring the guards

and the quelling *hiss* from the Snoprians at his side. "It's always 'bout him. Whaddabout us?"

All expression left Paul's face. "Hello, Jan."

Jan Terworth was a cousin, many times removed and usually in trouble of some sort, having poor taste in friends. "That doesn't," Paul told Lionel in a too-even voice, "make him less family."

"He stunned you three times."

"When we were young, he'd toss me in the creek." A wry smile. "Jan's a hothead. But he's—"

"Family," Lionel finished for him. "What do you want to do?"

Following Jan's little outburst the guards ordered they be separated, so the med-techs had moved the two of them into the adjoining recovery room. They'd have privacy until the prisoners had been checked over.

Or until those in command of the *Mistral* decided it was time to check on Paul Ragem.

"Get out of here." Paul refused to lie back on the cot, despite looking ready to collapse. "Failing that, locate our security." Neither of them mentioned Skalet, or S'kal-ru, by name. "She has the resources."

Relieved, Lionel stopped pacing. "She does—and that's who I meant. When I said I was sure the news of our rescue went out."

"Send a comforting message?" An eyebrow lifted. "You do know who we're talking about here."

Lionel frowned. "Paul, she rescued us." *And in the dark, cool lips had brushed his cheek.* Flustered, he went on, "Single-handed!"

"Did she?" with a snap. "Think, Lionel."

Unfair. "I am. Better than you are, at the moment. Sk—Security risked her life to set us free and capture five prisoners."

"Don't think me ungrateful, especially for the life of my rascally cousin, but—" Paul rose to his feet. He swayed, steadying himself with a hand pressed to the bulkhead before Lionel could offer help. "—she does nothing unless it's to her particular advantage. Make Es suffer, waiting for news? She'd call it a valuable lesson." Face set in grim lines, he took a step, sliding his hand along. "I'm getting out of here."

"No, no, you mustn't—" At the look Paul gave him, Lionel raised his hands and backed a step. No farther. "All right. Let me try once more to gain access to a com. If they refuse, I'll tell them I know where to find their wayward diplomat."

"Lionel—"

"I realize that might be a betrayal, but—why are you—?" *Why was Paul looking over his shoulder with that dumbfounded expression?* Lionel turned slowly.

"I'm already here," Evan Gooseberry announced with a wide happy smile. He was much better dressed than Lionel recalled, every bit the professional. *The slippers were an unusual choice.* "How are you both? They wouldn't let me through until the—" His smile vanished, bright green eyes studying Paul. "What's wrong?"

"Is Esolesy with you?" Paul asked urgently. "Or Esen?" However stressed, he didn't forget the little things. *Or was it years of practice?*

"No, we—"

"Do they know, Evan? That we're all right?"

Evan didn't bother answering. He went to the panel on the wall. "This is Polit Gooseberry to the bridge. Has notification been sent to the Library about their people?"

"This is the Communications Officer of the Watch. Which library, Polit?"

"The All Species' Library of Linguistics and Culture," Evan answered with commendable patience. "Has the notification been sent?"

"No, Polit. The *Mistral* remains under communications blackout until—"

"Send it now." The command in his tone made Lionel's shoulders involuntarily straighten. "Inform me when you have confirmation it's been received by the curator, Esen-alit-Quar, or her assistant, Esolesy Ki."

"At once, Polit."

The room fell silent. Waiting.

So the unlikely was true, Lionel told himself. This ship

was here for Evan, everything he'd told them about the Elves and Dokeci was factual, and the next logical assumption was the situation was worse than even Evan knew. None of which precluded Survey interest in their lost ship, official or clandestine, but he'd keep that hypothesis to himself, for now.

Evan's eyes locked on Paul. "It's my fault," he said suddenly. "I should have contacted them as soon as I arrived on board. I shouldn't have listened to anyone else. I'm so sorry."

Without a word, Paul returned to the cot and sat, looking down at the hands on his knees.

Lionel took pity on the now-forlorn diplomat. "Polit, why does the ship remain under blackout?"

"There was an attempt to blow up the Library—everyone's safe," as Paul's head jolted up. "But Johnsson and her lot—escaped afterward. Skalet said they took your aircar."

She'd allowed this—this child *to use her real name in public?* Lionel calmed himself. *Of course, she did.* It wasn't a Kraal name; anyone hearing it, if they connected the two, would consider it an alias for use with strangers. *Clever, as always.*

"Brilliant," Paul said, but it wasn't praise. "An escape and rescue, all in one day." He pressed the palm of his hand against his forehead, then sighed. "What a mess."

Evan took a worried step closer. "Commander Kamaara's personnel are keeping a watch on the landing field. They won't get away."

There was something dark in Paul's eyes. "I guarantee they haven't."

Before Lionel or Evan could respond, a voice came through the panel. "Polit Gooseberry, this is Com Officer Snead. We have confirmation from a person who identified themselves as Duggs Pouncey who, and I quote, wishes me to tell you, 'About damn time.'"

Paul looked at Evan, his mouth shaping 'Esen.' The diplomat nodded. "What of Esen, or Esolesy? Have they received the news?"

"Pouncey couldn't confirm that, Polit. Neither being has been located and there are search parties out—"

What was she up to? Lionel worried. *And as what?*

But the com officer wasn't finished. "—they found something else, however. It's disturbing news, Polit."

Evan looked at Paul. "Go ahead."

"An aircar, near the Library, with bodies inside. Commander Kamaara conveys that she's prepared to dispatch personnel to investigate, at your command."

Paul was on his feet, rigid, his face working.

Evan Gooseberry had no way to know the depths of the bond—the love—between this Human and his alien "friends." All Lionel could do was hope, fervently, that this young diplomat realized there'd be no keeping Paul from Esen, short of restraints and force.

And no friendship left, if he tried.

27: Track Night

I'D taken the Library train once before, the first time it had run. Paul and I had filled it with staff and their families, the journey more party than test, and there'd been hats and noisemakers, plus spontaneous outbursts of cheering whenever Brollo laid on the horn. It had been morning, that trip, snowy and crisp, with ice lacing the branches.

This time, it was the aptly named dead of night, and I'd still only taken the train once.

This time, I ran.

Waiting was overrated. I'd grown anxious with time—the wertowl had not helped there—until I'd begun twitching on the swing. That not being recommended, I'd begun pacing. From there, it was only a question of pacing with long loping strides and picking a direction.

I should have done this before. This me felt wonderful, running, though I had to curb the temptation to snap at bats. The unwary things swooped low, after the smaller creatures I startled into the air.

Also tempting snap-at-me targets. *This would be why civilized Lanivarians eschewed running on all fours other than at sporting events or the occasional discreet holiday with nature.*

The tracks were far from the shortest route to the landing field. We'd wanted our clients to enjoy the scenery while granting us time between arrivals. Also, there'd been some concerns expressed by the Hamlet of Hillsview Preservation Committee over our initial, more ambitious plan, involving two tunnels, a bridge, and a loop.

The loop had been my idea, scribbled on the plan in our kitchen after a very long day and a delightful bottle of wine. I'd dutifully erased it the next morning, with a few dramatically sorrowful sighs that might have also had something to do with the delightful wine.

Watching, Paul waited till I was done before telling me he'd made a copy. *Anything's possible, Old Blob,* he'd said. *Look at you.*

I'd be hard to see now. My fur was close in color to the gray-brown of the track bed, and I avoided the central rail.

Not the shortest route but the fastest, for this me, free of tangled thickets and nasty wet bogs, and every extension of my spine, every pull of muscle, brought me closer to Paul.

Or farther away. I wasn't so lost in *chase* mind-set not to be aware I could be going the wrong way. Paul and Lionel could have arrived home by now, and if they had, Paul would come this way after me. Perhaps borrow an aircar from the *Trium Pa.*

Ersh. Skalet would be insufferable.

What mattered was Paul would know this would be my route. I was determined, not foolish.

Not entirely.

The grade increased inexorably, the landing field set above the valley. My tongue lolled to the side, shedding this body's heat, and I was forced to slow my pace, if not walk.

I'd have to speak to Duggs about this track bed. Who'd thought small sharp stones were a good idea? Did Humans not walk along it for picnics in the hills?

Stars twinkled above. I wrinkled my snout at them, in case any were ships containing those who plotted against Paul and the Library, then stopped, because more likely they were stars. Around each would be worlds, worlds with life. Life that could be doing what I was at the moment. Running toward what was absolutely necessary to their existence.

Fearing it was gone.

It would be one day. He *would be.* I didn't need Ersh-memory to remind me my time with Paul was not only finite, but infinitesimal, in Web terms.

Some moments transcend time. She was proof, when it came to it. The little bust Lesy'd made and Evan now carried next to his heart was of such a moment within Ersh's millennia of existence. Ephemeral they might be, flickers of life in the darkness, but an entire species—more than one—remembered Teganersha-ki to this day. Lived by laws she'd put in place, in a peace she'd begun.

Not intentionally. *Whatever you do, don't be memorable,* being among Ersh's firmest admonishments to me. But sometimes—

I staggered and caught myself.

—sometimes, maybe most of them, you didn't know how you changed the lives around you. As Paul had changed mine. As I'd changed his.

Selfish, to want every possible moment, when already I'd gained so much, but I did, I did, I did—

I crashed into Paul before I saw him. "Whoa, old girl!" He couldn't keep his feet and fell back. I didn't help, jumping and climbing over him, sniffing and whining in the urgent necessity to be sure it *was* him and he was unharmed. The Human was no more sane, affectionately thumping whatever he could reach, and calling my name in a broken voice.

I stopped at last, standing over him, and bent to put my nose to his. "I knew you'd find me." A quick lick. Tears, dirt, sweat. Most of all, Paul.

Two hands dug into the fur of my neck and shook my head from side to side. "I knew you wouldn't wait."

And waste a moment? But there was no time, and no need, to be maudlin. I rose to my feet and helped Paul to his. "Is Lionel safe?" I asked then. "Is it over?"

"He is." Paul picked his hand light up from the stones. "If by 'it' you mean my mother's past, for now, yes. Hold this."

I took the light, aiming it at his hands. He brought out a com link and activated it. Calling a ride, I hoped. In the light, he looked more fragile than I'd sniffed. "Are you all right?"

"Cousin stunned me," without resentment. "Three times. Though I only," thoughtfully, "remember the first."

"Is this a cousin invited to the Garden?" I hoped not.

"He'll be locked away for a while." Paul sighed. "Jan blamed me, Es. That made it easy for someone to bribe him into causing trouble."

This Jan made his choice, I thought grimly, but didn't argue the point. I yawned as wide as I could. "Ready to go home?"

"Long enough to pack."

My ears pricked up. "Pardon?"

His fingers sought the soft skin behind one of those ears. "Field trip. Remember?"

Yes, but— "You were kidnapped. And stunned three times by a cousin." Not to mention been dropped off to wait for me on a train track in the dark—the details of that I looked forward to hearing.

"We've a job to do." Paul's voice roughened with emotion. "The job we started the Library to do."

Well, then. I licked his nose. "Let's go save the Elves."

Perception

THE pilot of the *Mistral*'s aircar had set her down, as ordered and with skill, by the side of the train rail leading to the All Species' Library of Linguistics and Culture, in the midst of what was otherwise a dense wild forest, in the dead of night.

To leave Paul Ragem, recently rescued, alone there.

Whatever she, and the rest of those from the Commonwealth ship—including Evan Gooseberry, who'd insisted on coming—thought of this, they were too well trained to show. Lionel Kearn was reasonably sure most thought Paul was crazy or in league with his captors, and Evan either a fool or exceptionally devious, to accede to his demand.

Lionel knew better. Paul had every reason to believe Esen-alit-Quar wasn't missing, but on her way to him, her patience over. That she would come this way and no other. That being left there, in the dark, would bring them together sooner than any aircar.

He'd wanted to be left with Paul. Had asked the other with a pleading look. Been refused with the barest shake of a head. And when Paul had staggered, climbing out, both he and Evan had started to reach for him, to help.

They'd sat back at the same time, to let him go.

"We gave him a com link," Evan said, abruptly but quietly. They sat across from one another on padded benches, two rows from the clot of security personnel sent by the ship. "The pilot knows to turn back at Paul's signal. We won't leave them out there. You have my word."

Lionel studied the younger Human. Evan, obviously used to being studied by puzzled senior staff—*given his recent history, not a surprise*—endured his scrutiny, face composed in the appropriate, bland "nothing unusual here, only helpful me" expression Lionel didn't believe for a heartbeat. "I've been briefed, Polit," he said even more quietly. "I know what you've risked. Why?"

Pale lashes swept down, then up. Green eyes, striking in their intensity, held Lionel. "It was the right thing to do."

Had he ever been this young? If he couldn't remember his own days of untainted fervor for the "right thing," Lionel reminded himself, he'd only to look at Paul and Esen to see it. Had only to listen to them to feel it again.

Regardless of motive, they weren't always right. He opened his mouth to caution this young, gifted diplomat against impulse. To make sure of his facts before acting. *To be trapped in indecision, then flounder in guilt—*

Lionel half smiled, then offered a gift. "Paul's done the same for as long as I've known him."

If he'd thought Evan's regard intense, that was before this sharpened focus. "How long—I mean—" with a charming, if futile effort to hide keen interest, "—have you been with him at the Library?"

Like that, was it? Lionel's smile widened. Countless before Evan had succumbed to Paul's unconscious nobility, the warmth he emitted like a small sun. A good test of character, that attraction, because there were others who judged Paul Ragem dangerous and a threat.

He was all of the above. "I've known Paul since his first posting to a First Contact Team. I was his senior on the *Rigus.*"

Evan's eyes rounded with delight. "What was—"

A call from the front. "Polit, we have the signal. Turning now."

"Thank you." The diplomat stared out the screen into the night as they banked. "Do you think he found her?" A whisper. "It's so dark out there. Wild."

"I know he has," Lionel replied with relief, happy to his core. Paul wouldn't call otherwise.

Something everyone close to him learned, sooner or later?

Nothing could keep those two apart.

Though a certain impatient blue blob might receive a scolding to sting her lovely ears in the morning.

The arrival of a footsore, panting Lanivarian—a species Lionel doubted any of those in the aircar but Evan would have encountered before—did what orders and protocols had not. From pilot to security personnel, the *Mistral* crew were all smiles, delighted to have done the right thing, too.

It didn't hurt the Lanivarian in question was glowing with joy and effusive in her praise. One of the armored security produced a spare shirt for her, even ripping a hole for her tail. Another produced water bottles for her and for Paul.

Who radiated his own joy, even with his head back and eyes closed with exhaustion.

Esen let him be, though her tail swung ever-so-slightly each time her eyes fell on him. As they flew back to the Library, she sat beside Lionel, a graceful if filthy paw on his knee. "I'm so glad to see you. Thank you, Evan. Thank you all," with such enthusiasm some of the security personnel blushed.

As well they should, Lionel thought, feeling a flicker of outrage despite knowing the *Mistral*'s crew hadn't had a chance of rescuing them. Unable to help himself, he whispered the words, knowing Esen's ears would pick up the sound. "Skalet saved us. On her own and at risk."

Nostrils widened, delicately sniffing the air. As if at a thought, those ears flattened, then lifted into a more pleasant position. Aloud, "And where's our Head of Security now?"

Evan glanced at Lionel, then frowned. "The last time I saw her was on the landing field."

"She wasn't welcome on the ship," Lionel countered.

"I'm sure she'll be waiting at the Library for us." He looked forward to their meeting. *Not that they'd speak of past events, no need, but he could share his speculation about the* Sidereal Pathfinder's *navigation system. Skalet would have fascinating insights—*

"If not," Paul murmured, eyes shut, "give her my thanks and let her know Esolesy and I will be in touch via com."

They couldn't—

"You're still willing to come to Dokeci-Na?" Evan asked, his face clearing. "I wasn't sure I should ask, after all that's happened."

One gray eye opened. "You need us—and the Library—don't you? Then we're coming."

They could, Lionel sighed.

Esen gave his knee a final pat before taking away her paw and looking at Evan. "I heard you wanted me to come, Evan, and I do wish I could." *Did she emphasize the "I"?* "It will work out for the best, though. While Esolesy keeps him—" her clawtip stabbed toward Paul who grunted contentedly "—out of trouble, I'm off to Grandine." Her dappled snout wrinkled. "The preservation committee has a very short list of approved restoration firms. Wish me luck convincing one of them to travel into the backcountry to repair our house."

Time to smarten up and get in the game, Lionel scolded himself. He was being given their cover story. One they relied on him to support while offworld. "You, dear Curator—could convince Ganthor to swim," he said, and meant it. "I can work with Duggs on the—other—repairs, if that's agreeable."

Her eyes sparkled. "It is. We're leaving you with your hands full, I'm afraid."

They trusted him. Lionel glanced at Paul, to be sure it was all real, to find the other smiling, his eyes warm and sincere. "Glad you're here, my friend."

Maybe Evan wasn't the only one, he thought, smiling back.

28: Starship Night

FOR my first five standard centuries of life, Ersh had been in charge of my training, and a significant amount of that dealt with eliminating the urge to react. In Ersh's view, *Web-beings did not take action, they observed.* My elders had adhered to this rule—if you didn't count Ansky's dalliances—throughout their long lives. I'd been doing my earnest, very best to follow their example until Paul showed up.

Not to say my slide into reactive and active Esen had been his fault. According to Ersh, those flaws had been part of my flesh from the start and, in her dim view, only a matter of the right stimulus to set me careening along. *Doing things.*

At this moment, however, I was happy to leave the careening and doing to the crew of the Commonwealth Survey Starship, *Mistral.* A fine, well-equipped ship indeed, and we'd each a cabin for the journey to Dokeci-Na, but first—"Mmmm," I said intelligently, my palate preoccupied with fudge.

Paul, as the more responsible of us, wasn't in the galley to fill empty stomachs, but to meet with Evan Gooseberry and learn all he knew. We were alone, being the only ones on the ship who knew why we were on the ship.

Feeling vastly clever—*and the kind of tired that promotes giddy joy*—I gave a little burp to cover the satisfied gurgle as food shifted from my third stomach to my fourth.

A dimple deepened on Paul's cheek, before he pushed his mug aside to concentrate on the display on the table. "Incredible," he breathed.

The Elves' moon, littered with the shards of their shelter-cities. *You saw one dead civilization, you'd seen them all,* according to Mixs. She'd never grasped ephemeral respect for ruins. In her view, you reused building materials or plowed them under.

I angled my big head to demonstrate I was looking at the image Evan showed us. Nothing elfish swam up from Ersh-memory. *Yet,* I warned myself. I did have her and Lesy's memories of S'Remmer Prime's gorgeous rings— Lesy interested in visiting the upcoming colony once established. *For her art.*

I closed the lid on the fudge container, no longer hungry.

"And the Elves?" Paul asked. He looked refreshed and alert, but his eyes were too bright for my liking. He'd taken a stim before we'd left the Library and, by my estimation, he'd another hour—two at most—until his body paid for it with a profound collapse. I hadn't argued. He'd needed the boost, having not only to pack, but provide sensible instructions to those of our staff who'd lingered.

As well as reassurances he and Lionel were fine. Lionel took over then, to our relief. I'd the impression staff were more willing to accept his authority, knowing he'd shared Paul's ordeal. Not that I'd much time to decipher emotions, Human or my own. I'd not only to appear as Esen the Curator—and give my reasons for departing at the crack of dawn, so please don't disturb me—but to reappear as Esolesy Ki and bid everyone farewell as I did the unlikely and journeyed into space with virtual strangers.

Much to the visible dismay of several staff; Botharans didn't travel as much as they really should.

Suffice to say, by the end I wasn't sure which me I was, only that I'd cycled enough times in succession to be free of the urge for weeks if necessary.

I'd find out that was just as well, later.

I did sneak a moment to take poor Lionel aside and tell him about our food dispenser operator. The parts I felt he'd need to know. Yes, that Lambo was a drive engineer by night, hunting for information on the *Sidereal Pathfinder.*

Yes, that he'd a newly minted access so the giant being wouldn't rattle around the collection after hours and scare staff.

No, about my and Paul's niggling doubts. We weren't convinced by the Carasian's assertion a twenty-year-old drive had value today. Something else was up.

Something that could wait.

I also decided Lionel didn't need to know our Carasian was a layer of chitinous shell away from deadly femininity. *Something else to wait.* Besides, he'd been doing much better lately around dire threats and catastrophe; it hardly seemed fair to leave him with a new one.

The trip to the landing field had been peaceful by comparison, Evan newly shy—or constrained by the clearances of his crew—while Paul and I needed no words. If I hadn't been exhausted and, by this time extremely hungry, I'd have bounced in my seat. We were off on an adventure. To meet a new species! And save them from a terrible mistake, if need be. *Fun and responsible behavior, all in one.*

Bringing us here. I sat forward, eager for my first glimpse. Evan changed the image—

"Es—what's wrong? Esolesy!"

—I was staring at Paul. Worse, I was backed against the galley wall, staring at Paul, my mouth full of bile. *Oh, no.* I looked down. I'd erupted the contents of my second and third stomachs. As if that weren't bad enough?

I'd erupted without noticing.

While my Lishcyn-self could do that, and obviously had, it was this form's most potent autodefense mechanism. *Against what?* I tore my gaze from Paul's upset but fortunately clean face to look at the image floating over the table.

DANGER! I closed my eyes, and jaws, frantically seeking the source of the dire warning before my fourth stomach became involved.

There.

Ersh-memory at last, if fragmented and incomplete. *A sense of running . . . THAT FACE . . . but not running . . . THAT FACE . . . digging . . . an endless pit . . . the EVER DARK—*

—I grabbed my jaws and held them together. Predictably, this form had overreacted, and inappropriately at that. *I really must spend time as something less risk-adverse.* When sure I'd gained control of my digestive tract, I let go and blinked woefully at Paul and Evan. "Sorry. I'm fine now."

Evan looked concerned—and possibly nauseous himself. Paul, on the other hand, looked grimly alarmed.

Hastily, I used my tongue tips to scrub my tusks before curling my lip to expose them. "I'll clean up," I offered, to deflect the *why* I read on Paul's face.

"I'll call the steward," Evan replied. Probably wise; I'd no idea where to look for a mop in this formerly gleaming galley.

My erupted supper, the yellow syrupy remnants plus chunks of fudge—*such a waste,* was confined primarily to where I'd sat and the table beyond. Oh, and some on the wall, sliding downward. If I'd been alone, I'd have licked the cleaner surfaces. Lishcyns had no issues with regurgitation and reuse. I wasn't so Lishcyn I didn't know the habit made Humans queasy in turn.

"Did I ruin your—the—" I waved at the diplomatic pouch and its contents, now more yellow than brown. Evan had shown them to us with such pride, too. They'd been left for him by his superior, secured in a vault, and my fifth stomach rumbled in distress at the look on his face.

"Let's get you cleaned up," Paul ordered. "Evan, I think it might be best if you join us in my cabin when you're—" his gaze fell on the pouch, "—ready to continue."

"The face was scary."

Paul rubbed my snout with a wipe. This close, only one of my eyes could see his thoughtful frown. "That's it?" At my sigh, he paused to stroke the skin under my jaw soothingly. "Take your time, Old Blob."

We didn't have time, not with Evan on his way. "The problem was this form's reaction to the memory—there was—it wasn't daytime," I finished firmly. It hadn't helped that I'd fresh and unsettling memories of night. This me was horrified I'd dared run along the track—

"Ah." Paul stood back to examine me for spots. "I think we've got it all. As for what you've remembered? Will it be a problem, on Dokeci-Na?"

"I won't eat," I promised, then wagged this form's short ears.

He laughed. "Hopefully we'll do better than that."

The door chimed, a pleasing reminder we were invited guests. While lacking the opulence of Kraal staterooms, Paul's cabin—and hopefully mine, across the corridor—featured a generous fresher stall, a table with a comfortable chair plus a fold-down padded bench for company, and an alcove with a thick mattress even my Lishcyn-self eyed with interest. There was a com panel keyed to our idents and, though we'd yet to test it, the same idents should permit Paul's access node to connect to the Library's collection using the ship's translight system.

Without letting the *Mistral*'s com-techs snoop. If they tried, the collection would retreat behind its walls, while continuing to appear interactive. *It wasn't as though we needed it.* But we were on board ostensibly to provide Evan with access to the collection, not the Web of Esen, and appearances mattered. Especially while on this ship. *At the mercy of strangers.*

When Paul opened the door, our host, who was alone, stayed where he was. Evan leaned forward to peer inside. "Are you feeling better, Esolesy?" *Translation: is it safe to be in your vicinity without an enviro-suit?*

I showed Evan my shiny tusks. "Thank you, yes." Then raised my lantern. "If I feel another urge, I'll use this."

He nodded gravely. "Good idea." He understood what many others wouldn't, that, for a Lishcyn, for me, having the ability to create light was more than a simple necessity in chancy environments—it was a talisman giving me courage. *More and more to like about this Human.*

"Come in." Paul went to the table, sitting on the bench with a relieved breath. Starting to feel the aftermath of the stim, I decided.

He wasn't the only one tired. My pretend-yawn turned into a jaw-cracking masterpiece.

Evan took the chair. The limp was almost gone, but he moved tenderly, and I thought rest would do us all more good than this meeting. As if reading my mind, he said, "I'm sorry to trouble you tonight, but this won't take long. First, you should know Captain Clendon's informed me the *Mistral* will reach Dokeci-Na the ship morning after tomorrow's."

"Impressive," Paul commented. "I'd expected two full days."

Perhaps thinking of his onerous trip to Botharis, Evan grinned. "Me, too." His grin faded. "The embassy would like us there sooner, which I'm told is within the *Mistral*'s capabilities, but the Dokeci won't allow a night landing."

Descent engines interfered with star-gazing. That wasn't all of it. "The Dokeci are stalling," I surmised.

He sighed. "I agree. They've cooperated within the Fleullen-ni, but from this—" he produced a now-clean, if damp, pouch, "—the only actions underway right now are ours. We were able to conduct an autopsy, and the embassy has acquired living rasnir-as—Esen discovered that means Devil Darts," with a challenging look at me.

Oh, no, you don't. "I'm quite familiar," I assured him, before Evan started pitting this me against the one he clearly preferred. *The eruption hadn't helped.* "I'd be happy to examine the autopsy results."

Evan reached into the pouch.

"Tomorrow," denied Paul, with feeling. "Unless there's a pressing reason to start at once?"

The diplomat looked disappointed but nodded. "Tomorrow it is. I'd like to leave a copy of the scans with you, however. I—" He fell silent, looking from Paul to me, then back again, and something in his expression made me tense.

"What's wrong?" Paul asked, seeing it, too.

"Senior Polit M'Lean put me in charge but the captain—I've no complaint," as if our now-worried attention implied one, "but I can tell Captain Clendon isn't comfortable about it. I'm really not qualified, you see, and to make it worse, I've granted civilians, you, access to mission parameters neither he nor his crew are allowed to have."

"You're afraid if the situation on Dokeci-Na changes, the captain might assume command and revoke our arrangement."

Evan nodded, looking miserable. "There's something else you need to know."

I'd a feeling we weren't going to like it any better.

"The captain left the *Dimmont III* to the Botharan authorities, but he refused my request to leave the prisoners behind. Commander Kamaara has him convinced the attempt to kidnap you and Lionel was aimed at my mission. She blames me for Skalet," unhappily.

"What's she done?" I blurted, with more anxiety than Evan expected, but then he'd only known my unscrupulous web-kin less than a day.

"I thought you knew. Skalet lied to us about having a tracker on Lionel—where the *Mistral* should go to rescue you." With typical generosity, he rushed to Skalet's defense. *Not that she'd appreciate the gesture.* "She did it so she could save you herself."

"Without harm to anyone," Paul said, as if not over his surprise about that. "Lionel and I expressed our gratitude." An eyebrow raised at me.

Too obvious, I agreed to myself. Something my web-kin never was. The list of topics to discuss at our next opportunity continued to grow; a regrettable number could involve yelling. *Later.*

"As long as these criminals are secured and brought to justice, does it matter where?" I inquired. Unlike the Library, the Survey ship would have provision for captives—if not a dungeon, then lockable doors and armed guards, hopefully well away from here.

I shrugged away Paul's reproachful look. One of us wasn't ready to forgive his stunner-happy cousin. *If ever.*

"It matters if they conclude Paul and Lionel staged their own kidnapping." Evan raised a hand, correctly assuming I was about to erupt, in words if not otherwise. "In the captain and commander's opinion, the *Mistral's* arrival flustered those taking advantage of my inexperience. You. The Library. They're welcome to think me that gullible."

His voice had an edge I hadn't heard before, and I decided this was a new Evan, perhaps even to himself. Someone whose anger didn't cost him control; it gave him purpose.

"The embassy knows better," he continued. "But those in charge of the ship suspect Paul and Lionel conspired with a Kraal to create an emergency in order to board this ship."

Paul rested his chin in his palms, regarding Evan over his fingertips, and didn't speak.

Leaving it to me. "Why would they do that?"

"I'm informed," from the twist of Evan's lips, it hadn't been a cheerful sharing in either direction, "the *Mistral* features several enhancements the Kraal wish to obtain by any means."

Plausible, on the surface. Even reasonable, I conceded. Except that the Kraal in question wasn't one, Lionel was former Survey, and Paul—

I slid my gaze over to the silent one of us. Ragem was a name we'd believed safe to use again. *I'd believed, to be accurate*, leaping ahead to buy the properties for the Library under that name and my own. My gift, to reunite Paul with his family and roots even as we began to build our future together.

Given there'd been no reunion and now, adding to the tally, a missing father, a mystery smearing the memory of his late mother, a cousin scamming our clients with gemmies, and another who'd stunned him three times? *My belief might have been premature—*

Paul put his hands on the table, then smiled, ever-so-slightly. "Thank you for your honesty. While their suspicions are unfortunate—and unfounded—"

"I know that," Evan interrupted. "They're idiots."

Paul's smile warmed. I showed a tusk to add my own approval. "Your officers are simply doing their duty. We're here to do ours. To help you on Dokeci-Na." He stood, not hiding his weariness. "Tomorrow, then?" He held out his hand in the Human gesture.

Evan took it. "Rest. I'll see you to your quarters, Es-olesy."

Remove the alien, so Paul could rest. "Thank you," I said brightly, despite my chagrin. I'd planned to linger and talk with my friend about what Evan didn't know: the *Sidereal Pathfinder* logs and Veya Ragem. That Paul hadn't brought them up told me I shouldn't. It didn't take away my own questions. Or concerns.

Though perhaps a night to think over what to share with my closest friend was wise. For I'd realized something more, as we'd talked to Evan. Something about what I'd experienced, seeing the Elf.

The memory had tasted of Skalet.

Inception

BELIEF is lost.
I am lost. Hope is. We are. The world is. Lost.
Yet...
How is it I can think such thoughts? We weren't taught
that there is something other than the Rise or the Fall.
Those stark choices. Survival or death.
Yet...
I feel no pain, which is good.
I cannot find up.
Which is not.
I am lost.

29: Cabin Night

IN hindsight, we should have looked for Skalet before assuming, as I had, that she'd gone off to sulk over the *Mistral*'s captain's adamant refusal to entertain a Kraal passenger.

If we had, my jaw wouldn't have unhinged and dropped to my chest at the sight of my web-kin stretched out on my mattress.

"Do you have everything—"

I slammed my jaw back into place and whirled in the doorway, positioned so Evan couldn't see into my cabin. "I do. Thank you, Evan. Good night."

The door closed on his reply, plunging me into darkness. I heard Skalet's soft mocking laugh as I fumbled to turn on my lantern, then used it to locate the controls for the room. *There.*

And there she was. "I should have known," I said in disgust.

She stretched like some bone-thin contented feline. "Come now, Youngest. Allow me to surprise you on occasion."

Oh, the pleasure in that.

I checked the rest of the cabin. She'd been through my luggage. Caftans hung from the chair and across the table, this cabin the mirror image of Paul's. With one notable exception. I was delighted to see a Lishcyn-sized box full of synth-grass. If they'd replaced the fresher with a mud wallow, I'd be exceedingly comfortable for the entire journey.

If not for my uninvited, unwanted roommate. Morose and grumpy, I began picking up my clothes. "What were you looking for?"

"Duras."

I humphed. "Survey ships don't transport biologicals." Skalet didn't need to know this ship was newly touchy on the topic, and my bag of those so-useful plants had been taken before lift and summarily left behind. "Besides, we arrive in less than two shipdays." I decided to hang my mistreated garments instead of subjecting them to my overtired folding skills, or lack thereof. "I won't need to cycle."

Nor would Skalet. Much as she pushed that envelope, preferring to remain as she was, our recent sharing had released the stress of excess energy.

"Aren't you going to ask me how I got in here?"

"No." I curled a lip to myself and gathered up another caftan. Piecing together what Paul and Lionel had said, at a guess? My brilliant web-kin had walked on board with the prisoners, then slipped away, either protected from scans by something she wore, or trusting the ship wouldn't bother with internal checks. *Protected*, I decided. Trust wasn't in her nature. "Though I would like to know why you're here, instead of the Library."

"Lionel is capable."

High praise, for a Human? However much he deserved it, and how unexpected the source, I didn't pay attention. Caftans rescued, I collected my scattered ointments, brought in anticipation of a lack of mud wallows. Scale junctions, particularly on my snout and armpits, tended to dry.

She hadn't answered my question.

My Lishcyn-self had superior peripheral vision. When Skalet left what I supposed was her bed for the duration to come up behind me, my scales, dry or not, began to swell in anticipation. Having had a sufficiency of surprises for one day, and still full stomachs, I turned to face her, mouth open.

It was, for this me, a threat display.

I watched her stop, the expression behind the hood shifting from smug to thoughtful. *No one wanted a Lishcyn eruption.*

"No need to get upset, Youngest," she said. "I brought you a gift."

"Does it blow up?"

She laughed, spoiling my attempt at sarcasm. "How did you know?"

Spoiling everything else.

According to Skalet, it was an Octarian Quandran Imploder. Mach II or III. Without dismantling it, she couldn't be sure.

I was. *This was a terrible idea.* "You brought an explosive device on a starship!" To be precise, she'd smuggled it inside a scan-proof bag.

"Stop repeating yourself, Youngest. It's unbecoming. And it's not an explosive device. The Octarians use them to concentrate deposits within asteroid fields. It implodes matter into a stable slag. A considerable amount of matter." No Human mother could hold up a newborn with more delight. "Excessive, to use on the Library. The field would have consumed—"

"I got that part," I gritted out. The Library, Garden, trains, farmhouse and barn, Ragem Creek and the road, the Ragem family oak, and conceivably several farms beyond that. Plus everyone and everything in that radius. *Would it have consumed me?* Not a question to consider while my web-kin hugged the thing. "What I don't understand is why you think *I'd* want it." *Inside a starship!*

"How many Ersh busts could Lesy have made?"

I swallowed the answer, *too many* being about the sum, consumed by a strange mix of horror and amazement. "Do you think we can somehow harvest them over the entire planet and colonies, collect them in one place and then, what, use that to slag them when the Dokeci aren't looking?" I charitably left out collateral damages.

My web-kin sat cross-legged on the bed, the imploder balanced on her knee. It was about the size of Evan's statue, and just as regrettable. "The first part's been done for us. Or didn't Evan mention Riosolesy-ki's Shrine to Teganersha-ki?"

"Ersh has a shrine?" *Of Lesy's art?* I wasn't sure which astonished me more. The Dokeci I'd known had preferred Lesy keep her work in the pods, the exception being the avaricious Cureceo-ki—but his interest hadn't been in her creativity.

Times and tastes evolved—not this fast or far. *We needed better data.* I squinted at Skalet. "How do you know about it?"

"I ordered Cieter-ro to arrange a purchase. A test. When he couldn't, he looked into the reason. For the two thousandth anniversary of Teganersha-ki's reign, all Dokeci were encouraged to contribute Riosolesy-ki's renderings." She smiled. "What our Evan carries around is possibly the last privately owned example, though I suppose there might be secret collections."

"Of Lesy's art?" I protested, unfairly to be sure, but I'd spent five centuries with beings who considered art something only the die-young did. *Lesy had puzzled Ersh most of all.*

"Inconceivable, I agree. Making this," she patted the imploder, "all the more useful."

I'd stripped and climbed into my box of grass, now warming nicely. It did nothing to warm me inside. Skalet wanted me to believe she'd smuggled herself on the *Mistral*—herself and imploder—to eliminate Lesy's leftover flesh.

That couldn't be the only reason. "This ship. You were never surprised. You knew the *Mistral* was coming." Thrills of caution coursed through my veins. "What she was."

"Of course. The *Trium Pa* reports all insystem traffic. I received an alert the instant the *Mistral* dropped into normal space." Another pat. "I'll admit to some surprise Survey came for your friend, Evan Gooseberry, but that proved convenient."

No Kraal allowed—"You're here to rob the ship, aren't you?" I glared at her. "In the middle of—" A burp. "—everything!?"

Skalet gave a *Tsk* of disapproval. "Don't be melodramatic, Youngest. I'm simply here to help the Commonwealth share its upgrades with those who'll put them to superior use. After all, House Arzul has indulged my interest in Botharis for a planet year. They feel a return on that investment is due. Unless you'd prefer I arrange something more—direct—to appease them?" A note of quite worrisome anticipation. "Perhaps undermine the Botharans' annoying government?"

Wouldn't Arzul love that choice, ambitious to be counted among the Great Houses of the Kraal? Skalet bore her allegiance to them over an eyebrow, the one she'd raise to admonish me. It was likely raised now.

"Steal the tech," I said glumly. *Not something Paul should know.* "Do us all a favor and don't let them find out. They'll think Paul and I—and probably poor Evan— were complicit." *Let alone the catastrophic potential of two Web-beings locked in the same brig—*

"Youngest. Trust me."

"Never."

I could almost feel her smile. "Good."

Though in this, I did. The *Mistral* hadn't a chance against Skalet's well-honed skills, bringing me, with sickening inevitability, to another conclusion. She'd called Evan convenient. *Something else had been more so.* "Did you hire those thugs?"

My lantern—*as well ask a Ganthor to stop drooling as my web-kin to keep up the lights for this me*—reflected glints within the deplorable shadow above the bed. Her eyes, aimed at me. At last, "Your Paul was never in danger—"

"Did you?" I persisted, soft and low.

"I didn't have to," Skalet replied without remorse. "Johnsson's backer provided her with on-site resources. Again, excessive, especially to acquire—" she'd been about to say *assets.* "—Paul and Lionel, when neither appears to know anything useful about the *Sidereal Pathfinder* or its reputed star drive."

Had that been wistful? "You didn't know about it?" I'd be pleased she'd respected our privacy by not installing her devices in our farmhouse or my greenhouse, except I'd a feeling that was about to change.

"I do now."

Ersh. And I'd left the image of the derelict ship in our cookie jar.

Time to deflect Skalet's attention, if that were even possible. I tucked my lantern into the grass beside me, set to a soothing glow, thinking of the Kraal com hidden under Paul's tea table. "I suppose you know about Evan's mission, too," I replied, snuggling down in case what she told me was scary. "The Elves on Dokeci-Na?"

"'Elves.'" Scorn, not surprise. "From the description of their so-called shelter-city, these can only be *Mareepavlovax*. The Ancient Farers. The Harbingers. If so, the Dokeci have no idea what they've brought to their living world."

Neither did I. I waited for the churn of Ersh-memory, a response to at least one of those names, in vain. I'd longed to meet a new species, not one new only to me.

Meaning Ersh deliberately kept the Mareepavlovax from me. Why? *She'd given me the rest of her terrifying, troubling memories,* I thought with familiar self-pity. But no. Here was proof there were more. I wasn't sure if I should be grateful or afraid.

No, I was sure. *Afraid.*

Skalet, used to my mental ruminations, waited the space of four breaths before snapping, "Well? Now you know what you're dealing with, Youngest, you can't tell me you're still going to help Evan."

I didn't know. But display such fundamental ignorance to Skalet of all my web-kin, past and present?

Wasn't worth the risk—yet. I'd names. Paul. The Library's collection. The rest of Evan's briefing. Autopsy results of a—a Mareepavlovax. *What was the singular?* part of me fussed. *Mareepavlova?*

Tomorrow.

"Yes. I am going," I said with great finality, "to help my friend."

Skalet's somber, "Courageous choice, Youngest," did nothing to help me fall asleep.

Perception

EVAN Gooseberry had set the cabin alarm to wake
him, judging—correctly, as it turned out—he'd need
it. He'd had trouble falling asleep, his mind too full to
rest. When he had, he'd dreamed—

*—of fire and acid-burned flesh. Of thieves in the night.
Of arriving on the bridge stark naked to give orders, only
to have—*

The alarm saved him from the rest. He sat up, curls
brushing the top of the bed alcove, and took a few steadying breaths. "Going to be like that, is it?"

Performance anxiety was an old acquaintance, one
he'd learned to recognize before leaving home to study
offworld. *You moved.* Accordingly, Evan rose and
stretched, doing one high-kneed leg lift before his feet
reminded him the soles had been burned the day before
and it was time to reapply the medspray as the med-
tech—and Esolesy Ki—had done.

After a good stint in the fresher stall. He'd set the alarm
well ahead of ship's morning. In a fit of sheer daring, he'd
also ordered his breakfast brought to his cabin and as
Evan stepped from the stall, a polite chime indicated it had
arrived.

Rather pleased with himself, Evan calmly wrapped yesterday's shirt around his midsection and answered the door.

Paul Ragem stood there.

Evan closed the door, leaning against it to keep it that

way, his heart pounding. *Why was Paul there?* They weren't to meet till midmorning, to allow a decent rest and breakfast for all, and giving Evan time to access any newly arrived material. Plus he'd agreed with Captain Clendon's suggestion to provide a coded report to Senior Polit M'Lean—

The door chimed again.

That would be Paul.

Who, come to think about it, had been holding a tray. *His breakfast?*

Evan went to the com panel. "A moment, please." As if Paul were the ship's steward, but what else could he say? He dressed with numb, if methodical, care, worried more about missing a fastener than the final result, then dug fingers into his hair, moist from the stall. You didn't comb the stuff, you poked it into shape, and Great Gran wore hers as a fabulous cloud, most often black, but she'd add colorful zigzags for special occasions—

The door chimed. Again.

Composing himself, fully dressed, Evan opened the door. "Good morning."

Paul's grin lit his eyes. "I hope you don't mind, but I waylaid the steward. I've brought my breakfast, too." He lifted the tray suggestively.

"Oh. Please come in." Evan hurriedly grabbed yesterday's clothes, then looked around for a secure dumping ground. Finding none, he tossed them in the accommodation and closed that door.

His guest, in the meantime, had made himself useful, setting out plates and utensils before taking a seat on the bench, the tray with its covered platter between them.

Timidly, Evan sat on the chair. *What was happening?* "Thank you for this, but it's—"

A lean beautiful hand reached over the tray, finding his, taking it in a warm grasp. "It's time we were alone, you and I, don't you think?" Paul said, his voice low and even warmer.

Then his other hand whisked off the cover and there, on the platter, steam coming from her nostrils, was the head of Esen-alit-Quar, dead eyes staring up at Evan with reproach—

"AIIE!!" Evan bent over his knees, half-retching. On some level, he realized his room was dark, that this was still shipnight—

That he'd been dreaming—

Whatever that was hadn't felt like a dream. It had felt *real*.

He cupped his head in his hands. It wasn't. There was no reason Paul had to choose between Esen and—and—

This wasn't about choice. What he'd witnessed last night: how willingly—eagerly—Paul had abandoned the safety of the aircar to wait out there, in the night, because he couldn't bear to let Esen be alone and worry about him—

How, reunited, they'd radiated such peaceful joy, the universe seemed to repair itself.

He'd never experienced a love like that. *Few*, Evan feared with an envy close to pain, *ever did*.

His dream was real in this much: he didn't belong in it. He rubbed his hands over his face. "That's it, then."

For no reason, every reason, Evan brought his holocube back to bed with him. He pretended to thumb it on. "Great Gran, you'll be proud of me." *He'd be professional and grateful and give up what had never been his to want.* "I've come to a decision." *One to make the rest of their time on the ship easier.* "I'm right about this. I hardly know him. He doesn't know me. But—you'd like him. I know you would."

Not just Paul. "You'd like Bess, too, Great Gran. She's—" somehow Paul's family, whatever their relationship. As was Esen, and Esolesy—

Evan could almost hear Great Gran's reply. "They'd make excellent Gooseberrys." *Unless, and oh, it would be,* "That Paul's a handsome lad. You'd make such beautiful babies together. Gooseberrys, of course."

They would, too—

He needed a real voice. Anyone's, to stop this—nonsense in his head. Evan's thumb moved again, activating the holocube. A pending message announced itself before he could call out and, desperate for distraction, he almost opened it without checking.

Almost. It was from Lucius. About to delete it, Evan hesitated.

Would it help, to make himself watch? Would being someone else's fantasy end his?

No. Nothing about this was the same. Gorge rising in his throat, he deleted the message and blocked the source. Nothing about Lucius deserved attention.

Everything about Paul earned it.

It was going to be a long day.

There being no question of trying to fall asleep again, Evan used the fresher, sprayed the soles of his feet, then dressed before calling the galley for a tray. The door chime sent his heart into his throat, but it was the steward, who gave him the breezy "not crew, but in charge" half salute and bid him good morning.

Evan ate out of duty, reading messages Trili had cued for his immediate attention. She had quarters on the crew deck, or he'd have invited her to breakfast—if it hadn't been two hours too soon.

And if what he was reading didn't cause him such intense and growing concern he forgot the mug in his hand, almost dropping it.

Another Dokeci had died, killed by a rasnir-as outside the spray zone. They'd resumed their spraying amid increased efforts to convince the Elves to allow them inside the shelter-city. Not by force.

That might come, Polit M'Lean warned in his analysis, if the Dokeci couldn't contain the deadly pests. He'd asked for, and been provided, more samples.

Evan wrote out a reply, then erased it. Another, erasing that. Finally, he sat back. If all he could report was what M'Lean already knew, that he was on his way back with expertise, there was no point. He'd write it after he met with Paul and Esolesy today, once they could ask the Library their better informed questions—any hope, however faint, could delay regrettable action by the Dokeci.

Evan opened the last message: a reply, from Commander Kamaara, to be conveyed to Paul Ragem. In it, she denied Paul's request to meet with one of her prisoners, a Jan Terworth, privately or otherwise.

Kamaara knew he could overrule her; perhaps she expected it, hence the blatant "follow the blame" routing of the message, but he wouldn't. If she'd concerns about such a meeting, it wasn't his place to dispute them. Not without a very good reason, which Paul might supply, or might not.

He checked his chrono.

There was, of course, a reasonable alternative. Evan rose, donning his jacket.

He'd speak to this prisoner himself.

30: Starship Morning

I stirred in my bed, working upward through synth-grass until I blinked in the room lights.

Skalet was gone.

That the lights were on went a good distance toward my not worrying what that meant: Skalet roaming the Survey ship.

It was what she did best, I thought fatalistically. Besides, I was hungry, craved a good long wallow in mud—or sand, in a pinch—and to talk to Paul. *Eat first,* I decided, listening to my stomachs.

Despite what I tried to make Paul believe about this form's requirements, a Lishcyn didn't need quantity so much as steady intake. Stomachs two through five grew irritable if allowed to empty. My first stomach was more a sturdy muscular gizzard, ready to pass along any inward discontent.

I'd packed snacks. I took an armload into the fresher stall to munch while I steam cleaned my hide. Singing being messy, I settled for thinking.

Mareepavlovax. As names went, it worked in a mouth able to handle comspeak. Always a bonus not to spit or need an instrument for accompaniment.

The Ancient Farers. Without knowing who called them that, other than Skalet, assigning meaning to the words posed risk, but I felt inclined to take them literally, if only because the Dokeci had deemed the Elves as "non-space-faring." Ersh had watched enough civilizations be born, reach the stars, and fall back again to make me wary of spot judgments.

The Harbingers. Skalet's term, or something more? I didn't like it. Species who arrived as portents or warnings were, in my opinion, exactly the species to be worried about arriving in the first place.

I swallowed my last mouthful, wrapping and all, and set the stall to warm mist. The dryer was out of the question for this me, much as my Lanivarian-self enjoyed a good fluff.

Some oil and my second favorite caftan, and I was ready to meet Paul for breakfast.

And start answering questions.

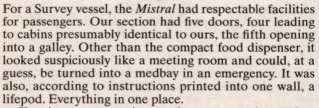

For a Survey vessel, the *Mistral* had respectable facilities for passengers. Our section had five doors, four leading to cabins presumably identical to ours, the fifth opening into a galley. Other than the compact food dispenser, it looked suspiciously like a meeting room and could, at a guess, be turned into a medbay in an emergency. It was also, according to instructions printed into one wall, a lifepod. Everything in one place.

Keeping passengers in one place, too, a point not lost on Paul. He'd smiled in greeting, then nodded to the upper corners of the galley walls. Being less suspicious, I'd have assumed the little boxes were fire suppressants or squirted fragrance to cover occasional flatulence. Not that I'd experienced an episode lately, but one had to watch one's diet.

The nod implied we'd be overheard, watched, and recorded. I curled a lip cheerfully. "You look better."

Clean helped us both, as had sleep. *Or had he slept?* Paul's skin had lost its unhealthy gray, but there were telling smudges below his eyes I didn't like. "I've set up our access to the Library. Once Polit Gooseberry arrives with his questions, I'd like you to work the interface. It's ready for you."

In other words, Paul had stayed up to modify our system, so my answers would appear to originate from the collection. "You should have slept," I chastised mildly. "But thank you." We could do this trick in the Library, but I'd wondered how we'd manage on the *Mistral*. I should have known he'd find a way. I looked at the empty table. "Have you eaten?"

"Waited for you." A dimple. "They have marfle tea."

"My compliments to the ship," I replied, showing tusks. *Life was good.*

We treated our watchers and ourselves to a blissfully normal breakfast scene, like any Paul and I shared. Our conversation flowed, more silence than words, entire phrases conveyed by the direction of a glance or the wiggle of an ear. It wasn't until we eased back with our mugs of tea that I changed things.

"The googly-eyed blue pony. With six legs?" In case there'd been other versions.

"Ah, yes." Paul surveyed me over the rim of his mug. "How did it get in my office?"

Try that, would he? "How did it get in Ally's basket?" I countered.

He took a sip, then grinned. "Remember your loop in the track?"

About to protest I remembered everything, I remembered our watchers also and settled for, "Yes. What has that to do with the blue pony?"

"Imagine it bigger. Imagine it in the Garden, near the patio. In front of the tree with the twisty red flowers."

Technically, the Garden had fifteen patios, if defined as an outdoor area floored in material suitable for tables, seating, or a Lanivarian stretched out in the sun. When Paul used the word, he meant only one. The large one by the greenhouse he used for family gatherings that hadn't as yet happened and as a landing field for an aircar I hadn't, till recently known we owned.

Now he wanted it to have a large googly-eyed blue pony with six legs? I regarded my Human friend a moment, then ventured cautiously, "Does it move?"

"The tree? Only in the wind." Eyebrows lifted. "Unless there's something I don't know."

"Not the tree. The pony." If someone was listening, they should be as confused as I was by this point.

"I hadn't thought of that." Paul's eyes twinkled. "What a marvelous idea, Es."

It was?

"I'd thought they'd climb on it. Maybe bounce. Maybe—" My stomachs gurgled, and Paul paused considerately. I waved at him to continue. "It's a toy I had," he explained with a faraway look. "The first one I remember. Starfield the Very Strange Pony. There was a happy little song about her visiting Botharis—my mother would sing it to me at bedtime. When she was fins down," with the simple acceptance of that long-ago child. "I looked for Starfield when you and I moved into the farmhouse, but such things don't last, Es." He smiled as though to prove it didn't matter. "The Garden could use a bit of whimsy."

We were missing a plant? But that wasn't what he meant. I knew the word, if not the full concept. Wait, was a hidden Anata close to "playfully fanciful or odd?"

I could almost hear Lesy's laugh. *She'd a wonderful, infectious laugh.* Alone of us, I suspected she'd understood whimsy as my friend did. *Not that Ersh would ever share it.*

"Then we'll put a Starfield in the Garden, bouncy or otherwise," I assured him, pleased to learn more of my friend's past, if still slightly confused. "But why have Ally make it as a Response?"

He pretended his tea was of absorbing interest.

Think, Esen, that was. Figure me out. Meaning this was about more than landscaping or childhood memories.

Studying the tumbling waves of his hair, an appealing if *whimsical* feature to my Lishcyn-self, whose own consisted of sensitive bristles surrounding each scale, I decided to view this as if I'd been a client, coming to the Library with a question. *What had I asked Paul lately?*

I'd asked him why his family hadn't come to the reunion. I'd asked him when would be long enough. And I'd been furious at them, for him. The googly-eyed blue pony, with six legs, was Paul's response: *his childhood, with this family, had been happy.*

He wasn't angry at all.

Unlike me, Paul was prepared to wait as long as they

needed and as he did, why not build what included his
family and put them at ease? After all, he'd bought
Moody-mood bracelets for the new Ragem children—
great-nieces and nephews and cousins—we'd yet to meet.

I'd known twins at that age. They'd squeak with joy
over a bouncy—maybe even moving—pony with friendly
googly eyeballs.

As Bess, I could, too.

*Not that I could risk being Bess, to play with Ragem
children*. I sighed aloud, this me's thick blubbery lips adding melodrama.

He looked up. "What is it?"

I showed him my tusks. "I wish I'd thought of it first.
What else should we add? To the Family Patio," I added,
so he'd know I had understood.

And to head off any attempt to put giant blue toys anywhere else in the Garden.

A Web-being had her standards.

Perception

EVAN pulled out a notebook and readied his stylo above a blank page. "Your name, please."

The prisoner looked at him as though he'd lost his senses. "Yer know. Yer guards took m'ident."

"For my records. Please," Evan insisted politely.

"Terworth. Jan Terworth."

Evan wrote it down in his neat cursive script, a habit begun as an exercise prescribed by his therapist—to record his thoughts, the words he used, above all his fears—and never stopped. He thought better when he wrote. Found connections he might have missed, and—on at least one occasion—the entire Commonwealth Embassy on Urgia Prime had relied on his somewhat obsessive notetaking when their systems were compromised.

Right now, however, his notebook was a tool. "Thank you, Hom Terworth. Place of birth?"

"What'yer doing there?" As if handwriting was a completely foreign concept—which it was to many Humans. When Evan waited, the other snapped, "Botharis. And if that's not partic'lar 'nuff f'yer, in an alleyway o' Burnston, Omameh Province, West Sceekok. Fifteenth o' Linderth, give'r'take, 242 AC." He rattled off the names, deliberately thickening his accent.

Evan merely wrote. "That would be years 'After Colonization,' Hom Terworth?"

"A'course after colonization. What are yer, stupid?"

He looked up.

Terworth sank back in his chair. "Yes, that's what it means."

"Thank you. Now, Hom Terworth, what is your relationship to Paul Ragem?"

His head hunched between his shoulders. "Who?"

Evan flipped to an empty page, made as if consulting it. "You called out to him, by name, in the medbay. Please answer my question."

"Scanned me, dinnit they? Yer know we're cousins." The other glared, blue eyes hot in his thin face.

It had been in the file the guard had shown him. She'd asked no questions nor checked with her commander before granting him access, suggesting Kamaara had left instructions. Whether that meant approval of his actions, or more "trace the blame," he'd no way to know.

There was no outward resemblance between Paul and this malnourished, morose Human, with his scraggle of light brown hair. The lobe of Terworth's right ear was missing, his knuckles enlarged and bent; given the muscles of his lanky frame, over the years he'd delivered as much damage as he'd taken. A rough life. Not necessarily a criminal one, Evan thought. *Was that why Paul wanted to see his cousin?*

"Ye're caus' a what he'd did, right?" Paul's cousin spat over his shoulder, the thick little glob a statement on the gleaming floor. "Sid'n with that Monster ov' his own kind n'kin. Pretending t'be dead all t'years since."

Stunned, hoping he didn't show it, Evan flipped back a page and raised his stylo. "Please continue, Hom Terworth."

He should have asked for another file. *Paul Ragem's.*

31: Starship Day

"**A**ND nothing." Paul leaned back, arms over his head. The posture was one of frustration.

An emotion I shared. "Yet," I said, for those listening. While waiting for Evan, we'd run the names Skalet provided through the collection, separately and in combination. Ancient Farer and Harbinger produced a wealth of myth from every species prone to exploring dangerous realms. Fear of the unknown being reasonable; fear of environments likely to kill you even more so. When we added Mareepavlovax, those results vanished. *Not helpful.*

"We need the autopsy." Paul glanced at the door, then his chrono. "I wonder what's keeping Evan?"

Considering the eager diplomat had been ready to stay late last night, I wondered, too. *On the bright side, there'd been no intruder-alerts.* I trusted Skalet's skills, but accidents happened. More if I were involved, possibly why she hadn't shared the details of her plan. *Not all were my fault.* "We could have—" I was about to say lunch, when the galley door opened.

Evan, at last. We stood as one, smiled.

Until we saw his face.

"Acting Senior Polit Evan Gooseberry," our friend told the ceiling, his voice tight and not his at all. "On my authority as Mission Head, terminate surveillance. Start-ing now." The little boxes winked white, then black.

Something was very wrong. His normally expressive face was set in unreadable lines, and he'd yet to look at either of us. He stood like a statue—*quite smart in that jacket*—and if I didn't know better, if I didn't know this Human better, I'd have thought we were about to be ar-rested.

When he finally looked at us, I changed my mind. *Maybe we were.*

Those green eyes could be shockingly cold. "Fifty-one years ago you—Paul Ragem of Survey—faked your own death," this to Paul.

Who nodded, his eyes alight with, of all things, curi-osity.

To me, "You—Esolesy Ki, lived with him, while he used the name Paul Cameron, during that time."

If Paul wasn't worried by this Evan Gooseberry, I was for us both. My inner temperature soared. Making it worse, my scales started to swell, making my reluctant nod more a forward tilt that clunked my lantern against the table.

Evan's gaze flicked to it, then came back to my face. For the first time, I saw something I recognized. *The need to understand.* "Are you a monster?"

Was I—what!? Feeling my jaw loosen with shock, I grabbed it with both hands and shoved upward. *He mustn't—couldn't—*

"You spoke with Jan," Paul declared before I could mumble a denial. "I take it my request to do so was de-nied?"

Like a lantern beam, Evan's attention left me for Paul. "I read your record, too."

Worse and worse. Dumping heat was difficult in this form, and I'd no mass, none—

Paul kept his tone calm and reasonable, as if we dis-cussed someone else, and I'd no comprehension how, in this fraught and dreaded moment, anyone could have such strength. "Then you know a mistake was made, fifty-one years ago. A mistake that linked my name with a creature—yes, a monster—that posed immediate, terrible danger. That did take innocent lives before it was stopped and killed—and that I helped stop it." He spread his hands. "But it was too late. Facts were confused, and by then rumor had spread, taking my reputation, my career. I'd one chance to keep the taint from my family."

"By dying?"

Ersh, a dimple. "Looking back, it seems extreme." The hint of a smile. "I was younger then."

Evan's age.

Nothing Paul said or did was ever by accident; I watched the realization cross the younger Human's face, soften it the tiniest amount before being replaced by a frown. "According to the report, Lionel Kearn continued to believe in your—those rumors. He believed this monster hadn't died. Pursued it to the detriment of his own career. If he hadn't resolved the Feneden Crisis, he'd have been discharged."

Ineffable grief filled Paul's eyes, turned down the corners of his lips, and had I been Lanivarian, I'd have whined in answer. "Lionel always does what he thinks is right. Whatever the cost to himself. Then and now."

"So when Lionel Kearn set the record straight, you decided to return from the dead and—what—take back your life on Botharis?"

Unfair. I burped, loudly. "We decided to build the All Species' Library of Linguistics and Culture because Paul and I—and Esen—do not want another mistake. By anyone. Including your Dokeci." I surged to my feet and did not curl a lip. *This was too important.* "Paul's family will come to terms with our choices, or they will not. If you're done dragging our past into your present, Polit, I suggest we go through the autopsy results for the Mareepavlovax. Because, yes," at Evan's start, "we kept working on what matters while you did not."

A soft breath. "Es."

"Fine," I grumbled and subsided.

"You're right." Evan eased into a chair at the end of the table. "I'm—I won't say I'm sorry," he said, rather bravely, under the circumstances. *I'd burped once already.* "I couldn't in conscience continue to work together without knowing."

"And now?" Paul asked gently.

Evan put his pouch and a notebook on the table. "Kamaara flagged your records for a follow-up. I'll ensure she's aware it's been done, with satisfactory results."

"We appreciate that," my friend said. "Truly." *There was an understatement.* And a memory not to share with Skalet.

"Well, then." Suddenly adorably self-conscious, Evan flipped the notebook open and produced a stylo. "How do you spell Mareepavlovax?"

Another Dokeci had died. Perhaps more Elves, though the report Evan had received this morning hadn't mentioned another ominous presentation. There was no mention of Elves—of Mareepavlovax, if Skalet was right—at all.

We were running out of time. I feared Dokeci-Na might be too, so when Paul and Evan grew engrossed tracing the etymology of "Ancient Farers" through the collection, I excused myself.

Having a source they did not.

I'd brought with me snacks from the galley, this form's appetite an excellent excuse. Skalet had no such flaws, able to function as Kraal when other Humans would faint from hunger or thirst.

She wouldn't turn down an offering. Especially when I came to her for help. Something I'd do more often if she didn't make each instance about what I lacked, why I lacked it, and how deplorably long she'd have to wait for me to *catch up*.

About three hundred years or so ago, I'd learned not to point out that catching up was a physical impossibility. Until then, I'd been able to hide behind Ersh.

I paused in front of the door. *Why haven't you given me this form, Ersh? Why Skalet and not me?*

Ersh's decisions about my education had never been about kindness.

Going in, I affected a nonchalant walk, Esolesy-the-carefree, not at all the walk of someone braced to find crates of stolen parts and a bloodstained web-kin. Far from the worst scenario I could imagine, which began with Skalet on the bridge, taking over the ship.

I closed and locked the door, my cabin free of any wrongdoing if I didn't count a pleased Kraal seated at the table, hood lifted above her eyes, with every one of my precious jars open in front of her. Which put asking for help well behind my aggrieved, "What do you think you're doing?"

"That should be obvious, Youngest." She stuck a finger into the nearest, scooped out the last of my very expensive sparkly pink Scale So Soft, and transferred it to her mouth.

They were edible? With a thoroughly Lishcyn urge to try for myself I dismissed with an effort. Some things were not snacks.

She gave me a wicked little smile. "Tastes like fudge."

I probably shouldn't buy any more, I decided glumly, even if Skalet wasn't teasing me. "You can stop eating my ointments. I brought you lunch."

Accepting the plate of galley gleanings, she put what was dry in a pocket of her uniform, bolting down the fruit with a dispatch that in other Humans would be rude, but this was simply Skalet, who didn't care about taste or texture, being efficient.

I'd tried to stay busy elsewhere when it was her turn to cook in Ersh's kitchen.

"Did you ask Evan about the shrine?"

"There wasn't a good moment." Between autopsies and dead Dokeci, not to forget *are you a monster*— "I'll take care of it." I eyed her, suspicious. "Are you finished stealing?"

A slow, contented stretch. "There's always more, Youngest, but yes, I have what will make House Arzul moderately triumphant. I'm sure they'll want me to stay at the Library."

Oh, joy. I didn't bother with the Human-shaped chair or bench, settling to the floor. "You don't have to, if you've other places—" *anywhere,* "—else to be. You could visit."

"And miss our chats?" Skalet in a good mood could be harder to endure than usual. An eyebrow raised, shifting tattoos. "Come now, you know you're here to ask my help."

Ersh. Should I try honest, or sneak around—

"Let me guess. Evan. Brave and good-hearted. I can see why you like him." Her eyes glittered. "He's a bright one. Too bright, perhaps? After all, he's met this you, that you, the other."

I rose. "Stop."

"Ah, but I won't, for your good and mine." This wasn't a mood—my web-kin had been thinking. She eased forward. "You may not want to admit it, Youngest, being *good-hearted,* but our Evan's jealous of Paul's affection. For that you and the other, at least." With a throwaway gesture that stung. "He has feelings of his own. Human feelings. You know that's true."

"I don't want to—"

"What you want—" her hand slammed on the table, making the plate jump and toppling several still-open jars to the floor, "—is irrelevant, Youngest. Tell me. Has our Evan asked the wrong questions?"

I couldn't help it, I flinched.

Faster than a striking Cloud Viper, she was on her feet, every trace of annoyingly amiable Skalet erased. "So, Esen-alit-Quar. Is that the help you need? To be rid of him?"

"How DARE—" I was overcome by the urge to cycle, to *demand* to share and *MAKE* her know Evan as I did.

Must not—must not. To my shame, my struggle wasn't to protect Skalet, but our secret. We mustn't cycle on this ship.

I hardly noticed my web-kin retreating until my bed-box hit the back of her legs. Hardly noticed her sink to the floor, trembling.

The superb hearing of this me heard her speak, however soft the words. "Ersh knows, I can't stop you."

Ersh. Who'd insisted her Web share when and where she wanted, yes, but who'd never used this essence of what we were as a weapon against us. *To inconvenience*

*and embarrass, absolutely, and to instill all those things
I'd dreaded to learn, but it had been for my survival.*

I'd forced Skalet to share against her will once before,
to save Paul. *I couldn't, again, not even to save Evan.*

The urge passed, and I gasped, cooling with the
breath. Skalet watched me, no longer trembling, but not
happy, not the least happy.

She wasn't a being who craved or comprehended an
apology. Or who thought much of those who felt the need
to apologize. Or—

Needless to say, understanding me in the absence
of Ersh presented my web-kin with unique challenges.
Family.

What I failed to consider? That the presence of Ersh
had been my sole protection from Skalet. *Such insights
typically arrived too late to matter.*

Here and now, I thought only of how to save Evan and
fix this. I gazed down at Skalet. What would Paul do?

*He wouldn't let family cower on the floor. Not even
Skalet.*

Restore her self-respect? A perilous line there, with
Evan on it. I sighed inwardly. Back to the old way, it was.

Let her best me.

"Evan isn't a problem, Skalet. He questioned Paul
about his past, yes, but only to understand it. He knows
nothing of our nature." I let the tips of my tongue hang in
humiliation. "I do need your help, urgently. With these
Mareepavlovax. Ersh didn't share the form with me. I've
only one memory of them: a glimpse of a face like those
Evan showed Paul and me. That and a sense of flight, and
dirt, and dark—" I paused to grip my lantern. "And you."

"Want it?" She showed her teeth. "I last used the form
before you arrived."

Putting it deep inside her web-mass. Skalet couldn't
do as I, or Ersh, did, and shift the memory to share into a
thin pseudopod, reserving the rest. We'd have to consume most of one another—assimilate almost everything.
Even if I'd been remotely willing to risk it?

"Skalet, we can't share on this ship. Or Dokeci-Na. It's
too dangerous."

"Glad you've come to your senses, Youngest," cold

and bitter. Skalet stood, brushed herself off, then went to sit at the table as if nothing had happened. "I'll teach you what I can. You'll have to obtain the form for yourself. There's one small complication."

There always was, I reminded myself, sitting with her. "What is it?"

"You'll need a *Vlovax*."

Perception

LIONEL sighed and wiped his nose, then dabbed the corners of his weeping eyes. He tucked the soggy wipe in a pocket bulging with others before resuming his examination of the morning's questions. *Ah, yes. The Odarian—*

"Ker-CHOOO!"

—with the— Another sneeze threatened. Lionel pressed a wipe against his nose and held his breath, fighting the urge. The wood of the temporary wall behind him was too fresh, oozing a pungent yellow oil that dripped to the newly cleaned floor—and offended his sinuses—but he wasn't about to complain. According to Duggs, it was all she could get her hands on quickly to keep out weather, mousels, and whatever else as they waited for a crew to make proper repairs to the outer surface. She'd added, bluntly, he should stay out, too.

He'd been blunt in return. Someone had to be here, in Paul's office, a visible working presence to help return the Library and staff to normal operations—or as close as possible.

Duggs had stormed away to work on the farmhouse, cursing inventively about offworld imports and offworlders. *She'd meant him,* he thought, touched.

"K-kk-ker-ChOOO!"

"Director Kearn?"

Putting away another wipe, Lionel looked up from Paul's desk. "Come in."

Director Kearn it was—if not from Duggs, who gave no one a title, or Lambo, yet to acknowledge his existence. Paul and Esen's easy informality wasn't his nor, in this instance, was it the right choice. While he might wish they'd call him Lionel, he was here to provide stability to a staff shaken by recent events. He smiled a welcome. "Yes, Senior Appraiser Steves?"

"Someone's here to see Paul—Director Ragem." Henri'd a clever, kind face; now it was troubled. "Ally says it's his uncle."

Lionel's smile froze; only for an instant, but Henri gave a sympathetic nod. "It's a shock to us, too, Director. Paul hasn't had—there've been no—" She stopped.

"I understand. Please show him—ker-CHOOO!!" Lionel pressed a wipe to his nose. "Excuse me."

"G'luck." The Botharan exhortation followed sneezing, coughing, and, as far as Lionel knew, any involuntary eruption.

"Thank you. Wait. Senior Appraiser—Henri—your advice. Should I meet Paul's uncle somewhere else?"

She knew he didn't mean the acrid wood. Henri considered the plank wall and her expression grew stern. "Everyone should see this, Director Kearn. Especially Paul's family. I'll send Carwyn with drinks."

"Thank you."

Because this would be a social call, however potentially awkward, Lionel tidied the tabletop and closed the node. He disposed of the used wipes and summoned his training. *Never sneeze in front of aliens* was, in all but a few remarkably messy yet instructive instances, the rule.

He walked to stand invitingly near the paired chairs. Paul's broken tea table had been replaced by a box of the same height.

The room would do. *He must.*

Carwyn appeared with a tray loaded not with the expected tea but three thumb-sized glasses and a clear carafe, each half filled with a dark amber liquid. She grinned at him. "Served at Ragem family meetings. Seems appropriate."

Lionel held up three fingers. "Who else?"

"Director." Henri stood in the doorway, behind her

shoulder a face Lionel recognized at once. The lines were deeper set, the hair now silver, but those gray intelligent eyes, uncannily similar to Paul's, hadn't changed. Sam Ragem, Veya's elder brother, and the most vocal of all in his outrage when Lionel arrived to tell him his beloved nephew was a traitor.

Following Sam into the room a face very few on this planet would know: Stefan Gahanni, Paul's missing father.

Lionel schooled his expression to polite welcome. Better than shock.

Stefan was shorter than Paul, with a heavier build, muscle curving his shoulders and upper back. The pallor of his skin and gaunt cheeks implied a recent illness. *Again, the eyes held the resemblance*, Lionel thought. The shape, if not the color. Paul's intelligent, driven curiosity, here also. At the moment, Stefan's were full of anger.

Both Humans were dressed in the long dark jackets Botharans wore to formal occasions, Stefan's borrowed by the strain at the shoulders. Neither looked surprised to see him instead of Paul. They accepted Henri's invitation to take the chairs and sit. Neither spoke, mutely taking their glass of whatever Ragems served on such occasions.

His in hand, Lionel leaned on the table, wondering where he could possibly start. *Paul should be here.*

"I'll bring another chair, Director," Carwyn promised and slipped out with Henri.

The door closed behind them.

"It's him," Stefan declared, rough and low. "He's the one who came after me."

"Lionel Kearn," Sam Ragem identified. He'd a deep voice. Now it had the heft of stone. He set down his drink and, with deliberate care, pulled a vintage Kraal disrupter from inside his jacket.

They really must increase Library security. Other than that wry mental note, Lionel remained calm. Sam was the one, of all the Ragems, he'd wanted most to see when he'd returned to Botharis to clear Paul's reputation. He'd tried, desperately, only to be rebuffed. Remembering, Lionel bowed his head briefly. "Hom Ragem."

"Is anyone listening?"

"No." *Not directly.* Skalet had given him access to her hidden security station so he could summon her Kraal in the event of more trouble; she'd pointedly not provided the means to disable her surveillance or recordings. Fortunately, she wasn't here. This was not, in any sense, a Kraal—or Skalet—situation. He'd a suspicion where she'd gone; hopefully, Paul and Esen weren't too upset with her.

"Is this your doing, too?" Stefan stabbed at the temporary wall with a blunt finger, the nail blackened. His hand trembled.

The aftermath of space sickness. Whatever had brought Stefan to Botharis, the trip had taken a severe toll and he belonged in bed—had likely been in one of Sam's, at a guess, until the pair came here to confront him. *Why?*

"This damage was caused by criminals, yet to be identified," Lionel answered carefully. "I'd no idea you were here, Hom Gahanni. I'm relieved you're safe—"

"Liar. You hired them, just like you did on Senigal—"

Lionel blinked. "Why would you think that?"

"I was there." Paul's father pulled up his left sleeve, exposing the gloss of medplas. "Back of my shop, in an engine to pull panels. Heard someone rummaging around—more than one. Decided they were welcome to whatever they were after and tucked myself inside to wait. Then they started a fire—" Wincing, he eased the fabric down. "The explosion sent the engine, and me, right across the street. I kept my head down after that." Stefan paused, then said grimly, "That's when you showed up at the door—Survey—asking questions."

"I've left the service—"

Stefan didn't let him finish. "Veya warned me Survey might come after her one day," furious and bitter. "That if they did, they'd go for anyone who might know about her work. Well, they did, didn't they? You! I followed you here to protect our son."

"From me?" Lionel sighed. "You both know I haven't a good history with your family, but I assure you, that's long over." And he hadn't left trust in his wake, with one exception. "If Paul were here, he would tell you I'm—" *his friend, now,* "—not the enemy."

"And where's Paul now?" Sam's eyes were fierce. "Taken

on one of your ships! Mal told me. We know what you're after—" He stopped when the door opened and pulled his jacket over the weapon in his lap, eyes sending Kearn a warning.

Carwyn, sensitive to the undercurrent in the room if not its cause, wordlessly placed a workroom stool near Lionel and left. When the door closed behind her, Paul's uncle brought out his weapon, holding it in a gnarled hand. Another whose body bore evidence of a lifetime of physical work. Sam the farmer; Stefan the drive mechanic. Both had loved Veya Ragem. Sam her brother; Stefan her first—possibly only—love.

He was slipping, Lionel decided. He should have recalled the links between them and looked for Stefan here, with Sam. Should have appreciated, much sooner, how his own actions might appear. "Paul and the Assistant Curator left on Library business," he stated firmly. "They'll be back in a few days. Ask any of the staff, if you won't take my word for it."

"Jets-straight, we won't."

Lionel put down his glass. "Contact Paul, right now. I'll arrange a translight link with the *Mistral*."

The pair exchanged looks, abruptly uncertain, and he reminded himself these were concerned relatives. He'd be surprised if Sam had ever fired the relic in his lap.

They needed help, not a target. "Please, Sam," Lionel urged. "I know Paul's been hoping you'd come to see him."

"Why would I? He's not come to see any of us," Sam muttered, half under his breath. "Too busy with aliens to make time for his own family."

Not how Paul saw it. Lionel didn't doubt his friend's lofty purpose for a heartbeat, but the Library was something else, too. Recompense, for his desertion. To Paul, his family had to see and accept the Library, his gift, before they could forgive him. Whether he realized it or not.

Lionel took refuge in his own drink, savoring the smooth burn of what was a very fine whiskey. The stubbornness of any or all Ragems was hardly news.

"If Paul is safe, our business is with you, Kearn," Stefan said, almost wearily. "If you didn't break into my shop, who did?"

"Janet Chase. A for-hire criminal."

They hadn't expected an answer. Sam's eyes narrowed. "We heard two male Humans were found dead near the house. With an Ervickian."

"Her accomplices." That the elder Ragem knew details only the authorities should? Staff, or Mal the helpful constable? Didn't matter. Right now it saved time. "Chase is no longer a factor." Those in the aircar had been poisoned. If Lionel trusted anything in this life, it was that Chase hadn't escaped. *Not from Skalet.* "Our kidnappers were taken into Commonwealth custody."

"Someone hired them. Someone offworld," as if Sam needed to make that obvious to Lionel.

No need to mention the cousin. "There's an investigation underway." The official one, and another by Paul's Group, likely led by Rudy. Lionel didn't doubt Skalet would take an interest, too.

"The Commonwealth." Sam scowled.

"Even if you're not involved, Kearn, Survey's the problem," Stefan said belligerently. "Always has been. You know that, Sam."

Who gave an affirmative grunt.

"Because of Veya and the *Sidereal Pathfinder.*"

Blue eyes and gray regarded him. Not startled. Wary.

The older the secret, the harder to let it go. To speed the process, Lionel offered what he knew. "Chase told us she was after the ship's navigation logs. She traced Veya's visit to your shop. When that turned up empty, she came here."

Stefan's hand fumbled for his glass, spilled a little before reaching his lips. He drained it, then stared at Lionel. "You think she followed me here? That's not possible."

Oh, it was entirely likely, given her skills, but Lionel didn't bother arguing. "Chase came here after Paul, to question him about his mother. I assure you he didn't know anything about all this before. Neither did I. You have my word."

After a long, hard look, during which Lionel managed not to sneeze, Sam Ragem put away the Kraal weapon.

"Sam!"

"Let it go, Stefan. Let it go." Paul's uncle refilled the

other's glass and his own. "We need all the friends we can get right now. Especially those with connections." He held out the bottle to Lionel.

Who accepted, because this had the flavor of ritual. "I'll do everything I can," Lionel promised after a tiny sip, adding no strings or conditions. "But I'll need the facts. Whatever you can tell me."

"It started with you, Kearn," Sam said, in a tone strangely free of accusation. "Veya didn't swallow what you told us. That Paul was a traitor. That he was dead."

"Refused to believe it, you mean."

"Stubborn as any Ragem," Sam admitted, glancing at Stefan. "My sister knew her son. None of what you said, Kearn, made sense to her. And Paul dying like that? Didn't fly either. She believed Paul was alive and in hiding for some reason. Out there." A nod skyward. "The night she left, she swore she wouldn't come home till she found him."

When Paul learned this—He couldn't think about it. "Alone?" Lionel shook his head. He'd had resources. Streams of information. Willing acolytes searching for the Esen Monster, all of them unaware they'd find Paul, too. "She had to realize it was impossible."

"'Impossible?'" Sam snorted. "Veya didn't know the word."

Stefan nodded. "Space was where she belonged. That's what made her such a great navigator. Survey knew it, too. Before the scandal over her son, she'd her pick of postings. Afterward? Dark times." He regarded Lionel soberly. "She even asked to serve on your ship, Kearn."

Paul's mother, on his ship? Lionel shuddered, recalling those days. He'd have mistrusted the offer, the person, the work. "I didn't know."

"You wouldn't. Veya said her superiors made it clear if she stayed in Survey, the only posts open to her would be as far from public attention as possible. The first few years, they gave her trivial, boring routes, probably hoping she'd give up."

Sam growled in his throat. "Didn't know her, did they?"

"Someone higher up did," Stefan countered. "Time

came Veya began to be posted to exploratory missions again. Test flights. The things she loved."

The *Sidereal Pathfinder.*

"Survey was lucky she stuck it out till then," her brother said with old anger.

Luck? Accomplished navigators, at Veya Ragem's level, were valuable commodities, Lionel thought. There were no interstellar signposts. No roads for travelers, only the curves of probability outside of normal space and destinations marked by unique gravity signatures. To follow those and find the others? Tried and tested routes could be flown by comp—but as far as he knew, every space-faring species preferred a living mind at the helm. In the case of Cyns, a Human one; reaching consensus at translight speeds had proved problematic for the species.

To go beyond the known, to explore? Humans had the itch, their fleet of Survey ships venturing forth in any unclaimed direction—few as they were. A map of known space was like viewing the insides of a body; all parts mattered to the whole, but each part crowded against neighbors.

By that comparison, Lionel thought, the Commonwealth would be a Human small intestine, looping through a host of others.

Even with a direction to explore, space offered an impenetrable vastness of choice. Look out in any direction, and you'd see a past growing older and less relevant the deeper you sought. Useless for explorers who could side-step such distances and arrive in days. Servo probes were too easily misinterpreted, making the polite option the safest. Go in person and talk. First Contact teams took care of that part. Survey navigators were the ones who picked the route and made it happen.

That wasn't to say other interests didn't go forth into the unknown; as a former explorer, Veya could have worked for any of them and been wealthy for life.

"Did Veya tell you why she stayed with Survey?" Lionel asked. "Did she think it would help her find Paul?"

Heads shook. Sam replied, his voice low and unhappy. "By then, she wouldn't have told us. We were the only ones who knew she'd kept looking for Paul. When she started getting good posts again, I—I'm sorry to say we thought she was being foolish to hang on to hope. That it was time she stopped and got on with her life. She argued, and I couldn't bear it anymore. I said—terrible things. It was the last time we spoke."

Then Paul Ragem arrives on your doorstep. No wonder this favorite of Paul's uncles hadn't rushed forward.

He'd guilt of his own. "There were others hunting Paul for their own reasons," Lionel said. "Dangerous. Unscrupulous. If Veya learned of them, she might have stopped of her own accord to protect Paul." He looked to Stefan. "Perhaps she chose those ships to put herself out of reach, so they couldn't use her to find him."

"Maybe," Stefan stared into his glass. "I'd like to think she made her own choices." He looked up, eyes haunted. "They didn't end well. Whatever brought her to that cursed starship, everything changed when it was lost. When she came to me afterward, she'd left Survey. She didn't say it in so many words, but—Veya was afraid."

Had she reason? Lionel firmed his tone. "Did Veya Ragem steal the *Sidereal Pathfinder's* logbook? And before you answer me?" He pointed at the plank wall. "Consider what she'd think of Paul being attacked in his home because of it."

"No." Sam sat back. When Stefan failed to answer, he turned to glare at him. "Veya'd never steal, especially not from her own ship. I know my sister."

"As she was." Stefan gave a little shrug, wincing when it jarred his injured arm. "The Veya who came to me wasn't the same. She was desperate and angry and, yes, afraid. She wouldn't stay—wouldn't explain. Went off and died in that stupid scow." His voice quieted. It was no less sorrowful. "Do I want to believe in her innocence? Of course. Can I say I do? It depends," he admitted, "when you ask me. Right now, it's hard, Sam. It's really hard. When criminals blow up my shop and then attack a library, of all places. When there are bodies—" He stopped and drained his glass, avoiding Veya's brother's anguished face.

"It can be argued," Lionel said calmly, dispassionate

because someone had to be, "the logs were the responsibility of the navigator to keep safe. Let's put aside for the moment whether Veya was on the right side of the law or not. Whether we believe what she told you then or not. Is there anything more you can tell me?"

Stefan, quietly. "Sam."

Paul's uncle shifted in his seat, focused on his glass. He put it down beside the carafe, then turned it.

"Sam, if it helps makes sense of this—helps protect Paul—"

"And what if it makes things worse?" More plea than protest.

"You don't know it will. That's not up to us to decide. It has to be Paul—and those with him." Stefan reached out, put his hand on the other's arm. "We talked about this. Agreed we'd do this for Veya."

"You agreed." The other tapped his glass against the carafe. "I was drunk. You made me drunk. We were," with gravity, "feet up and scuppered."

"I flew *in space* to get here, you ungrateful dirt digger, and was sick for days because of it, and we barely touched that awful dregs you call wine."

"'Dirt digger'? That's your best insult? You need to travel more."

"More? Bad enough I have to get home again!"

Sam chuckled, and something between the two eased.

Lionel, carefully quiet, could feel it. *Seize the moment.* "Tell me, for Paul."

So they did.

32: Cabin Morning

ACCORDING to Skalet, a Vlovax to a Mareepa was like a hoobit to a Ket. Simply put, you mustn't be seen without yours. What made obtaining a hoobit complicated, for imposters like ourselves, was that the intricate circlets were unique to individuals, created at birth and not removed even in death. From the Web viewpoint, it helped that Queebs regularly robbed Ket graves for hoobits to sell on the open market.

What made obtaining a Vlovax complicated? To start with, they were alive—a scavenger living below ground—possessed of sufficient smarts to know up from down and, like most living things, Vlovax resisted being captured, as Skalet told me I must do.

Because Vlovax were what the Dokeci called Devil Darts.

That was only the beginning. To wear your Vlovax in proper Mareepa fashion, you let one of the now-furious things lock its fang into your neck, then hang from it. Ideally, for the rest of your life, it being a status symbol among the now-named Mareepavlovax not to lose their acquisition. Presumably, the creatures wriggled in protest until they died, henceforth doomed to be an accessory.

Give me a grave-robbed hoobit.

The dead Mareepavlovax delivered for autopsy had a gaping hole in his neck. His, because Skalet had confirmed the correct pronoun after looking at the image, though she'd been vague on their reproduction and Ersh knew I didn't want those details anyway. The hole, in Skalet's opinion, marked where a Vlovax had been yanked out, so really we should call the dead a Mareepa.

I preferred Elves, but the name was no longer helpful, unless it reduced the chance of Dokeci taking actions we'd all regret.

Skalet closed the node. "I'm proud of you, Youngest."

I gave her a suspicious look. "Should I worry?"

My web-kin chuckled, acknowledging our shared, ever-tumultuous past. "Ersh saw more in you than I ever did, I admit. Until now. Permit me to amend my opinion favorably—this much." Her fingers described an infinitesimal gap.

"I'll take it," I said before she could change her mind. At that rate, in another few centuries, she'd approve of me, if not be ready to hug, but we weren't operating on a Web time frame. "I have to get back to Paul and Evan."

"To tell them?" Her eyelids lowered, obscuring her eyes. Her lips were a thin line.

I'd stood. Slowly, I sat down again, across from Skalet. "We came to prevent a potentially fatal misunderstanding. I can do that."

"Senior Assimilator, what is the purpose of our Web?"

"To preserve the accomplishments of ephemeral species. And," I added, "to prevent their loss."

"Bah. Extinction is natural." Her hand moved as though wiping something off the table. "It makes room for new forms." Her lids rose, eyes fixed on mine, and I was disturbed to realize I couldn't read their expression. "The Harbingers have had longer than most. These are most likely the last of their kind. Surely what remains is to preserve them in our memories."

"Once we save them, we'll have time to do that." *A lengthy task I'd happily assign my web-kin.* "First, we need to get them off Dokeci-Na."

Because the Mareepavlovax didn't belong on a living, healthy planet.

Being the Harbingers of Death.

It was a poetical name for a rather ingenious lifestyle. Other intelligent species went into space and sought worlds to colonize, ideally like their own. Since what appealed to one all too often appealed to anyone else in the vicinity, conflicts arose. The Mareepavlovax chose from the beginning to avoid the strife and danger of life-supporting planets.

Instead, they settled on those about to die. What the Dokeci called shelter-cities were traveling harvesters. According to Skalet, the Mareepavlovax she'd encountered remained inside their Harvester, safe within a minimal but complete ecosystem of their own, while Vlovax and other scavengers tunneled outward, returning with whatever life they could find. The harvesters stayed while the world beneath them became untenable, their departure timed to reap the most before the risk became too great.

Unfortunately—from their viewpoint—still-living worlds in the throes of ultimate destruction were rare, at least those with resources worth harvesting. Mareepavlovax hunted with slow patience, hibernating between finds to conserve resources, traveling in clusters of harvesters disguised as lumps of rock.

Skalet refused to waste time describing their culture, other than to call it "drearily profound."

Whatever that meant. I was fascinated and appalled. They traveled interstellar space, drawn to worlds in cataclysm, avoiding those with conflict. They were noticed, and named, and avoided by those with more appealing worlds to pillage. Now, from all Skalet knew, the Mareepavlovax were reduced to this remnant on a single moon, their nature forgotten.

Until the Dokeci decided to bring them home.

"That's the problem," I finished, looking from Paul to Evan. It was difficult to say which of them looked more unnerved. No, I could tell it was Evan. His eyes were bulging.

Paul? Had his *what aren't you telling me* squint. I returned my own *this time, that's it.* For what I knew, anyway. The spoken word had serious limitations; I hoped to get a meaningful bite out of Skalet the moment she was agreeable. *Polite and courteous, that was me.*

I really should have remembered neither of those were her.

"You're telling me this—this—"

"Harvester," I said, being helpful.

"You're telling me it's going to consume the life on Dokeci-Na?"

"I wouldn't put it quite like that." Catching Paul's raised eyebrow, I went on, "The Mareepavlovax will have realized they aren't on a dying world. I'm sure they're trying to restrain their—ah—partners, but the reach of a Harvester is determined by its tunnels. The Dokeci put this one on top of glacial till—a landscape particularly easy to dig through—so we shouldn't leave it there much longer."

An appalled silence. Evan buried his face in his hands. Paul kept his attention on me. I wagged my ears; he didn't appear mollified.

Finally, Evan put down his hands. "You want me to tell my seniors and the Dokeci they need Burtles-Mautil to come back, wrap up the Harvester and those inside again, and move it—and the Elves—again—to another, more suitable world as quickly as possible. Assuming they can find one."

Why did he keep repeating what I'd said? It wasn't as though the facts were going to cycle into some other shape. Summoning my patience, with an eye on my ominously silent friend, I did my utmost to reassure the young diplomat. "An excellent summary, Evan. Except for the part where we should find out if these Mareepavlovax are willing and able to hibernate. Certainly that would buy us considerably more time for relocation," I finished brightly.

"That's . . . Paul?"

My friend tipped his head as if hearing what I hadn't said. "I've full confidence in Esolesy's findings, Evan." To me, "How to deal with the situation will be up to those in charge on the ground."

Be aware, Esen, that was. Those in charge had minds of their own. Fearful ones. "My way is the only choice," I said firmly.

"Your way saves the Elves," Evan said as if agreeing with me, then confusingly shook his head. "You're assuming the Dokeci will want to save the Mareepavlovax."

Humans. "They're the same thing."

"Elves are bringers of light and joy. Storybook characters. What you've described is the antithesis. Horrific—terrifying."

He didn't like mousels either. No being was perfect. "Everything has its place, Evan Gooseberry. The Mareepavlovax didn't ask to be uprooted. They don't deserve to be extinguished because they were."

Paul stirred. "And the Dokeci shouldn't suffer for their kindness. Evan, what will you put in your report?"

He seemed frayed at the edges, despite the smart jacket, but answered with confidence. "None of this. I'll say I've pertinent, vital information and set up a meeting with Senior Polit M'Lean as soon as possible." Evan looked at me. "You've done more than I'd dared hope, Esolesy. I hate to ask this, but would you, both of you, come with me to the embassy? We may have more questions."

Perfect! I tried to keep a sober face. "What do you think, Paul?"

"We'd be honored, Evan."

"I've one request," I added quickly.

Paul gave me *that* look. In his relief, Evan didn't notice. "Anything I can do," he said warmly, if unwisely. "What is it?"

"The Mareepavlovax at the embassy? I want to see his body. And the Vlovax, too. Research," I explained. "For the Library."

Whatever argument Evan might have made faded before the joy of my curled lips and shining tusks. "I'll make the request."

"Thank you."

While Evan composed his report, we went back to our cabins. More precisely, I went to mine, and Paul crowded behind me into it. He continued to the accommodation and looked inside. Opened the closet and looked in there, too, before turning to me. "Where is she?"

Quicker than most, always. "I don't know," I replied honestly, torn between pleased Skalet wasn't here and worried she wasn't. A not unfamiliar conflict.

Paul sank abruptly on the bed. "Why didn't you tell me, Old Blob?"

"It wasn't as if I had a chance," I countered though, to be fair, I could have slipped him a note or used any number of key phrases—*hello, my less than reliable web-kin's on board stealing Commonwealth secrets for her Kraal backers.* "She never consults me."

As I'd hoped, my complaint made him smile in sympathy. "I take it Skalet was helpful, this time." His smile gave way to a familiar intense curiosity. "How could she know what you and the Library didn't?"

I climbed into my synth-grass box and leaned my big jaw on the side. "Ersh didn't share this form with me."

A sharp look. *He'd heard enough of my stories.* "Why?"

"I don't know. If Skalet does, she isn't saying." I rubbed my jaw pensively. "Her last experience as a Mareepavlovax was before I arrived. She told me what she could."

"What she wanted you to know," he corrected almost absently, knowing my web-kin, too. "That's why you asked to see the corpse. To acquire the form on your own."

And a Vlovax. *Not something to explain ahead of time.* "I must. You're right," I told him sadly. "So's Evan. The Dokeci and Humans will destroy the Harvester in order to save countless lives. They won't want to, but—" My stomachs rumbled. "I can hear the argument now: if the Dokeci hadn't planned a retirement colony in the neighborhood, nature would have run its course and the last of the Elves would have died on the moon."

Paul's eyes sparkled. "Then we'll present them with an eloquent, knowledgeable Mareepavlovax who can negotiate the extraction of her kind instead. What do you need, Es?"

"More than one sample would be nice. Hairs," I said wistfully. *Toenail clippings were a favorite, full of genetic material and rarely missed.* What I'd miss? The diversity inherent in any living things, and I'd no idea what that me would require. Then there was the ever-present concern about age equivalence. "I'll manage." This with all the confidence I could muster.

Didn't fool him for a heartbeat. "Don't worry. There should be more at the embassy. The report cited the species' genome, and they wouldn't rely on a single sample either. Leave that with me to verify."

"Gladly." I considered my inner list. Being Lishcyn, I couldn't help starting with, "I'll need clothes. I can sneak into the Harvester—"

"No. You can't," he said with alarm. "This time you don't know the culture and language. Too much could go wrong—for them as well," sternly. "Es, promise me."

It wasn't as though my promises ever worked, I thought, inclined to be stubborn. *Yes, I always tried my best to keep them, but something always happened—*

Paul softened his tone. "I know how much you want to learn about them. Trust me, I do, too. We'll have time if we save them."

What I'd told Skalet. Curling a tusk at my friend, I relented. "I promise I won't enter the Harvester." I showed the other tusk. "Until it's been moved to another world and they're safe."

At last, a promise I'd be able to keep.

I should have stayed with stubborn.

"Thank you. Now, what else do you need?"

I eyed his earnest, helpful face, one I knew better than any of my own. "There is one thing." Did I start with Lesy's stray bits, Skalet's imploder, or the shrine to Ersh—

The shrill of an alert through the com interrupted that complicated decision. Words followed: "Passengers and off-duty crew, return to your cabins and secure your doors. We have a developing situation in the lower decks. Please wait for the all-clear before resuming normal activities."

Paul and I looked at one another in perfect understanding. *Skalet.*

He rose. "I'll be in my cabin."

"Don't lock my door," I requested, settling into my box with a resigned sigh. Not that a lock mattered.

What was she up to now?

Perception

"THE prisoners got out of holding," Commander Kamaara informed him. Them, because Captain Clendon had leaned over his chair to listen. "I don't know where they thought they'd go," with disgust. "My people had them in minutes."

"How could they escape in the first place?" Evan asked. At her scowl, he added, "They didn't appear very, ah, clever."

The scowl deepened. "You a psych analyst now, Polit?"

The captain lifted a lazy hand. "We'd all like to know, Ne-Sa."

"So would I." She shrugged. "Locks don't fail. This one did. The techs have pulled the panel, but they tell me it could be a while before they've a cause." A grin Evan was glad wasn't aimed at him. "The prisoners are back in med-bay, under guard. Senior Med-tech Warford squawked about filing a protest. Sorry, Captain." She didn't appear the least apologetic.

Another lazy wave. "I'll talk to her." Captain Clendon straightened and checked the feed on the chair arm. He let out a low whistle. "Whatever you put in your report, Polit, it's got us the full treatment. Priority slot, with the embassy aircar waiting for you and your people."

"And two of mine," Kamaara interjected. "Under the circumstances, I'd prefer an eye on our guests." When

Evan opened his mouth to protest the embassy would surely send their own security, the commander said smoothly, "Unless you'd like four."

"Two would be appreciated," he replied.

The alert had rattled him, despite the prompt explanation he'd been provided. Actually, Evan thought, the explanation had made it worse. Escaped felons weren't what you expected to deal with on a starship. What if they'd attempted sabotage? Kamaara's continued suspicion of Paul didn't improve matters.

Nor did knowing what his friends, the very capable Lisam and Lynelle, would think of ship security piling into *their* aircar. They'd give him an earful, later.

Still, almost home. Evan pressed the call button by the door. "Trili? It's Evan."

The door whooshed open. "Are you all right?" she demanded, urging him inside. "I can't get anything out of the crew. 'Course, that goes both ways," with a gleam in her eyes. "Sit, sit. I've juice."

"I can't stay," he said, but he did take the seat. "Did you read the update?"

"The one you shouldn't have sent me? The one so far above my clearance level we'd both better hope no one else finds out?" She put her hands flat on the table. "What were you thinking?"

Evan forced a smile. "That I can't be the only embassy staff who knows. If there's a problem, Trili, blame me."

"Trust me, I will." But she wouldn't. His friend's face scrunched unhappily. "Damn, Evan. Any way this ends well?"

He gave her the truth. "I don't think so." Then rallied. "Senior staff will have better—"

Trili made a rude noise. "Senior staff will hide under their desks. M'Lean put you in charge. Fair, you've done more on this than any of them, but you listen to me, Evan Gooseberry. You've seen how it works. A no-win mess like this? They'll dangle you in front of the Dokeci as the

Commonwealth's foremost expert on these Elves. Whatever happens, it'll be your face they'll remember and your neck in a vise."

. . . spots and snake-arms and . . .

The *fear* sputtered, facing multiple Dokeci nowhere near as daunting as what he'd face them with—"We still don't know how much threat the Mareepavlovax and their Harvester pose. The valley is almost barren."

"Making them right at home, according to the Library." She reached out, touching fingertips to his wrist. "Before you hand this to M'Lean, be sure of your source, Evan." Her eyes searched his. "Be damned certain they aren't lying to you or holding back." Trili sat back. "No matter how handsome your Paul is," she observed dryly.

His face warmed. "That's—"

"Only obvious to someone who knows you like I do. Don't worry." Trili's smile was kind, but brief. "Just remember what's at stake. Ask the tough questions, Evan, before you put your neck where they can wring it."

Evan walked the empty corridor, the echo of his footsteps too loud, or was it the beating of his heart? Trili was smart and experienced—and the best kind of friend. If she warned him against blind trust, she'd done it for all the right reasons.

He'd reasons, too. Maybe they were mixed up with feelings, but he was, after all, Human. Instinct. Personal connection. Emotional response. They'd a firm place in any negotiation. Or relationship. If he couldn't reliably gauge his own kind, how could he represent humanity to what wasn't?

Great Gran said it was about layers. You met the outer person; you invested time, effort, and empathy to reach deeper. Above all, you reciprocated, layer for layer, because trust had to grow both ways.

At the time, she'd tried to help a painfully shy and anxious Evan endure the gauntlet that was his first school, but he remembered every word. *Believed them.*

He paused outside Esolesy Ki's door to press the call. "It's Evan. I wanted to see—"

The door opened, replaced by the Lishcyn's considerable bulk. She curled a cheery lip at him, inlaid tusk glittering. "And here I am. Did you come to tell me about that alert? Are we going to crash or something?"

On impulse, he tried to look past her. She showed the other tusk and moved forward, closing the door behind as she had earlier. "My room's a mess. The alert?"

"Oh. Yes. The prisoners managed to free themselves briefly. Security is upset, but I'm told all is secure. Sorry for the disruption."

"Thank you." She'd cup-shaped ears, so delicate blood vessels showed through like filigree. They waggled at him. "I feel much better now."

"Would you and Paul join me for a late supper? The guest galley in, say, a couple of hours?"

"Thank you. I'll be there." With an interested rumble somewhere mid-girth. "Will you let Paul know? I was—in the midst of a nap."

"My apologies for disturbing you," Evan said at once, though Esolesy wore a flowing silk caftan without a crease. "I'll tell Paul."

"Excellent! Before you go, Evan. Have you heard about my request? To see the corpse?"

He hadn't been sure she was serious, but there was a note to her voice that said she was, very much so. "They're confirming with the pathology specialist in charge, but my understanding is you'll be permitted if you are willing to wear protective gear." *Sammy having an entirely justified anxiety about Lishcyn stomachs in her lab.*

Tusks glittered. "Wonderful. I do enjoy dressing up. Till supper, then."

She slipped back inside more quickly than he'd thought a Lishcyn could move, and the door closed in his face. "Must need that nap," he mused aloud.

Then looked across the corridor.

Before he lost his nerve, Evan strode up to Paul Ragem's door and reached for the panel.

Which was when he lost his nerve. How long he might

have stood there, hand upraised, fingers curled in indecision, was anyone's guess.

Fortunately, a voice came from behind. "Evan. I've been looking for you."

It was Paul. Evan closed his eyes for a second before turning with a smile. "And here I am. Hello."

"That's it, then." Paul sat back on the bench to regard the itinerary displayed between them. "A meeting at the embassy to brief your senior staff. When they're ready, off to Riota-si to meet with the Dokeci. And they've agreed to Es and me coming along?"

"To everything I've asked for," Evan said glumly. "Trili's right. The embassy's sticking me out in front, whatever happens."

A wise glance. "It could go better than you think, Evan. Being in front, then? A career maker."

"I don't care about that." Words came out and, for once, he felt no urge to explain or justify himself. "I never have, Paul, no matter what I told Great Gran. What I want is to help. Make a difference. I want to find a solution for the Dokeci *and* the Mareepavlovax." He rubbed a hand over his face. "I just don't see one."

"Yet."

He looked up in sudden desperate hope. "Do you? Does Esolesy?"

For the first time, Paul appeared hesitant.

"Paul, if you've an idea, I don't care what it is, tell me. Please."

"We'd like to have a Mareepavlovax attend the meeting."

Who wouldn't? Evan was about to say, then saw the determination in those gray eyes. "You mean it. You think it's possible. How? They've locked themselves in—barely managed to communicate before that."

Lips quirked. "Esolesy's working on it. We won't know if she's succeeded in convincing a representative to join us until the very last minute—which means you can't tell anyone, Evan."

"But—"

Paul leaned forward, those eyes intent. "I'm asking you to trust me. To trust us. If this falls through," a grimace, "you know the consequences."

Trili wanted him to be sure of his sources—and he was, Evan realized, beyond doubt. "If we can have the Mareepavlovax's side, talk with them instead of about them—" He let his voice trail away. *This was the right way.* He could feel it. "Is there anything I can do, anything Esolesy needs—" he stopped and swallowed. "The body. Her request. It's about this, isn't it, not the Library."

"The less we involve you—" Paul began gently.

"No." Evan was on his feet. "I started this. I brought you into it. Trust goes both ways."

The other stood and came around the table. Evan hadn't realized he was taller until now. "It does," Paul agreed. "But so does duty. I'm protecting Esolesy. At the same time, Evan, I'm protecting you."

Drawn by the earnestness in that voice and face, Evan found he'd stepped close. Found he'd brought up his hands. Rested one on Paul's shoulder and the other—he couldn't help himself—didn't want to help himself—the other found the strong line of jaw, explored the faint pull of whisker, delighted in the warm softness of skin. "You don't have to protect me," he heard himself say in a stranger's husky voice. "I'm here for you."

And he watched the swallow, saw those beautiful eyes fill with—it wasn't pity, Paul was too kind for pity, but it wasn't what he wanted to see.

Evan tore away, breathing in heavy hopeless gasps. "I'm sorry. I'm sorry."

A hand gripped his shoulder, turned him with gentle strength. Arms went around him and held him close. "Shh." Warm, near his ear. "Never regret offering your heart, Evan. I'm flattered. Honored, deeply. You're a good brave person. I couldn't be prouder if you were my son."

He wasn't crying. That much at least. But he couldn't move away, not yet, so Evan mumbled into Paul's shirt. "I don't want to be your son. And my age doesn't matter."

He felt the chuckle. "No, it doesn't. What does?" Lips

pressed against his hair. "I'm the one sorry. There's some-one else."

Oh. Evan pulled back, not so far that Paul's hands couldn't remain on his shoulders. "I didn't know."

"No one does." As if willing to show Evan what he'd shown no one else, grief crossed Paul's face, followed by wistful longing. The first aged it; the second was a glimpse into who he'd been as a boy and Evan wished it would last. It didn't. "I'd given her up years ago, along with my former life. I thought I had," with a sudden, rueful smile. "This must sound quite foolish."

"It sounds romantic," Evan said firmly, and found he could, almost, smile back.

"Maybe. That, my dear friend, will depend on whether I'm brave enough to reopen an old wound—and whether she'll forgive me for it."

"She'd be a fool if she didn't!" he said hotly.

Paul laughed so warmly, Evan found himself laughing, too. "That sounded really—melodramatic, didn't it," he said when they were done.

"It was well meant and a comfort. Thank you. But, yes, a bit." He gestured to the table, then went to a bag and produced a bottle. "A toast, if you will, Evan Goose-berry."

Evan sat. "To fools?" he suggested wryly. *How could his heart hurt like this, and still be happy?*

"To those who dare to be." Paul poured a bit into a mug for Evan, then into a glass for himself. He lifted it. "You're far braver than I." His eyes softened. "I'd say I wished things could be different, Evan. But between us, the truth."

However cold and lonely it left them both. Evan sighed and raised his mug, touching it to Paul's glass. "To the truth." He took a sip and sputtered. "What is this?"

"A Ragem tradition." The burn didn't appear to bother Paul. He went to take another drink, then paused, "About what I've told you."

"I won't tell if you don't," Evan said quickly. "I mean— you know what I mean." He took a sip and sputtered again. "You do, don't you?"

"I think so." A finger came down on the table. "It's

Esen. And Esolesy Ki. They don't know I've someone—
that I hope I've someone, one day." He looked up. "They
can't know," more harshly than Evan expected.

Then again, he didn't live every day with a pair of too-
helpful aliens. "They won't hear it from me," he promised. "And I do understand. Esen told me—" *no need for
specifics.* "She told me you were available."

"Did she now?" A dimple.

Which he could enjoy, Evan decided, because whatever they weren't, they were this. Closer than friends.
Still, "You don't mind if I sigh, once in a while?" He demonstrated, exaggerating a little.

Paul burst out laughing again. "Evan Gooseberry," he
mock-scolded. "If you do that, everyone will think I've
broken your heart. And I haven't," he added, suddenly
serious. "No matter how it feels now. There's someone
out there for you. This?" He put his hand over Evan's
heart. "This is valuable exercise."

Evan covered Paul's hand with his own. "And a promise," he said, keeping his voice light, not knowing his
handsome face showed his soul. "If you find yourself
without someone—you don't have to stay that way, Paul.
You needn't be alone."

"Thank you. But I'm never that," the other answered,
with the oddest happy smile.

33: Cabin Evening

*T*OO *close.* I closed the door, sealing Evan outside, and turned to my web-kin. "Isn't there anywhere else on the ship you can stay?" *Did starships have a bilge?*

"Don't fuss, Youngest. We'll be gone in the morning."

I eyed the bundle on her bed, doubtless obtained during the so-convenient wanderings of the ship's prisoners. "And that's going to slip you past security."

"Not at all." Skalet's lips stretched. "Leave my exit with me. What have you done about the shrine?"

My third stomach protested, so I shifted contents from the second to placate it. "There's nothing I can do about the shrine," I said testily, "until this business with the Elves is over. That's why the Humans brought us along." *Because she tended to overlook such things.*

She did not overlook my tone. "What's wrong?"

"I have you in my room?"

"You told him, didn't you."

I waggled my ears at her. "I didn't have to—Paul knows you, too."

Her faintly satisfied "Hmm" was not a comfort. "Then he can help us reach the shrine."

"I haven't told him—" I stuffed my mouth with—*yuck, Human e-rations*—from the table to prevent worse than a rumble, not bothering to remove the wrapper, then mumbled, "—'bout Lesy."

"Finally, a sign of prudence. No others need know

about Lesy, thank Ersh. We will eradicate her leavings and be done."

I would never erase her laughter from my flesh. One of those thoughts best kept to myself. *Prudence, that was.* "We are not using the imploder on a Dokeci shrine."

"Of course not. I'm using it."

"We. You. No one. Not using it."

Skalet shifted her ill-gotten bundle to make room and lay down, closing her eyes. "Don't be tedious, Youngest. There's no other option."

"I'll find one."

"I suggest you find the shrine first."

Refusing to dignify that with an answer, I pried the wrapper from between my teeth and went in search of a full meal.

And better company.

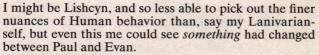

I might be Lishcyn, and so less able to pick out the finer nuances of Human behavior than, say my Lanivarian-self, but even this me could see *something* had changed between Paul and Evan.

Frustratingly, I couldn't tell what. Asking was out of the question, at least until I had one or the other to myself, so I contented myself, more or less, with observing.

And eating, it being the responsibility of a polite guest to appreciate what was offered.

"We've passage home when our business is done here," Paul told Evan, "including accommodations on the *Largas Regal* throughout our stay."

I perked up. Largas Freight was run by friends and allies—not to mention Joel and his family kept their ships in fine order. Paul must have been glad to find the *Regal* fins down.

Unless he'd planned it, not that I could see how, but my friend had surprised me before now. I gave him a look.

Paul responded with a tiny shake of his head.

A fortunate coincidence then, Dokeci-Na a busy and profitable hub for freight coming and going to multiple systems. *Call it luck,* I told myself.

"The embassy will cover your costs," Evan said. He looked relaxed, if drained. Perhaps a little melancholy. Until he caught Paul looking at him, then he'd smile.

Humans. If they'd become lovers, I'd need my other nose to tell, *not that it was*, as Paul would say, *any of my business.*

But it was, if only to reassure me our friendship wasn't costing him his own, Human, relationships. *Tactful questions remained a work in progress.*

We were lingering over dessert, always a favorite of this me, when I dared to broach one. "So will we be seeing more of you, Evan, in future?" I wagged my ears. "When you visit the Library, I mean." *Tactful Esen.*

The younger Human appeared to gag on his mouthful.

Paul smiled. "You are always welcome," he assured Evan, then gave me a quelling look.

Meaning I shouldn't ask questions when someone had a mouthful or don't ask questions about seeing Evan again? *Or both?* None of which actually settled matters, to my annoyed confusion, since Paul might be trying to convey I shouldn't ask prying questions about this relationship at all. *Also likely.*

I curled a lip brightly and, having learned long ago it was the safer course, changed the subject. "Evan, have you visited the Dokeci Shrine to Teganersha-ki? Esen told me you carry her likeness."

"I do." Looking as though he, too, appreciated a new topic, Evan pulled the bust from inside his jacket and set it on the table.

Ersh. I tilted my head to bring one eye to bear, having not truly looked at it before. The likeness was—well, the beads didn't help. The *taste* . . .

A foot tapped mine, snapping me out of it.

"There are shrines all over Dokeci-Na, Esolesy," Evan told me. "Is there one in particular?"

I pointed a thick finger at the bust. "I was told of a new project. One involving personal works?"

His face lightened. "Oh, yes. It's not that new. You mean Riosolesy-ki's Shrine to Teganersha-ki. It's in the capital—not far from Embassy Row." A hand cupped the statue possessively. "Only Dokeci were permitted to contribute."

"'Riosolesy-ki,'" Paul echoed, eyes locked on me. "Wasn't she one of the Dokeci artists killed on Portula Colony?"

He knew she was and who she'd been. Paul now knew Lesy was involved. Next, I told myself dolefully, my intelligent friend would deduce Skalet had snuck herself on board not to help the Mareepavlovax, but because she and I had some kind of unhealthy-to-others fixation on the work of our web-kin.

He wouldn't be wrong.

Rudy had a saying: *when in doubt, rush straight in.* Not the sanest advice, but I chose to take it. "A particular favorite of mine," I said truthfully. "I was hoping we could see her work."

Paul looked worried.

At least he didn't know about the imploder.

"It's quite the—" Evan seemed to search for the right word, "—sight. I don't believe there'll be time before we have to leave for the valley. Unless this is important to your endeavor, Esolesy," not only stressed, but with a lift of eyebrows I assumed he thought meaningful.

So I turned to Paul for an interpretation.

He winked at me.

Winking could be a good sign. When it meant *we know something no one else does.* Especially if it involved hidden presents or frozen treats about to be given to our mystified but deserving staff.

Winking, I reminded myself grimly, *could be the opposite.* When it meant *someone else knows what we know.*

They might not be lovers, but I'd reason to believe Paul and Evan had shared more than they should. *About me?*

With an effort, I curled my lip. "The shrine can wait, thank you. After all, I'm representing my kind here," *that* for Paul. "All Lishcyn must reinforce Dokecian recognition of the maturity of our younger members. Playing the tourist—under these circumstances—would undermine those efforts."

Evan nodded, well aware, I was sure, of similar problems faced by younger Humans on this world. The Dokeci did their best to grasp that, for most other species, youth didn't equate to sturdy, if nonverbal and barely intelligent, slave. Credit for that belonged to the Lishcyn, whose precocious, rapidly growing young worked as "adults" by their third year.

A significant plus to this form. If initially troubling to the Dokeci who found they'd opened into serious negotiations with "children."

Evan tucked away his statue. "Afterward, then, and with gratitude," with a disturbingly knowing bow of his curly-haired head.

This time I glared at Paul, who gave a little shrug and mouthed *later*.

Humans.

Tomorrow would be momentous. And possibly involve the extinction of a sentient species, risk the exposure of my own kind, and let us not forget the wanton destruction of art along with slagging most of the core of the Dokeci planetary capital.

I groaned and buried my head in synth-grass, an eye near my glowing lantern.

"Sleep," Skalet ordered. "That form needs rest, as does mine."

"I can't sleep if you keep talking to me." If Paul were here, he'd hum me a lullaby and rub my chin to help me sleep. I sighed very quietly. *As well compare the imploder to a fystia flower.*

Though I wasn't convinced I wanted Paul here at the moment. Before we'd parted for the night, he'd told me *what* he'd told Evan—that I'd the means to contact a Mareepavlovax and invite them to the meeting—if not why.

I could guess. Our earnest diplomat had lost hope; Paul, tenderhearted, had restored it. The problem was now Evan, in no sense a fool, would be on the alert, watching eagerly for this mysterious new being to arrive. My close-to-impossible task of cycling without being noticed had become impossible.

I still had to do it. I'd someone nearby who'd be delighted to turn on the lights and plan strategy till breakfast, all while chastising me for not having my own plan. If I had one, of course, Skalet would dismember it with glee then resume planning—*there was no winning either way.*

Or sleep. I sighed again.

"Youngest." Suspicion in her tone. "Is there something else you haven't told me?"

I pretended to snore.

And shortly thereafter, fell asleep after all.

Perception

A row of gleaming black eyes, each on their stalk, regarded Lionel with the sort of deep abiding malice that made survival unlikely unless he started running now.

Bluff. "Ah, you're here," as if he'd just noticed the looming mass behind the counter. "Good. I've a task for you, Lambo Reomattatii."

A great claw, shining and hard from the being's recent molt, rose in front of him, then snapped.

Bluster. Lionel blinked as air whooshed across his face. Another rule for first contact? Assume they know more about you than you know about them, though as it happened, he knew a considerable amount about Carasians and, thanks to Esolesy Ki, this one in particular.

He lowered his voice conspiratorially, despite them being alone in the Chow, rewarded when Lambo tilted closer. "I've been given a puzzle, and I'm told you have a fine technical mind. I've come to you for help solving it."

"My mind is brilliant."

"Even better," Lionel said agreeably. "What I—"

"Mine," with a smug rearrangement of eyestalks, "is the greatest mind on this planet."

An unusual boast for a Carasian, who preferred to point out their physical attributes. Especially for one larger than any he'd had the pleasure to meet—quite magnificent really, if less civil—

Too large.

Lambo spun about, handling claws moving in a blur over the dispenser. The lights winked out and a hum Lionel hadn't noticed till now was gone. The Carasian flipped up the counter gate.

Lionel didn't run because he couldn't, frozen by the realization he was nose to clawtip with a female of the species. Granted, prepubescent and prepredatory, but before Lambo's next, probably calamitous-to-others molt, there would have to be a talk about staff.

And a certain coy Web-being.

"What is your puzzle?"

Why a *female* Carasian was tending a third-rate food dispenser on Botharis—no, that wasn't a puzzle at all. Esen had explained this was how he—she could remain within the Library indefinitely, without being a client.

"How disappointing. You do not appear to have a mind at all." Lambo turned to resume her place behind the counter.

"Wait," he croaked. "Please." The Carasian clattered to face him again, claws half-raised as though to push him away. *Or chop him in manageable bits.* Lionel coughed to clear his throat. "Forgive me. I confess to being overwhelmed, Lambo Reomattatii. It is a state that happens to Humans when we encounter true magnificence."

A pleased rattle as her claws lowered. "Will you need more time to recover?"

"I will endeavor to persevere," he said truthfully, "because I do need your help. The puzzle I mentioned was brought to me by two visitors earlier today. They claim Veya Ragem entrusted them with a message for Paul Ragem. A message they gave me, for him. I would give it to you, for your opinion."

"If so, I would be, at minimum, seventh in this chain of transmission. The quality of information dilutes."

"That it does. I offer cross-verification, but I must warn you. It is necessarily in Human terms."

A troubled sigh. "I will cope. Provide it."

Lionel carefully didn't smile. "My visitors were males within the biological commonality that includes and produced Paul Ragem. All three exist within, and inform, the historical context of the life and actions of Veya Ragem. I give you their names. Sam Ragem of Botharis. Stefan Gahanni of Senigal III."

"I am astonished."

"As was I. Stefan—"

"You mistake me, Acting Director. It is your ability to communicate that causes my astonishment. It is superb."

Lionel bowed. "'To serve truth, one must begin and end with clarity.'"

A delighted *clickclick* of claws. "You quote Rampo Tasceillato the Wise! Bravo, Human!"

He really should be ashamed of himself. "While at the academy, I was privileged to attend several guest lectures on early Carasian philosophy," Lionel said humbly. "An enlightening topic."

"A scholar, indeed. I will hear what you've come to say." Lambo settled herself to the floor, eyestalks milling in content. "You were right to seek my help, Acting Director Kearn. It will be the best available to you."

Volatile and vain. The familiar traits put Lionel at ease, and he sat in her shadow, crossing his legs. "The message Veya asked Stefan to convey to Paul was this: 'What we believe is lost simply waits for better eyes to find it.'"

"I find no useful meaning in these words. Are they as cryptic to you, a Human?"

"Yes," Lionel admitted, "but the timing could assist our understanding. Veya gave this instruction to Stefan two years after *Sidereal Pathfinder* was lost, during a visit she did her best to keep secret. As, at that time, Paul was officially presumed dead, Stefan dismissed it as part of what he believed her delusion."

Eyestalks whirled in concentration, then aimed at Lionel. "If Veya made one secret visit, she could have made another, here, in order to leave the logbook for her offspring as Chase believed. Indeed something "lost" waiting to be found. A legacy, given its potential value."

Making Veya Ragem guilty of theft after all. A conclusion Sam resisted and Stefan feared. "Whatever her message refers to," Lionel cautioned, "we've no proof it's here, on this planet."

"Is there another location of meaning to both Paul and Veya?"

"No. Nor is there a more likely choice than here, where Paul met with his mother. I agree we should proceed from that assumption but, if so?" Lionel gestured to the smooth walls of the Chow. "Veya left it here before the changes to the landscape. These new buildings."

"I can confirm there is nothing hidden within the farmhouse stairwell."

There wasn't, according to Duggs, a stairwell left. "Good to know," Lionel replied. "The family buildings sat locked and unused for fifty years. I've gone over the initial location scans." He'd have to tell Paul that to get them, he'd hinted to Duggs about new construction in future. "Other than some animal activity, there's no indication of entry before Paul and Esen arrived."

"This is why you need me," with triumph. "Veya Ragem was a female of brilliance and technical expertise, uninterested in dirt. As am I. You wish to know where I would hide the logbook, if unable to know when it would be retrieved."

"Exactly." It was as good a summation as any, and superior to admitting Lambo was the only other staff member who knew about Veya and her ship, and so the only help he had. Lionel beamed. "Thank you!"

The Carasian rose with ponderous care. "I shall contemplate."

"Any results should come only to me, in person." *So he'd have a chance to soften any further blows to Paul, let alone*—Lionel gazed up at those attentive gleaming eyestalks. Human concerns weren't going to translate. "This is a serious matter, Lambo."

"Humph. I'll tell you what's serious." A clawtip indicated the pile of dirty dishes threatening to topple from counter to floor. "That is serious. My Celi deserted me. You are the acting director. You will fix this while I contemplate your puzzle."

What was a—He was not going to ask. "I'll see what I can do," Lionel offered, backing out of the room before this very clever Carasian could demand more.

34: Starship Morning

I woke blissfully alone. Wherever Skalet was, I trusted she'd get herself off this ship. Admittedly, part of me enjoyed the image of my web-kin languishing in a Commonwealth prison as a Kraal spy, but the rest of me was sensibly aware Skalet wouldn't "languish" an instant longer than she chose and why borrow trouble.

Keep her word? That I didn't trust. On the thought, I lurched from the box. It overturned, spreading synth-grass in a new, more alluring orientation, *because who really wanted to be constrained in a box*—not that I noticed, too busy rushing around the small cabin in a feverish hunt.

The imploder sat where my breakfast should be, snug in its stealth bag.

I kept a hand under my loosening jaw, in that shocked moment realizing how very little I'd believed Skalet trusted me. I'd have felt guilty, except I realized something else at the same time.

I was now the one stuck with smuggling the weapon off the ship, onto an alien world, and into the Commonwealth Embassy. Skalet's sneaky bag better work.

Family.

Time to pack.

"I'll carry that for you, Fem Ki."

I snatched my carryall from the reach of the too-helpful

ship's steward and clutched it to my broad scaly chest, appalled to risk discovery so soon.

The Human's eyes widened, then she composed herself. "I meant no offense."

Paul frowned at me, so I curled a wan lip. "Snacks." I hugged the bulging bag closer.

The steward, assigned to clean up the last time my digestive system had malfunctioned, stepped clear at once.

My carryall did contain snacks; I'd helped myself to a few items from the guest galley after breakfast, because you never knew when starvation—or queasy stomachs—might strike. It also contained my precious lantern, causing me no little anxiety.

Paul put his hand on my arm as we followed the steward. "We won't be back." He tipped his head toward my room. "Sure you have everything?"

Translated, that was *is Skalet out of the way?* "Yes, I'm sure. This isn't my first time packing," I said loftily, then added for the steward. "Loved the box. Very thoughtful."

She glanced back and smiled. "Glad to be of service, Fem Ki."

Not the moment to mention the synth-grass spread to every corner of the room.

We didn't gather Evan up in our procession but went from this corridor to a lift. After a quick drop, the doors opened on the spacious circular hold that served the ship as a staging area for those coming or going out the main air lock. Expedient and direct; I'd the distinct feeling Captain Clendon had had enough of strangers in his ship.

"Hello." Evan was waiting for us with his liaison, the Human Trili Bersin; both smiled a pleasant, if reserved greeting. They were dressed more formally, making Paul's dark jacket an appropriate choice. *If a tad dated. We simply had to go shopping offworld.*

My Lishcyn-self was fussing. I put a stop to it by arranging the three fingers of my free hand as a frame to my formal wear, the beaded neck bag that should hold my lantern.

Instead, it held an Octarian Quandran Imploder, snug inside a Kraal-designed anti-scan sac. *If I thought complaining to Skalet would be anything but futile, and possibly demeaning, I'd put this at the top of my list—*

With a sigh, I turned my attention to the others here.

Evan noticed and made introductions. "This is Commander Kamaara, the *Mistral*'s Head of Security."

I'd noticed Humans in such posts tended to develop frown lines. Kamaara's might have been carved into her broad forehead. They didn't ease when she gave Paul and me a nod acknowledging our existence and her dislike of civilians in general.

No names were provided for the two security guards standing at attention on either side of our exit from the ship, understandable given they wore the light body armor Rudy referred to as "let's intimidate," their faces obscured by black sensoscreens.

I curled a friendly lip anyway, because I'd noticed Humans smothered in pointless armor appreciated it. *And one of the matched set was probably Skalet.*

Paul thought so, too, by the way he ignored the guards. He took his bag from the steward and thanked her. "We're ready when you are, Polit Gooseberry."

Our friend nodded. He had the appearance of a being heading into trouble, braced for it, but above all hopeful it could be avoided. *Exactly right,* I thought, proud of him. Though I could wish the hope in his eyes didn't increase when he looked my way.

I'd a plan to deal with his attention. The sort of plan Skalet detested and that worried Paul immensely. That didn't mean, I reminded myself, it wouldn't work.

Make it up as I go.

Inception

*B*ELIEVE . . .
   I must, though lost.
I must, though alone.
I must, though all that remains?
Is the cold.

35: Embassy Morning

THE Human Commonwealth, operating under the tried-and-true principle that while predictable was boring, you couldn't get lost in the halls, built its embassies on alien worlds by one plan. This one.

Also by plan? That each embassy's exterior blend with the neighborhood. On Urgia Prime, there was a patio out front with a refreshing mist for any Urgians who might wander by. On Skenkran worlds, perches. On aquatic worlds, delightful free-form eddies, and so forth. While I applauded the Human proclivity to inconvenience their own staff to please casual passersby, at times their embassies blended a little too well and their hosts had to put up extra signage.

The Commonwealth Embassy on Dokeci-Na had elected to blend via artwork, surrounding itself in pavement cluttered with renderings of globes. Globes were the current popular craze, and they'd installed big ones, small ones, all depicting Dokeci-Na in the planet's present continental configuration, each coated in a unique tactile expression of—

I squinted.

—I'd have to be Dokeci to fully appreciate the humor within those wrinkles and dots of color, but I caught enough to chuckle. *Did the Humans realize the Dokeci had supplied them with a collection of jokes?*

Probably. A Human attribute I admired was their ability not to take themselves too seriously.

I'd one, granted highly personal, complaint with their landscaper. "What kind of embassy doesn't have a garden?" I muttered, turning from the window.

"This one." Paul kept reading the jokes, grinning to himself.

"I need," I said very quietly, well aware of the tendency of Humans to put surveillance anywhere public, "plants. After being in space."

He knew what I meant. Plants were living mass I could assimilate, troubling no one but the gardener. *I tried to prune when possible.* "There'll be plants in the Riota-si Valley. I'm sure you'll enjoy those."

I'd seen the report, too. Scattered scrub brush, pricklies, pockets of lichen. None of it concentrated in useful amounts in any spot discreet or safe. *Here I'd felt the foolhardy optimist, to expect a proper embassy patch of rose-equivalents.* "I miss the Library's Garden," I countered firmly. "It's lush. Abundant," I stressed.

"I've ordered salad," Paul informed me. "Fresh picked greens and those Dokeci berries you like."

Living mass. I regarded him dourly. "I trust you ordered a great deal of salad." The cycle into a Mareepavlovax wasn't the problem; it was resuming this more substantial form. Esolesy Ki the Lishcyn must reappear.

For one thing, I'd a ship home to catch and refused to travel in Paul's luggage as a Quebit. *Again.*

"You can have mine, too."

In this together, he meant, a comfort in every way but one. "Salad will be just the thing," I agreed, if reluctantly, only then allowing myself to look out the window for something else.

Where was Skalet?

I should have wondered *what.*

◆

The Dokeci expert on the Mareepavlovax—invited by me—was already in the embassy meeting room when Paul and I were invited to enter and join the proceedings.

Having invited no one, there being no Dokeci experts, I introduced "mine" to the only person who hadn't met her yet. *Maybe my stupefaction would translate as calm and collected.* "Director Paul Ragem, this is the esteemed Siokaletay-ki."

And my missing web-kin. I was gratified by the slight narrowing of his keen eyes as he caught on, though if Paul thought I could explain how she'd done it? Suffice to say "capable" described Skalet, and I hadn't a clue.

Predictably, as a Dokeci Siokaletay-ki was resplendently fit, the five arms springing from her thick neck taut with muscle and wide hips still fully fleshed and strong. Her trio of large eyes sparkled with health above her flexible beak. She required a grav-assist, worn beneath the usual cloak open to display her pulchritude. That enormous pendulous abdomen of middle age was unavoidable, dragging along the ground between your legs if you could budge it at all, and what were the young for if not to carry their elders?

Despite the impediment, this Skalet moved with dignified grace, poling herself like an Oieta. I wondered, to myself, how many weapons she'd managed to sneak into the embassy.

While I had an Octarian Quandran Imploder bouncing on my chest.

The embassy staff had accorded us full diplomatic privilege—meaning no physical searches, though unobtrusive tech would have scanned us from head to toenail. I'd had a small struggle with an overly helpful clerk, who'd wanted to store my carryall, likely because I'd narrowly missed a floor vase with it. Paul, the innocent, had stepped in to say we'd be going directly to our accommodations in the shipcity once done, so we'd need to keep our belongings.

"I was delighted to receive your invitation, Esolesy Ki." Her round head mottled pink to show that delight and even in this form, her voice had a rare, pleasant timbre that inspired trust.

Not likely.

A flurry of hasty introductions followed, the business at hand being urgent, and we took our seats. Siokaletay-ki lowered to the cushion provided for her, using her pulchritude as a chair; the sole advantage to her age in my opinion. As Riosolesy-ki, Lesy had enjoyed bouncing on hers, albeit in lowered gravity. Not that she'd bounce in front of our other kin, but with me she'd rock back and forth, mouthparts clicking in a blur of laughter.

Evan Gooseberry took a seat to the left of the Human ambassador, Cichally Hansen. She'd the darker skin, with large brown eyes that seemed to watch us all at once. Her bald head was painted, permanently or otherwise, in a striking pattern of pink-and-yellow whorls. The effect was intricate and pleasing—and a compliment to the Dokeci, who would find this pattern attractive, if politely reserved.

When on Dokeci-Na...

Skalet, as a Dokeci, could split her attention. In a meeting such as this, with a designated Personage—the ambassador—her leftmost eye would remain on that individual, watching for visual cues, leaving the right and upper free to roam where they would. Naturally, one stared at me.

The other locked on Evan when he stood to speak. "I will be conducting this meeting at the behest of Senior Polit M'Lean."

An older Human who appeared, in my opinion, a little too at ease. If they planned for Evan to take the blame if I failed?

Add more to the list of why I mustn't, I told myself with an inner sigh.

"Our thanks, Esolesy Ki, for bringing the expertise of Siokaletay-ki to our attention." He faced her directly, his normally amiable expression stern. "That said, why have you come to Humans, and why wait till now, if you're an expert on the Elves?" Annoyed, was our Evan. It looked good on him.

"I am no such thing." She bristled, aquamarine highlights chasing away the pink, then amber notes appeared, signaling pride. "I am the foremost expert on the Mareepavlovax. The Harbingers of legend." Her arms stiffened. "Esolesy knew to contact me using the correct classification."

Technically, Skalet had invited herself at every step, but right now I wasn't inclined to argue. If she was willing to help—*if help was her plan.* If I wouldn't let her use the imploder on the shrine, here was an even better opportunity for mayhem and destruction on a massive scale. To remove the threat posed by the Harvester.

The Dokeci would, in all likelihood, thank her for it.

I resisted the urge to touch my beaded bag.

Evan appeared satisfied by the explanation. That, or he'd used up what time he had to establish the credentials of this new arrival. "We've been granted permission to add the three of you to the Fleullen-ni in effect concerning the Elves in the Riota-si Valley. Please state for the record you are aware how this agreement binds you and accept its terms." When we'd done so, he went on. "On my authority, Burtles-Mautil Intersystem Holdings and its personnel have been reinstated. Hom Hymna Burtles has provided a reasonable contract and terms."

The ambassador frowned. "For the Dokeci. If they agree to relocation. I assume you've consulted with Ekwueme-ki?"

Evan, clearly of Rudy's *leap ahead* mind-set, didn't blink. "We will consult later today, Ambassador Hansen. In the interim, I've authorized the release of embassy funds so Hom Burtles can transport equipment and supplies to the valley with all urgency."

Senior Polit M'Lean winced, pursing his lips as though holding in the urge to take over and stop this madness.

Typical elder. *You put Evan on the spot,* I thought without sympathy. *Don't be surprised when he does something about it.*

"Within a Fleullen-ni, all parties must act to expedite a resolution." Siokaletay-ki's eye on me shifted to confront the Human ambassador. "I am gratified by such bold partners. Splendid!" She actually let the rings around her eyes glow green with excitement.

Paul, possibly feeling the dynamic of the meeting shifting Skalet-ward—*never a good thing*—coughed in that way Humans did to attract attention. "Truth between all parties is expected as well. I read your reports and there's something I don't understand. How the Dokeci came to find and rescue the very last of the Mareepavlovax—and just in time."

I blinked at him, as did Evan, and even Siokaletay-ki

lost some of her green and pink, fading to a nonplussed beige.

When no one answered, Evan spoke up, his troubled gaze fixed on his senior. "We can't assume altruism in our sense of the word. If the Dokeci have another motivation, Polit, any history at all you haven't told me, I must know before I face them. Or the chance of a resolution we can live with tomorrow diminishes."

Senior Polit M'Lean leaned on the table, fingertips together. "This goes no further than this room," he warned, his tone somber.

I couldn't help a purely selfish inner rumble. *What now?*

Perception

NONE of this should be happening.

The realization kept Evan Gooseberry cool and calm when by rights he'd be ready to faint. Him, in charge of a meeting with the ambassador present; Paul and Esolesy Ki present, too, looking to him for answers; a Dokeci expert on the Mareepavlovax, a stranger who gave him the oddest feeling of familiarity.

Concern for her arms or spots hardly ranked on that scale.

"I can't agree, Polit," Evan heard himself say in a voice more like Great Gran's than his own. The one she'd use when approached by a fake Gooseberry, thinking to slip into the Lore. "Their motivation could be essential to my negotiations. I must be free to speak."

M'Lean glanced at the ambassador, then back to him. "Very well, Polit. I leave it to your discretion. But please, be discreet. The Dokeci aren't proud of this."

What had they done? Evan looked at Paul, seeing his expression grow dark. He knew—or suspected.

"The Dokeci are responsible," his senior confirmed grimly. "The architect of the proposed S'Remmer Prime Station asked for the planetary ring to be refreshed—something about more enticing views for clients. The plan was to destroy three of the smaller rocky moons and add their material to the ring. When the last of those didn't break apart as planned, they landed to plant explosives."

M'Lean's face was like stone. "Suffice to say the Dokeci discovered they'd almost obliterated a civilization. If there was altruism at work, it was that they didn't destroy the moon and the Elves to cover their crime."

"They couldn't," Evan murmured. His hand pressed over the bust of Teganersha-ki in his pocket. "A mistake isn't immoral. To knowingly kill the innocent would have been."

Siokaletay-ki's skin flushed with amber mottles. *Pride.* "You are correct, Polit Gooseberry. However, it is the definition of 'innocent' that will be at issue once we provide the facts about these Harbingers. Expect stiff arms and calls for dire action."

Fear, in other words. "Then we'll provide more than facts." He could almost *feel* Paul's tension. He did hear Esolesy's anxious rumble and finished quickly, "We'll provide both with options." Evan turned to Ambassador Hansen, dipping his head in acknowledgment. Meetings were the lifeblood of the embassy.

They were, he feared, *running out of time for more.* "With your permission, I'd like to adjourn, Ambassador, and proceed to the valley once Esolesy Ki has completed her—" *whatever she planned,* "—examination of the specimens in the lab. We," his wave included Paul and the Dokeci, "will finalize what remains on the way."

A gamble? *Not really,* Evan thought as he waited for her answer. Hansen was a career diplomat; she'd worked with Prumbins before the Dokeci. Before either, the Panacians of D'Dsel and her success with such disparate species—not to mention the Humans surrounding her— told him she knew when to follow the manual and, more importantly, when to let instinct take over.

Her hand lifted, made a shooing gesture. *Go.*

Senior Polit M'Lean stood. "Full and frequent reports, Gooseberry," he ordered. "And," with the hint of a smile, "trust yourself. We do."

As if this wasn't about pinning blame for a risky no-win situation on an underling, but as if he, Evan Gooseberry, was the right diplomat for the job.

If they believed that, Evan thought numbly, *one day, he might.*

36: Morgue Morning

IT was going to hurt.

"Excuse me?" The embassy security guard pulled off her helmet, tucking it under one arm. She'd short brown hair and unexpectedly twinkly eyes. "I didn't catch all that, Fem Ki."

"Sorry. Talking to myself," I explained, glad I hadn't muttered worse.

"Just like our Evan. I'm Lisam Horner, by the way." She looked almost shy. "Thanks for standing by him. Trili spread the word."

An embassy being a community like any other—and Evan being what he was—I'd have been surprised otherwise. I nodded gravely. "We'll do our best."

"This way, please."

As I followed, I realized it wasn't the *going to hurt* that bothered me. The real me. My web-self, Esen-alit-Quar.

It was the *biting* involved.

Technically, if I did obtain my very own Vlovax, alive and in biting condition, it wouldn't bite me, it would strike.

An irrelevant distinction. There'd be a fang. There'd be my flesh. One would enter the other with force and malice and pain, making the entire process *biting.*

I clutched my bulging carryall tighter to my chest.

"Would you like me to carry that for you, Fem Ki?"

Where was a rude Hurn when you wanted one? *Save*

me from the courtesy of Humans. Aloud, "Thank you, but no. I'm fine. Snacks," I added mournfully.

She'd a nice smile. "You may not want those in here." Lisam used her ident to unlock what looked like the door to food storage.

Which was what the insulated room behind the door had been, until the embassy needed a morgue and xeno-pathologist's lab onsite. Given Human squeamishness, they'd probably repurpose yet another room for that, rather than return their food—mostly dead—into a space recently housing the dead—and mostly dead. All mass, but I'd yet to convince Paul.

The temporary morgue was brightly lit, with ample countertops and cupboards. Sterile, efficient, and empty.

"Hey, Sammy!" Lisam called.

A tall cupboard opened, and a tousled red head appeared. "Here," the person announced, the rest of—undecided, I chose her—emerging from what wasn't a cupboard at all, fog flowing out over the tiled floor.

A stasis unit. Or walk-in freezer. Not every embassy dared rely on tech that needed local maintenance.

Sammy was tall, slender, and a Mod. My first, in fact, though Ersh had made sure I knew of this personalized evolution. And its risk to us. We couldn't be this type of Human.

Few Humans could either; my elders were prone to exaggeration.

"I'm Esolesy Ki," I said, stepping forward with my three-fingered hand out in the Human gesture.

Costing me a secure grip on my bag, but the security guard swooped in to catch it before it fell to the floor. "I'll hold it."

Oh, dear.

"Sammy Litten." The hand that gripped mine was longer than Human extremes, with paired opposing thumbs. She'd opted for a lightly furred skin except for her face. Or his. The reason an easy pronoun eluded me was neither were completely right. Mods chose whatever combination of attributes suited their inner nature.

"Your preference?" I asked politely, giving up the struggle.

Bright red lips stretched over reassuringly average Human teeth. *Biting on the brain.* "I'm more fem at the moment," with the comfort of someone who'd made their own skin.

Gender was fluid in the species, Ansky'd taught me; more spectrum than either/or and less affected by age than situation and experience. Despite being prepubescent myself, my Human-self was female. Web-beings were. I'd debated the topic with Ersh—*actually, she'd lectured after a too-smart remark I'd made, chiming with irritation*—but the gist? We Web-beings were female not only because we reproduced on our own by fission, ergo female by default, but because when we cycled into another form, we were the reproductive gender of that species. As Ansky herself discovered in multiple forms, there could be consequences.

My being one, Ersh had finished, assigning me to sweep her greenhouse and ponder.

Fascinating as Sammy was to me as a study in variety, Mods—be they Human or Hurn—weren't a form any of us could assume. We assembled a genetic profile across a species, assimilated as much sample material as we could, then cycled. Only then did we discover what we were, as that form. From then on, form-memory was absolute.

Bringing me to why we were here. "Thank you. Were you told what I need?"

She nodded, the lobes of her ears swinging gently against her graceful, elongated neck. I thought I glimpsed gills and would have asked, but Sammy turned and led the way. "Evan sent word. You want to view the specimens alone."

Her wary tone suggested Evan had employed what Rudy called the *Bizarre Secret Alien Ways* cover story. While uncomplimentary to those of us who worked diligently to uncover what we didn't understand about one another, there were, it had to be said, enough bizarre secret non-Human ways to fill a substantial portion of the Library.

Let alone the Human ones.

I curled a friendly lip at the security guard and reclaimed my bag, my lantern and snacks in hand.

The opening of the cupboardlike door proved a tight fit. *Or I was paying for those calm-the-nerves treats.*

Before I had to ask for a push—an embarrassment sure to be added to the *bizarre-not-secret alien ways* file—I popped through with an effort that left me wheezing. And—I checked—a few scale gouges in the doorframe, an embassy built of softer materials than, say, a starship.

I couldn't apologize for everything. "Where are they?" I asked, looking around. Four sterile white walls, another door, hooks, shelves—definitely food storage in a previous life. Cool, not the cold I'd braced for; this would have been the chiller. Then where were the salads Paul promised?

Worry later, I told myself.

Sammy stood possessively in front of yet another counter, this one covered in neatly labeled oblong cases. "The Elves' biochemistry is—it's adaptive. Unlike anything I've seen and that's outside the unusual blend of senescent and youthful features. Fem Ki, this species could take years to fully comprehend. Will take years."

I hated to disrupt true passion, but years we didn't have. "Senior Polit Gooseberry is waiting."

"Yes, yes. I've prepared the species' genetic profile for you." She held out a datadisk, then hesitated. "I'd be happy to assist you with interpreting it."

Useless and pointless and—what I needed was to be alone.

"No, thank you." Instead of taking the disk, I leaned to look around her hungrily. "Those are the samples?"

"My source material, yes." She didn't budge. "I don't see why—"

And I couldn't possibly explain. "You have your orders," I said, sorry to take that approach. I wasn't sorry to have to destroy her source material, not if it saved the still-living Mareepavlovax, but scientists were touchy about such things. Especially a scientist qualified to investigate a new species, surrounded by hard-to-obtain precious samples.

Best, I told myself, *be gone before this one found out.* "Please show me where.to find the Elf and the rasnir-as, then leave."

The oval pupils of her eyes widened in dismay, overwhelming her purple irises. Like Chase, an augmentation to a purpose, in this case biological. "But—"

"My orders are to ensure you do as Fem Ki asks," the security guard said from the doorway, her voice no longer that of a friend. "Are we going to have a problem, Sammy?"

I winced inwardly, but there was no choice.

A glower from those purple eyes. "This way."

The inner door led, at last, into a large freezer. My scales swelled in response, keeping me warm if ridiculously stiff. There remained food packages on the shelves; I was sympathetic, familiar with the issues around finding a spot for a freezer of any size, let alone getting it installed before your food thawed. *Quaint farmhouses came with attitude.*

A sheet covered the body, supine on a table.

Sammy hadn't accorded the Vlovax the same respect. A series of glistening dissected corpses—shelled, fanged, clawed—floated in midair, lit from two sides. Another lay in its tray beneath, awaiting its turn with the knife. The delightful inner goo of life—or death—didn't bother me. For some reason, this display did, however vital it was to the Humans' understanding.

I'd my own approach. *Admittedly no less messy.* "Where's the live one?"

The scientist hesitated, telling me she'd clung to hope I'd not want her prize. As a living Vlovax was mine, if I believed my web-kin, I tilted toward the security guard.

Without a word, Sammy bent to retrieve a cloth bag with handles from under the table.

I blinked. "You've got it in there?"

"It's a cryosac, Fem Ki." She put the bag on the counter beside the tray and spread the handles to show me the palm-sized control panel.

With my scales firmly interconnected, bending was out of the question. *If Paul were here, I could lean on him.* Not a possibility, given Sammy's expression suggested she'd prefer to dissect a Lishcyn next.

Flashing a conciliatory tusk, I braced myself with a hand on the table, and tipped awkwardly to bring one eye to bear on the panel. "How does it work?"

"The display shows the specimen is in good condition. Not full torpor, but in a state in which—"

I didn't need Vlovax Sorbet. "Show me how to wake it."

"Fem Ki?" Lisam, with alarm. "Those things are dangerous."

"Oh, I won't wake it here," I assured the guard.

"You're taking it?" Sammy's reach for the bag was too slow.

Not the best plan, I realized, finding myself with a bag of deadly Vlovax in one hand and a carryall containing my precious lantern in the other. At least the deadly weapon was safe around my neck.

Exhibiting a fine grasp of the moment, Lisam heaved a dramatic, weapon-rattling sigh. "This is ridiculous, the pair of you. You know what Evan said, Sammy. Show our guest how to work the bag. There're more of the things out there anyway."

Ah, I told myself cleverly, *but this one I'd caught!* Skalet would be amazed. Or less critical. There could be a modicum of approval, I decided, triumphantly holding my Vlovax.

If only I'd known . . .

Long fingers, the nails modified to black, tool-like tips, pulled the cryosac from my hand, replacing it on the table. "The cryo system is active as long as the top is closed. To revive the specimen, you open it. To open it," this with a purple glare of doom I blithely ignored, "you tap twice here, then once there. In a secure location."

I curled my lips, showing tusks in a cheerful smile. "Thank you."

"Fem Ki—" Whatever the scientist wanted to say, she decided against it. She went out the door, the security guard following behind at my nod.

I waited until I heard the outer door close before I moved.

First things first. I pulled the sheet from the corpse. As I'd hoped, the Mareepavlovax—*Mareepa, being without Vlovax*—was naked. And . . . if I were a researcher frantically searching for cause of death and thus uninterested in clothing I'd put such things . . . *there*. I went to the open bin and aimed an eye downward, almost falling in the process.

Out of the freezer would be an improvement.

Tissues, bits of moist-looking nasty, and there, balled in one corner, a familiar-looking fabric. I retrieved it, glad the streaks were of the dirt variety, and gave it a shake. My Lishcyn-self's fashion sense might be offended, but I was relieved to find the woven strips intact. What was sized for an adult should work for me in this form.

Regretful but resolute, I discarded my snacks and ointment jars, pushing them deep in the bin, under the nasty bits. Into my bag of belongings went the fabric, along with an unreported anklet of what might be smooth ceramic, and matching fist-sized bead on a rope I discovered wrapped inside. I fingered the bead for a moment, having no idea how it might be worn.

Later.

My first stomach lacked digestive enzymes, making it an excellent storage pouch for those moments when my other four stomachs were full. Assuming I could refrain from erupting, but as I'd told Paul, *you could only plan for so many disasters at once*. He'd laughed.

He wouldn't laugh now.

I went to the corpse.

Tracks of shiny glue marked where Sammy had closed exploratory incisions. Otherwise, thanks to the freezer, the Mareepa was much as he'd been in life. *If a tad wrinkly and frozen*. The skin was dark brown, except for the pale stripes that encircled the neck and torso, extending down the upper arms and thighs. They became vivid where they passed around the sides to the back, but I'd no interest or time to roll the body over to see the result. His face wasn't peaceful, lips drawn back in a rictus, exposing thick, grinding teeth, and I was glad not to see the hole where his Vlovax had been attached.

I ran a fingertip lightly over the skin of the abdomen. Hairs there were, short and plentiful; I harvested a few using a clean blade beside the dissection tray, then popped them in my mouth and swallowed, saving them in my first stomach.

That done, I replaced the sheet and blade, then tucked the cryosac into my carryall. *Because who didn't pack a venomous creature with their clothes.*

I left the freezer for the relative warmth of the chill room, relieved to close the door. Without giving my scales time to warm and shrink, I headed for Sammy's specimens.

I emptied each little case into my mouth, swallowing the contents, delighted to find more here than the number of corpses presented to the Dokeci. Not just hair. I applauded the techs, of whichever species, who'd diligently preserved whatever Mareepavlovax products they'd encountered on the Harvester. *There was Web thinking for you.*

I considered closing the cases again, but it would only delay Sammy's outrage at the theft by milliseconds. The better plan?

Leave the scene of my crime, quickly.

So I did, gouging the doorframe again.

Perception

LIONEL folded his clothes and put them on the box. Henri and Ally had insisted on ordering him more, to be delivered within the next day—or three, this being the start of lambing season—because their acting director must look his best.

Their matter-of-fact care of him was—it was more than reassuring. Warm inside, Lionel smiled as he stretched out on the cot. *Gods, he was tired.* That good tired, of a day's work done and done well. There'd been some humor, too, though how even a Queeb could mistake an ardent, if confused, Heezle's proposition—*the species had no observable boundaries when it came to sex*—for an offer to have a scholarly debate on the origins of the Human head shake for "no"?

He chuckled into his pillow.

"Lionel."

At the rich voice—*her* voice, he bolted upright, pillow flying, staring into the dark. "Skalet?" *Who else could it be.* "I'm here."

"I know," with underlying impatience. "Have you and Lambo made progress?"

She'd overheard—or had a report. Lionel sank back with relief. "Not yet." He'd had second thoughts, doubts, all too late to stop the Carasian who was either not searching for whatever Veya had left Paul or doing so with a caution even a Kraal should appreciate. "You approve of our search, then."

"I expect such valuable initiative from you."

"I am gratified." Lionel put a hand to his cheek, *that cheek*, and felt the heat of a blush.

"Matters on Dokeci-Na approach the critical point. As expected, the Youngest has been headstrong."

"She mustn't fail," he said, now concerned. He'd been right—Skalet had gone on the *Mistral*, somehow. "I'm glad you're there. You'll help Esen save the Mareepavlovax. I'm sure of it."

In the pause that followed, Lionel fussed to himself. He'd been too bold. Pushed his opinion into their business. Offended—

"This result is important to you, Lionel." Softly. Not a question. A factor, considered.

"Of course! But so is your—" about to say *safety*, he rephrased, "—privacy."

"We remain secure. I will do what I can—" Which relieved him. Followed by, "—but the Youngest must learn."

Which did not. Lionel pulled the blanket to his chin. "What must she learn? May I ask that?"

"You, may. She's grown complacent, here. Careless." Her voice, velvet made sound, sharpened. "Esen-alit-Quar must learn the true cost of ignorance."

Silence, then, as if even Skalet had nothing more to say.

Lionel closed his eyes, then opened them, no longer tired.

But there was nothing he dared do but wait.

37: Valley Afternoon

Once the embassy's aircar lifted through raindrops and clouds into clear sky, Siokaletay-ki left her assigned spot, grabbing seat backs with her several arms to launch herself toward Evan Gooseberry.

Who, I was pleased to see, didn't immediately launch himself toward his now-alert security team, though one hand locked white-knuckled on his seat arm as if the notion had occurred to him.

Taking advantage of the distraction, Paul leaned close. "No salads."

I tightened my own grip, this around my beaded bag. Thus far ignored. *Or we wouldn't be on this trip.* "Plan B?" with a hopeful ear wag.

By the sober look in his eyes, there wasn't one. Not a Human one, anyway. I stared at the back of Siokaletay-ki's head, pleasantly mottled in pink. She'd inserted herself. Maybe that meant she'd come to help.

Or not. I focused on the deceptive mountaintops billowing white to every side.

"We might not even need—" Paul tugged gently at the red-gold silk covering my knees.

"You know we will." And while I didn't want to be critical, especially of my first best friend—*who, to be fair, didn't criticize my mistakes*—I wasn't the one who'd told Evan I'd produce a Mareepavlovax for his meeting.

If there'd been leaves handy, I'd have stuck some

between my scales and moped. *Paper worked.* "Do you think Evan has a spare notebook?"

A perceptive glance. "We aren't there yet, Es." He bumped his shoulder against me. "And you aren't alone."

"That's the problem," I muttered under my breath, but rallied to flash a tusk at him.

My web-kin returned during this exchange, her eye rings tinged with color. *Someone was pleased with herself.* "The Dokeci have agreed to move our meeting to an entrance into the Harvester."

I'd have been pleased, too, but a helpful Skalet made me nervous.

"That wasn't the arrangement." Paul kept his voice down; that didn't take away its sting.

Her skin grew lumpy with displeasure. All three eyes riveted on the Human. "It is now. They'll take precautions against the Vlovax, naturally. A solid floor should—"

"No." His eyes narrowed. "Change it."

Lumpy skin with, yes, those were black spotted wrinkles rising to the surface. Before Skalet—or Paul—grew angrier, a prospect guaranteed to risk my sample-enriched first stomach, I interposed, "Our guest will appreciate the convenience." I then curled my lip at them in a frantic attempt to convey we weren't alone. "Isn't that right, Evan?"

"Siokaletay-ki made that point, Fem Ki." Our diplomat leaned against the bench in front of us, swaying with the aircar. He appeared resolute, if uneasy. "I wanted to be sure you agreed."

I didn't look at Paul, knowing what I'd see on his face. *Yes, it was risky, but we hadn't brought salads, had we?* "I do."

And if after our meeting I happened to saunter inside the Harvester with other Mareepavlovax, say into a dark corner where there could be mass to spare?

I was not going home as a Quebit.

Evan led the way, his shoulders tense. I could see why. The Dokeci, with Human help, had made significant changes since his first visit. There was now a thick wall, head-high, surrounding the outstretched arms and lofty towers of the Mareepavlovax Harvester and extending up one side of the valley. The base of the wall disappeared into the ground, that ground stained yellow with sealant for a considerable distance on either side. Along the top, at regular intervals, were messy clumps of pipes and wires. At a guess, sensors.

Or weapons.

The tent with awnings Evan had described had been replaced by ranks of waiting aircars, each with a pilot waiting nearby. Evacuation protocol.

The Dokeci weren't afraid; they were terrified.

On a happier note, I spotted heavy equipment being unpacked by Humans. Our best option, should we be able to stave off the alternative.

That was on display, too. Behind the portion of wall that looped up from the valley was a line of menacing objects which were, indisputably, weapons. Aimed at the Harvester. Aimed everywhere. The Dokeci didn't need what hung from my neck. The Riota-si Valley was no longer a resettlement; it was a death trap.

The Mareepavlovax? No one knew if they'd noticed, or if they cared. By all reports they'd remained quiescent inside their ancient ship.

For the Harvester was—or had been—a starship. I'd asked Skalet for details; she'd professed an unusual disdain for their technology. Then again, if you built a ship to function as a complete-unto-itself city, only to wrap it in rock and hibernate inside for however long it took to reach a world worth visiting? *Not a lifestyle for most.*

How old was this one? I wondered suddenly. How long could such a ship, a Harvester, continue? Those able to answer these and so many questions were inside, waiting.

If only I knew how to ask. I refused to worry about my lack of knowledge, firm in my belief that what mattered was the Dokeci understand one of the Mareepavlovax. After all, if this went well, I'd meet them myself in their new home.

The Devil Darts, on the other hand, had been increasingly active. Blots of red and black dotted the yellow, marking where they'd broken through and been dispatched. Armed Dokeci and Human guards, in envirosuits, patrolled in pairs—an interspecies' harmony I'd appreciate if it were for any other reason than to combine senses and tech against a little scavenger.

One with a fang and venom. I shuddered inwardly. *Biting.*

Ekwueme-ki, the leader of the project and, by virtue of not having run fast enough, newly appointed leader of the Dokeci effort to contain their fanged problem, met us before the entrance to the Harvester selected for our meeting. It was the only unsealed entrance; I didn't know if the Mareepavlovax had opened it, or the Dokeci breached it, but I suspected the latter.

Their leader stood before a group of ten, numbers being a comfort. Ekwueme-ki was an older Dokeci, visibly worn by stress and responsibility; little wonder she responded to Siokaletay-ki's presence with a flattering display of pink mottles. After all, a new face meant the blame could be shared that much further.

And meant the possibility of new, better ideas, I reminded myself sternly. The poor Dokeci didn't want to blow the Harvester and occupants to component atoms any more than we did.

As befitted his temporary promotion, Evan stood slightly to the side as the other Human in our little group, Petham Erilton, made the introductions on behalf of the embassy. Petham, a bright-eyed, scholarly person, was the embassy's senior administrator, here to put the necessary official stamps or whatever on any agreements involving Humans.

That wasn't all he was, I thought, seeing the attention Paul paid him, and Skalet's wary second eye.

When my turn came, I gave a subdued bow. "I will strive to be of assistance, Project Leader."

Ekwueme-ki's eyes refused to aim at me.

Too young, was I? I flashed a tusk. "The beings you mistakenly call Elves are, in fact, the Mareepavlovax." We'd decided not to mention their wearing dead Vlovax as ornamentation. As Ersh would say, *not the appropriate time.* "The Harbingers," I added helpfully.

The skin of every Dokeci in sight, except for Siokaletay-ki, flickered with agitated pseudolightning, splots of violet rising. In the back row, I saw forward arms stiffen to fend off danger—hardly the optimal response in a crowd where your superiors were in front. Ekwueme-ki had to grab her neighbors to stop from being toppled over.

Oh, dear.

Siokaletay-ki rose on her anti-grav unit, magnificently smooth, with swirls of rose. "Attend me." She went on to give an impassioned speech in Dokeci the rest of us could only grasp in broad strokes, lacking the tubal pumps.

She basically told them their troubles were over, the Fleullen-ni adeptly crafted by their leader held all concerned, and to disregard my disreputable youth for somehow I'd found a solution, improbable as it seemed.

I glared at the eye turned my way.

One of Ekwueme-ki's eyes found me, too. "We will be grateful." Grudgingly, and with an *if it works* implied, but I wouldn't get more from a Dokeci with this much flabby abdomen.

"Then let's proceed," Evan announced. He'd a little twitch by his left eye but was otherwise composed. Impressive, given he faced so many Dokeci, though I'd a suspicion the twitch was more his version of *if it works*.

Metal sheets had been welded together to make a Vlovax-impervious floor. Soft little carpets protected the tender portions of dignitaries and the Dokeci had provided folding stools for the Humans.

I stood, none of those close to supporting my weight.

The embassy's security guards went to join—

The DARK!! Averting my gaze, I found myself locked in place, scales swollen in response.

Paul moved into my line of sight, tapping his nose with a finger. *Watch me,* that was—a lifeline—so I stared at his nose as he took a step to the side. A second. At the third, the dark loomed behind him, but I was safe, as long as I stared at his nose.

The tricks we played on this me, I thought with a sigh, wishing to be braver.

My problem was where the floor ended: the entrance to the Harvester. The plug had been removed, leaving the ropelike metal frame. Guards, Dokeci and now the embassy's, stood watch to either side. Though the sky was overcast—the storm approached the range—all was bright.

Except *inside* the Harvester. I focused beyond Paul for a horrified instant, seeing nothing but a BLACK *ABYSS!*

"There's no time for your fussing," my web-kin whispered, a sinuous arm indicating the beaded bag that should contain my lantern.

And, because of her, didn't.

I'd been too disturbed to think clearly, but now everything snapped into focus. I didn't dare open my carryall, with its cryosac and clothes from a corpse, to find my lantern. "Does anyone have a—"

"Here." Evan handed me a Human portable light.

"Thank you." I wrapped my fingers around it. Paul smiled encouragingly, but his smile didn't reach his eyes. He was worried, deeply so. None of us had known the interior of the Mareepavlovax Harvester was unlit.

Other than Skalet. Who hovered nearby, the epitome of helpful concern.

She was up to something. I knew it and so did Paul.

So was I, as it happened. Evan and the rest expected a Mareepavlovax to walk out of the Harvester to join our gathering and discuss how to save the day.

They'd get me.

Meaning I had to get my frantic Lishcyn-self, light, and carryall of ill-gotten Mareepa goods and Vlovax inside the Harvester.

IN THE DARK! My scales were swelling and that was nothing compared to the uproar brewing in my fourth and fifth stomachs—

I heard Paul's voice and snapped out of it.

"—We will bring forth our guest."

We?

Before I could open my mouth to object, Siokaletay-ki had me in her very strong arms. With a boost from her grav unit—*cheating!*—she shoved me into the abyss.

Perception

"YOU can't go in there, Polit," Lynelle told Evan. The security guard put her gloved hand on his arm.

But—he stopped, staring into the darkness. Warmer air came from it, like an exhalation. Moist, fetid. Not a sound, not a glimmer of lantern light. After their first few steps, Paul and Esolesy had vanished.

"There's a sharp turn, just inside." Siokaletay-ki stood beside him. "They won't be long."

But it was already too long.

38: Harvester Afternoon

I shone the beam over corpses, neat in their rows. "We're too late," I heard myself say.

"Here!"

My beam found Paul, kneeling beside a Mareepavlovax. This one lived, if barely, her hand rising to block my light. I lowered it at once, reducing the intensity despite the gibbering of instinct, then played it around us.

They were—stacked. As far as my light reached in what appeared a wide corridor, there were bodies, some still, others shifting in reaction but none well, none active or fully conscious. *They hadn't come out again*, I thought with a cold inner fury, *because they couldn't*.

"Esen—" Paul, a plea.

"We'll fix this," I promised him grimly, setting down my carryall.

"Wait. What if what's hurting them hurts you in this form?"

"Then we'll know."

He made no further objection, trusting I knew my own capabilities, well aware I'd take the risks I must. That didn't mean he liked it.

Nor did I. I pulled out the fabric strips. All those in sight wore the same. The bead and anklet came next. Near me was a corpse, bead in his left hand with the rope wrapped around the wrist. Another bore an anklet on the right leg. They were clearly personal, so I put those back in my carryall, with my beaded bag and what it contained—*appropriate timing*—and brought out the cryosac. I handed it to him.

"What's this?"

"A Vlovax. A living one."

My friend looked confused, then suspicious—a pleasantly normal sequence. "What haven't you told me, Old Blob?"

"They do it." I pointed to a half-sitting Mareepavlovax. The segmented body of a Vlovax hung behind her back. "It's like wearing a hoobit." With a lack of conviction even I could hear in my voice, but we were in the dark, and I was Lishcyn.

"The hells it is," he said with a growl and started to toss the sac away.

"No, Paul. I have to do this. Here." I showed him the controls. "And be careful," I warned. "It's me the Vlovax has to bite."

His eyebrows lifted. I conceded the point with a shrug.

I stripped off my caftan, setting aside Evan's light with an effort.

Definitely time to be something braver. To return to this form? I loathed having to find an almost dead Mareepavlovax but, as Skalet would say, *mass was mass.*

"Ready?"

In no sense. "You'll know when."

I erupted the contents of my first stomach into a tidy if slimed pile, then loosened my hold on this form and cycled into web-mass.

I lost sight, sound, and touch, replaced by my fuller, deeper senses, the universe around me improved immensely . . . then became . . . confusing . . .

I could sing with the pulse of gravity from Dokeci-Na and her moons . . . feel coursing waves of magnetism . . . but sense no power within the Harvester.

I could taste the molecules in the air flowing over me . . . *Paul's sweat, the richness of decay* . . . and knew.

The dying and dead were everywhere.

Assimilate . . . I took in the samples, *learned them* . . . and cycled.

. . . becoming Mareepa . . .

And *SCREAMED* . . .

Inception

*B*ELIEF *restores.*
 I am free!
 Here—here is up, the up of all our dreams, the culmination of hope. The up of soft and tender and warm.
 I Rise.
 I plunge my tooth into what Awaits and give my Offering gladly.
 Then, at last, I can say:
 <Hello.>

39: Harvester Afternoon

<HELLO.>

I stopped screaming. Stopped—worrying. For filling me, restoring me as warmth after a chill, as drink after thirst, as food after famine, and yes, as love after loneliness—was *Presence*.

"Who are you?" I asked, but I knew, didn't I. It wasn't pain throbbing my shoulder, but pleasure. Completeness. *The Vlovax*.

"Esen! Es!"

My poor friend. Screaming and a bloody bite? I formed a Human-shaped smile with an effort that told me these lips didn't make that gesture, offering my new hand. I felt his grip it. Felt the distracting *difference* in our shapes.

"Give us a moment, Paul." I closed my new eyes, needing to adjust inside first.

"'Us?'" He fell silent; he didn't let go.

<We have all our lives.> With such sincere gladness I felt my own heart swell. <What shall be our name? You are strong and beautiful and—you are so special. So special. I believe I am fortunate above all.>

With my free hand, I reached up to touch it, feeling the hard slick of shell. I squeezed Paul's fingers at the same time. "Can you understand me?"

<Always. We are one!>

From my viewpoint, it was as though the Presence

stood next to me, whispering in my ear, somehow able to project emotion, too. But here was more. I'd a circulatory system and could feel paired hearts pumping what might be liquid heat, but soothing, throughout this body. "What am I feeling?"

<My gift. My Offering. I tasted through my climb from the Ever Dark, even into the Lost, so you may thrive. Is it enough?> With a tinge of anxiety.

Sammy's adaptive biochemistry. The Vlovax had sampled this world's life. Somehow was able to shift my inner workings to fit, explaining much about the Mareepavlovax lifestyle. *Fascinating.*

Terrifying. But I'd worry about this me later. "It is," I replied warmly.

A dizzying delight. <Our name?>

Names mattered. Language did, too, and I decided it was high time I'd some help. I opened my eyes. "Paul?"

The Harvester was unlit because these eyes detected infrared. Paul showed as a pattern of cool grays and warmer yellows, with attractive red highlights limning his face. Allowing me to see the beginnings of a dimple.

"You've attracted a crowd, Old Blob."

Perception

EVAN stared into that opened entrance, black and empty and what he saw was a gaping mouth, one that had swallowed beings he cared deeply about.

The scream, brief but chilling, had made it worse. The opening would become a new *FEAR* if he wasn't vigilant in his thoughts and reactions—

"This is a home." A strong arm encircled his. Siokaletay-ki hovered close. "What is dark to your eyes is not to theirs. Do not presume, Human."

A scolding. *One he needed.* Evan found himself gazing into a stern amber eye, its judgmental gaze so like that of the little bust in his shirt he thought he saw a resemblance to Teganersha-ki. "To your greater knowledge, for I rely on it, Siokaletay-ki," he said quietly, careful of other ears, "is there concern in this delay? Esolesy made it sound as though they'd be right back."

A beak clicked once, in dark amusement. "She tends to extraordinary belief in her own abilities. In part deserved, do not mistake me, but I fully expect this—encounter—to take more time than she predicted." The arm tightened, then let go. "Patience."

Evan looked over at Ekwueme-ki and her clump of Dokeci. The mottled red skin corresponded closely to worried frowns in Humans, though the lack of deep wrinkles showed they were still willing to wait. *So be it.*

"I can see why Esolesy brought you here," he told Siokaletay-ki. "I'm glad she did."

All three eyes shifted to regard him for a long moment, then, with a strange bristle of aquamarine. "She won't be."

The Dokeci poled herself back to her kind.

40: Harvester Afternoon

MAREEPAVLOVAX surrounded us. I couldn't see an end to them, though they didn't crowd us, or block our way out. It was as though everyone who could still move had come.

<We are welcomed!>

The Presence had a refreshingly positive outlook. Much as I preferred it, I'd Paul to concern me. The Human stood out, an ominous shadow to these eyes, and I made sure to keep his hand in mine. "The Vlovax is intelligent and benign," I told him quickly. "Able to communicate clearly and display emotion."

<This is a surprise to you?> With worry.

"It's worried by my describing it."

<I am not 'it.' I am us!>

"I'm sorry. My describing 'us.'" I managed a helpless shrug. "My head's a bit full at the moment."

"You said benign. Are you sure?"

<I hear with you. Understand what you understand. I believe this speaking creature, whatever it is, to be a good influence.>

The sense that came with *good influence* was one of profound respect, even affection. I wanted to smile. In response, my beaklike nose glowed, making me try to cross my eyes to see it. "We approve of you," I said to Paul.

He ran a hand through his hair and I didn't need to see his eyes, shadowed to this sight, to know they'd hold that exasperated fondness. If we'd been alone, he'd have launched into questions.

We were not.

As for those who lived here?

They were beautiful. The striping of their skin in sunlight was here reversed, what was pale now a deep gray, the dark flushed with glowing violet. The fabric of their clothing emitted subtle sparks of what I perceived as white, creating elegant patterns particularly around the join of shoulder to neck that housed—I could think of no better word—their Vlovax. Dead or alive.

Clothing! I let go of Paul's hand and snatched up the strips I'd brought, holding them in front with no idea how to dress.

Purple flashed along their noses. <You are funny.>

"I don't know—" I stopped, because the amused purple disappeared with my first word. "Can you tell them I don't understand?"

<They know.>

A Mareepavlovax taller than me—taller than Paul— came forward from the rest, uttering a sequence of high and low trills.

"What does he say?"

<You are not to fear. They come to greet us because they know what you are. With pride. I have Risen as far as it is possible. You are the Youngest.>

Skalet's name for me.

I knew her deep, abiding despair, to be subordinate yet responsible. She did her best for our Web, in her blunt, callous way, and now I realized with a sinking feeling why she'd sent me here without warning. Learn, Youngest.

The Presence's cheerful <They will teach you!> came a little close for comfort.

Two Mareepavlovax and Paul, whom they treated without noticeable difference, helped wrap my torso and upper limbs. Against this skin, the material was irritating and scratchy. *Clothing or their version of funeral shrouds?* Not a happy thought.

Not a happy place, despite the irrepressible joy of the Presence. I saw grim lines around Paul's mouth. Understood them. *Had the Dokeci done this?*

The Dokeci were waiting, along with Evan and the Humans. I needed to know more.

<I hope we will have a name soon.> Wistfully.

Start simple, I decided. I pointed to Paul, enjoying the suppleness of my four digits. "Paul." I touched my chest. "Esen."

More trills. The two who'd dressed me consulted a third, the tall individual who'd spoken first. When they were done, he faced me and said in passable comspeak: "Not Esen only."

So, simple it wasn't. I hoped they weren't like the Iftsen, who added the names of their ancestors to their own and recited them in rhyming couplets as a party game. Taking a guess, I touched my Vlovax. "Do you have a name of your own?"

Confusion. <I was one of many, now I am us.>

"May I give you a name and add it to mine?"

<Yes! We will have a special name!> With such innocent delight I felt a pang of guilt for not taking this as seriously as perhaps I should.

What did I call a creature hanging from me by its fang—which didn't hurt at all, come to think of it, though Paul had insisted on wiping blood from my back.

Dart?

No. Whatever the Presence was, I couldn't name it after a monster. If anything, it deserved to be named after something unexpectedly precious—something you'd be surprised to find inside an ominous exterior. *A pearl.* I liked it, not that my feelings mattered when it came to a workable syntax. "If I call you Pearl, together we could be Pearlesen. Is that a good name?"

<It is beautiful. Is it to be our name?> Wonderingly.

"We can hope, Pearl." I repeated my gesture, hand to my chest, and said to the tall Mareepavlovax, "Pearlesen."

He pursed his lips and gave a short, sharp whistle, the small beak of his nose glowing with what I took for approval—or good humor. Suddenly the air filled with complex trills and even a few shouted "Pearlesen!"

Fair enough. I'd a name for this me they'd accept. *Now to figure out the rest.* I looked to Paul, waiting for me to do just that. He was calm, though surrounded by aliens—living and dead—the lantern's dim glow all he had against what to him would be the dark and to this me, a world lit by those in it. Calm, and I knew curious. Above all, wise.

"Paul?"

He gave the slightest nod of his head toward the row of corpses. The living Mareepavlovax appeared to ignore them, except for those who sat with them, as if waiting their turn.

Understand this first, he meant.

I'd a clue, perhaps. I addressed the tall individual. "We understand your speech," I told him, though it was a good bet he knew that already. "Why am I the Youngest?"

His four-fingered hands moved in the first overt gesturing I'd seen thus far, as if collecting all those present, to end at me. Then he trilled. It was like listening to a Human flute, the notes as able to convey grief as joy.

"Pearl, tell me what he says."

Completion

*B*ELIEF *fills me.*
    The Esen is perfection. She is all I require and more. I, who am now of Pearlesen!

I hope only to be worthy.

She asks me to interpret, being so young and new she has not acquired language. Though she is not young or new and has language of her own. I enjoy being part of someone so special.

I see through her eyes, for mine, burnt and useless, no longer trouble me. I no longer am, for what brought me to her is empty now, the Offer given and accepted. It dies, as it must.

I listen with her ears. Mine no longer hear. "You are the Youngest. You are the Only, for there has not been a new generation created since the Last Decision was made."

The One Who Speaks For All says more. He says more and such terrible things I stop.

I am afraid to repeat them.

"Pearl, please tell me. We need the truth, you and I. It is what we are."

What she asks of me, for my help, I must do, though with each word my hope falters . . .

I fear my belief will go next . . .

41: Harvester Afternoon

WHEN Pearl finished, I waited a moment, digesting, then said gently, "Thank you."

It was true. The Mareepavlovax—these few—were the last. They'd known it and, instead of protests to the fates or some desperate action, they'd made a decision, together. To end, together. Harvesters had set their course, landed, and disabled their engines. They'd been ready. Content.

Until the Dokeci plucked these from their final resting place and brought them to a new world.

They were dying, still. The evidence was all around us. Not so their partners. Stimulated by the new and alien biology beneath the Harvester, a fresh generation of Vlovax had emerged. Determined to seek partners and make their Offer. To live.

In numbers certain to terrify the Dokeci.

I finished, having recited the translation word-for-word for Paul.

No wonder Pearl had been distraught. I couldn't imagine the Mareepavlovax were any less so. Some, I could see, had accepted a new Vlovax, answering the instinct to adapt to their changed environment.

Perhaps the bodies left for the Dokeci, with an open wound where their Vlovax had been torn out, were those who'd refused to adapt, wanting only to end.

Or had they been a response, understandable only to

those who knew this species? *"We will not be forced to live, when our civilization has died."*

"Mareepa. Vlovax." Paul spoke, and his grim voice was like the tolling of a bell. "Two sentients in mutualistic symbiosis."

<What is that?> With playful curiosity.

What had never, to my knowledge, been seen before. "It means we depend on one another," I said, feeling Paul's fingers gather mine. Knowing.

<We do depend! We do!> Pearl was, I could tell now, younger even than I. New to life. Full of its possibilities. <It is the joyful Culmination.>

It was Skalet's lesson.

I could see it in its entirety now. She'd watched how I'd prided myself on knowing more than any ephemeral. Worried when I'd made my memories the ultimate authority of our Library. And when, time after time, I dared assume I could solve everyone's problems with my wit and charm and some Human luck?

Had she been afraid?

She'd been right to be. Now, as if I'd failed a client, my ignorance would have tragic consequences. I'd wanted to be Mareepavlovax. Insisted on it. Boasted to myself of my cleverness in obtaining a Vlovax of my own, without once asking why one was necessary.

Symbiosis. We were locked together now, one being, but I was a false partner. This was why Ersh hadn't shared the form: Skalet must have found it, been this, and only then learned the terrible truth. The Web of Ersh, my Web, existed to preserve, not destroy sentient life.

When I cycled—

<You are being quiet, beautiful Esen.>

<Is something wrong?>

Everything was.

My *education* would cost this dear little being its life.

Fingers unlike mine pulled once. *Save the rest,* that was, Paul making sure I kept my mind on what we could do. Must do.

I squeezed, then reclaimed my hand, still thinking of Skalet.

What would she do? Do not assume comprehension. Test and assess.

Fair enough. "I have something to offer," I said, using their term. Going to my bag, I rummaged in my bundle of clothes—unpleasantly slick to these fingers—for my little beaded bag and what it held. I tucked away the empty cryosac before standing.

"If you want to end?" The Kraal sac drifted onto corpses as I freed the imploder. "Here is the means." No need to worry about an explanation. To these eyes, it had deep menacing glow, and if I'd realized Skalet had powered the thing for quick use—*a little late to worry now.*

Paul stiffened. *We were going to have that talk about secrets again.* The thought was cold, rather than warm, and I wasted no time in regret.

Because, as one, the Mareepavlovax backed away, hands out in horror.

Then suddenly began to *SCREAM*.

<We must not Fall, Esen! We must not return to the Ever Dark!> As if Pearl screamed for me.

"You won't." I handed the imploder to Paul, blithely confident he'd know how to shut it off.

Test complete. Assessment?

Despite their decision, the Mareepavlovax weren't ready to end without a struggle after all.

"How would you like some hope?"

<Hope is why we climb.> With satisfaction.

"Then let's go outside."

Perception

THE screams from inside echoed across the valley. Human and Dokeci stumbled away from the entrance, not slowing till they reached the yellowed ground.

The Human guards stood facing the Harvester, weapons drawn despite a lack of target. Petham Erilton, his credentials as a mere administrator in shambles, stood with them, a com to his ear and a small needler in hand.

Could they hear his heart? In the sudden quiet, its heavy sickening beats were all Evan could hear. Heartbeats and the distant creak of something moved by the freshening breeze.

The Dokeci, guards included, clustered, skin black with horror, arms stiff and outstretched so their mass resembled Great Gran's pincushion. The sole exception was Siokaletay-ki, who leaned on her poles where sun met the dark shade of the tower overhead, so it was impossible to tell her color.

Her arms were relaxed. Normally a trigger to his *FEAR,* this time Evan was relieved. He summoned his courage and went to stand beside Petham. No one else was to use a com link without his authorization, but with that scream? Chain of command wasn't his concern. *Help for Paul and Esolesy was.* "Are you in touch with the embassy?"

The needler disappeared, whisked inside a jacket. The other gave him a straightforward look. "I've Commander

Kamaara of the *Mistral* on standby, Senior Polit. Awaiting your orders."

Survey. Meaning additional security—well-equipped
security—at their disposal. Meaning someone offworld
paying attention. Evan saw and understood the tension in
his team. Lisam and Lynelle trained with the Dokeci.
They'd be aware what a serious breach of protocol—say
deploying armed Humans who were not signatory to the
Fleullen-ni—could mean here.

As was he. *They weren't adding a second interspecies
issue to the mix.* "End your call, Administrator Erilton,"
managing not to stress the title. "Contact Senior Polit
M'Lean at the Embassy. Apprise him the situation is unchanged." Spotting the flicker of resistance in Petham's
eyes, Evan went on firmly, "We've heard a sound the
Mareepavlovax have used—peacefully—before. Startling, yes, but not cause for alarm."

"Precisely," Siokaletay-ki reinforced, poling silently
toward them. Two of her eyes faced the entrance. "I will
calm our colleagues." She wrapped two arms over her
face, wiggling their now black fingerlike tips in flagrant
disdain. "Hysterical fools."

The coarse display reassured Lisam and Lynelle, who
put away their weapons.

This was why Esolesy wanted her here, Evan thought
suddenly. To intercede with these less informed Dokeci
if—when—the strangeness of the Mareepavlovax overwhelmed them. "Thank you."

"I'd best hurry," she said, turning at once.

"Polit."

At Lisam's urgent tone, Evan looked to the shadowed
entrance.

Their guests had arrived.

42: Valley Afternoon

I led the way, inner eyelids shuttering down the, *to this me*, over-bright light of Dokeci-Na's overcast sky to bearable levels.

Paul walked beside me, empty-handed. Whatever he'd done to the imploder, it was now in three small—presumably harmless—pieces, none glowing, so I felt comfortable leaving it behind. Along with my carryall and what I'd need—

I wouldn't think about it.

The Mareepavlovax followed, their spokesbeing leading. Those too weak to walk on their own also came, supported by their fellows, and I suspected they'd have brought their dead along as well, if there'd been sufficient living hands for the task.

<We are in the Bright.> Anxious, overstimulated, but not afraid. <Does Paul live in the Bright?>

"Yes. Pearl," I murmured, foreseeing a problem, "I must speak now to several others. When you hear your name, I'm speaking directly to you. I'll need your help to translate the words of One Who Speaks. Do you understand?"

<You will find and Offer hope.> With appalling trust. <I understand and will help. We are Pearlesen!>

I halted within the tower's shadow, on the metal floor. Being disconnected from the earth was a *wrongness* to this me, and most unsettling, so I used gestures to indicate the other Mareepavlovax should stand beyond it.

They didn't look pleased by whatever the Dokeci had painted on the ground either, but none hesitated, spreading out to either side along the wall of the Harvester. The weak among them were eased down.

The One Who Speaks stayed with me. His Vlovax was little more than chunks of shell connected by dried threads of cartilage; this close, I could hear how his every movement disturbed those remnants, producing a delicate clatter as if he consulted with the dead.

But his Vlovax wasn't dead; it had discarded its outer shell and moved inside him, to be part of him. It starved, too, unadapted to the biochemistry of this world, and that was part of my problem. My instinct, as an individual, was to treat them as two separate entities. In a sense they were, as I'd learned with Pearl, but they weren't independent.

What happened when a new Vlovax rose from the ground? Did it replace a predecessor, or join it? Or fail.

Between worlds, did Vlovax hibernate within their partner?

Or die.

Not questions for Pearl.

Paul went to Evan, pointing to the entrance. I left it to him to explain why Esolesy Ki the Lishcyn hadn't come out of the dark in a way that wouldn't result in a laudable, but unhelpful flood of Human rescue-the-helpless. Wonderful species, but predictably focused on relationships.

Predictably, mine arrived first, tipping respectively forward at One Who Speaks, but also at me.

I could *feel* Pearl's growing curiosity, so spoke quickly. "My name is Pearlesen."

No more than a splot of aquamarine betrayed my web-kin's. "Siokaletay-ki is how I am called," she replied graciously. "We did not expect so many."

What have you done, Youngest? that meant.

I couldn't smile in a way a Dokeci or Human could see. One of doubtless numerous points on which we couldn't communicate, so I settled on how we could. "I

am fluent in comspeak and will interpret for the
Mareepavlovax as necessary." That, in case she thought
to circumvent me, but at this of all times I needed whatever help I could get. "Correct me at once if I make any
errors."

"Be sure I will. You are—" a pleasant pink mottling,
"—young for such responsibility."

Some things never changed.

"Greetings." Evan Gooseberry approached with Paul,
his eyes wide with wonder. "You understand me?"

Bowing appeared to cross species, so I dipped my
head. "I am Pearlesen. This is One Who Speaks. It is he
who will call for a decision when we are done."

Evan looked so relieved I wanted to hug him, but I
refrained. "I am Evan Gooseberry, representing the Human species. This is Siokaletay-ki and," with a bow of his
own, "Ekwueme-ki, who speaks for this world."

Black fading to gray, arms suspiciously rigid, the
Dokeci came forward nonetheless and tilted politely.

Nicely done, Evan. Widen the discussion to the planet.
Make clear what's at stake. Next we'd settle, conduct the
style of meeting best calculated to soothe the others, then
I'd bring up—

<Beautiful Esen.>

I turned away and whispered into my palm. "Not now,
Pearl."

<It is now.> With truly alarming triumph.

"What is?"

<They Rise.>

"We accept your hope." I whirled on the tall Mareepavlovax, who spread his hands in that inclusive gesture, then
trilled emphatically.

<He says the others must leave now.>

All at once, I felt it for myself, despite the metal floor,
having senses attuned to movement below ground. *What
had I done?*

"Evan, evacuate the valley!"

Inception

I climb in hope.
*   And I . . . and I . . . and I . . .*
We all climb for hope . . .
I believe!
And I . . . and I . . . and I . . .
We all believe . . .
For all are taught to fail is to Fall . . .
To Rise is to leave the Ever Dark behind . . .
And live!

43: Valley Afternoon

IN hindsight, ever flawless, I should have seen this coming.

As no one but Mareepavlovax ever had, I forgave myself, too caught in what was happening to worry about the details.

For the valley floor had erupted. If the Dokeci thought they'd contained the Devil Darts, they'd been woefully mistaken. In every direction, shells shed dirt, claws dug in, and the creatures dragged themselves toward the Harvester.

Not the Harvester, to those waiting alongside it. And it wasn't a march, it was an urgent demanding flood of life. Magnificent, yes, but to those hovering in aircars?

Terrifying, too.

<Some will Rise.> Pride tempered by resignation.

Somehow, I understood. "There aren't enough Mareepa, Pearl."

<There are never enough.> Pragmatic. <It is the way. Most will Fall.>

Evan had made sure the decision-makers were in this, the embassy's aircar: the Human contingent of himself, the administrator, and security; Siokaletay-Ki and Ekwueme-ki, with the latter's foremost staff squished in the back; Paul, and—much to the Dokeci's dismay, me.

While below, a sea of Vlovax flowed inexorably forward,

climbing over one another in waves. Their fangs glittered, moist with the Offering.

This me felt warmed by the sight.

The rest believed nothing worse could have happened. The Dokeci were too quiet. Evan and his people too still. Who would be first to burst out and insist the cause was lost and the valley be purged of alien-to-this-world life?

I looked at Paul, wishing he knew this me, seeking what comfort I could.

He looked back, gray eyes full of trust. *Trust I didn't deserve.*

Then I heard a too-familiar voice and tensed, knowing Skalet wanted this outcome most of all.

"Peace, everyone. This isn't disaster."

I stared at her. *Was it a trick?*

"Go lower," Siokaletay-ki ordered quietly, no eyes on me. "This isn't a threat. What you are watching is hope."

"Hope of what?" Evan asked, quieter, a whisper.

"Rebirth."

Why wouldn't she look at me? What was she planning now?

Evan ordered the pilot to descend. On either side, the other aircars did the same. We hovered low enough to look down—and did.

<They Rise.> With joy.

Pearl didn't mean the Vlovax this time, or not only. The Mareepa were on the move, too, tearing out the withered remains of their former symbiotes, those who could walk wading eagerly into the oncoming mass—not that they needed to, for the Vlovax poured in and around, climbed them, and BIT.

Which this me found meaningful and ever-so-slightly titillating—

"Look!" Paul pointed to where those sitting or lying on the ground had begun to stand. "They're recovering."

Blood oozed down their backs and I doubted anyone else presently watching felt anything but nauseated by the sight of a Vlovax with its fang sunk deep into a neck, but that wasn't what he meant.

Those who'd sat or collapsed were on their feet.

Stretching. Even from here, by this light, I could see their renewed vigor. They touched one another, as if amazed by themselves. Were stroked by passing Vlovax.

Who knew when a Mareepa was claimed. Who, when there were no partners left, curled into despondent lonely balls and went still.

Before our eyes, the Mareepavlovax walked into their home as if aircars carrying their fate didn't hover overhead. They continued to touch one another as if unable to believe themselves.

Until all that remained was the churned earth and silent balls of those who'd failed.

<It is done. You have done this, beautiful Esen.> Tenderly, with such pure love and gratitude I trembled inside.

"Es." A breath, full of wonder.

Him, too? This wasn't over, I thought grimly, and for once, I couldn't meet my friend's eyes.

My web-kin addressed Ekwueme-ki and the Human, but one eye found me. *She spoke to me.* "The Mareepavlovax have decided to live. Because of you, this species has a chance to survive. I suggest they do not do so here." Dryly.

Ersh, was that . . . approval? She dared . . . ?

Skalet was helping, I reminded myself. Beyond hope or belief—and certainly with no aid at the moment from me—Skalet the bloody-minded, who valued secrecy above ephemeral life, was resolving the day as I'd wanted and she had not.

What had changed her mind? Given what she could see attached to my neck, ringed in dried blood, it wasn't mercy.

"Burtles and his people are standing by to remove the Mareepavlovax and their Harvester from Dokeci-Na." Evan sounded prepared to move them by hand if necessary. "We are willing—"

"WE are willing," Ekwueme-ki announced, all at once smooth and bold and confident. I supposed seeing the remaining Devil Darts on her planet die hadn't hurt. "We will, of course, work together within the Fleullen-ni," she added belatedly, perhaps calculating the cost. "Will you, Pearlesen, convey our plans to your people?"

"And I've the appropriate farewell offering," Siokaletay-ki said, her skin and voice unreadable to anyone else. "You'll take it for me, won't you, Pearlesen?"

There it was, the pin behind the smile.

"I will," I told them both.

Whatever Skalet wanted me to take to the Mareepavlovax, I'd check it first.

Paul and Evan, the latter watched by his guards from a distance, walked with me to the entrance of the Harvester. The Dokeci, including my web-kin, weren't ready to come close to the dead Darts, leaving them for Humans to collect. *They'd need heavy machinery.*

I paused where the shadow let my inner eyelids open. Evan's face was pale and cool; Paul's vivid with heat. "I'm coming with you," my friend repeated. "Esolesy will want an escort. And I've this." Siokaletay-ki had produced a white box I distrusted on sight and couldn't open without breaking. *I'd tried, discreetly.*

<The Good Influence must stay out.>

"Why, Pearl?"

Paul's eyes narrowed; he knew to whom I spoke, or to what, and suspected a new problem. Evan hesitated, curious but unwilling to ask.

<Beautiful Esen, you have a wonderful plan. All to Rise together and begin anew. I do understand.> This with a fervent *pay attention to me* I understood completely, being young myself. <If all accept, first comes the Sleep, to travel without need for offerings. The Good Influence must stay out.>

"You should know," I told the Humans, "that if my people accept this plan, we will sleep."

"Why? You didn't sleep on the way here." Evan heard himself and had the grace to look abashed. "My apologies, Pearlesen. I ask what I shouldn't."

"On the way here," I told him bluntly, "the Mareepavlovax wanted to die. The moon was to be our final resting place."

"Why there?"

Ersh, save me from curious Humans. But this question, too, I decided to answer. "The Rings of S'Remmer. Who would not want to end bathed in such beauty?" Something I'd like to tell the Dokeci architect who carved up their moon, but aesthetic congruence wasn't uncommon. *And made no difference now.*

His eyes lit with more questions. I waved them off with my digits. "I must go. My gratitude to you, Evan Gooseberry. To all of you. Paul Ragem—"

He was already in motion. "Are you coming?"

Save me from stubborn ones, too.

The corpses were as we'd left them. I supposed I'd hoped the Vlovax could revive the dead, but that wasn't how it worked.

<The Good Influence must leave.>

Pearl's growing anxiety fed my own, but Paul? Fearless as always, he'd let me guide him into the darkness, to my carryall and the lantern within. Sitting in its light, he'd taken the box from me.

His palm on the box had opened it, the Human as concerned by a Skalet-gift as I.

The duras plants packed inside surprised us both. *Always have an exit, Youngest.* I should have remembered.

Paul retrieved my caftans from corpses, selecting one for me with purposeful haste. *Be done,* his every move begged of me. *Let's be done and gone from here.*

"He'll go very soon, Pearl." I turned to face the three who'd been waiting here. "Do you agree?"

I'd had my doubts on how—using Pearl for help—best to convey the complexities of plucking the Harvester from this world and sending it through interstellar space, but I'd forgotten to whom I spoke. This—other than having another species volunteer propulsion—was what Mareepavlovax did. Casting themselves into the unknown was, in their view, safer than staying on a world where, to put it mildly, they'd end up digesting neighbors who'd object.

From the Dokeci? The sooner the Harvester was bagged

and in space, the less chance of a new generation of quest-ing Darts. This time hungry and preset to their biology.

"We agree," the Mareepavlovax said in unison. Then, the tallest, "He must go," with a gesture to Paul. "We begin the Sleep, Pearlesen."

<I have said so.> More than anxiety now, fear.

"I'll remain here to ensure the Human leaves."

"We understand." One Who Speaks stepped close. His stripes glowed brighter now, his voice richer, and when he touched my cheeks, then the Vlovax, I felt cher-ished. Without thinking, I did the same, and watched a new expression light his face. Joy. He trilled.

<He says 'We will have our own new youngest, Pearlesen, because you came as our beacon and guide. To restore our hope. You will always be special to us. We will remember your name.' Why does he say that?>

Because the Mareepavlovax knew. Somehow. Knew I wasn't one of them.

What could you say to those about to sleep?

What could I say, to those I wished I'd never met?

"Believe," I told him, wishing them a future.

At last we were alone, Paul and I, but we weren't alone at all.

"It's time," my friend said. "Es."

<He MUST go!> Near panic and I could feel it now, the gentle urges to lie down. To sleep.

Soon, this me would.

"You should go—"

Human hands grabbed these arms, shook this me as they'd done to shake sense into other mes. "We go to-gether, Old Blob, or not at all."

He'd known, I thought fondly. Known that without him to save, I couldn't bring myself to—

With a snap Ersh would envy, "Now!"

I pulled away, not to reject Paul, but to protect him. *He was right.*

<Something is wrong, beautiful Esen. Isn't it. Have I been wrong? Am I wrong?> With *worry*, with *dread*, with

all the things I didn't want this dear, special being to ever feel.

So I told Pearl the truth. "You are special and perfect, Pearl. You will be part of me, always."

And I waited to feel the surge of *love* and *belonging* and *bright happy HOPE*—

Before I cycled, and they were gone.

I'd ended an intelligence before. Murdered. If you call letting a rogue Web-being eat more of me than was wise, and solidify under its own greed, murder. I'd grieved for it, nonetheless. I'd grieved for Lesy, Mixs, and Ansky. For Skalet—until she'd reappeared. For Ersh and for any and all those lost.

This?

I was empty as I'd never been before, my every motion clumsy and uncertain. Paul helped me dress, grabbed my carryall, then put his shoulder under my larger one. He held the lantern to guide us because my fingers wouldn't close, and it wasn't until our first halting steps that I realized he cried, as this me could not.

For me.

Something made it easier to move then.

And when he staggered, gasping, and I remembered Pearl's warning, I picked up my first friend before he could fall, this me being strong.

And when my lantern smashed and we were in the dark, it didn't matter, because though I was empty and grieved . . .

I wasn't alone.

Perception

"YOU saved them." Overcome, Lionel closed his eyes, then opened them. "I expected nothing less."

"I am gratified by your confidence." Though whisper-soft, her glorious voice found the corners of Paul's office, filled them, as it warmed his heart. "You should know Paul and Evan performed capably."

"And . . . Esen?"

"She learned the lesson I intended. A hard one." *Was that remorse?* Before he could be sure, Skalet's voice sharpened. "She will not be grateful. The Youngest never is. Fortunately, she has a task to occupy her until we leave this world, so I needn't listen to her fuss."

"But everyone's all right. Aren't they?" He frowned worriedly. "You're safe?"

The pause stretched until Lionel assumed she'd ended their conversation and fussed to himself. He'd been too forward. Implied doubt in her ability, when no one was more *capable*.

Been too Human—

"We are never safe, Lionel."

And he didn't know if Skalet meant their safety—

Or warned him of his own.

44: Shrine Evening

THE Humans insisted on caring for their own, and I listlessly agreed, leaving Paul at the Commonwealth Embassy. He lingered between unconscious and incoherent, having inhaled a complex of Mareepavlovax pheromones presumably designed to promote a hibernation state, and flat in bed was safer. The med-tech described his condition as nonthreatening and "blind drunk, with a good hangover to follow."

Sammy was happy to sample his blood. Not at all to see me again and, if not for the success in the valley this morning, I daresay the scientist would have me arrested for destruction of embassy property.

Pearl hadn't been property.

"Here we are," Evan announced cheerfully.

He'd been nothing but cheerful, despite being assigned the vastly unimportant duty of keeping me busy and away from Sammy. I felt a vague curiosity. "Shouldn't you be writing reports and whatever?"

A lighthearted shrug. "Senior Polit M'Lean and the Ambassador decided I deserved the rest of the day off. They're heading to the *Libstry-ni*—it's the nearest large festival hall—for the Dokeci celebration of our success."

Ah. Human politics. "They're taking credit."

"They're welcome to it." He grinned as he waved me through an ornate metal gate, looking happier than I'd ever seen him. "It's chain of accountability. The Senior

Polit's name is on the request—and expense—to send the *Mistral* to Botharis. My—let's call it a temporary field promotion—was his gamble and the ambassador's."

I harrumphed. "And your success?"

His grin softened. "Ours, Esolesy, and I'm beyond grateful to you and Paul. And you, Siokaletay-ki."

I'd tried to ignore the ticktick of her poles behind us as we walked along Embassy Row.

"Your superiors will remember your achievements," she assured him. "Your grace in accepting reality high among them."

If she meant that for me, too? My stomachs rumbled angrily. To forestall an eruption I might enjoy, if no one else, I focused on our surroundings.

Riosolesy-ki's Shrine to Teganersha-ki.

There was the gate, through which we passed, though no fence. As one we stopped to appreciate the shrine itself.

The long low building was shaped like a greenhouse and as transparent as one. Rays from the setting sun entered from behind—

—to be refracted by gems into a cascade of rainbows. The effect was breathtaking.

If you didn't know the gems were Tumbler excretions. Ersh's to be precise.

To enhance the play of light, the Dokeci—never ones to say "enough is enough"—had installed ponds and fountains around the building, creating a confusion of colored sprays and twinkling reflections. Light poles in the conceit of trees stood ready to shine over it all once the sun no longer cooperated or, I supposed, to sparkle on cloudy days.

At least there were real flowers, plus a dense soft turf underfoot.

"Teganersha-ki would hate it," Skalet said. I glanced at her, unsurprised by the dismayed wrinkling of her skin.

She wasn't wrong. *That wasn't the point.* "Riosolesy-ki would love it," I countered. Could Skalet *taste* the webmass here, as I did. Feel its pull?

Did she grow *hungry?*

"It's only open alternate weeks now. I'm sorry I couldn't

arrange for you to go inside, Esolesy." Evan nodded at the large double doors at the end nearest us. They were transparent, too, allowing full view of a life-sized bust, floating serenely above a glowing ring.

Of Ersh.

"Like all exhibits, popularity wanes when the next arrives." Siokaletay-ki waved the tip of her pole at the empty paths and vacant hip cradles. "I predict there will be something new here soon, given the excellence of the location."

And her intention to destroy it. Skalet didn't know her imploder, in pieces, was about to lift from the planet in the Harvester. To be fair, I'd my carryall clutched to my chest. Snacks remained a useful excuse, though I hadn't eaten—

I burped as my stomachs gave an unhappy lurch.

Evan patted my arm with cautious but sincere affection. *In that much, I'd improved his opinion of this me.* "You must be exhausted, Esolesy. Let me call you an aircar, to take you back to—" At a guess, he'd been about to say the embassy, then remembered Sammy. "—to your accommodations in the shipcity. I'll stay with Paul."

That wasn't the plan.

"What I really need, after today, is a good wallow." I waggled my ears in charming fashion. "Like that one." I pointed to the larger pond, edged in floating plants. *Should be mud in the bottom,* I decided, halfway excited to find out.

"But—" The poor diplomat was horrified.

I regarded him with all the wide-eyed *bizarre secret alien ways* innocence I could muster; Paul would be proud. *Or concerned.* "Surely the Dokeci expect Lishcyns such as myself to visit and appreciate their shrine. Why else would they provide such excellent facilities?"

"But it's a pond—" Evan turned to Siokaletay-ki. "Isn't it?"

My web-kin regarded me with suspicion, well aware what I wanted. *Them gone.* "Art must be appreciated to truly live," she mused aloud, as though giving his concern serious consideration, and not trying my patience.

I eased toward the pond.

Evan came along, as if he believed he could stop this larger me from doing what came so naturally I grew dizzy with longing. Maybe he also believed he knew all the ways this could go badly. *I could tell him a thing or two.*

"Wallowing to view art is a Lishcyn custom familiar to us," Siokaletay-ki said, finally helpful, if lying through her beak. "This—art—clearly needs someone to care about it."

I glowered for Lesy as I removed my caftan and put it on a bench with the rest of my belongings, then showed Evan my tusks. "Exactly."

A Lishcyn didn't step daintily into a promising wallow; a Lishcyn leaped.

The resulting splash missed Skalet, who'd been ready for it and moved; it did soak Evan from the waist down in glorious mud and plant bits. I submerged to my snout, savoring what was indeed a delightfully deep layer of ooze and organics, and waggled my ears at him again.

Being Evan, he chuckled. "How long will you need to fully appreciate the shrine?"

While I could wallow for a good long time and—*ahhhh, the relief from all the itches*—would love to do so now, we'd a starship to catch. Granting Paul was space-ready by morning. I sighed to myself. *Duty called.*

Before I had to answer, Siokaletay-ki did. "Leave Esolesy Ki to care for herself, Evan. She looks—" three eyes stared down at me; I waggled my ears at her, too, "—comfortable. Come with me. We'll go to the Libstry-ni for tonight's well-earned celebration."

We both blinked at her. Evan recovered first. "I would love to do that, Siokaletay-ki, but I'm not on the guest list."

Smug. "I am. You shall come with me, as my guest. After—" with a flash of amused pink, "—you procure dry clothing."

He wanted to go; I could see it. Deserved to celebrate. Being Evan, he worried about leaving this me.

I settled things by sinking below the surface, blowing languid bubbles.

And waited until I was alone.

The Ycl and a Web-being had something in common. Or I did. I hadn't noticed my elders ever thinning themselves to a few molecules; then again, they'd cycled in closets until I'd caught them at it, on the notion I'd continue my attempts to hold a form without exploding if I believed it was easier for them.

A considerable amount of my early years involved deception along those lines.

The shrine's doors were designed to keep out the rain and art thieves, not a thinned Web-being, so it didn't take me long to find a gap and slip myself through—a reminder I really should add such useful gaps to the Library doors when Duggs wasn't looking. *She was a little too good at her job.*

I condensed into my proper teardrop before the bust of the infamous Teganersha-ki. Alas, to my web-senses, the statue was so much inert material and uninteresting, despite a shape I knew.

Ah, but the *taste?* I extended thin pseudopods, following the gradient. Yes. *Lesy. Lesy . . .*

LESYLESYLESY!

Had I been more fluid, I'd have frozen in shock. As it was, I sloshed a little, torn between choices. Web-mass close enough to touch.

Web-mass enough to drown in, beyond the next door.

Skalet had been right. Here could be all of the busts Lesy had signed with her own flesh.

Except Evan's. I'd already decided to let his alone. Paul carried a scrap of me in his pendant. If Evan carried a scrap of Lesy when he traveled, as he had?

I could find him. If I were close, and probably would need to be in web-form to be sure, which was its own complication because Evan was not ready for that much me—

I was dithering. As a tactic to help me resist the powerful instinct to consume all the Lesy I could *taste* as quickly as possible, it was helpful. As a means of making a decision what to do with it? *Not so much.*

And I didn't have all night. Evan would change, go

with Skalet, attempt to enjoy himself, then bolt at the first
hint he'd been noticed by his seniors. *Using a wallowing
Lishcyn as an excuse.*

Leaving Lesy's bits here was not only distracting—and
likely impossible for my web-self, now that I was here—
but dangerous. This much web-mass available to be ana-
lyzed was the risk. The time would come, if centuries
from now, when Lesy's careful dabs of glue would dry
and flake away, when the Ersh excretions large and small
would either be collected or lost, and some clever ephemeral grow curious about the immutable blue left behind.

*It was up to me to protect my Web—now and as long as
we existed.*

To work, then.

Like many, if not most of my plans, it wasn't until after I'd
committed myself past the point of no return that I noticed a problem.

The reason my elders didn't thin? Because it was hard.
Hard to resist the hysterical compulsion to resume my
normal shape. Hard to control a wide, thin, extended *me*.

Above all, hard to maintain a sense of self.

Fortunately, web-flesh hungered for more of itself. I
didn't need control as I reached the giant pile of Ersh
heads. *Lesy-taste* drew me irresistibly along.

All I had to do was remember one thing: not to assimilate any of it. Not yet. I'd no idea how she'd affixed
smears of herself to the statues and I'd no intention of
absorbing that knowledge and find it somehow affixing
me to them, too.

My shudder caused a localized avalanche. I supposed
I should be grateful the Dokeci hadn't glued the little
busts together.

I thinned and thinned . . . found *Lesy* . . . gathered
Lesy . . . and shunted that web-mass toward one remote
portion of mine. Pulse after tiny pulse, collecting, carefully apart from *Esen*.

I started at the top, spread like a blue blanket over the
entire exhibit, letting gravity and appetite draw me down

and through, flowing like blood through every cavity. By the time I reached halfway, I'd lost any understanding of what I was doing, only the *hunger* and the primal caution to keep apart—for now.

When I reached the floor, I'd lost myself, but who I was hardly mattered because there was more web-mass *THAT WAY!*

I condensed through the channels I'd taken and made, growing thicker along this line and that. Ersh busts began tumbling and bouncing. Air rushed in, *new tastes, new sensations*. Had I been sufficiently condensed to think, I'd have realized my now-frenzied contractions into myself were sending Ersh busts flying merrily through the glass walls of the shrine and into the ponds outside.

But I was only instinct and wanted MORE.

I flowed back and into myself, reclaiming every precious bit of *ME*.

Teardrop again.

Aware, again. I'd been clever, leaving the life-sized bust till the last so its *Lesy* would draw me—

Something was wrong . . .

Wrong with me . . .

TOO BIG! Ersh-memory was precise, the instinct of what to do about it clear, if not at all reasonable considering I was still inside the shrine.

Give birth? Not an option, even if all I had to do was bud off that annoying lump of *not-me*—because I couldn't carry it through locked doors, could I?

Be rid of it, then. Use it. Change that useless web-mass into energy and, what, fly? *As if that would work*, I thought crossly. Paul had the part of me that knew how. For Good Reason.

I could use it to cycle into something bigger—then what? Use Ersh's head to try and break out of her shrine?

Ersh . . .

The realization I'd a much larger problem than a large me struck like lightning.

Ersh . . . ?

It wasn't a word. It was memory.

And it wasn't mine.

Perception

PAUL Ragem winced, stopping when they walked out into daylight. Evan paused with him. "You're sure you're ready for this?"

"I'm ready to go home," the other said, shading his eyes. He glanced at Evan and half-smiled. "Don't worry. I'm sure I feel worse than I look."

Sorting that out, he had to laugh as Paul intended. "If you say so. The med-tech's cleared you and Esolesy's waiting on the ship." Evan hesitated, embarrassed. "Please apologize to her. I meant to pick her up at the shrine." He didn't remember too much about last night, not a fact to share. There'd been a quiet spot to observe without attracting the wrong attention. *Excuse me, Ambassador Hansen, you didn't want me here, but I thought I'd crash your party.* Why had he gone in the first place?

There'd been a drink. Admiring amber eyes.

"I don't know what happened," he admitted.

"Don't worry. My partner needed some time alone." Paul's smile faded. "We'll both rest on the trip."

"Lucky Esolesy left the wallow before the plumbing broke and disturbed so much of the shrine."

Paul's eyebrow rose. "'Plumbing?'"

"It was in the newsfeed this morning. I'm glad she saw it as it was," Evan added, though he agreed with Siokaletay-ki. *A degrading misuse of personal treasures.*

He'd put his bust of the infamous Teganersha-ki on the table by his bed at home, where it would be safe.

He'd been tempted to give it to Paul—then realized any gift was selfish. He'd no right to push something of himself into Paul's life. Evan straightened and held out his hand. "Thank you for coming, Paul. For everything."

"Don't be a stranger," Paul Ragem ordered, taking his hand in a tight clasp, gray eyes bright. "We'll expect you to visit."

"I will," Evan promised, managing to smile. "I wish you luck with your someone."

"And you." Paul smiled, leaned close, and kissed Evan firmly on the mouth.

And if it was the kiss of a friend?

As Evan watched the groundcar—and Paul Ragem—pull away—he decided it was still the best kiss of his life.

45: Freighter Morning

IF Paul was surprised at what was sharing his cabin on the *Largas Regal,* he did me the kindness of not showing it. "Hello, Bess." He tucked his carryall into the locker with mine, then took a moment to pour us glasses of juice from the container young Lance Largas—one of Joel's numerous great-grands—had left.

Giving me time.

I'd wrapped myself in blankets, Human skin not as good with synth-grass as scales, and had done my best to worm myself deep in the box. It wasn't comfortable.

I didn't care.

He did. "That won't do, Old Blob." Paul put our drinks on the table, then reached in to gather me up, blankets and all. Synth-grass whispered as it fell to the floor and I made a broken little noise of my own as he cradled me in his lap, both of us sitting on his bed, and tucked my head under his chin.

"Now, Es," Paul said, his voice as gentle as any voice could be, his arms around me walls of comfort, *which was silly, because they were flesh and frail and wouldn't always be here . . .*

"Tell me about Pearl."

"Together, you showed the Mareepavlovax they could have a future," he said when I was done, and when I'd dried my tears—that being the *why* of my being Bess, which he'd known, of course. Paul had shed tears with me.

Pearl would have liked that.

"An easier demonstration would have been nice," I mumbled into my juice.

His eyes flashed. *Not pleased with Skalet, not at all.* And I thought to myself, *be careful, web-kin.*

But all Paul said was, "We're on our way home."

Neither of us mentioned what waited for us there. It wasn't the time for mystery and missing ships. Corpses and puzzles. Recalcitrant family.

A home primarily in splinters—but, I perked up, there was a plus.

My Lanivarian-self loved renovating.

There might come an appropriate time, as Ersh would say, to share with my friend what bulged inside my luggage.

Or, I decided, *not.*

Perception

*T*HERE *was much to enjoy about being a Quebit.*
Skalet adjusted a handling appendage, then tightened the annoyingly loose nut. *Gratifying*.

The form was focused, unlike some. Identified goals and proceeded to act rationally to attain them, unlike some.

Was *safe*.

Unlike some.

As a Quebit, Skalet had no difficulty putting the Youngest and her reckless *proclivities* aside. They could be considered. Dealt with.

After she tightened every bolt. *Satisfying*. Next, she would check the ventilation ducts for lint.

She should be a Quebit more often.

46: Home Afternoon

TO my chagrin, the All Species' Library of Linguistics and Culture hadn't fallen apart without us. Paul and I took the crowded train from the landing field. We walked through the doors within a mass of eager clients, bags in hand, to find ourselves surrounded by focused confusion. Henri saluted from her counter, too busy to talk, and Paul waved back, chuckling.

They hadn't missed us at all. I stopped in my tracks; a trio of Ervickians muttered "scaled blots" and detoured around me. "I expected a—"

"A party?" Skalet, again Kraal, stalked past, her reappearance startling us both.

Well, yes. I sighed, making it a good long one.

Paul chuckled again. "It's a sign of good staff, Es," he assured me. "They'll be all over us when they've time. Did you want to get something from the Chow first, or to head straight home?"

"Chow!" My stomachs rumbled in agreement. "You?"

"I'm going to check in with Lionel. See how things are."

Being time to share him. Familiar, this jolt of feeling when we reentered Paul's world and I realized how many others relied on him. Yet this wasn't the same. Suddenly, it occurred to me that here, in our Library, others relied on me—on two mes—as well.

"I'll stop by and see Ally. She'll—" No, she didn't need me. This place didn't, and that was fine.

I needed it. Them.

"Ally might like some help," I said instead, and burped peacefully. "After the Chow."

We parted as easily as letting the determined Heezle with a wrapped *something* ooze between us, on its way to Assessment.

Another client. Another day at the Library.

Another chance to prevent a mistake caused by ignorance.

Because the cost was too high.

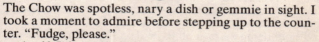

The Chow was spotless, nary a dish or gemmie in sight. I took a moment to admire before stepping up to the counter. "Fudge, please."

As if I'd startled the giant Carasian—*who'd risk that?*—Lambo spun around with a roar, but I'd seen a sly eyestalk aimed my way. If this was a new game, I'd no problem playing. "Eek! You startled me!"

"I didn't." Without the usual surly undertone.

Pleased, I curled a lip. "Not really, no." I gestured to the gleaming countertop. "Looks good. I take it you've a replacement for Celi?"

"Changed my mind." A claw landed possessively on the counter. "I take care of my own place."

This was *new*. "What about the dishes?" I'd a sudden horrid feeling Lambo was now refusing to let dirty dishes back in the Chow at all, in which case where were they piling up?

"Do you want your fudge or not?"

Treat! I most assuredly did. "Please." I waited as she did her blur of control tapping, surprised anew when the bowl spat out and offered to me was, indeed, filled with cubes of fudge. *Was it her recent molt?* "Thank you," I said suspiciously. "Why are you being so—so tidy?"

"I have much to do." A claw snapped. "An important task. Keeping tidy is efficient and saves valuable time."

Something even Paul hadn't been able to drum into those thick head plates. "May I ask what task you've acquired?"

Eyestalks converged. "No."

And back we were to normal. *Almost a relief.* "Then thank you for this," I raised my bowl. "We'll talk later."

"No. I talk to Esen." Lambo turned with a clatter, leaving me facing a black shell rump.

Also normal, so I wasn't offended.

I wanted to be Esen again, too.

My Lanivarian-self would "return" tomorrow from the other side of Botharis, where, according to staff, *that me* had succeeded in obtaining what we needed to restore and, hopefully, improve the Ragem family farmhouse. I left the details of how "I'd" accomplished such a feat without being there at all to Paul and his Group. *Though it was occasionally disturbing how adept they were at scripting my life.*

Until then, I nibbled fudge and listened to Ally Orman's report on the past days, paying more attention to the fudge and less to her words, since I could tell from her tone all was well.

"Esolesy?"

Might have missed something. I hastily used my forked tongue to remove any evidence of fudge from my tusks. "Yes?"

"Don't you think it's strange?" At my doubtless blank look, Ally made that noise Humans used to show exasperation. "You weren't listening."

"Fudge." I held up my now-empty bowl and curled a pleasant lip. "This is the Library. The strange is our business." *Clever that.*

Or maybe it wasn't, for she made the noise again, this time rolling her eyes in emphasis. "This is important. Esen would know that."

I could grow jealous of myself. Which was confusing an already confusing moment, so I showed her my most serious face. "I apologize."

Ally looked contrite. "No, I should. I do. You and Paul—what you accomplished for the Mareepavlovax was wonderful. You've proven the worth of what we do here, and I bother you about this—this family thing of Paul's. It can wait."

Veya Ragem? It all came crashing in again. The *Sidereal Pathfinder.* Chase, the attacks, Paul's office. The disk in the cookies. My scales began to swell in alarm, and my voice squeaked. "What's wrong with Paul's family?"

"Goodness, Esolesy. It's nothing like that. Henri and I, we were talking and—we found it strange Paul's uncle would visit while he was gone. That's all. I'm sure it was a misunderstanding." With the too-hopeful look of a Human who didn't think that at all.

Meaning—I'd no idea what it meant. *Strange* covered it. I picked up my bag. "I'm sure you're right," I told her. "Time I unpacked anyway. Unless you need help?"

"Lionel's kept up nicely while Esen's gone," Ally assured me. "You go and rest. Thanks again for coming."

I was already gone.

Paul's office door was closed. I knew the code to open it, which—according to my dear friend—wasn't polite, and could chime for attention, which was—

Unless it wasn't. I lowered my hand from the panel, doing my best to think like a Human despite this me being thoroughly upset and about to waste my fudge. If Paul's uncle, most likely Sam Ragem, had come to see Paul and missed him, Lionel would say so and they'd talk about it. The result might be a happy Paul.

Unless Sam had come when he had in order to not see Paul, making none of us happy. In which case, Lionel would still tell Paul what had happened.

Adding me to either instance wouldn't help.

Families.

I hefted my carryall.

Time to deal with my own.

The Garden hadn't missed me either.

Nonetheless, it welcomed me home in a way nothing

else could. I wandered its paths, drew the fragrance of living things and healthy rot through my nostrils. There were plants this me found tasty—a good garden plan considered its caretaker—and I plucked leaves and flowers to nibble, but I wasn't hungry.

I was at peace.

Until Skalet stepped from between shrubs. "Youngest."

My fingers tightened on the handle of my carryall. Her gaze dropped to it, then lifted. When she didn't say another word—*a tactic my Elders had used regularly*—I merely curled a lip and waited, too.

To my surprise, she dipped her head in a short bow. "You did well."

"I murdered Pearl."

Her face might have been carved from old ice, her tattoos trapped there for centuries. *Some had been.* "I named mine *Flittertee.*"

Flittertees rose from Signat's dark seas at the year's highest tide to mate. Their fragile gauze wings twinkled like stars by the light of the three moons, wings shed as the tiny creatures plunged back down, drifting afterward like forgotten clouds. Beneath, ripe bodies opened, their final act to release luminescent eggs that transformed the still water into an ocean of light.

A good name for a Vlovax. Making whatever I could say cruel, and if Skalet counted on my kindness and compassion—it'd be the first time.

Oddly uncertain who we were, I gestured at the path ahead. "Walk with me to the greenhouse?"

A cautious nod.

She'd no idea what I intended. Knew what I carried—there was no hiding the *taste,* even inside a cryosac—but appeared fully in control. *Good.*

I'd a surprise for her.

As two, we were antagonists, pushing and pulling. To simply walk side by side like this, her long lithe legs must shorten their stride to mine, and I—I had to control this form's too easy anxiety. When we attempted to work together, as on Dokeci-Na, it was her nature to keep back and manipulate; mine to rush forward and trust.

What if we were three?

Skalet opened the greenhouse door for me. I half-closed my eyes as the rich aromas within flowed over me, settling my nerves. My Lanivarian-self loved the Garden and greenhouse because all of me did, but I'd yet to be another form that reveled in growing things as much as this one.

My web-kin, to my knowledge, hadn't entered willingly other than for her customary "it's new, be wary" inspection and to use the greenhouse to host prisoners. Who'd died of her care, but that was Skalet.

As I put my bag on the cleanest section of workbench, I watched her wander in a very un-Skalet manner, pausing to stare at pots and piles of warm mulch. *Criticism or curiosity?*

They didn't preclude one another.

I closed the door, having hung my flag for privacy, then returned to my carryall. Skalet came to stand near, but not close. Rather than prolong the moment, I unfastened the bag and dumped it upside down.

The cryosac rolled out, stopped by a pot. It had held Pearl with room to spare, but I'd stuffed it with *Lesy*-bits until the seams strained and popped open, an upsetting moment till I'd realized the sac was constructed to expand. It was close to popping again, the handles stuck out at angles.

Instead of a Kraal beside me, suddenly there was a Web-being, glorious and blue and deadly. Skalet kept some control. She'd hadn't formed a mouth—yet.

I held form, dumping heat. Impossible to talk to her like this. Yes, she'd detect the vibrations of air molecules affected by the energy of sound, but—so I rapped on the bench. Twice.

The teardrop extruded a pseudopod to slyly collect mushrooms from beneath the bench, then Skalet stood there again.

Naked, because she'd cycled without thought and the components of her uniform—and any weapons—were now so much water puddling the tiled floor. I handed her one of my caftans and waited till she'd put herself together—clothing mattered to Humans, even Kraal. "Lesy's still here."

She glared at the cryosac, then at me. "No." She shook her head vigorously. "That's not possible. We'd know." Hesitation. "Wouldn't we?"

As if I'd have answers. While refreshing, all I could offer was a sigh. "When her mass came together, I sensed a memory."

A frown. "What do you mean, 'sensed'?"

Another reasonable question, because we tasted and assimilated memory. *Were memory.*

Her frown deepened. "You aren't still—this isn't from being—"

I saved her the effort. "No, this has nothing to do with my having a symbiotic partner who talked in my head. I'm telling you the truth. How I know? I can't explain in Web terms. But there's something alive in there. Something of her."

We both looked at the sac.

"We could be three," Skalet breathed. When I turned to face her, she went on defensively, "It'd be better if we were—even if it was Lesy." Who'd troubled this, her younger web-kin, all along. "You know I'm right."

What I knew was my life would be easier if Skalet believed this was her idea. "We have our differences, but—"

Her attention went back to the sac. "We'd be a Web again, Esen." With raw, naked hope.

Without another word, I tapped the control panel and pulled the handles apart. "Stand back. And don't eat her."

Skalet gave me a wild look. "Don't you!"

At last, we agreed on something.

Perception

"**M**Y father was *here*."

The way Paul said it, eyes stunned and lost, made Lionel burn with outrage for his friend. He kept it to himself, saying calmly, "With your uncle, yes. From what I gathered, they hadn't met in person before Stefan arrived on Botharis."

"But they knew each other. Through my mother."

He nodded.

Duggs had installed what she called a "scenery window" in the plank wall, there continuing to be delays in a full repair. Paul went to it; stood looking out on a landscape that hadn't changed at all, even if those living on it had. Lionel couldn't begin to imagine how he felt. "Do you—" There was no easy way to say it. "Do you believe it? This message they brought for you?"

"That it's from my mother?" Shoulders rose and fell. "Or that she's a thief."

"Paul—"

The other turned, his expression composed, if drawn. "It's all right, Lionel." A small, pained smile. "I shouldn't be surprised it hadn't fooled her. My playing dead. Mother could always see through me."

"And if she'd met Esen?" Lionel asked carefully. "Would she have understood?"

Paul let out a slow breath. "I'd like to think so. Who

am I—what matters to me—she's responsible, Lionel. My values are hers."

"Then as far as I'm concerned, there's no question. Veya would have approved," the older Human said, brisk to cover his own mix of emotions. "Leaving us with what she left for you. If it can be found—I've had Lambo searching after hours, to no success."

That expressive eyebrow rose in question.

"Esen said she could be trusted."

Both eyebrows. "'She'?"

Flustered, Lionel pointed to his desk—Paul's desk. "I prepared a memo. Concerning staffing in future—" Spotting the grin, he relaxed. "You knew."

"For some time now." A nod of appreciation. "And that Lambo wouldn't fool you for an instant."

"She fooled me long enough," Lionel retorted. "I must be slipping."

Paul walked over to the chairs, inviting him to sit with a gesture. "The best experts can be fooled," he said, once settled. "Let me tell you about our 'Elves.'"

Intrigued, Lionel leaned forward. "You succeeded." Should he mention Skalet contacted him personally? *Not where she'd overhear.* Not, he decided suddenly, at all. Paul and Esen needed him to work with Skalet, for everyone's sake, making her continued—deserved—trust essential. Instead, he said, "We got the news. The Dokeci announced the Harvester is now in orbit, being prepared for translight. They'll send their own ships with it and have declared their willingness to watch over the—" *what would you call it,* "—resettlement once it happens."

Paul nodded. "Dokeci morality won't allow them to abandon the Mareepavlovax—who've no remaining space capacity. Wherever they're put will be it. The odds . . ."

"Are better than staying where they were," Lionel insisted. "You've done marvelously."

"We did our best." Paul's eyes were hooded now, inscrutable. "Have you heard of symbiotic intelligences before? True mutualists. Each unable to exist without the other."

"Only in theory—it's difficult to envision such a partnership evolving without one member regressing in favor of—oh, no." Lionel felt sick inside. There was only one reason Paul would mention such a partnership. Only one possible outcome if—"Esen."

A shaky breath. The next, steadier, then, "Our friend's asked us to incorporate her knowledge of such species into the collection. As a lesson. She thought it worth learning." This last dark and grim as he looked up.

Lionel realized Paul spoke to someone else.

Skalet.

47: Greenhouse Morning

"**Y**OU'VE been busy." Paul looked around the greenhouse. As his knowledge of gardening was a match for Skalet's, I wasn't worried he'd see anything out of place. Or know it if he did.

"We've been gone," I pointed out, patting the soil around my seedling. "Duggs won't let me near the farmhouse since I asked for a slide." Sniffing, I lowered my head to look more closely at him. "You've been climbing through plants." Which he didn't do.

"I can show you. If," with a nod to the pot, "you aren't *too* busy."

This return of the playful side of my friend was promising, if true, but I'd only been Lanivarian for a day. Echoes of my Lishcyn-self advised caution. *Pranks were possible.* "What's this about?"

"Uh-uh." Fingers flicked my chin. "You'll have to catch me, Droolycheeks!"

And he was off, running out the door while I stared after him, dumbfounded. Paul couldn't possibly think his Human legs could outrun mine. *Definitely a prank.* Grumbling to myself, because the last time had involved balloons filled with *water,* I picked up the next pot.

My ears pricked back. His, "You . . . can't . . . catch . . . me . . ." came from a good distance.

Meaning Paul was running after all. He was fast, for his kind.

I took my time removing my gloves and taking off my apron, tongue lolling in anticipation.

So was I.

Paul cheated. He'd hidden a powerless wheeled contraption the Botharans called a getaround bike and must have leaped on it, peddling with all his might, to get as far as he did.

Before I launched myself through the air and brought him, and the bike, to the ground. "Do it again," I urged, between licking his ears in the way that made him giggle.

Which he did, before grunting in surrender and trying to push me away. "Stop. Enough. You caught me. Esen-alit-Quar!"

My wet nose being *in* his ear. "Fine," I said, jumping back. I'd not had such a grand run in—well, ages, both of us busy in the Library. "Again?" With my best pleading face.

"Depends on what we find. C'mon." Suddenly serious, Paul brushed himself off and led the way.

I growled menacingly at the fallen contraption as I passed, still in hunter mode. My successful attack brought it—and Paul—down in the midst of the field behind the barn, a field fallow this year. The tender clover and other plants would be plowed under by Rhonda, who worked the land for us in return for crops to feed her elk. *The Library tended to such arrangements.*

More importantly at the moment, it was soft underfoot and gave out a fragrance even a predator enjoyed, so I didn't so much walk with Paul as I gamboled around him, once in a while "happening" to trip and roll.

He smiled at me, but didn't vary his path to join in, indicating there was purpose to whatever we were doing out here. *Gamboling!*

It soon became clear our purpose was to go to the abandoned outbuilding in the far corner. It was more, I decided, pot than building, what remained of the walls holding the soil and leafy debris—and roots—of the great family oak.

Which wasn't one, but you didn't argue. I'd tried.

We'd visited it before, so Paul could show me. I'd traced the initials I could reach. Most were two letters, an unsurprising majority being "R," but there were "Ls" and a smattering of others. Plus anatomically inaccurate hearts and other shapes. The oak hadn't improved my understanding of Human art or family, though I had liked it when Paul showed me his initials.

Until he'd grown quiet. We'd left soon after.

Guessing this might be another such visit, I stopped gamboling, rising to stand and walk the rest of the way beside Paul.

When fallen stones began jutting through the ground, he paused to look up, so I did. The sun peeked back through the massive crown of fronds, swaying in the light breeze. I spotted a family of *weaslings*, arboreal relatives of the mousel, and a nest of stingers and was about to show Paul, when he spoke.

"It's grown."

Obvious yet mysterious. My tail drifted sideways, unsure of his mood. "And is growing," I observed, to be helpful.

"No—yes, you're right." He shaded his eyes, looking intently for something.

Not, I decided, *for weaslings or stingers.* "Why are we here?"

"Ah!" Ignoring me completely, the Human scrambled over the rocks and began climbing the trunk.

Lanivarians did not climb. Oaks or anything woody.

A young Rrhyser, however?

I dropped my clothes and prepared to cycle.

"Got it!" Down Paul came, ruining a perfectly good surprise.

Then I saw what he carried.

Veya Ragem and her son had a hiding place where they'd leave one another surprises. A letter. A gift. Whatever could fit inside a knot of the oak.

"Especially," Paul told me, "before she left for space." This time, he wasn't sad or wistful. Simply remembering.

We stretched out on the clover, both on our stomachs, to regard what Veya Ragem had last left her son. "'What we believe is lost simply waits for better eyes to find it,'" I said, having heard her message.

Googly eyes looked back. Starfield the Very Strange Pony had been wrapped in a piece of spacesuit material, proof against the elements. That said, the toy had been loved to a shabby splendor, missing most of its glitter and a toe. The eyes, however, were fine.

"Mother didn't need proof I lived. She knew," Paul said then, his voice full. He reached out to touch a googly eye. "She found this. Kept it with her all that time, then left it here, for me, in case she didn't get a chance to tell me herself."

Not to lose your favorite toy? Which had traveled a considerable distance from home in the process. I reached to sniff it, detecting the suit fabric, Paul-scent, and, perhaps, a whiff of another's. *Or was that whimsy.* I pulled back. "Tell you what?"

A tender, peaceful smile. "That why I disappeared didn't matter to her, so long as I found my way home."

Families. Secrets become history. History—could become pain. I was silent, thinking such things as we returned home. Paul was quiet, too, thinking his own thoughts.

I doubted they included a cookie jar.

There was someone who could unravel the threads of Veya Ragem's past. Who'd follow the scent of truth without hesitation—or compunction, for that matter, but you worked with what you had. Being family. At least I could rely on her utter discretion.

I'd given Skalet the image from Chase and shared my memory of that dreadful conversation. *Set her loose.* It had seemed necessary to take charge of this—secret. Now? Now I'd a different image of Veya Ragem to consider. One to protect. I whined softly.

Paul's fingers dug into my neck fur. "Thinking about the big version?"

The—? "The pony," I said. "Of course. Yes."

And nothing would do but we go to the Family Patio, right away, to see where to put it. Laughing and, yes, gamboling, down the path, Paul pushing his contraption while talking so quickly it was as if joy had waited to spill out of him.

Only to fall silent when we found we weren't the first to arrive.

Perception

PAUL appeared out of nowhere, covered in leaf bits and dirt, laughing till he saw them. Esen, tongue out and panting, was right beside him, naked and on all fours. She growled in startled reaction more like some crazed beast than a civilized being and if he'd wanted to create a worse impression of their relationship, Lionel couldn't imagine how.

No, he thought abruptly. *This was them. Happy and together. What better impression than the truth?*

"You've wonderful timing," Lionel exclaimed and smiled. "Paul. Esen. We've special guests." He gestured expansively, including those with him. "Sam Ragem and Stefan Gahanni. Didn't I say we'd find Paul here?"

The pair might have been frozen in place. Sam shifted. "Aie."

Esen rose to her feet, wiping her paws on her thighs. He saw uncertainty in the look she gave Paul.

Who appeared as transfixed as his stunned relatives.

Lionel smiled to himself. He'd sent a request ahead, and there it was. "If you please. Carwyn has prepared a family welcome. Over here."

A table with three chairs waited. On the table, the bottle and glasses of a Ragem family meeting, along with a simple bouquet from the Garden. The plantings to every side were stunningly beautiful but the Botharan

Blue-eyed Daisies—according to Henri who'd asked a cousin—had been Veya's favorites.

First contact, or second. Meaningful props eased the moment.

Esen smiled at Lionel, her tail swinging from side to side. "Perfect. I'll go freshen up while you—talk." This with a gentle push at Paul, who gave her a startled look, then nodded.

She knew to be absent for this.

So should he. Lionel gave a short bow. "I'll get back to work now."

Paul nodded to him, too, then visibly braced himself. "Uncle—"

"We're not here to bite you, lad." Sam Ragem strode forward and took his nephew in his strong arms. Stefan hovered close, then grabbed the two.

Lionel faded back.

Esen?

Already gone.

48: Greenhouse Afternoon

PAUL had his family again.

My tail wouldn't stay still.

They had Paul. I'd meet them later, I'd no doubt.

Being Paul's family, too.

First, however, to be sure of something.

Having quickly washed and changed—regrettably I'd no time to mend a broken nail, but after all, Sam and Stefan had met me naked and on all fours and so might not notice—I went to the greenhouse, put out my flag, and closed the door.

She was hiding.

A good habit, as far as Skalet was concerned, it being impossible to explain a Web-being in the greenhouse to anyone else. Especially Paul, without significant preparation and probably a good fortifying meal.

"Lesy." I went to all fours, mindful of my clean clothes. Web-flesh had no scent, so I followed the faint-to-this-me *taste.* "There you are." Under the bench, near the back.

She was in a pot this time, a large one I used for transplanting young trees. It was comfortable and a comfort, having an imposed shape. I'd left a variety of containers around, trying to discern any favorites. So far, it was mostly pots.

"Will you come out?"

A ripple in the blue. *No,* that was. Probably just as

well. Web-flesh consumed other living matter. I'd had to start hanging the plants I didn't want her to assimilate.

She was larger. *Still far too small.* To augment the plant material, I gave her my flesh in careful doses, taking nothing in return. An appetite for web-flesh wasn't one to encourage, I knew, but what I gave her were the memories she'd shared with Ersh.

She'd yet to cycle. *I'd taken my time, too.* And had no intention of dropping her off a cliff to hurry matters.

Skalet remained dubious there was enough of Lesy to *be* Lesy. She might be right, and this someone new.

Being Skalet, she worried there was enough here to make an Enemy, like Death. I refused to believe it, being me.

Perhaps it was time for something different. "Are you hungry?"

I put aside my clean clothes and cycled . . .

Share . . .

. . . then I fed wee Lesy my memories of her laugh.

Perception

HER hand flattened on the table, palm up, holding a disk.

Above it, hovering in the room's light, appeared an image. Lionel caught his breath, studying it.

It was rendered in the cooler end of the light spectrum, framed in what might be script or decoration. What held his attention lay within—

"A ship." He looked at Skalet. "Survey, despite the damage. This could be the *Sidereal Pathfinder*."

"I concur."

"Where is it? Do we have a location?" Stars showed, but were there sufficient?

"Not yet. Hear me, Lionel. How the *Pathfinder* reached this place has become secondary. Do you see why I say so?"

She challenged him to understand. *The image.* He looked back to it. "What's this—around the edges? It's unfamiliar."

"To us as well," she replied, chilling his heart.

This wasn't about star drives or navigation tricks. "This is a message," Lionel said, his lips numb. "From someone who encountered a Human ship. Someone who sent this image into Human space, in a format we could interpret. It could be a warning."

"Or a request to remove unwanted debris. We two are aware of the danger of assumption, Lionel." Skalet reached across the table. A fingertip traced the vein along the back of his hand, like a kiss of ice, and he knew not to move. Didn't want to move.

"What can I do?" he offered, feeling breathless.

She smiled, sitting back. "We will work together, Lionel. Solve this mystery left to us by Paul's female parent and present the answer—at the appropriate time, of course."

Work behind everyone. Survey. Paul. Esen. For the right reason, he told himself. To protect them. Guard them.

Lionel met her cool, measuring gaze and nodded. "Together."

"Admirable."

Completion

<BELIEF comes first.>

"I've that." Vanekaelfien ate a fruit made safe and familiar by the Offering. "And hope, as you would say next. You are a good influence."

<As are you.>

"Remember there are no promises. This life won't be easy." Vanekaelfien gazed outward, Elfien using her eyes. Hills rolled into the distance, covered in vegetation. Creatures moved, easy to see in the night, in herds or flocks. Scaled. Feathered. "It is beautiful."

<That is good, too. All will strive to be worthy of this life.>

"Together."

<Always.> With *determination*.

It would be so, here. Their beloved Vlovax need never again be sacrificed after the Sleep, in order to adapt to a different place. The old way, first and best. Always.

Comforted, at peace and pregnant, Vanekaelfien let herself laugh, fluorescence painting her nose with joy. "The Others named this world Miranda Prime, but it is ours now. That is the decision."

<It was a silly name. Our name is much better. Our name has spirit and hope.>

"That it does." She liked saying it. "Welcome to Pearlesen."

<Welcome home, where all shall Rise.>

Main Characters

Web-beings (in order of arrival in known space)
Ersh
Lesy
Ansky
Mixs
Skalet
Esen-alit-Quar, Esen in a hurry, Es between friends
Death *Author's Note: Esen wishes you to know the stranger was named by those attacked. A Webbeing not of Ersh's Web.*

The Trusted Few (who know of Esen, her abilities, and the Web)
Author's Note: Don't blame me. Esen wants their loyalties made abundantly clear for you.
Paul Antoni Ragem—Human; former First Contact Specialist, Survey, Esen's first and best friend; went by the alias Paul Cameron while pretending to be dead for fifty years to protect Esen's secret
Lionel Kearn—Human; Paul's boss while in Survey, former First Contact Specialist; led the hunt for the

so-called Esen Monster (Death) while Paul was pretending to be dead to—you know the rest. Now in Paul's Group and dedicated to protecting Esen's secret

Rudy Lefebvre—Botharan Human; Paul's cousin; former patrol; searched for the truth while Paul was pretending to be dead, etc., now captain of the *Largas Loyal* and in the Group, etc.

Staff of the All Species' Library of Linguistics and Culture

(those named in this book, in order of responsibility)

Director: Paul Ragem

Curator/Head Gardener—Esen-alit-Quar (Esen as Lanivarian)

Assistant Curator/Gardener—Esolesy Ki (Esen as Lishcyn.)

Author's Note: Esen hopes you've noticed this means she does twice the work. Oh. Now Paul points out she's only one of these at a time and leaves the conclusion to you. Also, the staff wish to add that while they adore Esolesy, she's more a big softie than boss.

Assessment Desk—Henri Steves (Botharan)

Response Room—Ally Orman (Botharan)

Greeter/Coordinator of Intersystem Passage—Carwyn Sellkirk (Botharan)

The Anytime Chow Inc. Food Dispenser Operator—Lambo Reomattatii (Carasian)

Head Contractor—Duggs Pouncey, Botharan who built the Library and remains on staff and in charge of structural maintenance/repair. *Author's Note: Esen's convinced Duggs stayed to make sure no one—especially Skalet—messes with her work. Paul agrees.*

Head of Security—Skalet (as Kraal but doesn't use S'kal-ru among non-Kraal). *Author's Note: Skalet is in no doubt that Duggs remained in order to make her life more difficult.*

Train Operator—Rhonda Bozak (Botharan)

Greeter—Quin (Botharan)

Paul's Family

(those named in this book, in alphabetical order)

Char Largas—Paul's temp contract partner, mother of their twins, Tomas and Luara

Delly Ragem—Paul's grandmother on his mother's side, now a sofa in Sam's attic

Jan Terworth—cousin

Kevin Ragem—cousin

Luara Largas—daughter of Paul Cameron and Char Largas, sister of Tomas

Sam Ragem—Paul's uncle on his mother's side

Stefan Gahanni—Paul's contracted father; drive machinist; lives on Senigal III

Tomas Largas—son of Paul Cameron and Char Largas, brother of Luara

Veya Ragem—Paul's mother, starship navigator: died on the *Smokebat* 18 years before Paul stopped pretending to be dead. *Author's Note: Esen reminds us Human relationships are complicated.*

People of Importance to Evan Gooseberry

(those named in this book, in alphabetical order)

Author's Note: Evan adds those from his first adventure* with Paul and Bess as set out in the e-novella "The Only Thing To Fear."

Bess*—Human; the "Esen" Evan meets and befriends on Urgia Prime. *Author's Note: Esen wants to remind everyone this seemed an excellent choice of form when she picked it.*

Aka M'Lean—Human; Senior Political Officer, Commonwealth Embassy on Dokeci-Na and Evan's boss

Dorton Freeny—Human; juniormost, Commonwealth Embassy on Dokeci-Na

Ekwueme-ki—Dokeci; Leader of the Mariota Valley Project on Dokeci-Na

Evan Gooseberry—Human; Political Officer, Commonwealth Embassy on Dokeci-Na; one of the few accredited Gooseberrys of his generation. *Author's Note: His Great Gran wishes everyone to know Evan is the most eligible and sweetest Gooseberry.*

Interested parties should get in touch with her directly.

Gooseberry—The only surname with an unbroken legal line of descent from fabled Earth, as set out in The Lore.

Great Gran Gooseberry—Human; keeper of The Lore and responsible for assessing the legal status of claimants to being real Gooseberrys; raised Evan

Hymna Burtles—Human; manager for Burtles-Mautil Intersystems Holdings on the Mariota Valley Project on Dokeci-Na

Justin Gooseberry—Human; Evan's cousin, eldest son of his Aunt Melan

Lisam Horner—Human; security at the Commonwealth Embassy on Dokeci-Na; friend of Evan's

Lucius Whelan—Human; acquaintance of Great Gran; friend of Justin Gooseberry

Lynelle Owell—Human; security at the Commonwealth Embassy on Dokeci-Na; friend of Evan's

Malcolm (Mal) Lefebvre—Botharan; retired patroller and now constable for the Hamlet of Hillsview; Rudy's uncle

Melan Gooseberry—Human; Evan's aunt

Ne-sa Kamaara—Human; Commander of the security detail of the Survey Ship *Mistral*

Ny Wimmerly*—Human; Ambassador at the Commonwealth Embassy on Urgia Prime

Petara Clendon—Human; Captain of the Survey Ship *Mistral*

Petham Erilton—Human; Admin Staff at the Commonwealth Embassy on Dokeci-Na

Pink Popeakan*—Popeakan; nickname Humans give Prela on Urgia Prime

Pre-!~!-la Acci-!~!-ari*—Popeakan; also known as Prela or the Pink Popeakan; Evan encounters this individual on Urgia Prime

Prela—Popeakan; Esen's nickname for Pre-!~!-la Acci-!~!-ari; she and Evan encounter this individual on Urgia Prime

Sammy Litten—Human/Modified; xenopathologist at the Commonwealth Embassy on Dokeci-Na

Sendojii-ki—Dokeci; artist particularly famous in capital of Dokeci-Na

Simone Arygle Feen*–Human; Senior Political Officer at the Commonwealth Embassy on Urgia Prime; Evan's first boss

Snead—Human; Comm Officer on the Survey Ship *Mistral*

Teganersha-ki–"Dokeci"; historical figure: the infamous leader who united Dokeci-Na and established their moral system as well as plumbing; in reality: Ersh's name in this form. *Author's Note: Esen has her doubts Ersh would appreciate Evan carrying her image—a small bust—with him for inspiration, but she has yet to figure out how to tell him.*

Terry Koyak*—Human; Evan's coworker and friend at the Commonwealth Embassy on Urgia Prime

Trili Bersin—Human; Political Officer at the Commonwealth Embassy on Dokeci-Na; Evan's closest friend there

Warford—Human; Senior Med-tech on the Survey Ship *Mistral*

Others Who Appear

Author's Note: Esen wishes several didn't, but admits every past has its trouble spots.

Bob*—Human; alias Diale gives his Sweat Provider and colleague

Celivliet Del—Anatae who refuses to leave the Library. *Author's Note: Esen firmly intends not to let another being hide in her Garden. Firmly.*

Cieter-ro—Kraal; Captain of the *Septos Ank*, a ship affiliated with S'kal-ru

Cureceo-ki—Dokeci; curator of the museum on Dokeci-Na about to host a show of Lesy's artwork

Diale—Hurn; security tech specialist from Minas XII; worked with Paul to set up the Library; has history with Cameron & Ki, Paul and Esolesy's company

Elfien—Vlovax

Janet Chase—Human; was captain of the *Vegas Lass* while Paul was pretending to be dead, but turned out to be a criminal; alias used by Victory Johnsson

Jumpy Lyn—Ervickian; henchbeing of Chase
Lance Largas—Human; crew on the *Largas Regal*
Osmaku Del—Anatae; "head of off-world inquiry" who led delegation to the Library
Palrander Todd—Human; henchbeing of Chase
Pearl—Vlovax
Pearlesen—Esen's name as a Mareepavlovax
Rampo Tasceillato the Wise—Carasian; philosopher quoted by Lionel Kearn
Riosolesy-ki—"Dokeci"; Lesy's name in this form
Ses-ki—"Dokeci"; Esen's name in this form
Siokaletay-ki—"Dokeci"; Skalet's name in this form
S'kal-ru—"Kraal"; Skalet's name in this form
Sly Nides—Human; henchbeing of Chase
Tallo—Iedemad; Library client and entrepreneur
Thielex—Lexen; Library client and musical prodigy
Tory—Human; alias of Victory Johnsson
Vanekaelfien—Mareepavlovax
Victory Johnsson—Human; birthname of Janet Chase/Tory

Ephemeral Species

Author's Note: Esen would like you to know this is far, far, far from a complete list. Her universe is a large and lively place. Also, that as a Web-being, she and her kind are not ephemeral, being semi-immortal and originally from space.

Acepan—species extinct before Humans arrived in this part of space, multilegged and not fond of the cold

Anatae—herbivorous species who have yet to live down mistaking performers dressed as edibles for edibles during a Festival of Funchess

Articans—inhabitants of Artos. *Author's Note: appear Human but have significantly different biology.* Xenophobic religious fanatics who view the boneless as sin; responsible for the death of Ansky.

Botharan—a Human from Botharis. For example, Paul Ragem. *Author's Note: In Esen's opinion the finest of his species. She admits to prejudice.*

Carasian—species with hard carapace/shell, claws, multiple eyes, and significant sexual dimorphism

Cin—one of two communal species (see also Rands); in their case, varied cognitions are present in a roughly humanoid body. *Author's Note: Esen points out Ersh forbade taking this form, citing "one personality is enough."*

Crougk—largest land-based sentient species, horse-like. *Author's Note: While Paul disputes this, Esen remains convinced.*

D'Dsellan—insectoid; a Panacian from the home-world, D'Dsel, or living there. Mixs' preferred form under the name Sec-ag Mixs C'Cklet.

Dokeci—species with five arms/three eyes; pendulous abdomen drags with age; Ansky's preferred form for cooking; Lesy's preferred form for art, as Riosolesy-ki. Esen as a Dokeci is called Ses-ki, being too young to be taken seriously.

Efue—species about which the Anatae come to the Library, there being confusion about certain substances and good taste

Elves—what the Dokeci call the aliens they find and transplant from the moon around S'Remmer Prime (see also Mareepavlovax)

Engullan—species with a cinnamon tang; bright yellow makes them wince

Ervickian—species with two brains, two mouths, and pliable morals; most are con artists or petty thieves

Feneden—species new to Esen until Ersh memory informed her this is a species Ersh preyed upon; locate themselves using polarized light

Ganthor—species vaguely like warthogs; tough, with a herd instinct; often mercenaries; need implants to use comspeak-otherwise use olfaction/physical gestures/clickspeech

Grigari—species known for their music; black-and-white stripes, two pairs of feet, three tails (one prehensile), long-fingered hands; mane collects sensory input; Ersh considered them "show-offs"

Heezle—species resembling pillars of ooze; no interspecies hang-ups; bats eye covers to assess interest in mating, and inattention means "come hither"

Human—humanoid species, bipedal; wide variety of shapes and sizes; prone to curiosity. They are loosely organized with a Commonwealth, although at the far reaches a new Trade Pact is forming. For example, Paul Ragem. Esen as a Human is called Bess.

Hurn—species enamored of Human sweat, ring of lip-smacking mouths around the neck; For example, Diale, security expert on Minas XII.

Iberili—species that hibernate for 300 years at a time. *Author's Note: Esen has no intention of wasting that much time asleep, even if Ersh found it restful.*

Iedemad—sluglike species that must wear osmo-suits to tolerate anything but a water-saturated environment

Iftsen—theta-class species, but live in such a chemically "rich" environment they use non-oxy facilities; known for "party" habit; several subspecies (See also Mobera)

Jarsh—extinct species with memorable voice; Esen sings to Paul to show him what the Web remembers

Jylnics—aquatic species; tentacles; move with reckless speed; one made advances on Paul

Ket—species, humanoid but extremely sensitive hands; work as masseuses and always have a hoobit. Esen as a Ket went by Nimal-Ket, the name on her acquired hoobit.

Kraal—Humans belonging to the Kraal Confederacy; strict hierarchy organized by affiliation to Houses; do not interbreed with non-Kraal Humans and may go extinct or become a subspecies. Skalet's preferred form, in which she is known as the Courier S'kal-ru.

Lanivarian—canidlike species known for its loathing of space travel; Esen's birth-form. As a Lanivarian, her name is Esen-alit-Quar.

Lexen—species who employ respiratory tubes in their music

Lishcyn—species with scales, five stomachs liable to react violently, and poor night vision; their homeworld is a Dokeci protectorate; as Paul's business partner and friend, Esen remained Lishcyn while he was pretending to be dead, under the name Esolesy Ki.

Lycorein—aquatic species resembling a very large otter

Mareepavlovax—species the Dokeci discovered and called Elves; also known in Web memory as

Ancient Farers and the Harbingers. (See also Vlovax.)

Mobera, Moberan—subspecies of Iftsen (there are several); frilled face

Modoran—species, feline, dirty (except under UV) white fur, aggressive and large, needs implant to speak

Nabreda, Nabredan—subspecies of Iftsen (there are several); protruding forehead

Nideron—species that inflates a nostril hood in disdain; aggressive toward weakness; seven-digit hands

Nimmeries—aquatic species; thrum when impatient; engaged in border dispute with Oietae

Octarian—species with multiple chins, pouch, auditory tentacles

Odarian—species with trunk (sputters in conversation by exhaling moist air) and elbow pouch

Oieta, Oietae—aquatic species; filter feeders (shrimpesque); color changes with emotion; size of a Human. Esen's name as an Oieta is Esippet Darnelly Swashbuckly.

Ompu—species Ansky watched go extinct

Panacian—general name for insectoid species living in the Panacian system and elsewhere. (See also D'Dsellan.)

Popeakan—arachnoid species known to be reclusive and to work within groups: to interact with other species requires the Offer; twelve jointed limbs, three eyes. For example, Prela.

Poptians—species who deals in gems on Picco's Moon; gloved tentacles; green faceted eyes

Prumbins—species that grows larger with age; vertically pupiled eyes; not aquatic

Quebits—species that resemble little vacuum cleaners with extruded flowerlike appendages; work as janitors/repair crew on starships; known for their intense focus on minutiae. *Author's Note: Esen will not travel as a Quebit again. Unless she has to, and if so, she expects something to fix.*

Queeb—species with tentacles and six eyes, forked tongue

Rands—one of two communal species (see also Cin) who travel/live in clusters of less than 20

Refinne—massive aquatic species; lives in deep water and is blinded by light

Rrhysers—species that are standard tripeds, thump chest plates, broad nostrils, infamous for their temper and will let offspring play anywhere

Sacrissee—species deer-esque; evolved from solitary, shy herbivores; architecture is designed to provide peepholes and prevent interaction

Screed—species with knees at height of Human waist

Seitsiets—species who generate internal hydrogen while asleep so need weights or will float away

Skenkrans—space-faring species with leathery wings (not skyfolk)

skyfolk—non-space-faring species with wings; gliders; doleful and solitary

Smoot—species who illegally homesteaded the waters under the south polar cap of Urgia Prime

Snoprian—humanoid species, similar to Humans except for their voices and vestigial feathers

Tly—Humans who live in system of the same name

Tumbler—crystalline species native to Picco's Moon; excretions considered rare gemstones; Ersh's preferred form and Tumblers called her Ershia the Immutable.

Urgian—species with no calcified skeleton, four arms; hosts of the Festival of Funchess. *Author's Note: Esen experienced her first festival with Evan in "The Only Thing to Fear".*

Vlovax—small creature that rises from the ground to complete a Mareepavlovax (see Elves); named Devil Dart by the Dokeci

Wz'ip—species like stone; graphite filaments and exterior vents; what Esen sometimes becomes to sulk. *Author's Note: Esen points out she doesn't sulk. She mopes. Cutely.*

Ycl—amorphous coalition of cells; obligate predator of "living flesh" so their world has been declared off limits to anyone tasty

For more information, visit the All Species' Library of Linguistics and Culture on Botharis. A fact for the collection, delivered in person, will be required in exchange. Please refer to the Library's guidelines before planning your trip. Pamphlets are available on Hixtar Station.

Julie E. Czerneda

Esen

Esen is a shapeshifter, one of the last of an ancient race. Only one Human knows her true nature—but those who suspect are determined to destroy her!

"A great adventure following an engaging character across a divertingly varied series of worlds." —*Locus*

Web Shifters

BEHOLDER'S EYE	978-0-7564-1351-4
CHANGING VISION	978-0-7564-1195-4
HIDDEN IN SIGHT	978-0-7564-1350-7

Web Shifter's Library

| SEARCH IMAGE | 978-0-7564-1244-9 |

"*Search Image* is the guaranteed most delightful and fun SF read of the year." —Marie Bilodeau

To Order Call: 1-800-788-6262
www.dawbooks.com

Julie E. Czerneda

The Gossamer Mage

"*The Gossamer Mage* is full of life and quirky, complex characters doing things that feel important...both because they're described with deft skill, and because you care about the characters as people." —S. M. Stirling

"A wonderful book—rich language, strong world building, interesting characters, and a magic system that both pinches and soothes the heart.... I think it is Julie Czerneda's finest work so far." —Anne Bishop

"*The Gossamer Mage* is like eating chocolate—smooth, addictive, and fabulous. And deliciously dark." —Kristen Britain

"Every so often, a book comes along that is pure magic. The Gossamer Mage is such a book. Julie Czerneda's spell binding take on magic-with-a-price is enthralling and exhilarating—a joy to read!" —Sarah Beth Durst

"Oh, but this book is good! Grab it, take it home, and lose yourself in it!" —Ed Greenwood

978-0-7564-0890-9

To Order Call: 1-800-788-6262
www.dawbooks.com

DAW 61